Visions
of
Dragons

Cover Design: Vanda Pinto

Map Design: DiceCoven

Editing: Shalini Gopal

Proofreading: Vivian Kross

CONTENTS

WARNING

GRAPHIC AND TRIGGERING THEMES.

NOT SUITABLE FOR ANYONE UNDER 18.

READERS DISCRETION IS ADVISED!

18+

N
W E
S

THE SEA
OF
ROSES

WATERGRALE

■ ONRAKAR

SLUMBROUS
SEA

RINGTEN

GOLD SEA

PROLOGUE

ONCE THERE WERE two Dragon brothers; one, a breather of fire and the other, a breather of ice.

They have dominion over life. The Ice Dragon, Kari, embraced man, thinking them to be wondrous beings while his brother, the Fire Dragon, Ori, opposed them. Hating the flightless creatures, he considered them small, foul, and worthless.

Kari and Ori have never agreed with each other since their creation, but they were always true to one another. Their loyalties to flesh and blood never waned despite the years they lived.

Though the coming of man placed an unamendable rift between them, causing an argument that could never be resolved. So, Ori parted from his brother's side with the other Dragons, leaving Kari behind with mankind.

Abandoned by his kind, Kari turned into the ice he breathed. He caused the lands to turn cold, killing crops, animals, and the beings he overlooked. Man was forced to huddle around their fires to stay alive, and they gradually grew resentful toward him.

For a long time, Kari continued his onslaught until, one day, a brave woman climbed the mountain to kill the Dragon that was plaguing her people and the land.

As the beast slept peacefully, she took a spear and pierced him through the chest, slaying the great Dragon Kari. He tumbled to the earth below, thrashing and bellowing, cursing the land and man until his last pained breath.

Victorious, she expected the lands to warm, but the cold never ceased, the storms became fiercer. As a result, the people became desperate as food had not filled their bellies for an age, so this mysterious woman led man to Kari's final resting place.

There, they disturbed the snow and ice clinging to his body. No more was he the great Dragon that terrorized them, he was a mere shadow of himself, listless and distorted due to the fall from the rocky cliffs above. Axes raised, man hacked the flesh that defied the elements, refusing to freeze, and it seemed his magic still lingered in death.

The woman who slew Kari was the first to consume him. Upon devouring, a change overcame her. The cold stopped fazing her and stripping herself of her clothing, she showed man they would not perish from it anymore.

The others too began feeling different, less human.

But immunity to the cold was not their only blessing. They obtained the power to wield ice. The Dragon's ability now belonged to man, yet, unlike the beast, they remained beautiful.

When the Fire Dragon, Ori, learned of his brother's death, he was outraged and mad with grief. He vowed to eradicate man because, to him, they were the beasts.

Fire, claw, and teeth he sent to man, but man fought back with their newfound powers, refusing to be under the tyranny and mercy of Dragons any longer.

Ori was surprised to see the feeble creatures his brother had loved become such strong rivals. He tried as he might to end man, but the lands his brother cursed proved too much, too hostile, despite the Fire Dragons' advantage in strength, numbers, and the skies.

And with no Dragons having the powers of ice to combat them after his brother's demise, Ori was forced to withdraw. Kari was the beginning of a lineage he never started, no wife and no children and due to his folly, ice was lost to Dragons. Fire was not as Ori sired many children.

Slowly, as the ages went by, man became known as Mages. The war continued between the races. Many deaths occurred on both sides, each generation unable to forget the past.

To end the war, the current King of Ice Mages asked for a treaty. For ten years of peace, he would give the Fire Dragon King one of his precious daughters.

Now, the time had come for King Orval, a descendant of Ori, to decide if he wanted to take a daughter and keep the peace. It was a decision that could change everything forever.

ONE

SUMMONING

THE STONES ARE cold beneath my fingers; the winter air creeps in through the wooden shutters, blocking my only warmth from the sun.

The tower is frigid as usual, but Ice Mages are numb to it, so why wasn't I? It must be a myth or a lie that I have been told by my father. Falsehoods have often left his lips.

I can feel the coldness - so bitter, it makes me tremble. I hold my body tight, and I don't hear anything but the constant howl of the wind as it rattles the shutters trying to reach me.

So cold...

I'm lonely too...

When was the last time I held a conversation with somebody? Anybody?

It is the guards' fault, they've recently forbidden speech. Prisoners are to remain silent so we can repent for our sins. They have taken our last joy from us.

They take everything from us.

When was the last time I was touched? I can't recall... I don't even remember my exact age.

How long has it been since I've been placed in this tower?

I know I am now a woman or at least, close to being one. I can't see for myself, but my breasts feel ample, and my face and body have changed with time, or so I can tell.

I don't know if I have grown taller. Feels like I have, perhaps just a little. My dress is shorter and tighter, has been for a long while.

Sometimes I forget why I am here... until I remember that day so many years ago.

I wouldn't be suffering if not for my curse. Because of it, I don't have control over the magic that flows through my veins. A sudden strong emotion and I can freeze an entire nation, they say. Maybe it is because my vision was stolen when I was a babe.

My mother used to say I would cry every single second I was awake since my birth, and I wouldn't stop until I was held by her.

The warmth from her body, or perhaps her affection, was the only thing that prevented me from falling into complete madness.

It is a strange feeling. Everyone around me can experience the world in colors and sight, but I have never been blessed with such.

Darkness was the only thing I was gifted. It took time to get used to. I often got hurt easily since I was very clumsy, but I have learned with sounds. Now, I can move around with ease, with a click of my tongue. And it is in that way sounds are a miracle; I don't know what I would do without them.

There is a sudden noise as I hear a door shut directly below me. Strange... It isn't time for the maid to bring me food. She doesn't come until the bells ring twice, signaling morning has become midday.

They feed me once a day as I don't need much sustenance for being confined in such a small room. Usually, my plate consists of stale or moldy bread, and if I am lucky, soup. It is usually cold but still a delicacy on my tongue.

Over and over again, it is boring and hardly satisfying. I faintly remember being spoiled as a child. There were times I would feast on rich meals filled with flavor, but even if I try, I can't recall how it tasted or what I ate.

I listen to the person's footsteps all the while becoming tense and rigid. Even my shivering ceases.

Their footsteps are heavy, and they walk with confidence. I can hear a small presence fall behind them.

Who is it? I'm frightened, excited, and curious at the thought of who could be coming to see or have anything to do with me. This is a tower full of prisoners after all; no one has visitors, not of the pleasant company anyway.

I wait. I listen.

My back is straight, and I turn my head toward the door as it is unlocked and pushed open, the hinges squeak in response to the motion.

I stand to my feet.

"Who's there?"

My voice sounds odd. I don't use it very often after all. Before I used to sing the songs I have heard from other prisoners but with the new rule, it gives the guards more reasons to hurt us – they are always watching and listening.

I am barely alive. I'm not even a person to them, just like the other prisoners in this tower.

I hear there is a young boy they captured months ago who is of Dragon blood. I am interested in him, and I hear the guards talking about him as they roam the halls.

They are saying he was detained by the royal's best Mages after he entered our Kingdom Yulor. It is another victory for the King, my father, another praise in his name.

Dragons are our enemy. They are beasts meant to be hunted down. They are harmful, large, and bloodthirsty for Mages since the start of the world. Tales are told of the humans who killed the first Dragon and how they are gifted with the abilities of magic after eating its flesh.

To this very day, the Dragon's magic runs through every Mage. We are no longer called humans but Mages, specifically Ice Mages due to the nature of our powers.

The boy of Dragon blood is young, barely a man, so the only way the royals could have taken him down so easily is because of his age and inexperience.

The Dragon is even below me in status, which is saying a lot, and when I sleep at night, I can hear his screams, and within the darkness of my dreams, I am able to see a shape. A shape that eventually turns into something, something powerful and frightening.

I realize that for the first time in my life, I am able to see something other than funny shapes in the blackness. That something is what I imagine to be a Dragon, although I don't know the true shape of one.

It is humongous, with teeth longer than my body and colors I cannot describe due to the fact I have never seen them. I have been described colors, but in my world, they are strange and impossible to understand. And in a vision, I saw this creature, what I believed to be a Dragon in color.

I am in denial, but every time the boy screams, I see the scary Dragon in my head, bellowing in pain and thrashing as it tries to escape the chains placed around his body.

I quickly grow used to those screams. I feel connected with a boy I've never met when I dream at night. I believe it is my magic or even his, linking us together.

Even though I have been taught that Dragons are evil, including their menacing King, the boy I feel is not. In my last dream, the Dragon saw me, and it didn't look happy. I could feel its fear and since then, I haven't seen it or heard the bellows or cries of the boy below me.

A person speaks to me, a man from the sound of his voice, "Princess Vrai, you have been summoned by your father, the King. You are not to say anything unless you are asked and are to keep silent otherwise. Understand?"

I nod my head, wondering why I am being called by my father. I begin to feel fear as I cannot imagine it being for a good reason.

The other person with lighter footsteps grabs my arm and drags me forward. The fingers are dainty, leading me to believe it is a woman, and the man takes the lead.

She follows him while maintaining her hold on me, and all I can think of is how her fingers are as cold as ice, but we are naturally cool to the touch.

Each step I take down the descending stairs, my throat feels tighter. I feel as if I want to run back to the cage I am imprisoned in. It sounds crazy, but at least I have the comfort of the walls and routine. I feel safer inside those walls than outside of them.

I hear thumping, moaning, and crying. All sounds come from the prisoners. My legs start to tremble, and it's hard for me to move. I want to ask why my father has summoned me, but I remember the promise I made to keep silent.

We move outside and the bitter cold instantly freezes my bare arms and feet and I miss the tower already. I feel exposed, almost naked, the rags I wear thin.

As we walk, I hear noises in the street - whispers and mutters from the townsmen and women. I hear sounds from animals, too - grods barking, tiggs oinking, and rickens clucking. It must be hard for them during the cold winter months, but I imagine that no one truly cares about them.

These are the noises that comfort me, sounds that I haven't heard in such a long time. *People... Animals...*

I slow my steps to enjoy the fresh air, but I am immediately tugged forward by the woman holding my arm. I imagine she thinks ill of me since she is showing me no remorse. Everyone knows who I am, I am the King's bastard daughter.

It is hard to miss me... I wish I weren't so noticeable. I know they stare as I hear their feet slowing as they pause to look at me. I tense, feeling uncomfortable as I assume more people begin to gather.

Maybe I am overthinking it, but it is as if I can feel their gazes burning my skin just like Dragon's breath.

We move through more of the town, and my stomach growls loudly. I have had no food for about a day's time. I can tell it's morning as the bell has only rung once, and the rays of the sun are low and strong.

I may be the way I am, but I am able to see light. If the world is dark, mine is even more so. If the sun is out, the darkness is somehow brighter. I can even tell if a room is well lit with candles or fire. However, I am unable to make out shapes, faces, or even bodies.

It isn't long before I grow weary as the long winding roads and hills are exhausting. My bare feet are sore, the road unkind. I want to slow, but I'm forced to keep up with them. Every time I fall behind, I am jerked violently forward. Sometimes I am even thrown off balance.

We eventually stop, and I can sense it is a quiet and peaceful place. I can hear another man's voice at a distance.

"State your business!" His voice is loud.

"We are here with the King's imprisoned daughter, Vrai, who has been requested by his majesty himself." The man replies in a booming voice, which bothers my ears.

It isn't long before I hear the gates creaking open and men's feet scurrying across the stone ground. The sounds eventually stop, and we move forward abruptly. I'm barely given a chance to catch my breath or even try to take the chill from my flesh by rubbing my arms with my hands.

Another door opens, and we enter. I know it's the palace because the floors feel different. It is warm underneath my feet; the stones are said to be mined from the Silvertop Mountains carried here by our ancestors. It is a relief to my battered feet, and the chill starts to disappear.

I hear a woman's voice and the click of a heel as it hits the stone floor, which creates an echo within the silence of the palace.

"Is this Vrai?" a woman questions. Her voice is like silk, and I hear her heels snap closer.

"Yes, Your Majesty." The man responds instantly.

Majesty... So this is father's real wife and the Queen of Ice

Mages. I wonder if the rumors are true and she is as cold as the ice powers she wields.

She is quiet, and I can feel her stare as she stops in front of me.

"So, it is true..?" Her words are slow as if she struggles to believe it. "It's the first time I have seen a blind Mage unless their eyes have been gouged out of their skulls." I attempt to pull back, not liking her words, but the woman on my other side keeps me in place.

Even though my eyes are useless, I still like the fact that I have them, and I am not eyeless. I made sure to check one day, feeling the wet gloss on my eyes and pushing slightly to make sure I did have them.

"Close your eyes, dear. Why keep them open if you do not need them? You will just creep everyone out with eyes like yours." I hear her walking away, and the woman pulls my arm silently, telling me to go forward with them.

We continue walking, and I close my eyelids like I am told. Are my eyes...creepy? I have never been told what I look like, but when I feel my face, it feels normal. When touching, I can only imagine what I look like. It seems colors matter to them....

Colors.

The only time I have seen colors is in my vision of the Dragon. Is this how it feels like to have sight? My dreams have always been strange, but the one where I imagined a Dragon is the most abnormal.

I can still feel the cold gaze of the Queen even though she is walking ahead of me. I wonder if she is staring at me.

Suddenly, the two guards stop and the woman who has a tight grip on my arm lets me go, and I hear both of them sink to the floor. I realize I must be before the King and I follow suit and carefully lower myself and bow before him.

"Your Majesty, we brought her just as you requested." The woman's voice is light and airy as she greets royalty.

He doesn't reply instantly, and I hear the click of the heels stop along with the swishing of clothes. I imagine the Queen is now seated by the King, "You may leave us."

I hear them rise and walk away, and I ball my fists as they move further away, leaving me alone before the King - my father - and his now-wife and my step-mother - the Queen.

"Vrai. Stand!" he orders, and I get up from my bowing position. I turn my face toward the direction of his voice.

I feel like a grod, but I have always been treated like one since the death of my mother.

"May I ask why I am here?" I question nervously. Wondering if I am going to be sentenced to death or perhaps a worse fate, but I cannot think of what during this time.

"I summoned you here before me because of a war," he replies in a serious tone.

"A war?" I ask with uncertainty. Maybe he wants to use a new science on me and extract my powers for his own or give them to one of my sisters. I have heard rumors from the overly loud guards of such new sciences going around.

I don't have anything to live for... Yet, I still yearn to live in this world.

"Yes, the Dragon King, Orval, has declared war on us once again. It seems the one Dragon shifter in our possession has sent him into a fit of rage," he announces. "But it does not make up for the hundreds of our people he has slaughtered. I wish I had done much more than torture a young boy to his death."

So that boy is dead...? My heart pangs in my chest, and it tightens. A meaningless death.

No, I shouldn't feel sad over a Dragon. Remember, they have killed hundreds of us Mages.

"So... What does that have to do with me?" I am afraid of what his answer may be.

He doesn't hesitate with his reply, "Well, if there is one weakness the Dragon King has, it's women... Or so I have been informed. Hence, I have offered him to take one of my daughters for ten years of peace."

I grow cold and ask, "So even though I'm just a bastard... I'm included in this?"

"Yes. You're still my daughter. The Dragon King does not need to know you're a bastard or a curse." He stands up, his clothing rustling. "Maids, come clean the girl and get her in some decent clothes. Have her ready before nightfall. At least try and make her seem... presentable." He orders loudly.

From either side of me, there are footsteps and in unison, I hear, "Yes, Your Majesty."

"This way, Princess Vrai." A maid's soft voice announces, and they guide me from the room.

I never thought I would be back in the palace, much less being offered to a King, but I imagine that if by some chance the Dragon King chooses me, he wouldn't want me for marriage like I am currently praying.

Maybe my curse is a blessing and will save me from a monster of a King. *Why would he want me as a wife?*

My father said *take*. That the Dragon King is to *take* one of his daughters for a wife.

It doesn't sound too promising.

I don't want to become a toy for a sadistic Dragon to play with, but now that is all I can imagine...

TWO

THE KING OF DRAGONS

I HAVE HEARD stories about the Fire Dragon King told by those lucky enough to see him and live.

They say his eyes are the color of rubies, and hair is as dark as the night. The white of his skin is covered in black tattoos from head to toe. The tattoos, too, tell stories - stories of his power and the power he holds over his people.

It is said the Dragon men use markings to show how powerful they are, the more they possess, the more they are feared. So, if you see a Dragon with a tattoo only around his finger, he is weak, but if his entire body is covered in them, you are most likely going to die in battle fighting him.

They say they use such markings not just to show off their status but also to seduce women of their culture, who know very well what the markings mean. Some say the Dragon King shows his off only for the women rather than the status.

I think about him and the Dragons as the maids scurry around, helping me bathe, fix my hair, and dress me. I am not used to such treatments, and I find myself recoiling from their touches.

There is no physical touch in the tower, and baths are only once a year – a bucket of water and a sponge. Help does not exist either; washing is done by oneself. There is also my struggle with such things as dressing.

Sometimes I wear my dresses backward or wrong. The guards and maids always let me know, but it doesn't matter as they are the only ones who come to see me.

They are cruel to me.

The guards sometimes messily throw my food to the ground, and the contents of the tray litter the floor. I barely will get a chance to sip the soup, most of it spilling out. The maids ignore me; I am nonexistent to their eyes.

The ever so lukewarm water feels good as I bathe, and the bathwater smells of roses which reminds me of my mother.

I vaguely remember the scent as my mother loved those flowers when she was alive. Roses are considered a luxury here where it snows most of the time. We barely have a spring or summer where flowers have enough warmth to blossom or grow.

Currently, it is winter, it being one of the warmest we have had in a long time. Usually, the winter's air is brutal and enough to kill any animals outside, but they are out today. It is definitely warm enough.

I wonder if perhaps our lands are beginning to change ever so slowly, or this has something to do with the Fire Dragons preparing for their war against us.

By the time the maids are finished and have pulled my hair up into a tight bun, I am a different person. I feel fresher and clean, and they've trimmed my hair, leaving me lighter.

My hair has always been long. I believe it is to my waist and all of it, they have somehow placed on top of my head.

It is time for the final touches, so they wrap something around my eyes that feels like silk. It is most likely to hide my eyes away from the Dragon King and the others in the palace. They rub something on my lips, which feels smooth, and I wonder what it is.

It smells of something sweet, and I am tempted to lick my lips, but I don't let myself. Something tells me it is for decoration rather than tasting, else they would have told me to taste it.

But decoration means nothing to me.

Once the maids escort me out of the room, they place something around my shoulders. It feels heavy, and they take one arm each before slipping it into the sleeve.

Not only is it heavy, but it's also warm. The slight chill I had in my bones fades with whatever they have slipped over me.

"This way, Princess Vrai," one of the maids says as they guide me by my arm through the palace.

Princess Vrai...

When was the last time I heard that term?

It's been a while.

Even from the start, not many addressed me by that name. I am just a bastard child, but my father had loved mother... I heard rumors she is the only woman he has ever loved, even now.

When my mother was alive, he would often visit, but he was a different man back then. I used to hear him laugh, and I could imagine he was always smiling.

My mother used to tell me that when an Ice Mage loved someone, they only loved once and never again, not truly. When my mother died, he also died with her that day, making him a real Ice King.

We were cursed. Our hearts grew as cold as the Dragon named Kari when we lost that love. We inherited the curse from our ancestors, from when they consumed his flesh. I always believed it's true, especially with my father.

As I walk through the halls and travel downstairs again, I hear scurrying of what sounds like panicked feet. Women's heels, men's boots, stricken and fast breathing, along with whispers and mutters.

"He's here!" A woman screams from the bottom of the stairs. "You have to hurry!"

The maid grips my arm too tightly and questions nervously, "The Dragon King...? Already?"

"Yes, now hurry! The King is already outside with the other Princesses," the woman snaps.

The maid quickens her steps down the stairs, and I nearly trip, but I grab the railing. I want to beg her to go slow for my safety, but I doubt she will listen to me in her state of panic. Also, to her, I am not truly a Princess.

After catching the rails, she tugs me further down the stairs, and when I reach the bottom, I am relieved to be on flat ground. Yet, she pulls me forward, not stopping or giving me a moment to rest. I need to sit down.

Please, I wish to sit...slow down. I am begging her in my thoughts.

They are scared. I am more so – I am to be thrown to the King, not they.

"Sorry, Princess Vrai, but we must hurry." We continue to move forward as we slip outdoors. The wind blows against my face.

"I don't understand why it is so important that I must be there. I'm only a bastard and not even loved by my father as my sisters are," I mutter to the maid, whom I probably won't see after this.

"I think that is why, if I may speak frankly, Princess." She grows quiet afterward.

Ah, I see. The reason why my father is so adamant about this is that I am the least loved, and he is secretly hoping I will be picked by the Fire Dragon King, whom I've heard so many unpleasant things about.

He is a lustful woman lover, hateful, hotheaded, and temperamental. Some say even the weather can affect his mood for the day. He sounds like he is a very unpleasant man overall. A man that I do not wish to meet.

I don't say anything more, and I hear people talking at a distance as we draw closer to our destination. A chill runs up my spine as I feel very strong magic, a feeling that I've never experienced before.

I stop in my tracks; the more I feel these strange presences, the more I feel I am in danger. I faintly see something within the darkness of my eyes. I see the shape of a beast again, but this one is different. It is larger and meaner looking.

I do not need to feel his magic long to know it is the King, this being his Dragon.

The thing has piercing eyes, another color I have yet to see, but perhaps they are red as people have rumored. The color of his body is dark, perhaps the same midnight black people spoke of when it came to the King's hair. The beast's tail is long and spiked, the ends deadlier than any soldier's sword. If I have to guess, his scales are smooth and shiny.

It bares its teeth at me almost immediately, knowing it has been seen. The beast charges at me, mouth open, and I prepare for an actual attack. But before it can reach me it bursts into tiny particles.

The vision is over, and I am dazed by it. *It felt real. How is it not?*

The maid's voice calling out to me is background noise. "Vrai! Vrai! Princess, please move! We must hurry, or I will be in trouble."

I snap back to reality as the cold breeze blows against my body, the winter air nipping at it. "Sorry..." I begin to move forward to their suffocating presences. It is then I realize there is more than one Dragon; I see them in my head.

Each of them is unique, but they only show themselves quickly before slinking back into the darkness. They, unlike the Dragon which charged at me, are unaware I have stolen glances of their true and monstrous forms.

Perhaps I am able to see these beasts due to their magic. As a child, I was always able to sense magic in a person, even seeing different colors in my head if I concentrated enough. It looked like smoke, a distinct color from darkness, and they were also in the shape of a person.

My father's color is bright – just like my mother's when she was alive. They have always been different from the others I've seen

Just beyond me are three similar colors that resemble my father's stand in a row. They are probably my sisters. I never really got to meet my other siblings even though I know I have them. It is true, even if we'd met on official terms, they would have never acknowledged me.

Once I'm standing next to these three presences, I am still. The maid lets go of my arm before scurrying off. "Good luck," she whispers to me, then I hear her feet quickly retreating.

"You're late." My father's voice is gruff.

"I know," is all I can mutter. There isn't anything else to say.

There is a short silence before I hear a rumbling snicker coming from a distance. I hear a man speak; his voice is as deep as his laugh "So, this is what you have to offer me? Four skinny and feeble women... one seems to be blind."

Ah, this is the Dragon King. He has taken the form of a man.

"Yes, these are my beautiful and healthy daughters." My father seems to take offense, his voice snide.

"You do know my people are at the borders of your country, just waiting for me to give the signal for battle, to eat you little Mages up or crisp you alive... They're just itching to win a war our ancestors couldn't and kill all of you Ice Mages." The Dragon King's voice is cold. "I really shouldn't be wasting my time playing games with you, Mage King, when I could be..."

"What about your great ancestor, Kari? The legendary Ice Dragon. Hasn't the power of ice been lost to your people?" my father questions the King.

There is silence from the Dragon King before he says snidely "And...? What is your point? I hate these meaningless stalls. Do not waste my time."

My father ignores his rudeness and continues to explain, "And if you marry one of my daughters with Kari's magic, perhaps your future heir will inherit and receive the power of ice once more. There can be a Dragon born with the power for the first time since Kari."

"Each of my daughters has a powerful source of magic and is healthy and strong enough to carry a Dragon child... I don't even care if you take a second wife amongst my daughters or even harm one of them. She'll be all yours to do what you will with. I think this is a good deal for you and your people to consider for just ten years of peace between us. Don't you think so, King Orval?"

So, if I am to be picked, he can get away with hurting or even killing me. I realize that my father does not seem to care about what happens to his daughters. If I fall into the hands of the Dragon King, I may as well have a death sentence attached to me.

The minute I give birth to a healthy male heir with ice magic, I will be tossed away like trash, perhaps even tortured for information regarding my country, although I am not very educated about the country like my sisters are.

The King is quiet, and I hear low whispers in foreign language from another man at his side, most likely discussing the best options.

Minutes pass as I continue to hear murmuring, and the Dragon King switches back to our language to questions us. "So, she will be mine? And say, if she dies from my hands in the ten years I have her, what will you do?"

"Nothing... We will both be signing a treaty," explains my father. "Once it is signed, my people cannot attack yours and vice versa. And once my daughter is handed over to you, she is technically a part of your Kingdom Oria and no longer mine."

The Dragon King steps forward, his magic drawing nearer.

"Then let me get a closer look at your four lovely daughters," he says with a little too much excitement.

"Of course," my father replies coolly.

He starts from the left, his feet shifting and stopping, examining each of my sisters. He seems to be disinterested as he moves on rather quickly, from one sister to the next.

He stalls and asks, "May I touch them? I'm concerned you're giving me a man with this one. She has no breasts, and her face is mannish. I wouldn't doubt you are trying to trick me so you can make a fool out of me."

My father is quiet. "You may touch them, but all my daughters are, indeed, female."

I hear a startled gasp coming from one of my sisters, and the Dragon King laughs. "Seems she is really a female..."

He moves on, his feet stopping at the sister next to me. I can tell he is somewhat more interested in her as he examines her longer than the others and doesn't make any rude remarks toward her.

"I do have to say, this is your best daughter so far, Mage King. Beautiful face, healthy body, nice hips... But she just doesn't do it for me," the Dragon King remarks snidely.

"You're running out of luck," he coos as he moves to me slowly, "you better hope I am interested in this last one, or you have some secret daughter that I can see."

His feet finally stop in front of me, and his magic is so close that it causes the hair on my arms to stand. I can feel his gaze on me, and he's quiet once again, surely uncertain what to make of me. I am definitely different compared to my sisters.

"Blind and unfed... This one doesn't look healthy. Perhaps she is sickly," he says. "I've never heard of a blind Mage before. Is she really blind, or is the thing around her eyes just for decoration?"

I feel his hand reach for the cloth over my eyes, and in my head, I see a vision of the Dragon roaring in my face. On instinct, I draw back even though I shouldn't and slap his hand away.

I hear laughs coming from behind him, but the Dragon King himself doesn't laugh and is rather quiet.

"Well, Princess, consider yourself lucky. You're the first Mage to touch me and live to tell the tale.... But I am still interested in those eyes of yours," he says almost in a growl, his temper surfacing when his comrades laugh.

He quickly reaches toward me, snapping the lace ribbon from around my eyes. On impulse, I open them, and I can tell it is nightfall now.

"Ah, so she is blind... There's no color to her eyes," he laughs. "Guess this thing isn't just for show after all."

He leans in toward me and this time, I stay still. "You're all bone. If you gain a little weight, you will be more desirable. If I didn't know any better, I'd assume they are feeding you scraps." I feel the warm breath fan against my cheek at his proximity. It smells of liquor.

"You're either sickly or mistreated... Which is it?" he questions me.

I am quiet, unsure of how I should reply. Instead of speaking, I consider how he smells strongly of leather and how he must be wearing it.

"Princess, you are very rude," he coos. "You should answer a King's question immediately." I can hear the impatience in his voice.

"Are you deaf, too?" He blows in my ear, and I cover it with my hand.

"No..." I finally reply. "I can hear you."

"Ah, she speaks. Guess she isn't mute either." He draws back to his people, and I can hear some of them laugh again.

He turns silent, and so do his people. He announces, "I think I have come to a decision."

I swallow, preparing to be mixed into some war and having to flee or fight for my life. I clench my fists, and even my father is quiet.

"I will accept your treaty of ten years of peace," the Dragon King announces to my father.

I freeze and I am in shock, but there is also relief that there will be no war.

"I see. Which daughter of mine have you taken an interest in?" My father sounds gleeful that the Dragon King will not be declaring war on our people and the Kingdom Yulor.

I wait to hear his reply, thinking he will most likely choose the sister standing next to me. She'll be his best option even though he has said he isn't attracted to her.

The Dragon King replies, "I want the blind woman to be my

wife, the one you have treated so poorly." It is like I can see an evil smirk gracing his face at this announcement.

My heart clenches in my chest, and my sisters begin muttering to themselves, probably thankful to be not chosen, but curious to know why he would choose me. I wonder the same myself.

I can't believe it; the Dragon King has declared me as his wife... Me. A blind bastard child of the King.

Do I secretly wish for this? To be chosen by him?

There is a part of me that feels special, that I was the one chosen over my sisters. Me – a King has really picked me to be his wife.

Is it my beauty that made him choose me? Does he perhaps feel pity for me? There has to be a reason for everything – *or is it random?*

He may be labeled a monster, but there is a possibility the Dragon King can give me a better chance at life – a life outside of my bitter cold tower.

"I wish for her to be prepared for me to take to the borders of your land by dawn. Meanwhile, you and I will discuss this treaty," the Dragon King addresses my father.

"Follow me," my father says, retreating from the group, not giving any further instructions on what I am to do.

The Dragon walks behind my father, with what sounds like two other men. "The rest of you go home, you two included. I am in no need of escorts. Tell the army upon your return of the news, Ukiah first. I don't want there to be any accidents... I am sure they will be delighted that I am bringing back a bride tomorrow night. All should be in good cheers, happy moods."

They listen and retreat without saying a word. I hear their footsteps disappearing. I stand still, wanting to fall down and breathe deeply. But I don't know of any place to rest but the ground.

I have been picked by the Dragon King. One who will be bringing me to his country of Dragons. They hate Mages. I will be with a King who can do anything to me once father and he sign the treaty.

My breath is shaky. I am panicking. I grab my chest, trying to get over my thoughts and calm myself down. But it is difficult.

I am to be the wife of the Dragon King... I am cursed. That is no longer a question, but I guess it is better than being thrown back into the tower. Surely it is.

I hate that tower, at least now I have a chance at some freedom. But I realize I will never get to taste what it is to be truly free.

THREE

YEARNING TO BE FREE

THEY SIGN the treaty in blood at midnight after going over every section, down to the smallest details. The two Kings despise one another, but they manage to tolerate each other for hours in a single confined room.

In those hours, I should have been packing what few belongings I have; instead, I spend the time outside. All I have are the clothes I am wearing.

I used to have other belongings, but I learned long ago that I would never see them again. They have either been thrown away or stolen by my sisters and the maids. Because of that, I have nothing left to remember my mother by. I care for nothing else that has been lost – old clothes or children's toys.

I need to focus on other things. I should enjoy the last bits of cool air as I hear the land of the Fire Dragons is hot, the ground sometimes even catching fire on its own from the sun. For an Ice Mage like me, it will be silent torture and hell. I normally despise the icy air, but I believe I will eventually miss it.

I can't help but wonder why the King chose me yet again, these thought never leave me.

I wish I could read his expressions and thoughts, but without sight, I cannot see his face. I don't know anyone who can read minds. I will never know his reasons for choosing me. If I ask, he will lie. Besides, does it really matter?

What do I know about him? *Very little...*

I know the army of Dragons at the borders finally retreated when they received word from the King. I can imagine the bloodthirsty men not being happy with his decision. I wonder what their reactions will be on discovering he is bringing home an Ice Mage for a bride... Perhaps they will be confused, happy... Or angry.

And upon their King's return, what faces will they show him? What faces will they have on seeing me, their future disabled queen?

Perhaps being blind is a blessing. I will never see their looks of disgust or hatred. However, I will hear their words, I am sure they will not hold their tongues. Maybe initially they will, but eventually, given time, they will not be shy with their thoughts.

It is already well past midnight and soon, I will be amongst the Dragons and in the lands they rule. The lands I will soon be ruling. Shortly, I will be around those who hate me for different reasons. I don't have anyone to bid farewell to; my absence will not be missed by a single person. Even those in the tower will not miss me. Maybe they won't even realize that I am gone.

I am traveling on horseback with one of my father's men to the border. It is the first time I have ridden on a horse; though, I am not alone, the man sits behind me, guiding us to our destination.

I decide that the experience is enjoyable. The beast is warm, his fur long and coarse, and his heart thunders in his chest as we ride. The sound is reassuring and pleasant.

His breathing is heavy but not labored. He is working hard, the pounding of his hooves against the ground grows louder as the land changes and is rockier than I expected.

I weave my fingers through the fur. It is too bad I will never see my surroundings and experience the world in different colors as others do. I will never see the sun rise or set, the flowers blooming, the snow falling, or even my person.

I feel like an empty vessel with no face or personality compared to the many others I am surrounded by. Sight is everything to them, even to the person I ride with, and I'm sure even to the Dragon King.

I wish magic existed to cure me, to make me see again. As a child, my mother would tell me grand stories, fairy tales, to make me hopeful about magic which could cure anything, even my blindness.

My curse makes me think too much. I am so caught up in my thoughts and memories, I didn't realize we have stopped riding. I am hoisted down from the horse, all without a word being spoken to me.

The horse paws at the ground with its hoof, loud snorts expel from his nostrils, impatient to be moving again. My feet are stationed on the earth, while my heart races. Everything is moving so fast that I am struggling to get my thoughts together.

I hear a snap of the reins and feel the spray of small pebbles pelting my dress as the horse turns and gallops off, leaving me all alone. I listen for a long while until I can no longer hear it, which tells me I am finally by myself.

I listen carefully for any signs of life around me, but I hear absolutely nothing. The air is still and vacant of even winds. I try to control my fear, but I am unable to. I panic and start walking, hoping to hear signs of life. Someone who can help me.

This is the very first time I have been left alone for a long time. No, if I am honest, this is the first time I have been completely alone. I have always been surrounded by people, even if separated by stone walls. I could hear the noises of their life from talking to breathing. This silence is comforting in a way.

I have no idea what is coming next, but I recall the Dragon King's words of wanting me at the border by dawn for him. I assume or maybe hope that it is almost dawn. I didn't want to be left alone; even a terrifying Dragon is better than no one...

I click my tongue each time I step forward to get a feeling of where I am. It seems that there is no life here around me, no trees, birds, animals, nothing but stretches of barren land. Even the smallest of life has traces of magic, and there is nothing here.

My heart pounds faster with worry, but I reassure myself that everything will be fine. Yet deep down, I knew nothing will ever be okay again. I am putting false hopes in my head like my dead mother, so long ago, gave me one that my vision will be cured with miraculous magic.

After walking aimlessly for what seems like hours, I stop wandering. *If I go too far, will the Dragon King find me, or maybe someone besides him? Someone or something wishing me harm?*

The Dragon King obviously does not care for his new bride. I am sure a blind Mage wandering around lost is a joke to him. Unsure of what else to do, I listen more intently to my surroundings. I hear nothing at first, but when I concentrate, I can hear something. The sound is almost nonexistent.

In the far distance, I hear the something that can be easily mistaken as heavy winds. Though that's not an apt description, it is more like a loud hum resonating through the air.

As I try to figure out what the noise is, it gets louder and closer, approaching fast. Before I have a chance to react, I feel strong winds gust past me and lift my dress.

It finally clicks in my head.

A Dragon.

Those sounds are the flapping of its powerful wings, disturbing the air around me. I crane my head up toward the source, and as I concentrate, a large mass of magic hovers over me.

It looks like the Dragon King's magic, which I faintly saw during our first encounter. This must be his Dragon in the flesh.

I feel startled as the mass of magic lowers to me, the beat of its wings slowing to a rhythmic beat. I feel like death is descending on me instead of a Dragon.

What is he doing?

My muscles tense in apprehension as I feel warmth and vibration begin to enclose around my shoulders. Spindly long clawed fingers slide between my arm and body before tightening quickly. I feel my dress tear as the claws accidentally snag the loose fabric.

The claws are so sharp that the fabric gives way easily. If his claws accidentally touches my skin, my flesh will be torn asunder. The thought is terrifying, but somehow, he manages to avoid my skin.

My breath is caught in my throat as the wings, which were beating gently, begin to pulsate the air violently. I am lifted off the ground, my feet dangle over vast emptiness as his wings propel us higher in the air. I am frightened, yet I don't find myself moving. I am frozen with fear at the thought he may drop me.

I wouldn't be able to do a thing if he dropped me from this height... I will surely die. Maybe he intends for this to be a joke and he is going to drop me, making my death a symbol that nothing will appease him, and he will have his war in ten years. Or he will go back on the treaty and declare war anyway.

I grab the Dragon's skin, trying to find security in something that cares nothing of my life. The scales on his hands are smooth and soft. It is an odd texture for me when I was told their skin is slimy or so rough that touching the scales will rub away my flesh.

I can't stop my mind from returning to the thought of falling to my death. Learning rumored stories to be false is not on the top of my list. I may have my magic, but it will not do me any good. My powers of ice will not blanket my fall at this height.

More pressure is applied to my shoulders, making me stiffen. My body's weight is already a discomfort to my shoulders from being carried by my torso. He is soaring through the skies with ease as I am in his grasp, suffering. Struggling.

I cannot enjoy the feeling of the wind pressing against my face. We are too high in the atmosphere; it's where only God should reign from.

Most would be crying in my situation, but I find no tears forming. I cried for so long in the tower that I do not think I have any tears left. Crying is something shameful with our kind, or so I have been taught by the people around me.

Dragons must think the same, tears are weak...

Drifting through the air would not be so bad if I wasn't being carried through the skies within a Dragon's clasp, a Dragon who seems to despise me and my kind.

My hearing is drowned out by the wind whipping past us and the beat of his wings propelling us forward. I cannot perceive anything but those two things.

After a time, the ache in my shoulders becomes unbearable. It is my ears that hurt. Soon, the Dragon King's wings begin to slow, and his hold on my shoulder lessens until I am completely let go of. I feel panic and start to think my beliefs are true about him killing me by dropping me.

I begin to plead for my life against my better judgment. "Wait! Please don't! Don't let me go! Please!" I shout.

My pleading doesn't work as before, I know it. I feel myself falling through the air. I tense, clenching my eyes shut, knowing the fate that awaits me.

I hit the stone ground hard, but the fall was shorter than I imagined, even the pain was lesser than expected. I thought I will be in terrible pain as I hit the ground. Surprisingly, I am not.

I slide my hand out and run them along the smooth stone ground as I try to make sense of everything. I can still hear him above me, his wings beating gently.

Where am I?

I know, in theory, I was to be brought to the Land of Dragons. But am I really here, or have I been taken someplace else?

I dare not move, not knowing my surroundings or what is going on. I can still be very high off the ground as strong winds are causing my dress to flap around. These are not being caused by the beat of his wings disrupting the air.

The stone under my fingers feels extremely hot, just like his scaly flesh. It feels like a fire is raging beneath just like the fire within each Dragon and the sun. A fire I feel I cannot escape from.

This place must be the Land of the Dragons.

I hear him land. It is loud as his body is massive, the ground quakes underneath him. I can almost see him in my head again. The scary Dragon is a shining mass of darkness, or what my mind tells me is black. This is the Dragon King.

I stay lying in the same position, too scared to move or say anything, in case I somehow anger the temperamental Dragon. All I can do is listen.

I tremble, hearing loud crackles and snaps, noises that a raging fire would make. I feel the air vibrate. *Is the Dragon King shaking his head?* Then comes the hissing and spitting like a tea kettle left on the fire too long.

I feel hot burning pellets hit my arm, which stings painfully before cooling down quickly enough. A sizzle informs me the pellets hitting my dress are burning holes into the fabric. They are bouncing everywhere.

I reach to touch the one that burned my skin only to feel the pellet disintegrate under the light touch of my fingers. *What are these things?*

The next thing I hear is of something melting and hitting the ground in splats. It frightens me as it feels like the skin and flesh has been carved away from the body. I imagine it is the Dragon shifting back to a man.

Then there is silence, and I hear the whisper of bare feet drawing near. I sit up slowly, straightening my back as I face the man who I believe to be the Dragon King. I am prepared for just about anything in my thoughts yet for nothing in reality.

He is so close to me now his body feels like a smoldering fire, the warmth just as impressive as the land itself. The heat does not radiate off his being like the first time I met him.

Is it from shifting?

The feet stop, and I curl my fingers into my dress. Which is now probably frayed after the pellets. I hold my breath again.

"You are no longer in the Lands of Mages, Yulor," he states, his voice indifferent.

"Am I in the Land of Dragons?" I ask, unsure. I have a good idea where I am from how hot it is, but I want confirmation.

"Yes, my Kingdom, Grand Oria. You are in the capital, Viss," he replies, "A place you won't ever be leaving unless it is by your death."

His words chill my bones. Many, like my father, have threatened my life before, but somehow the Dragon King makes it even more intimidating.

What will it be like to die by his hands? The hands of a powerful Fire Dragon...?

I can only guess that it will be extremely painful, the worst pain one can feel before death. Our powers don't mix - ice and fire. I've heard horror stories about Ice Mages torturing Fire Dragons with their magic, the ice and cold slowly killing them, sometimes even from the inside out.

There are so many tales of Ori, the Fire Dragon, and Kari, the Ice Dragon. Many stories told of when they were children, how they would hurt each other. Then there are other tales of how Kari would accidentally hurt other Dragons when he played.

I remember one story spoke of Ori having a permanent scar running down his face from his brother lashing out at him, using ice over a petty argument.

If there is something Kari and I have in common, it is the fact that neither of us can control our magic very well. I can't help but imagine the Dragon King torturing me in the future. I imagine he will use his fire to get revenge for his people by slowly burning me alive. My flesh will bubble, and my insides will boil until they melt. My hair will be gone, long turned to ash, my eyes will get so hot they will run down my already melting face.

I don't want to die so horribly. I stand on my feet, my balance wobbly. He can do anything he wants to me. And there is no way of escape.

Anything... I can be some toy he can break over and over without any consequences. There is nothing I can do. Nothing. Even If I were to protect myself from the Dragon King, others are sure to kill me. There is no hope in my situation.

He has said I am going to be his bride... A bride is someone you love or will come to love. I am not that to him. I will never feel that way toward him either.

The Dragon King can probably feel nothing but lust, and I'm sure the lust he feels for me is very little. My body is thin and boney, my eyes colorless, unable to see, and I lack the intelligence to hold a decent conversation.

But, then again, there is the heir father spoke of. He will probably use me just to get a male heir with the power of ice, to get back what was stolen from his kind. But I also know I will suffer in the meanwhile.

Children, I have never thought about them before. I never thought there is a possibility, but I may be barren. *What if I am? What will he do then?*

I move back, each step I take on foreign land is slow and cautious. I have no idea where I currently am, other than being in his Kingdom, the Land of the Dragons, and on the stone ground.

He has said we are in his capital called Viss. *Is he telling me the truth?*

My heart beats madly against my ribs as I hear him moving, walking toward me. I keep getting visions of his Dragon, roaring and threatening to burn me alive until there is nothing left of me but ashes. I see visions of him abusing me, using me to just get what he wants.

I have had enough of abuse.

What did I do to deserve any of this?

To have something stolen from me since birth that I should have had... To be thrown in a tower for most of my life, to have no connection with people either by word or touch, to be given to the Dragons, then tossed away.

Life is unfair.

To be treated like a monster, only to be given to a true monster.

I clench my teeth as I listen to him approach me again. I don't want to be here, I regret saying anyone at all is better than being alone. I hate how he can see me floundering.

"I wouldn't run if I were you... It's useless... You will either die from the cliffs or by the hands of my people. They know I have to take a Mage as my wife, but they see you as an enemy. It's your choice," he hisses.

I don't care to listen. His words mean nothing to me.

I have the sudden urge to flee. I want to survive and to be free.

Freedom is my only wish.

I will only be a prisoner here just like I was in the tower.

I start running and suddenly, I feel nothing under my foot, and I begin to lose my balance. *Where is the edge?*

My heart stops as I feel myself fall backward from trying to turn on the balls of my feet to go back where I came from.

I cannot see it!

There is nothing I can do!

I fling my arms in the air, desperate to grab a hold of anything, and when I do, I feel a warm hand catch me.

I dig my nails into the arm as it pulls me back onto my feet again. I hear the Dragon King snort. "Didn't I mention cliffs? Or are you not only blind but stupid as well?"

Once I calm down, I feel a little better having both my feet planted on solid ground. I whisper loudly with urgency, "I just want freedom."

He is silent as he processes my words, giving me some hope. I hope maybe he will send me off with some money to the edge of his land so I can live peacefully. It's a very big hope.

"I don't want to be your prisoner. I don't want to be trapped," I explain to him, hoping he will understand, hoping he isn't as vile as the rumors say.

He laughs, the laugh more mocking than anything, "Well, I am sorry to inform you, Ice Princess, queens are bound to their lands and husband. You will not be a prisoner, but neither will you have your freedom. No king or queen truly has a sense of freedom."

My nails dig more into his arm, and he takes my hand off, applying slight pressure. "And another thing, Ice Mage, to make things clear, if you have any strange ideas, I will never love you or treat you as a real queen should be treated. You will only be by my side until you give birth to a male heir with the power of ice. Only then, will I think about what to do with you."

My nails no longer dig into his arms, and only when I wince, does he let go of my hand. I feel a sorrow wrap around my throat, choking me. I can't find a voice. What am I to say? I swallow.

"For now, I will have a maid come to collect you and show you to your room. Then tomorrow we have a wedding to attend, unfortunately for you and I. More so for myself," he says before I hear his footsteps travel further away.

"Oh, and until then, don't try and run. I'm afraid the cliffs here have seen one too many deaths of Mages. I don't want our soon-to-be queen to be one of them." He laughs as he disappears, and I can no longer hear his footsteps.

I feel another strong gust of wind, and I just stand there, knowing one misstep can lead me to my death or a serious injury.

Once again, I feel trapped with nothing I can do. There is always nothing I can do.

Helpless is what I am.

FOUR

EVIL MAIDS

My eyes burn, smoke fills my lungs, and everything feels hot. It feels like I am burning everywhere, not a place spared. I scream out in pain and wiggle only to realize I am bound tightly to a beam with rope.

I can't break free...

I don't know what's happening.

I can't use my magic either.

Why can't I use my magic?!

There are so many voices murmuring in a crowd, too, some excited while others talk in hushed whispers.

I hear a snarky voice above the others, a voice belonging to the Fire Dragon King, "Are you enjoying our wedding, Ice Princess?"

Is he burning me alive?

Is this what he had planned all along?

This is insane. I just want to go back home. I want to curl up against the cold stone floors of the tower and never leave. I am scared of death! Death is something unknown; death is the end of life as we know it; there is nothing beyond death. Everything ends in one single moment.

I can only scream in response to what the Fire Dragon King has asked, the pain too unbearable. Everything hurts.

"It appears like you're enjoying it. I'm glad... I thought long and hard about how I wanted our wedding to go." He laughs, other voices follow suit. The whispers soon die down.

"Please let me down! Please!" I beg in pain. "It hurts!! IT HURTS!! IT HURTS!" I finally scream, even my face is getting hot. My flesh feels as if it is melting. My voice is rough from the smoke.

"Now this is what I call a wedding!" he hollers evilly to his men, and before I know it, I somehow break free of the ropes because of my thrashing, and as I hit the ground, I am jolted awake.

I fling myself out of the bed, sweat dripping down my body. I can hear someone else in the room with me, not too far away. I gasp, panicked, not used to anyone being near me as I sleep. I was never once caught off guard in the tower where everything had a routine. I am especially startled by my nightmare.

"Are you alright, my lady?" a maid questions, her voice uncaring. The King, after all, assigned the maid to me last night. The very moment I met her, she led me to my room and left shortly after.

The maid appears very detached and cold, but that is to be expected. I don't even get to learn her name, and neither is she interested in telling me. But that is to be expected as oil and water never mix. I am their mortal enemy. Then again, my people are nothing less. They would have never accepted a Dragon queen had my father taken one.

I breathe heavily and grab my chest. The room is unbearably hot, even my clothes feel like they are suffocating me. It must be the warmth of the room that has triggered my nightmare.

"I'm fine," I reply even though I felt the complete opposite of fine. The frightening nightmare has knocked me out of my bed and landed me on the floor, my toes curling into the rug beside my bed.

"Good because we must prepare you for the day," she says, walking toward me. She grabs my arm and pulls me forward.

My legs move with her, but my muscles are extremely tense. I can even feel the touch of her hand and how warm she is when I compare her to Ice Mages.

She stops and I feel the presence of others. Their magic is easier to sense unlike the maid who has spoken to me thus far. There are more people here. *Are they all maids?*

The maid lets go of me. "Girls, come in. It's time to dress the queen. I beg your pardon, she is still a princess and only at the wedding, will she become a queen." She laughs.

Their mocking hurts me, but this is to be expected. I harden my mind like the stone floor of my room and stand still, trying to take in everything with all my senses. The girls filter in. Their magical presences reach me before I hear their footsteps. They were three of them.

"You will help her wash, dress, then do her hair and makeup. Everything must be perfect even though she is an Ice Mage. The King has picked her to be his queen, therefore you will treat her as one of our own. After you're done, send her down to the King for breakfast," the woman announces in a stern voice.

"Ma'am, the King has informed us that he does not want her to join him for breakfast. He wants to keep her in her room until tonight and only because of the wedding," a girl speaks up, her voice soft.

The woman laughs, "Oh, is that right?"

"Yes, ma'am."

She stops laughing, "Have you spoken with Advisor Rhys about this matter?"

"No, ma'am."

"The King's wants don't matter in this case. It's Rhys we must please. He knows what's best for the King," the woman snaps. "Go, ask him what we must do with the Queen. Now, Catherine!"

"Yes, ma'am," she says before scurrying away, the door shutting after her with some force.

"Now, girls. Get going. She isn't going to wash herself, she's blind. It will take our lady forever to do it, and our time is limited." Not only her words state her impatience but her tone, too. "Hurry!"

I can wash myself, but they speak the truth. Everything is new here, making it difficult for me. It feels shameful regardless.

"Yes, ma'am." The two girls chorus before they walk toward me.

I do use sounds to get me by, but I cannot tell them. It will only lead to future mockings. A queen who has to click her tongue to perceive others as she walks, not her sight.

I hate the humiliation my blindness brings, most of all. I remember when I was in the tower, growing from child to woman, the guards would comment on my growing breasts each new day they saw me. Their words were vulgar, comparing my breasts when I was a young girl to praisins and as I aged, to dropapples, then icemelons.

They would always snort and laugh, especially when I got my first blood. They told me I was dying from some made-up disease – Dragon Rage.

The maids here are also not so gentle with me, instead they are rough as one pulls off my clothes while the other fills the tub. This is nothing like the treatment I received back in my land on my final day there.

Once the clothing is removed, I am yanked into the tub. The hot water scalds my skin, and I grab each edge of the porcelain tub in shock.

"It's hot!" I cry out in surprise and move, only for one of them to grab my shoulders, holding me in place.

One of the maids giggles. "Oh, is the water too hot for you, Ice Mage?" she asks snidely.

"I forgot Ice Mages are sensitive to the warmth," the other jibes while taking a cloth to my flesh, scrubbing so hard that it hurts.

I try and get out of the steaming water. I am only pushed back down, the water splashes around me. "Now, my lady. We must cleanse you for tonight, and from what I am taught, Mages are filthy. The King does not like dirty women."

"Please, it's too hot! It burns!" I start panicking at the scorching sensations on my skin; it is like I am reliving my dream. The dream where I was being burned alive at my own wedding by the King.

"Stop being a baby, my lady," a maid hushes me, forcing me in place, "it is only hot water." She spits out her venom.

I feel tears sting my eyes, and I suck in a shaky breath to try to calm myself.

Please just let this be over soon...

As the maids clean me, there is a knock on the bedroom door, and the woman calls, "Who is it?"

"Catherine, ma'am," the first maid replies.

"Come in."

The door creaks open and the maid steps in, and I hear her shutting the door quietly behind her.

"What has Rhys said?" the first one questions.

"He wants her to dine with the King. It is a formal thing for him, and they should get familiar with each other before the wedding. He's also said the King can't avoid her if he expects children from her. And..." Catherine replies, pausing at the end.

"Go on, spit it out, I am not going to be cutting your tongue off," she responds haughtily.

"He... He... He...." she stutters. "He said the King is not a boy and shouldn't believe the tall tales of Mages freezing the pricks off men who bed them."

"I see," she laughs, "it is probably in your best interest to keep it to yourself, seeing as our King will not be so keen of you spreading such rumors. You might just lose your tongue yet." Then her tone changes. "Girls, don't mess around with our lady too much. We don't want her skin to be all red and blotchy for the King to see, though I'd imagine he wouldn't care too much."

"But it is you who told us to cleanse her of any filth," one of the maids remark.

"Mages are dirty, yes. But, unfortunately, she is our Queen, and we must respect her to certain levels, Yanmei."

"I see." The maid, Yanmei, lets go of my shoulders. The restriction of her hands is gone, and I am tempted to push myself out of the tub, only for her to warn me in a rotten tone, "Don't even think about running, my lady."

"Yanmei, be nice... And Catherine...?"

"Yes?" replies the soft-spoken maid.

"Watch these two and make sure they don't cause our lady too much grief. I have other things to take care of." She exits the room.

Will I be treated better with her gone? Or worse? She seems to be in charge.

"Yes, ma'am," Catherine shouts just as the door closes.

Once the woman has left, Catherine, Yanmei, and the unnamed maid get silent.

The unnamed maid continues to wash me, and Yanmei speaks up, "Catherine, you will not get in our way, right?"

"Miss Selene has told me to watch you two," she says.

"Watch us do what?" questions Yanmei snottily.

"I won't let you or Ava slack off on the job. So I will be watching for that... I don't care what else you do." Her voice seems to change with the disappearance of the woman, Selene. "Now, let's get to work. I will help her with her hair and makeup. I will also be picking out her dress... If I let one of you two dress her, she will look like a spawn of the circus."

"You're such a wench, Catherine," Ava says, wringing out the washcloth and tossing it aside. "I am better at picking out dresses than you. Let me help."

Yanmei laughs and says, "Do you think Orval will sleep with her tonight? She is so thin..." She pokes at my ribs and continues, "I can count every single one of them. I can't imagine she would be desirable to him."

I get a flashback of how the King commented the same about my weight. Yanmei is right about deciding me to be undesirable.

"If he does sleep with her, it is only for an heir," replies Catherine.

"True, just don't forget about that, Ice Mage," Yanmei pokes her finger into my rib painfully, "our King will never truly fall for one of your people, especially one who is so pitiful and weak."

Their words continue to be hurtful. There is so much to think about. I am going to be sleeping with the King tonight, the first man I am going to be laying with. It is too much to think about.

It is scary.

Everything is scary.

I still want out of this scorching bath.

"Besides, who are we to judge who our King brings to his bedchambers or who he takes as a queen? We should not bother to think what the nobility does. Our minds will be boggled by only a quarter of what they do," Catherine mutters.

Yanmei takes her finger away from my ribs, and I can only sit in the steaming water, trembling like a small child.

Pitiful... She is right. For an Ice Mage, I am. I don't want to use my powers, and I don't think I ever will... Not unless I have to.

"Let's wash your hair now, my Queen," she says, and before I can protest, I am pushed violently under the hot water. I clench my eyes shut along with my mouth. Her tone and actions are more violent now after bringing up the King.

Is she jealous?

She keeps me there for a few seconds before pulling me up by my hair, and I cough violently. My eyes and throat burn, not only from the boiling temperature but from the soaps and oils in the bathwater. My tears and drool mix together.

She keeps my head stretched back, her fingers woven in my hair, a tight fist pulls and tugs at them, threatening to scalp me. Slowly, my gagging becomes less, but I gasp still, unable to believe that I will not be drowned in the bathwater.

While gasping, I question her, "What are you jealous of?"

The maid grows quiet, her fist loosening, the reprieve a small gift. "Jealous?" She pauses before she snorts, "Are you asking if I am jealous of you?"

"Yes," I squeak, acting not like a queen, but a mirromouse in a room full of skalagins.

Her fists tighten in my hair again, and she hisses, "I will never be jealous of a whore who charades as a queen."

She plunges my head back under the water, my hands struggling to find something to grab, but there's nothing. I don't even have the chance to get another gulp of air, only hot and soapy water.

I hope and pray, but she keeps my head under. My head pounds just as my heart does. My body is desperate as it wants to live, and I try to inhale air. Water rushes in, and the last bits of air escape my lungs. Bubbles form, I feel them brush against my face, rushing to the surface.

I don't feel weak as time passes, I feel... relaxed, and I stop struggling against my oppressor. My hair moves through the water as I imagine the wings of a bird flying through the sky. What an odd thought...

Perhaps it is my fate to die today.

And maybe in the next life, I will be a bird... With wings, able to fly where I please and to see the whole world from the skies. Yes, I would like to be a bird.

My mother used to sing to the birds.

She used to bathe me too.

The memory is like a dream, but I know she bathed me a few times. Her hands were gentle and soft. When she washed my hair, her nails would skim across my scalp ever so lightly, her fingers weaving in and out of my wet tresses. Then, like the birds, she would sing to me, her voice kind and filled with love.

She loved me...I should be happy that I was loved by one person in my lifetime. Love was all I ever wanted. The King will never gift me with such pleasure; hatred will be the only thing I'll receive from him... *Never love.*

My mind slips away to nothingness as it always does when I lie and fall asleep. Maybe I am fated to die... At the hands of my maids...

Dragon maids... Dragons... It is for the best... Sparing me of a lifetime of pain and suffering.

I close my eyes, giving up, but fate has different plans.

I am yanked back, my hair whipping behind and hitting my skin with a slap before plastering itself against me. I gasp, water gushes out from my lungs, before gurgling as I try to breathe. I cough and snort as I claw at my face, my hair sucked partially into my mouth as I try to inhale as much air as possible.

I continue to cough, expelling water from my lungs. My desire to live seems stronger than the temptation to die a peaceful death. *WHY DO I WANT TO LIVE?* I will suffer. I am so angry and frustrated. *WHY ME?*

I hear screaming and sense tense hands on my shoulder. They are rough and calloused, the nails dull and uneven. These hands knew hard work. The grip they have hurts, their fingers curl into my skin.

I am gasping. I begin to pay attention to my surroundings; my body realizes it is no longer in danger. Somehow, I have managed to find the sides of the tub, and my fingers wrap around them and hold on for dear life.

"You could have killed her, Yanmei! Do you not understand that she could have died?" Ava snaps, her voice rises with each word.

"I wished she did," Yanmei hisses.

At the same time, a hand leaves my shoulder, and I hear a crack a moment later... Then silence.

Was someone slapped?

I try not to breathe, try to be silent, but my attempt is a failure. Snot travels down my face from my nose and drips into my open mouth, where my teeth chatter.

"You are Theka, mind your place. You will never be of nobility; you are merely tolerated by them. Do not place yourself on a higher pedestal than the rest of us because our King took pity on you," Ava growls out.

"Ava..." Catherine murmurs, her voice soft.

"Don't... I don't need pity from you... I need it from no one... Ava,

I might be a Theka like you, but I am not lesser than anyone because of it," Yanmei says with bitterness and venom. "Wash the whore. Wait... I was wrong... She is not even a whore, just a mare to be bred. Why don't you tend to her like stall boys?" She laughs.

I hear the click of Yanmei's shoes as she turns and continues to laugh. I expect the door to be violently slammed, but she closes it quietly, and her aura eventually vanishes.

"Next time, I will not be responsible for her actions. She will not live much longer, with behavior like that. They will not tolerate her," Ava whispers.

"Ava..." Catherine murmurs again, not knowing what to say.

"Enough! We have more work." Ava exclaims, her demeanor changes, and her hand leaves my aching shoulder from where she has been digging in too hard with her fingers.

I am scared, but I remain silent. The two maids I am left with chat about all the work they have left. Each time they run a cloth over my skin, I shake and tremble. I try to shrink into myself, but they became rougher with my refusal of letting them bathe me.

"Please, no more..." I sob, pleading as a last resort. If only the Mages at home knew I am begging Dragons, I would be shamed further...

"Don't worry. I think you have suffered enough for one day, Mage. Though, there will be more days to come like this, worst days. And it is not only Yanmei you should worry about because as you are aware of, you are also surrounded by enemies, enemies you can't even see."

"Why?" I ask, not even sure why I am bothering.

"Why? It's the way it has always been and will be for eternity," Catherine says. Her words are cruel but true.

"Why Yanmei? She hates me not just because I am a..."

"Partially," replies Ava. "That's why most will hate you, but she has a far greater reason to do so..."

"She wants to be you," Catherine murmurs, "She loves our King more than her status allows."

She loves the Fire Dragon King... She considers me no better than a thief, but she will not want to be me. I don't want to be me.

Ava speaks up, "But we also hate you, Mage. Just because I warded off a danger does not mean I love you as I should love my lady. To be serving a Mage is the most disrespectful thing Selene could have done to us. We will much rather be serving a true queen rather than a false one."

Selene must be the head maid.

Catherine runs her fingers through my hair. "But let's try to get along, for now. We are to take care of you until the end of our days or yours, but I believe yours will be much shorter than ours. Yanmei doesn't have to drown you when so many others around us are eager to kill you."

How long will I last? Her words frighten me. If my maids try to kill me, *who will be the next one? The cook?*

The maids start giggling in unison, and Catherine's hands find my hair again.

"Such pretty hair, my lady," Catherine giggles.

"Do not worry, my lady, we are true to our words. We will always be so. You can take what little solace in that, yes, you can." Ava giggles more.

I nod my head. I can only remain in the bathwater, frozen in place, small tremors shaking me as my entire body starts to throb.

If the maids are this evil... *How will the Fire Dragon King be when we are alone?*

I get visions of his Dragon, breathing fire and having skin hotter than any flame. My fear can only grow.

FIVE

THE GIFT OF FLESH

One hundred and forty-nine steps, four turns, and one flight of stairs I have descended since leaving my room.

I walk the unknown halls of a foreign castle, and the sound of my feet in shoes is also alien to my ears.

They are new to me; I never had shoes in the tower. I can barely remember what they were like before I was locked away. It is joyous in a way.

I have a maid to my left and one to my right. They have not once left my side. What a strange sight we must be. If only I had eyes...

One hundred and eighty-one steps...

My evil maids are not so cruel in the eye of the public. They are kind, friendly, and even respectful if I dare say. They are entirely different people, but this all is a facade, a show.

Every king and queen is respected. I will be the first one who isn't. It is horrible to think I will be queen to people who hate me and wish me dead. But the fact is I do not want to be their queen. If it is my choice, I would flee far away.

I have no doubt these women will not change; I can feel the tight grip of Ava to my right and Catherine on my left. Ava has long and slender fingers, musician's fingers, while Catherine's are small and pudgy, what I have often heard people call cook hands. Ava is tall and thin. Catherine is shorter and slightly overweight, yet not chubby.

I could tell their features when they bathed me, their bodies coming in contact with mine despite how much they disliked doing so. The slightest brush has given me so much information, even their words have told me a little of how their nose and mouth are.

I yearn to know more visually. I want to feel their faces, but I dare not ask. They will not grant me such permission either.

I remember feeling my mother's face; she is the only woman who allowed it. She seemed so beautiful. She had such full lips, a small and dainty nose, and really big and round eyes. My mother used to tell me I looked a lot like her but with my father's hair.

I wonder if her words are true still...

Every time a brush is run through my hair I am reminded of her words. And I am always left pondering them. I hope I still have her beauty.

Two hundred and five steps mean that I am one step closer to the Dragon King.

I am tired, and my body feels heavy. How much more terrible will I feel by the end of the night? Especially with all this walking.

We turn sharply, and my steps are silenced on a carpeted floor. I still have a wedding to attend, and events of this morning has proved to be exhausting.

My skin is still burning from the bath. The only relief I have is the warm air touching my exposed thighs, but they rub together as I walk, so the relief is limited. What is worse is the suffocating feeling as the tight corset clings to my torso – my midriff is soaked with sweat already.

The dress is unlike any others I have worn before, though I do not have a long list to compare them to. I don't remember much of what I wore as a child when my mother was alive.

The dress feels light and airy, and the back of the dress is ruffled and frilly yet feels silky. The only fat my corset has to push around is my breasts. It squeezes them so much that I feel if I bend over, they will fall free for anyone's view. I do not wish for that, so I walk rigidly, my stiff knee boots seem to help a little.

Two hundred and eleven steps, all the closer to my doom.

The hair ends tickle my open back, making me shiver. I am used to my hair being down, but they insisted on a high ponytail. It is as tight as my corset when they pulled and tugged roughly to do so.

I still can't believe how much my hair reminded me of the dress I wore - light and airy. The difference between my hair before and after is that they have washed and brushed it, and now it almost feels magical. It is much softer than before.

I'm not sure I am keen on the idea of having such a painful experience every morning just to prepare for the day. My eyes have watered plenty of times just for this preparation. The maids don't seem keen on preparing me either. They kept complaining while applying my makeup. A lot.

Two hundred and twenty steps and we stop.

Catherine lets go of my hand and walks forward, her movement muffled by the carpet. I hear her reach for the handle followed by the creak of the door opening wide.

As soon as the door opens, I am gifted with an array of different smells. My stomach lurches, clenching in hunger at the smell of freshly baked bread and other goods in the dining hall. I can almost taste the food, items I have never tasted before or if I have, they were moldy and stale.

The bread here will be warm and soft. I can almost imagine pulling a piece off and placing it in my mouth. Feeling it melt on my tongue, tasting divine.

When is the last time I ate anything fresh?

I've occasionally smelled such wonderful aromas when I was in the tower. Those came from the main castle when they had to cook for the parties. They teased my stomach more than once throughout my stay in the tower, the torture silent.

My temporary paradise of imagination is ruined when I hear the

King's voice growl as a screeching chair pushes hard against the stone floor signaling he is now standing. "I thought I told you maids that I don't want any guests during breakfast."

Ava pushes me forward by the small of my back as she walks me into the room. "Rhys ordered us differently, orders that came after yours. He deemed for you to dine with the soon-to-be queen, my lord."

"Rhys said that? That bastard's audacity..." he snaps and slams his hands on the table which causes the plates and dishes to rattle. I flinch at his anger and begin to envision his Dragon again, this time with a darkened aura and evil eyes. "Send her back to her room," he orders.

"We can't do that, my lord," Ava states.

"You can't or won't?" the King asks sharply.

"I can't and I won't," Ava replies smoothly.

"Why, because Rhys ordered you to? Am I not your King, or do you think Rhys is your King? Which is it?" he screams.

"Rhys knows what is best for you. Everyone is looking out for you, worrying about your well-being, my Lord," Ava explains.

Why is she arguing with him? Why is this man named Rhys over-ruling him? Isn't he their King? *Do they want to die?*

"Then explain how this helps me, maid?" The King stretches out the word maid as an insult.

"He said best to be familiar now before the wedding," she replies, somehow managing to keep her confidence, her voice never once wavering.

The King becomes quiet before he 'tsks,' and I hear him sitting down in his chair, which creaks with his weight. His silenced tongue makes me think he is pondering what to do with me or how to be rid of me and my maids.

"Seat her, then leave us. I will not argue with you halfwits any longer," he says annoyed but seems to accept what has occurred – if only a little.

"Yes, My Lord." I am guided forward until she stops but only to pull a chair out from under the table for me. I hear her move dishes around along with silverware, and I begin to wonder if she is setting a plate for me.

My hand clumsily finds the back of the chair, and I make my way slowly to its side, feeling it out. I do not want to ask for Ava's help; I don't want her mockery or her treating me like a child anymore. It is bad enough she is placing food onto my plate, the same way you do for a child.

I think back to how the maids have treated me thus far, and I can't help but imagine my life with them for the next ten years will be cruel. I am thankful for the breakfast, I can't wait for Ava and Catherine to be gone so that I can dine with the King alone.

I wonder who is worse - *my maids or the Dragon King?*

Well, I will find out, won't I?

"And, maid..." the King says.

"Yes?" Ava stops in her tracks.

"Don't you ever listen to Rhys over me... I am your King. Never forget." He gives a subtle warning which sounds ominous.

"Understood," she replies.

"Now go," he hisses and throws something past my head toward her. It hits the floor and makes a clatter. I think he just threw a knife or fork at her.

I now see that this breakfast will go well. I may die.

Catherine must have been the first one out; she probably stood by the door. I hear the hurried footsteps of Ava before she slips out, the door closing quietly behind her. The Dragon King and I are now alone.

Everything is silent, and I remind myself that I have not eaten properly at a table since I was a child. I don't know Dragon culture either. I have many questions I want to ask.

What food are we eating?

How do we eat?

What are your – our – people's customs?

All questions I want answers to, but I get the idea – especially from his magic spiking – that he is angry. I cannot be sure if the anger is directed at me or the anger stems from something else. I cannot believe his magic. I have never seen magic do such a thing.

I can feel him gazing at me in silence, his stare deep. It might be only a feeling, but I am not usually wrong about someone's eyes on me, watching me.

I touch the table before hesitantly touching my plate. I have no difficulty finding a large dish. I smooth out the tablecloth and graze my hand over the surface until I locate the base of a glass cup. The glass is cold and somewhat bumpy, perhaps it is the design.

I touch my plate, feeling the same bumpy ridges as the cup, only on the perimeter. The plate and glass must be from a matching set.

I hear the King pick up his silverware and start to cut into something noisily. The knife and fork scrape across the plate, a horrible screech emits each time. His stare still lingers as I can feel it, never once has his eyes wavered from me.

I'm surprised he hasn't spoken thus far to me – maybe he hopes to annoy me with his poor etiquette. As I think that, he begins to chew loudly, grinding his teeth over gristle just like the guards in the tower.

I wonder what it is we are eating, and my fingers skim over the food. I know there is meat from shape and texture – tough and tender and thick with a roundish shape. Then, to the right of the meat, I feel a warm stringy food somewhat slimy to touch. To the left, a piece of bread, hot and soft, and it is the only thing I know I will like just by touch alone.

I pick up the bread and split it in half. I bring one half to my face and inhale the smell and let the warm steam roll over my flesh. The bread smells wonderful, even the warmth in my hands delights me.

I am okay with food being my only comfort here.

I part my lips to taste this divinity, but the King interrupts me, his question is snotty. "Do you always have such odd habits while eating, Mage?"

Mage?

I am getting sick of everyone calling me everything but my name, whether they call me Ice Mage, Mage, Ice Princess, my lady, or other names, some of them vile and tasteless. All of them bothered me.

"My name is Vrai," I announce, unsure if he knows my rightful name. He may have forgotten, so I hope this serves as a friendly reminder.

"Are you... telling me to use your name?" he asks.

"Preferably," I reply.

"I can use whatever name I see fit, Mage, and Mage is a very suiting name for you," he growls.

"Do you have a preference of what you want to be called?" I question before taking a small bite of the bread, very much tempted to stuff the rest in my mouth like a truffle trigg. I can moan from the mere flavor alone.

While some may call bread bland, to someone such as I, who ate cold and stale food for the last ten years, I say differently. The bread is rich and full of flavor.

He seems to take to silence, and I give him a list of options. "King of Dragons? Dragon King? Maybe just King? Your Majesty? My lord? Your name? Something else?"

"Just call me My Lord... like the maids," he grumbles.

"Alright... My Lord," I chew and swallow my food as quietly as I can. I was locked in a tower for my entire life, and my manners are better than his.

"And I want to be clear, Mage... You are never to call me by my name," he says. "You will never receive the pleasure of my name rolling off your tongue or hear me speak your name, Mage."

I hear him stand as he pours himself a drink, the liquid splashes into his empty glass. It has such a sweet smell and its aroma fills my nostrils.

Listening to him pour his drink reminds me of my bath and the maid trying to drown me and how scared I felt. Shivers run up my spine, and I smash the bread in my hand. A sound so simple is able to trigger terrible memories of recent events.

I hear him place the metal canister on the table, and the sweet-smelling liquid swishes around inside. The sound is soft but enough to draw me back to reality and stop tormenting the food in my hand.

I slowly finish off the bread, wishing for more, but I dare not ask, so I move on to the next item on my plate. I pick up my silverware, having to feel the tips to know what the fork and knife are. The utensils feel odd in my hands as it has been a few years since I have eaten with cutlery.

Though I haven't eaten meat for a much longer time, once I cut a small piece of meat the best I can, I carefully bring the tip of my fork to my open mouth – which is watering from the smell alone.

The meat is salty, smoky, succulent, and so tender that it melts in my mouth. The bread is good, but if I dare to say, the meat is far better.

Despite almost melting in my mouth, I must chew, if only a little. I feel disheartened as my teeth are sore and sensitive from not having much food over the years.

"What food is this, that I eat?" I ask after swallowing.

"Meat," he replies in between taking giant gulps of the liquid from his glass.

"I know I eat meat... But what kind of meat is it?" I ask, beginning to cut another piece.

"Do you need to know?" He puts his glass on the table before asking.

"Yes." I take a second bite.

"It's Dragon flesh," the King replies and by the time, he answers, I have swallowed the second bite. He can't be serious, can he?

He continues, "Of course, the flesh comes from a prisoner. One who committed treason, no one innocent by far or could ever be presumed innocent. I thought why not let him honor us at least once by giving us the gift of flesh," he chuckles. "He accepted although he didn't have many choices. All in all, he wanted to be accepted by the Sky Gods and be eaten by his king... and in a turn of events, his queen."

I drop my utensils, and the Dragon King laughs, "Why so pale,

Mage? Didn't your ancestors once eat the flesh of Kari? Isn't eating the great Dragon Kari's flesh the only reason why you peasants received such divine powers given to us by the Sky Gods?"

My stomach turns and rolls with disgust. I stand up, placing my hand over my mouth, the thought of eating Dragon flesh, or the flesh of any being, is horrifying and disgusting. I try to keep the food down, the food that I have barely taken two bites of.

"You are sick," I mutter. "How can you eat your own?"

"I'm sick?" he questions. "What of your people, Ice Mage? Don't they use us Dragons as decoration? Use our scales as armor against us in battle? Kill our children and women? And much more. All the things you know about."

"I know nothing of what you speak!" I snap, this being the first time I have raised my voice against a man... A king, no less.

"Oh, I see. Because you are blind, you are blind to the actions of your people." The King gets up from his chair, and I hear his footsteps approaching me.

His boots clump against the hard floor, click, and tap... *Click, tap...* A slow approach, he wants me to know he is stalking toward me with heavy and powerful steps. *Click, tap.... Click, tap...*

He stops behind me. His leather jacket squeaks with the movement of his arms. I only know this noise because one of my guards always boasted that the jacket he wore was from a Dragon he killed.

I see his magic growing brighter as he closes the distance between us.

I remove my hand from my mouth, waiting for his next move. I must be prepared for anything; the Dragon King is unpredictable. I have no idea what he is going to do next.

His shoes have become silent, his aura gone. He is circling me like a predator. I have made a mistake. I am going to die. I am foolish for aggravating him.

He grabs my face with his hands and yanks so we are face to face. Only then do I feel his hard and sharp nails scraping against my cheeks.

"Now tell me this. Are you just a sheltered Princess or simply an ignorant fool? Or perhaps both?" I feel the tips of his fingers grow hotter than the rest of him, maybe he is threatening to burn me if I don't answer him this time around.

"I am neither," I reply.

"Neither?" he questions, his grip around my cheeks loosening. "Then perhaps I am a poor judge of character? Well, my good lady, give me another jab at guessing.... Were you perhaps locked in a tower most of your life like some fairytale princess, waiting to be saved by a kind and handsome prince?" He strokes my cheek with the back of his hand, but this act of his is not comforting to me.

He is right... I was locked in a tower most of my life, the second part about wishing for a Prince to rescue me is not.

Mages have often told tales of what he spoke of, about a knight or prince in shining armor saving a princess who has been locked away in a tower by an evil, menacing Dragon who burns those who draw near the beautiful maiden.

The knight or prince is described as wholly handsome and saves the beautiful maiden after slaying the hideous Dragon in a vicious and long drawn-out battle. The tale ends usually with the last sentence, 'And so after being saved from the tower and the Dragon slain, the two wed and are granted very beautiful children, living happily ever after.'

Real-life is all but tragic, and there are no happy endings. There is truly never a happily ever after. Those stories spin false hopes in the hearts of the children who hear them.

The world is sad and unhappy, and this is the reason why story-tellers write such tales because they crave happy endings, and they also want those hearing their stories to be happy too. If I was a story-teller, I would try and make everything happy, maybe even the Dragon.

I think I lived too close to that story, but instead of being locked away by some evil Dragon, I was locked in a tower by my father. Then instead of being saved, my father gifted me to a Dragon.

I guess you can say the Dragon I am to wed breathes fire and is just as menacing and evil. I will never have a prince or knight braving the Dragon's castle to rescue me. I will be marrying the Dragon, he himself being the Prince or well... the King.

I don't answer him, and he laughs as his nails drag across my skin. "I'm interested in your story, Princess. Maybe you won't bore me like some common whore. I even wish to hear the story from your very lips. You may not know much about us Dragons besides terrible tales, but we do enjoy a good story."

"And finish your breakfast, you are skin and bone. All you are good for is using your bones to pick my teeth of leftovers, Mage," he chuckles.

I stand still before I decide to sit back down slowly, still disturbed about the origin of the meat on my plate, meat I must finish, or I risk offending the King. Dragons are not my people, but regardless, a person is a person whether they are Mage, Dragon, or some other being.

But then again what differs between feasting on this man and dining on a trigg? It is disturbing how quickly my thoughts turn dark. It is disgusting and worrying.

I have no words left for the King, and we eat the rest of the breakfast in silence. On occasion, a breeze blows in from the balcony; the doors must have been left open.

I still can't believe I will be marrying this man by the end of the night. The wedding is fast approaching and also creeping up on both of us. Also, neither of us seem to be prepared for the event.

I do not want to marry him. I do not want to be queen. I do not want anything to do with Dragons. The food in my stomach sours. I feel sick.

I'm also scared of what tonight will bring. Suddenly, I remember the words of my maids.

'Death is everywhere.'

SIX

MIDNIGHT WEDDING

ONLY WHEN THE sun has set do the maids and the people in the palace begin preparing for the night – a wedding and a celebration. Everyone is speaking, whispering, and not a single person seems to be excited for the upcoming nuptials, least of all me.

I hear whispers such as, "Is the King really marrying a Mage?"

Yes, he is, unfortunately.

"Are you sure this isn't some kind of joke?"

I wish it was.

"I can't stand the thought of a Mage as our queen," one exclaims.

I am still stomaching the idea of marrying a Dragon.

"Has the King gone mad?" asks another.

He already is.

"Is she at least... pretty?"

Perhaps...

I have spent most of my day in my room, only listening to the talks outside the door while trying to come to terms with what is happening. I will be a queen by the end of tonight. I think of my nightmare and how there is always a possibility it will somehow come true.

In my twisted visions, they do, over and over. There is no way to stop it. It is inevitable. The King is the kind of man to do such things. There is no doubt in my mind he wouldn't enjoy the pleasure of burning me alive, my screams making him and his people happy as they will never be truly pleased with me as their queen.

I am never going to be accepted.

There is a sorrow I feel – as the breeze from the balcony brushes past me like it did at breakfast, I can only think of suicide despite my ongoing struggle with wanting to live.

Will I finally be free? I wonder.

At sunset, when the Land of the Dragons is finally beginning to cool, the maids return to my room and this time, they are much gentler with me. I wonder what has changed.

They release my hair from the ponytail, running sweet-smelling oils through each strand, and a brush follows once more.

This, I can come to enjoy.

"The King loves hair. The smell, color, softness... Hair as white as snow," Ava whispers into my ear. "Only the Mages must have such a thing. Perhaps that is why he chose you. This is the only thing I envy about you, my lady... And perhaps your chest."

She then gropes my bosom, making me gasp. "I would kill to have your size."

I slap her hands away, feeling revolted. They are no better than the guards.

Catherine snorts as she slips jewels around my bare waist and legs, the cold metals pressing against my skin. "Nothing to be envious of... and someone's sensitive."

"Yes, she is indeed. Her kind is known to be prudish," Ava says snottily. "And Catherine! You only have a chest because you are fat. If I were, I would also have one."

"Shut up!" squeals Catherine. "I thought we agreed upon only picking on the Mage tonight."

"Shh! Not so loud. You have a big mouth, just like your body. Selene is about," Ava shushes Catherine.

"Yeah, yeah. my lady, you're so quiet, is everything alright?" Catherine questions in a worried tone.

She is a fake – a bully. She does not care about me.

"Yes," I reply.

This makes Ava giggle. "Is she being cocky to us? I heard she was at breakfast with the King. Is that true, my lady?"

"I was only being respectful to my lord," I whisper back softly.

"I can't hear what she's saying. She's mumbling. Are queens supposed to do this?" Ava asks.

"No, only the bland ones with a personality more fitting for a doll," Catherine replies.

They giggle in unison, and my mind goes blank as they continue to dress me and carry on a conversation I am no longer in tune with.

A doll.

I sit here like one, being dressed and adorned with jewels.

I have no personality...

I've been alone in the tower for so long that it is odd I have so many thoughts and emotions. Here, I am unsure of what and when to feel them, pain is all I know.

Is this what it's like to be normal?

I barely register what they do any more. I note I am dressed after a while. Jewelry is on my waist and legs. I am wearing no bra, only a flimsy string like underwear and a thin fabric dress.

I feel like I am getting dressed for a whorehouse rather than my wedding, but I don't question them about it. There is no point in arguing with them. I must do as the King and the maids say. It is the only way I can survive living amongst Dragons.

I know very little about the whorehouses, only that my Kingdom has them on the very outskirts as they are not allowed in the Capital Zolis – my great grandfather banished them, and the law has stayed enacted ever since.

I only know of their existence because the mad man above me in the tower talked incessantly about them. He said he enjoyed the ice whores, bold enough to wear very little clothing in ice and snow to lure travelers in, and how they even danced on blocks of ice and in blizzards.

I imagine I am wearing something similar to those 'ice whores' as he called them. At least they don't put me in the awful corset as they did at breakfast. I am glad to have my waist freed from that thing. I'd struggle to breathe in it.

The maids finally come to a decision to leave my hair down, only braiding a single strand at the back. And when I stop talking completely, they decide to ignore me.

I did hear one thing from their talks that stood out amongst the rest, a compliment, that was from Ava. She had said I looked prettier with my hair down.

I assume initially she has whispered lies, but Ava had said she would always be truthful with me, no matter what, so perhaps what she said was true. I have caught Catherine lying – *I cannot trust her.*

The maids have long since left my side, and now I await the King. It is the custom of the Dragon people that he must accept the queen before bringing her out to be formally seen before the general public.

The Ice Mages have different customs, where the groom has to wait to see the bride. It is a bad omen if he sees her before, either the marriage will fail or the woman will be barren.

I know the marriage between us will fail, so it doesn't matter much to me about my customs and beliefs. They will not respect them either way.

I wait in the courtyard and sit on the ledge of the fountain as I run my fingers through the water; it is lukewarm. I miss the cold... As much as I hate the tower, I think I associate it with a lack of touch, or maybe it is something more than that. I cannot be sure anymore.

I pull my hand out of the water, and it drips off my fingers, craving to be with the earth again. I place my hand back on the stone and flinch when I feel something soft and warm touch my skin. It almost feels like velvet.

I brush it off, only for another to fall on my skin, each one of them holding its warmth. It is odd. I have never felt a petal like this.

I hear the Dragon King suddenly speak, "They're petals from a Hearth Tree."

I jump, the fact I didn't hear him at all until this moment startles me. He must have been quiet... too quiet for me to be able to hear him approach.

"They're warm," I whisper back as I take one off my skin and feel it. I rub the soft petals with my thumb and after a while, it no longer holds the warmth it did before.

"Yes, they're known to absorb any heat, but after the petals fall from the tree, it doesn't take long for them to lose that warmth. They're much like a dying man or woman. Some say each time a Hearth Tree loses a petal, someone dies in this world." The Dragon King walks toward me, his steps more pronounced than before.

"Do you believe in that?" I ask him.

"No," he replies.

He stops in front of me and grows silent, probably inspecting me and looking for something to complain about. I remember Ava's words right before she brought me to the courtyard. 'Remember, silence is good. Silence means acceptance.'

Catherine's words soon after were, 'If he speaks, that usually means he is unhappy.'

He lifts a strand of my hair and even then, he is silent. He seems to like hair as the maids said he would. The strand falls softly back on my shoulder, and he begins to walk away, his feet carrying him to the door, his steps once again light.

"Follow me," he commands.

I stand up and follow his footsteps, knowing that where he has walked has no obstacles, and I am right. I do not bump or trip into anything as I cross the room to join him.

He is waiting for me and when I reach him, he grabs my arm and pulls me to his side, interlocking his arm with mine which surprises me.

"For the wedding." In other words, he is saying he won't be doing this otherwise. *Why does this not surprise me?*

He pushes open the door and walks confidently into the room. The hall is silent, but I can feel the people around, some whose presence is much stronger than the others. I can see their magic, though the strongest remain more toward the back of the room while the weaker ones are upfront.

I breathe in and out slowly, the penetrating stares of people going right through me. The silence is suffocating. I suddenly feel nervous about being on display. I wish I could see their faces.

The Dragon King's arm begins to unlink from mine as we slow our steps. "We must take our vows. Just stop and face me when I do."

I give a slight nod, and our arms drift apart as the Dragon King stops. I turn toward him; his magic tells me where he stands, and I focus on that.

The silence is broken when the Dragon King speaks in a loud and booming voice. "I, Orval, the great Fire Dragon and King of Oria, offer myself today in marriage to the Ice Mage, Vrai, in the presence of my people and of the Sky and Fire Gods."

Once he is done, I repeat what I hear. "I, Vrai, Ice Mage and Princess of Yulor offer myself today in marriage to the great Fire Dragon and King of Oria, Orval, in the presence of his people and of the Sky and Fire Gods."

More silence follows my vow, and much to my surprise, my voice does not crack or quiver once.

Did I say the right vows? No one told me what I must say.

Did I humiliate myself? There are so many people.

They are too quiet. Did I misspeak?

"May the Fire Gods bind you together in the flesh, and may the Sky Gods bless you with divinity... May both Gods bless you with children of fire and ice." Someone says to our right, their voice nasally and masculine.

"Both of you, put one arm forward," the voice instructs. I lift one of my arms, and a metal bracelet is snapped around my wrist, and I hear the other snapped around the King's.

"Now we must welcome our new Queen." Everyone claps and applauds around us, and I put my arm back down to my side.

It is heavy, a symbol of my entrapment.

The Dragon King links his arm with mine after coming to my side once more. It has been such a long time since someone touched me like this. I take comfort in this small gesture.

"Now we must celebrate in honor of our King and Queen!" A man hollers from the crowd and everyone cheers.

The hall that was once silent is broken by excitement, and the Dragon King explains to me, "We must sit through the celebration. You will be given gifts as will I, in honor of our wedding. Then, at midnight, we will leave to go to our bedchamber."

I can only nod as he leads me up the small stairs, and I feel him let go of my arm to walk a few steps away from me. His boots stop as he sits down on a chair, his clothing rustling slightly.

I walk forward and feel for the back of my chair before I seat myself. Once we both are seated, music starts to play.

The music is loud. Drums beat and people sing, and I can imagine they are dancing as well. Their auras are twirling and spinning, sometimes combining briefly to make a new color – *it is beautiful.*

As we sit in silence, I see a presence approach us. The magic is there, but it is faint.

"For my Queen," a man speaks in a heavy accent. Two others walk forward, and a heavy box is set down. I hear the stuff inside rattle and imagine this to be jewelry or perhaps gold.

The Dragon King lifts his hand and sets it back down quickly and heavily. I think he has shooed them away. I hear them scurry off and wonder if I should have thanked them for their gifts, but I was not given a chance.

"My King," another man says, "may I present the finest of swords forged by the greatest of masters?"

"Yes, yes, leave it and go." The King is now cranky, and I imagine he wishes to leave.

Time passes, more gifts accumulate. The King occasionally voices complaints about what we are receiving.

He sighs loudly. It is clear he is getting tired of the gift-giving as much as I am. I wish to go back to my chamber – but not with the King.

A confident voice pipes up. "I congratulate you on your marriage, King Orval. For a Mage, she is a fine beauty."

"You will find the ugliest of women beautiful, General Cell." The Dragon King laughs heartily.

I feel the King is calling me ugly, although in not so many words. *Why did he choose me then?*

I feel conflicted about my looks. Everyone says something different. I certainly do not feel beautiful, but I want to be like every woman, or so I want to believe.

I hear the man laugh. "No, you're mistaken, Your Majesty. I am very picky about who I call beautiful."

"Well, then you have fooled your King greatly." The King shifts in his seat, unamused by the man.

"I have a gift for Queen Vrai. I think she will enjoy it." General Cell steps forward. I can tell as I hear his soft footsteps on the stone before me.

He is the first to approach and to treat me like a queen.

I faintly see light-colored magic, nearly transparent, and he places something gently on my lap. Much to my surprise, it moves.

I hear the Dragon King hiss in disgust. "Great! You have brought her a scaly mutt."

"Not just any mutt," Cell declares. "It's a pup from a liwolf. You got lucky, Queen. My girl just gave birth to these wonderful pups early this morning, and this one turned out to be white just like your hair. I thought it will be a perfect gift for you."

I feel the creature called a 'liwolf' move on my lap, its tiny claws curling into me as it raises its head, chirping.

I hesitantly touch its back to feel the smooth and soft scales. I ask, "It's just a day old?"

I continue touching it. Its ears turn sideways, and while its claws are sharp, it also has a reversed one that is sharper than the rest.

"Yes," Cell replies. "He won't need his mother. These pups start eating meat from the minute they are born. Sometimes the pups are known to devour their own mother which is why I had to separate them as soon as possible... So, make sure to feed it meat soon."

"Disgusting. Cell, take it back," the King hisses once more. "They are not pets. These things are used for the army and the army alone. How did your mutt even get pregnant?"

"King, I do not expect you to know. They're asexual creatures. They don't need a male to reproduce. That is why males are less valuable than females. We have no need for them. The males die out quickly as they fight to death with each other. Unless it's strong, it won't survive as even pups kill each other, given a chance," Cell explains.

The thing in my lap cozies up to me before nibbling at my finger, and I feel a sharp pinch here and there but nothing too drastic.

So, you are unwanted just like me. Poor creature, I will love you. I do not care what others say. I hope the King will let me keep you. It is not much I am asking.

"Well, I wish you luck in raising it. Upon turning into an adult, liwolves are extremely loyal to the person who raises them, so loyal they will also die for that person. But if they don't like you, they can end up eating you, too." Cell chuckles before stepping down.

His magic disappears into the crowd of people, and I hear the King question me. "You aren't considering keeping that thing, are you?"

"Please, I want to keep it," I murmur as the liwolf doesn't stop suckling and nibbling at one of my fingers, its sharp claws still curling into my thighs.

The King falls silent before he expresses his disgust by making an accompanying noise. "Don't cry when it ends up dead or when it bites off one of your fingers."

"I think I can replace one of my fingers..." I say, unsure, knowing others in the past have done it. But maybe I can't, I have not used my magic in a long time.

The Dragon King doesn't say anything, but I feel his stare. Is he looking at me oddly? Maybe the Dragons can't do the things like we can…. replacing a limb takes a lot of magic from us, but it can be done.

I feel a strong connection to the small liwolf on my lap; the feeling is almost like the bond between a mother and her child. I try to think of a good name for him but fall short. Perhaps it can be called 'baby' as it is one. Although it won't stay small forever, it is big for a day-old pup.

"I hate weddings…" mutters the King, expressing his hatred over what he is doing. "Always have. I don't understand why women are so excited about them. What is there to enjoy?"

"I never dreamed of having a wedding," I say to him. "Not all women enjoy them, but I imagine a wedding is different if you love the person whom you are marrying."

"I doubt they would feel any different even if you love the person," he says. "They have no purpose. Why take vows that will end up broken? Or why would others want to celebrate the love between two people who aren't themselves or celebrate a love that will never exist? If it were up to me, I would have just given you the title of queen and fucked you by now."

My heart clenches. That's right. We still have to do that by the end of tonight.

I have never kissed a man or loved one or even touched one. Like many princesses back in my Kingdom, I am still a virgin. I know that Dragon people don't care for such things, some even thinking it strange as most Dragon women bed their first man by the age of sixteen, or so I hear.

Stranger yet are the rumors that spoke of the Dragon customs and how it is better to sleep with men early so you will be able to please your husband when you are older.

The same can be said for the Dragon men, and I know for a fact the Dragon King is no virgin. It is like I can smell the women off his clothes, such strong perfumes don't belong to a man.

The music suddenly comes to an end, and the King stands up from his seat. "Oh, I nearly forgot. We must end the night with a dance. Another annoying thing," he mutters under his breath.

"A dance?" I feel startled, and one of my maids comes over to pick up the Liwolf pup from my lap, taking it in her arms before walking away with it.

I do not like how they took him from me.

"Yes, a dance," replies the King.

"I don't know how to dance." I don't move from my seat. My heart pounds in fear of making a fool out of myself.

It is usually expected of royalty to know how to dance. I'm sure this is what the King and his people must think as well.

He clicks his tongue. "I should have expected no less from a blind Mage. Just follow my steps, you seem to be good at mimicking. Now, stand before we are looked at any longer."

I stand and he slides his hand along mine, guiding me down the steps once more and on to the floor. We stop once we are far enough, and he lets go of my hand to stand in front of me.

The music resumes, and the King begins to move across from me. Our hands meet once more, but this time they are lifted in the air, and we encircle each other. I attempt to mimic him like he has told me to do, and I wonder if this is what he means.

We spin around each other once again, but from the opposite side, before his hand circles around my waist to the small of my back, making me dance with him from the front.

We continue to dance to the pace of the music. The King spins me around time and time again. I step on his foot a couple of times and, much to my surprise, no patronizing or no sarcastic or no condescending words or sounds of displeasure leave his lips, though I am sure he is scowling. I am glad I don't have eyes to see; it saves me from having to peer at his face in these moments.

I feel like I am a small bird learning to fly, and I need help to glide through the skies. I wonder if this is how Dragons feel when they are flying. I am light as I glide, barely using my feet to move. I'm curious if the scary Dragon King has been taught to dance when he was a little boy.

It is hard to imagine, but that is what I am currently getting visions of – the dance instructor lecturing him and trying to teach him how to dance with a woman. Telling him that one day he will have to perform in front of his audience.

As the dance comes to a close, he dips me slightly before gliding me back to my feet once the music comes to an end.

I hear the snide and snotty voice return, the one who spoke at the end of our vows. "It's midnight, sire."

"Yes, I know." He grabs my arm and begins to lead me slowly away from the crowd. "Now comes the easy part."

I swallow, knowing all too well what will come next, a part which will not be so easy for me. I wish I could avoid this, but I know I cannot.

I wish our dance could have been longer.

SEVEN

FIRE & ICE

EVERYTHING IS silent in the bedchamber – all but the rustling of clothes. I inhale sharply, mostly in fear as my gown hits the floor, and I am left bare in the eyes of the Dragon King. All but the delicate charms touching my skin and the flimsy underwear.

I shiver, not from the cold, but a strange sensation. *Is it fear or anticipation?*

The air is hot and humid, and there is a thin layer of sweat covering my skin. My cheeks flush in this heat as if I have a fever. The sweet-smelling oils, that my maids have rubbed into my skin, evaporate, shrouding us in an aromatic cloud. I can't stop the heat from traveling through my body; my mind keeps wandering over the possibilities. I feel nauseated at the prospect, but a part of me is hopeful too.

His gaze lands on my body, as heated as the land he rules over. Even in the darkness of my world, I can feel it on my naked skin, *scorching*.

A whisper of movement, a touch, the back of his hand grazes my breast. I gasp, it is so unexpected. My nipple hardens at his touch. A tremble starts deep within me. It seems my body is reacting differently than my mind, which is frightening and unknown.

I long for another caress, but his touch gentle ceases, and he pushes me back. I land on a bed covered with what feels like soft fur, my breasts bouncing, and my hair fanning around me.

He doesn't stop, making haste with his next actions. His fingers hook into my underwear before he drags them down my legs. His hands pull away, the vacant air swirls around my body. *Is it a moment of uncertainty or perhaps... repulsion?*

The Dragon King is always so confident and outspoken, profound with his words and actions. *So why now?*

He has said before that this is the easy part. Then it must surely be me making him turn away. His hands return to my body, but they are still. He is hesitant. But he has no choice just like me.

Eventually, the awkwardness fades, and his fingers slide through the dampened oils on my skin, the sensation odd. Heat follows his touch. He seems undeterred by sweat, for any Ice Mage, it is unappealing. Perhaps these Dragons are different.

I can hear the rumbles around the room. There are people surrounding the bed, the ones who have to witness the consummation of the King and the Queen.

I can see their magic, so many of them, their flames shimmer behind my sightless eyes. My heart pounds in fright not only from the King's touch but also the alien stares. Their eyes seem to pick apart my body, each part is analyzed and categorized, perhaps too thin, too ugly, or too inept.

How am I supposed to be comfortable doing this? How is he?

I don't know much about sex, but it feels that everything is moving too fast. My eyes tear up with the force of my emotions.

Is this going to hurt? Will it happen quick?

I don't know if I am supposed to have a say in this. Perhaps not. In the tower, I fantasied, having heard snippets from the guards. They were uncouth, some utterly crude. But I learned and took comfort where I could. A slight touch here and a caress there, places forbidden and pleasurable. But this is different.

I can feel the tension thick in the air. In the silence, the sound of the zipper echoes through. I have never seen or felt a naked man before. I don't know what to do, but he does. He has felt the body of a woman, the arms of many whores. I'm sure he prefers them over me, given a choice.

I am just to be bred, that's all.

I wonder if I will come to desire him in our short time together. I feel his hands on my body once again, and they are like pinpricks of flames to my skin. Melting the ice inside me.

He spreads my legs forcefully, in these moments, I am so much of a doll that I don't move and let him do what he wishes with me. I can hear the murmurs go around, their mockery, the truth in their words.

Let him be quick...

Tears well up and fall on the bed. My throat tightens as I try to keep a check on them. Dolls do not cry, but I am not one. My mind is in shambles, my emotions leading my body astray. I want this, but I don't want it this way. The King's hands tighten around my ankles for a fleeting moment. *A warning or uncertainty?*

A nasally voice, which has been with us over the entire course of the wedding, pipes up. "King Orval, just be done with it. Put it in her. We all want to rest, yes?"

Tears spill at his words. *Done with it?* I feel worthless, nothing but a vessel to keep their royal lineage alive.

"Yes, we all want to rest. Are you having performance issues, my lord?" Another voice joins in as the others snigger.

Is this normal? Have the other queens in the past suffered like this? Did my father do the same to his current wife, the queen, in my country? Or is it just me who is feeling like this?

Please, just get it over with. I want this humiliation to be over already.

"Rhys, silence! And you too, Gregory! You insisted on this lunacy! Perverts!" The King barks angrily at his subjects. He clicks his tongue, muttering to himself. "And here I thought this is the easiest part... I didn't know I would have you assholes in the room with me... Watching me with your beady little eyes."

His ranting has not ended when his fingers loosen around my legs, and he slides up my hips and pulls my lower half toward him, a foreign warmth poking my inner thigh.

The movement is so sudden that it makes me gasp.

Is this his manhood?

It is hard, warm, and erect against my leg.

Will this go inside me?

I wish we could at least have shared one kiss before this, maybe then I would feel less scared or worried. He presses forward, and an uncomfortable feeling settles over me. I want to push him away; I do not want to continue with this. It doesn't belong there.

However, the next moment, a pleasurable tingle courses through me. The warmth of his manhood rubbing against a part of me that wants him. It is a short pleasure and is gone instantly. He eases inside of me, past the lips that part so easily. I tense, there is something stopping his movement.

Stop... it hurts!

He is being slow with his actions, but it induces more pain. He is doing this on purpose. The word 'stop' travels to my tongue, but it never leaves my mouth. It hurts so badly, no one told me there would be pain. I grip the fur wanting to tear it apart. The warmth of his penis sickens me, disgust crawling up my spine.

My womanhood burns when it is normally so cold. This feeling is foreign and uncomfortable. I'm sure the King dislikes it as much as I do, but he must keep silent and bear through it, acting as a true king.

I too try to mimic him, gritting my teeth. Over time, the burning fades, yet the pain lingers. *Is this how all women feel during their first time?*

He eases out of me, and I feel him shiver as he pushes back inside. He is clearly feeling the effects of my coldness. The King keeps up with this motion, easing in and out of me. His hands on my hips tighten ever so slowly with each thrust he gives. Small claws dig in, adding a new pain.

He hates me, his body is so stiff. What am I to expect – a touch full of compassion? I should be thankful he isn't being rough. I bite my lip, the pain is lessening with each thrust, but I can't help but keep thinking of their eyes watching us. Watching me.

Those who said sex is great, are liars... What is there to enjoy?

Why does the King enjoy such activities with whores, why does anyone? Perhaps it is only enjoyable for men...? Then why do the women here talk about how enjoyable sex is? Sex is... confusing.

His manhood feels strange, and it brushes against spots I don't entirely understand. The touch of it feels like velvet... silk-like, smooth, and slick. It also has a heart of its own... it throbs. *Is it a Dragon thing, or do all men have a second heart in their manhood?*

Another shiver leaves the Dragon King. I can feel his trembling. He is so close, our breaths intermingle. We probably wouldn't be doing this if the tiles of 'king' and 'queen' weren't pushed on to us. I imagine that if we were just normal people on our own lands, we would never have crossed paths, much less force ourselves to have sex.

He gradually picks up the pace, his thrusts becoming quicker and he grunts. Maybe this is a sign of the pleasure he is feeling. Maybe a sign he wishes to be done and is in a hurry to finish... But, before I know it, we are back at a slow pace, and he growls in frustration.

The Dragon King finally snaps and stops moving. "Fuck! How am I supposed to fuck her with Rhys and everyone else breathing down my fucking damn neck?"

"It's something that must be done, Your Majesty," replies Rhys.

"Well, you can see that I'm fucking her, can't you? Do you not have eyes, Rhys? The Mage doesn't, and she knows I am fucking her," hisses the Dragon King. "Isn't this enough??"

"No. We must see you give her your seed to complete the ritual. Sire, how do you think you were born? Even your mother and father had to complete—" He doesn't finish the sentence.

"Alright, enough! Are you trying to make me go soft?" He yells one last time, "I won't be able to finish with your mouth running."

This is torture.

Rhys falls silent and the King pulls out of me before he plunges back into me making me whimper softly, the first noise I have made tonight.

My cry is a pained one, not that of a woman enjoying the touch of her husband. He begins thrusting in and out of me once more, but much quicker than the last time, soft grunts leaving his mouth with each thrust of his hips.

I spoke too soon; this touch is not gentle. He is truly in a rush to get the job done, no doubt. He does not want the eyes of others on him, just like me.

He leans forward, almost crushing me, and sniffs my hair, inhaling sharply. The heat in his body increases, he is now on top of me, more aroused.

What has changed?

He draws my hips closer to him, this time making himself slide deeper, and a rather odd feeling sparks within.

What is that feeling...?

"The rumors are true about his Majesty having a hair fetish," a man comments, and the King growls as he tries to concentrate on his release and for the act to be finished.

His breathing escalates and his thrusts become erratic. With one last grunt, something warm fills me. It travels to my stomach or so it feels like. He pulls out of me. His torso separates from mine, and I hear him pull up his pants as he continues breathing heavily.

A liquid begins to seep out.

Is that it...?

Is everything over?

I close my legs slowly, his warmth no longer keeping me still. I push myself up on the bed reaching for the closest thing near me which is a blanket and use it to cover myself.

"There! Are you all fucking happy?" The King is still panting. "It's done."

"Yes, very glad," Rhys answers sarcastically. "Now we can all go to our rooms and homes and get to bed."

"Rhys, call the maids to get her cleaned up. That is your job tonight for your big mouth," he says and walks forward, his feet can be heard plodding on the floor. "And Lucius?"

The next thing I hear is a punching sound. "Didn't I order everyone to shut up? None of you fucking listen."

He huffs and slams out of the room shortly after.

The King is gone... now I want all of them gone.

"Him and his temper, how cute," says another man further in the room before chuckling. He sounds older than the rest of them.

"I wonder how cold his dick is to make him run out of the room like that," snickers a younger man whose voice came from the same corner of the room.

"A virgin... He will need company tonight..." says a different man. He is the next to leave behind the King.

"I hadn't noticed she was. I was too busy staring at her tits..." the older man responds before shouting, "Ukiah, your sister's tits would be just as lovely to watch them bounce if the King—"

"Enough, Zachariah! All of you, out!" hisses Rhys.

"Okay, okay, you bald prick, before you open your yap again, I heard you the first time. Come, Fonzell, speaking of pricks, mine needs a whore. Let's go before the good ones are taken."

After Rhys yells at everyone to leave, Zachariah and Fonzell exit. The last grumble comes from Lucius who complains of how his jaw hurt from where the King punched him.

I grip the blanket tightly, feeling awkward that the King and his men have all seen me nude. I feel violated and dislike the way they spoke about me as if I didn't exist.

"What insolence! All their tongues should be removed. I never get respect around here. And you, Queen, I will call the maids for you later," says Rhys, the 'queen' sounding hateful on his tongue. "In the meanwhile, lie back and let his seed sit a little while longer. It will increase your chances of pregnancy."

Rhys walks to the door, his heels clicking against the floor. I am glad when he leaves. Once I am fully alone in the room with no sounds, magical vibes, or stares, I lie down slowly, doubting it will help increase the chances of pregnancy, but I do it anyway.

Then a thought crosses my mind. *If I don't get pregnant from this, will it happen again?*

It must... Maybe I should hope for pregnancy to arise from this as I can't possibly stand being looked at by others in the room like that.

Tears slip down my face, and I wipe them away with the edge of my blanket. The feeling of being scared has dissipated, but the feeling of humiliation lingers.

For once in my life, I am glad to be alone and for a little while, I want it to stay that way.

EIGHT

NEW BEGINNINGS

THE SUN FEELS POWERFUL TODAY, its heat beating down on the land, making me swelter. The Fire Dragons very rarely sweat; they thrive in this kind of weather—after all, it is their homeland.

Unlike my world of ice. I don't think the Dragons would survive in my land as perhaps, I won't here. The ground reflects the intense rays at me, and there probably isn't a day when I am not sweaty.

I do get some strange looks, especially now when I am sitting at the table with the ladies of the court, waiting for my tea to cool while fanning myself. I listen to them chatter about the inane things in life, or probably they sound silly to me – makeup, clothes, jewels – anything they can show off.

And the gossip!

I thought it was bad at the tower, listening to the guards talk. But these ladies can beat them in the rumors they have heard and the inner delight they get in spreading those around the realm.

I hear a woman speak up. I think she introduced herself as Amelia earlier. "It must be so hard for you, Queen Vrai, to be born and raised in a Kingdom so cold and full of snow, then to be brought here."

Another woman joins in. "Most of us have never seen snow as our husbands mostly do the traveling and the wars. Such protective brutes are they not, but men will be men. I am curious though. What is it like, the snow, that is?"

I answer both women. "It's hard here. As you can see..." I nod, referring to my drenched appearance. "Snow is snow, sometimes soft and dusty and other times, hard and crunchy due to the ice. And it's cold every day throughout the year in my land, the completely opposite of here. Spring, summer, and fall are icy. But the winters are especially rough. The northern winds that blow freeze the land and kill everything but the Mages, including our animals, so we have to keep them inside to protect them."

There is a collective gasp from the women. "Oh my goodness. Your land sounds harsh. I mean, we have a few fires here occasionally, but deaths do not arise from them unless it's one of us causing them deliberately. Like our King sometimes does during one of his rampages, but it is mostly setting trees on fire. The worst kill count during his rages was when a few birds or those annoying things that feast on ingonuts were killed in the blazes."

Amelia asks, "How is King Orval, by the way? Treating you well, I hope." She giggles softly as if teasing me, but I can hear the sarcasm in her tone. She already knows the answer to that.

My silence says it all. I think about how the King has been toward me lately. Since the wedding night, which was over two weeks ago, he has been quiet and aloof, doing his best to avoid me when possible. I am happy with his indifference; it means we don't have to share a bedchamber.

Although a part of me feels rejected and used.

The only occasion we actually spend any time together is during breakfast and sometimes dinner, but not a single word directed toward me leaves his mouth. It is mostly the servants or maids he speaks to, at whom he lashes his ire about the food prepared. Throwing dishes at them, and always informing them the head chef is fired. He does provide me with some entertainment in those moments.

Apparently, Dragons don't have lunch. Tea parties and snacking between breakfast and dinner are the only way they survive. I don't mind the snacking in between as the pastries are delicious.

But the tea parties are something new to me, something I have never experienced before. Rhys told me one day that it was expected of the queen to get acquainted with her people to gain love and respect.

But what is the point? I am a temporary queen. *Do I need to get acquainted and know my... his people?* It isn't that these women like me... and much less the people in this Kingdom.

I look up, and I can feel their Dragons leering at me. I understand that they are forced to endure this gathering and having to speak to me with mock respect. Yes, respect is definitely lacking. I am a novelty to them at the moment until they get bored.

"He has been fine," is all I reply. I believe her husband is a Duke of some land or something like that. I didn't bother to remember the details, something that I should probably do. A queen must know her subjects.

"How is the sex?" Amelia does not seem to care that she is asking inappropriate questions. "Fire Dragons are passionate lovers if they love the woman, even their flings can be intense. The kisses of a man who loves you are divine. I should know. And from the rumors of his favorite whore, Red, the Dragon King is quite thrilling in bed."

Again, I don't know how to reply. I recall the sex we've had on our wedding night, quick and to the point. I know that I didn't get any pleasure from it. He didn't even kiss me... Maybe he reserved his kisses for another woman, a woman I will never be. Perhaps for that whore, Red.

We have not had sex since the wedding night and for this, I am grateful. Now it seems that a whore is more appealing to him than me. I should not be upset. There is no love lost between us, so I cannot expect him to be faithful.

Our marriage is one of convenience. But it still hurts when I am the subject of everyone's gossip. I feel used by all, past and present. My father, the Dragon King, his people, these women here.

Resentment rises in me, not only for these Dragons but also for my own people. They locked me up since childhood, then gifted me... no, more like tossed me away for their convenience, to ward off a war.

I am said to be a curse in my land. I wonder if I still am because the Dragon King picked me, not my sisters. I did save my country as, without me, Zolis would have been scorched to nothingness.

I am a savior, but they do not realize this as they go about living their happy days. Their callousness sickens me. But what can I do now?

"Fine," I respond again, fanning myself quicker, the movement of my wrist not keeping up with the waves of heat.

No fan can cool me. The fire is too much. I bathe in ice, but the heat does not stop plaguing my body like an illness. The effects, too, do not last long, and I find myself longing for another even before I have finished dressing.

"Just fine?" giggles another lady in question.

"Yes, it is fine." I feel my anger increasing in tandem with their mocking giggles. I decide to set them straight. "We, Ice Mages, prefer not to speak about such matters." Being their queen, I expect them to accept my answer and respect my wishes.

"I see," Ameilia says. "As I thought, Mages are a bore. It seems they're not only that but prudes, too."

Bore? Prude? I am tired of these words. Even if I were a free woman, I would not spread my legs for every man. I am not a wanton Dragon or a whore.

The doors in the room swing open, and a boisterous woman barges in, her heels clicking sharply on the ground. "Sorry, I'm late. I could not decide what dress to wear. It took my maids forever to get me ready. You see, I'm too kind and lenient with them sometimes." She lets out a small laugh. I know she is nowhere that. But she does sound quite confident.

But wait... *This is different!*

I do not think she is as confident as she portrays. Her Dragon is not. I can see it shaking and trembling. *It is scared. Is she?*

"Good afternoon, Queenie," the woman greets as she approaches me and slides into the empty seat close by. "My name is Beatrix. Yours is Vrai, correct?"

"Yes." My reply seems empty, emotionless. I am drained by these women.

"I never thought I will see an Ice Mage as our Queen, or much less, a live specimen." Beatrix is impudent enough to lift the untouched tea off my plate and take a sip of it. "Yet here you are. The Gods are always gifting us with peculiarities. At least let us all be thankful a criminal of blood has not become our queen."

After taking another careful sip, she places the cup back on the plate with a clink. Criminal of blood... *what's that?* She confuses me. *Is there someone else who was to be their queen?*

"I presume you and the King have lain together on your wedding night?" Beatrix says.

Great! More questions. *What is it with them, needing to know all the details? Do they not have anything else that they can talk about?*

Amelia cuts in sarcastically, "Yes, they have, but our dear queen does not like to talk about such matters. Mages don't. Her own words."

"Oh, I see." Beatrix hums. "Do you feel any signs of pregnancy yet, Vrai? I knew right away when I was pregnant with my little one."

Vrai...

She is the first one to call me by name. *Acceptance or mockery?* She must not respect the title I have over her as the others do.

"I think it's too early to tell." I want to take a sip of my tea but remember her slurping from it. I dare not drink from the same cup. I do not want diseases.

"You probably aren't pregnant if you feel no signs. Unless the child is to be a Theka," Beatrix says. "But you do realize what will happen if you are infertile, correct?"

Theka? That word again. I've heard it once before from my maids. *And what does she mean? What will happen if I am infertile?*

"No," I mutter.

"If you're infertile, you will be killed. Without a doubt. We once had a queen who was unable to breed, and she was sentenced to death. She was a Dragon. Can you imagine what they'll do to a Mage?" Beatrix sounds too gleeful with the information. "The Kingdom has always gotten rid of the nasty queens. I think the King should have picked a woman who has already given birth. At least then we would have known that she will be able to produce an heir."

"Like you, Beatrix? Then he will have to take care of your bastard," a woman called Willow says. "A child who isn't his, no less. Whose child is that, Beatrix? Jon's? Jon, the drunkard?" Willow's questions have decidedly become more hateful. "Now you make your noble parents take care of the bastard child for you."

There is silence after, and I can feel the anger seeping out of Beatrix as she scoffs. "I would at least be better than an infertile queen."

"Well, she isn't confirmed to be infertile, is she?" hisses Willow. "And for the sake of the Gods, it's only been two weeks. Amelia didn't even know she was pregnant until twelve weeks and if the Queen isn't pregnant in another eight weeks, she and the King can try again. Both of them are still very young, and they have only tried once." My sex life seems to be public news; now they are all talking about it.

"Amelia also gave birth to a Theka," Beatrix taunts hatefully.

Amelia stands up and growls, the noblewoman turning into a fierce animal within seconds. "I dare you to say that again, Beatrix," she snarls out.

"Your little boy is a—" Beatrix goes on to say but is interrupted when someone enters the room.

"My lady, it's almost time for your lessons." Ava walks in, and I wonder if she has been outside the entire time, listening to the conversation.

"Lessons?" I am not aware of any that I have to take.

"Yes. Rhys wants you to get properly educated about our lands as well as other things. Today you will meet your mentor," Ava explains. "So, we must get going. He likes his students to be punctual; he is such a man."

"I see," I say, standing. "I'm sorry, ladies, but our time has been cut short. Have a good day."

"You too, my Queen," they chorus.

Ava grabs my arm and guides me out of the room. I let out a heavy sigh. The silence outside is so much better than their chatter and bickering. It was beginning to get on my nerves. I do not have time for such pettiness.

Lessons... I have never been educated. My people did not care about me and gave up on me because of my lack of sight. In the tower, all I did was sit and allow my brain to rot. I guess, in a way, I am simple in the head because I wasn't taught anything.

How will this man teach me something useful?

I guess I will find out now.

I FIND MYSELF SITTING AT A DESK IN A SMALL ROOM. IT IS stuffy as there is no fresh air coming through the windows. The place smells of musk and old books – it is rather suffocating and difficult to breathe.

My hands run over the surface of the desk; it is so smooth. I can even feel something engraved – some kind of writing, it seems. I don't know how to read and write, so I am unable to decipher what it says.

Nobody bothered to teach me lessons after my mother's death. She was the last, the one who never gave up on me. The other prisoners in the tower taught me all that they knew because of their own boredom.

The door creaks open, and someone steps in quietly. "Good afternoon, my Queen." His voice is soft and gentle. "My name is Dakari, and I will be your tutor."

He drops some heavy books onto the desk, and I narrow my eyes in confusion. *Can he not see I am blind? How are books going to be useful to me?*

"I will teach you how to read and to some level, write. We will begin simply, learning each letter of the alphabet and how to write your name. Are you ready, Queen Vrai?" he questions me.

"I thought we are learning about the lands. Sir, I am—" I start to say, but he interrupts me.

"You can feel touch, can't you?" He grabs my hand, his fingers ever so warm but not as hot as the Dragon King's flesh.

"I can," I mutter.

"You already felt the engraving on the desk, right?"

"Yes."

"That is your name." He guides my hand back to the inscription. "I engraved it in the wood before you arrived."

I feel the word once more, and I am shocked. "This is my name?"

"Yes," he says. "Now, I want you to take your time and feel each letter. Memorize it as best as you can."

I carefully go over and follow the lines gorged on the desk. They are all different and confusing. My name feels rather short in length. But I am excited. New possibilities are achievable. Soon I will not be called stupid.

He opens one of the tomes on the desk. "This entire book will teach you through touch. It was made by a tutor a long time ago. He slowly lost his vision due to age, and he decided to make this book for those who lack sight so that they can also learn words."

My hand slides from the engraving on the desk to the book to feel the tiny bumps all over the pages, each a different shape with loops and lines. It feels confusing and exciting, both at the same time.

I am going to learn how to read and write! I have dreamed of this all my life, and now it is becoming true.

"I am going to ask you again, Queen Vrai. Are you ready to learn?"

I am quiet for a few seconds before I reply, a small smile gracing my lips, "Yes!"

I never thought I would be able to learn.

I am eager to get to my lessons.

I am so ready.

NINE

BANDAGED WOUNDS

THE LIWOLF HAS GROWN. He is still so young, but his paws are as big as my palm, his claws longer and sharper.

How big will he get? I caress his back, wondering.

I do know he enjoys my cool lap when he wants a place to lie down, away from the hot sun. He is quite loving despite General Cell's words about them being quite terrors as pups. He is calm and affectionate and enjoys the sound of my voice.

Every time I sing to myself in my room, he uses his claws to pull himself up on my bed and lie next to me, his presence my only comfort. He is not big enough to jump on the bed yet.

The scaly, yet smooth, warm creature remains with me transiently, visiting me oftentimes in the day before he scurries off. I wonder how his siblings are doing. *Are they all calm like him or terrors as the General described them?* I haven't asked about them. Maybe next time I run into Cell, I will.

The liwolf stands on my lap after getting comfortable with his body temperature. He stretches his limbs before springing off me. The reversed claws on his hind legs dig deep into my flesh, drawing blood. I feel my muscles scream in pain, and rivulets run down my legs.

Perhaps, next time, I should keep something on my lap; although, I do not know what I can possibly use to stop him from hurting me accidentally. It's not his fault; it's his nature.

It won't be long before he grows too big for my lap. His appetite is also huge. He can eat almost constantly yet never get enough. He enjoys the meat the maids serve him, despite them not wanting to. But he is the Queen's pet, so Yanmei is forced to do her job. Anyway, she would rather care for the beast than me. Those are her words from what Catherine and Ava tell me at different times.

I wonder if Baby is also fond of Yanmei just as he likes Catherine and me, though Catherine is scared of the liwolf due to their reputation. Her litany of complaints never ends. According to her, his eyes are like serpents and she is his prey, stalking her as she goes about.

Serpents, Dragons – *are they so different?* Ava doesn't seem to think so. I have also heard rumors from the East that there are serpent-like Dragons who live above ground in all the four seasons of the weather.

Four seasons... Back in my Yulor, there are only two - cold and colder, and this land is the same - warm and warmer.

Catherine worries that the moment he gets big and confident enough, he will try to eat her. Ava and I tease her about being careful as it would take Baby many days to eat Catherine and by then, he would then have no desire to eat Ava or me. I know it is wrong, but it feels great to scare her for all the taunts she gives me. I find it amusing.

The two often fight about weight and beauty and bicker about silly things, but I can tell, even with all that fighting, they are best friends. Through thick and thin, they are there for each other and always will be.

Yet, they are not my friends. I am just envious of their relationship. It must be nice to have a friend like that. I can't imagine having someone who will stand by me. Everyone here is my subject. They have to respect and wait on me, as per the Dragon King's orders.

As I get up, my leg twinges. The warm blood trickles down my thigh, probably staining my dress as well. I can feel the rip from Baby's claws.

I hear him jump down from the stone bench we are sitting on and wander off, having free range of the castle even when I don't. I am not allowed in the towers or the west wing or the King's private quarters and office. We may be wed, but unlike other kings and queens, we are not close to being equals.

I hear footsteps, and my eyes drift to where the sounds come from. I smile softly seeing the light aura. The magic is so pure and soothing that it can only be one person.

I love his aura, and the one thing I have never seen is his Dragon. It is there, hidden, but I know it will be beautiful. I wish to know his Dragon like I wish to know more about him.

"Vrai," calls out Dakari, his steps growing closer.

"Yes?" I question eagerly, excited. I wonder if we will be starting our lessons early today. I enjoy studying, and now I even know how to write my name. After practicing it many times. I believe I have perfected it.

He comes to a foot or so close to me, telling me my schedule, "For today—" And he stops abruptly. "What happened to your leg?"

"Oh, it's nothing," I say. "Really. It's Baby's claws. Sometimes they cut into me. He's getting too big for my lap."

Dakari knows I have a liwolf named Baby from our short talks in between lessons. He laughed at the name when he first heard it. I still don't understand how the name is funny. I think it's rather cute and suits him well too.

He is a baby, *my baby*.

He sighs. "Sit. It isn't nothing. You're a queen, not some child playing with a pet. Let me get some bandages. Stay here until then."

I sit back down on the bench that is hot from the sun, and I frown. Dakari must have gone to get the doctor. This is the first time he has ever really lectured me like this. During our lessons, he is always calm and patient. I start to worry and grip my dress convulsively.

I am a queen... I guess I should always consider my appearance and health.

I haven't seen the doctor yet, but I know from the gossipy ladies of the court that he is handsome and foreign. He is also the older brother of General Cell. Both of them are not Fire Dragons but Water Dragons.

Why are Water Dragons in Oria? It seems odd, but then, I am also here, an Ice Mage.

I know very little about them. The ladies of the court have described them both having hair much like mine but not silky; theirs is wild and unkempt. I thought only the Ice Mages had white hair, or so I was told.

Their skin is lightly tanned, General Cell being way fairer than his brother. Cell is said to take better care of himself despite his brother being a doctor.

Their eyes, if I remember correctly, have been compared to sea glass –a precious gem for the Fire Dragons.

Cell's eyes are light blue like the sea glass Beatrix wears around her neck while Amelia's jewelry resembles the color of the doctor's eyes, sea green.

The women almost got into a fight over it the other day, but their attention turned to me as soon as I mentioned that looks mean nothing if their insides are ugly. Luckily, I escaped their wrath since I had lessons to attend as usual.

I suppose I will be meeting the doctor soon for a checkup too. Rhys has been complaining of this at dinner. I assume he wants to know if I am pregnant.

The Dragon King is never enthusiastic about the idea, telling Rhys to stop grumbling and that everyone will know soon enough. It seems he despises the word 'doctor,' probably it is just my imagination.

It has officially been a month since the King and I last slept together. I haven't bled yet, which gives the maids hope, but I also don't have any signs of being with child either.

I am still unsure of everything. I do not feel ready to be a mother, though I must become one despite my feelings. A child must come soon, a son to become the next king. Women can't rule in Oria.

Dakari returns from the medical wing quickly. The doctor is not with him. He lifts my dress, which startles me but also makes my face flush.

"Wha... what are you doing?" I question, stuttering.

"Caring for your wounds," he replies. "Liwolves claws can be dirty and can lead to infection. Perhaps our next lesson will be medical related... You also need to change your dress. As a queen, your appearance matters."

I am quiet as his lecture continues, and his fingers brush against my thigh. I recall the Dragon King's touch the night of our wedding. Men's fingers feel... good on the skin. It isn't like when the maids touch or bathe me; this feeling is different.

He cleans the wound first, which stings, before wrapping them tightly.

"What did you want earlier? I ask.

"Oh, just to say today's lessons are canceled," he announces, which makes my heart sink.

"Why?"

"I have things to take care of. That's all."

He sounds abrupt.

"I hope everything is ok," I whisper. He has nearly finished wrapping the bandages around my leg.

"Everything is fine, Queen Vrai. There is no need to worry about me," he assures as his fingers slip away.

I feel another presence nearby. I have failed to notice, being distracted by Dakari. Chills run down my spine as I realize, to the right of us, I can see the magic of the King.

He is steadily approaching us, his footsteps quiet, which is unusual for him. He always likes to make himself known.

In my head, I can see another frightening image of his Dragon, its eyes observing me carefully. I am wary of his appearance. Dakari stands, also noticing him. I pull my dress down over my knees.

"My King," greets Dakari, deciding it is best to address rather than ignore him. I'm sure he is also bowing.

I notice another person behind the King. It is Rhys if I am not mistaken. He is never too far from the King. He seems to ignore our presence as he grows closer, but at the same time, his Dragon keeps its eye on me, watching me carefully and causing me to stiffen. I suddenly feel very self-conscious.

"How lewd," Rhys says, letting out a chuckle, which is short and mocking.

The look in Orval's Dragon grows worse, more hateful as it wrinkles its face in fury. Once the Dragon King comes close to Dakari, his feet stop, and there is a brief silence. Rhys also comes to a halt behind the King.

Suddenly, I hear gasps. The sounds are coming from Dakari, and I see in my head that the King's Dragon is enraged, snarling and almost consuming the light aura of Dakari.

He is choking him!

I stand, startled by the noises, and yell, "Stop it!"

No response comes from the King, and I can hear Dakari struggling. All I can do is scream, finally finding my voice, but I feel helpless.

"I said, stop it!" I yell again and go to grab the King, but an arm pushes me back. It's Rhys.

"It's his fault," says Rhys. "He has touched you in places he shouldn't have. If the King decides to kill him, he has a full right. Dakari has been rude and indecent toward the King's wife."

"He was only wrapping my wounds," I shout, struggling with Rhys.

"He could have brought you to Doctor Viggo," replies Rhys. "He was being perverted as well as you were... You let it happen."

I feel bad as I did have indecent thoughts when he touched me. I caused this... I am the reason Dakari is being hurt... I am the reason he is fighting for his life.

Suddenly, a body hits the ground, and Dakari starts coughing and gagging.

"Consider this a warning," growls the King, his Dragon's eyes focusing on me rather than Dakari. "Rhys, send the queen to her room. I think she has had more than enough freedom lately."

"Happy to, Your Majesty," replies Rhys giddily.

I hate him! He is enjoying my suffering!

The King strides forward, leaving the courtyard. I immediately go to see if Dakari is alright, but Rhys has a tight hold on me. He pushes me toward the direction where the King has gone.

"Come on now. There is no need to worry over a replaceable mentor. If he dies, we can just get you another one." Rhys grips my shoulders tightly. "Though he is smart... It will be a shame to lose him."

"I'm so sorry," I whisper as I turn my head to where I last heard Dakari gasping for air.

I feel awful, tears stinging my eyes. *This is cruel.*

Rhys pushes me out of the courtyard, and my heart wrenches more. I can no longer sense Dakari's pure magic. I worry.

Not only has something happened to him, but I have also angered the King and made him unhappy. If dinners aren't already bad enough with him, they will now certainly be a lot worse. I do not look forward to tonight's meal.

I am sorry, Dakari.

TEN

DRAGON'S CANE

ALL I CAN THINK about is Dakari.

Is he okay? It is a question I have asked myself many times in the silence of my bedchamber. That is all I can do or think. Ever since the incident with him, I have been locked in my room, the King's orders.

I have lost my freedom again. It is like I am back in my prison cell in the tower, albeit a much nicer prison – except for the scorching heat.

Sometimes, when I am lucky, I receive a nice breeze through my window. The maids are permitted to come and go as they please. They are the only company I have, not that they are much for conversation.

I am also allowed Baby, but he is not a person. I wish he were. At first, Baby was banned, too. Though this was soon reversed when Baby drove everyone mad. His screams were so loud that no one could sleep. It was not just the noises he made; he went on a path of destruction, where nothing was safe.

They tried to capture him but failed. He would come back at

night, waking everyone with howls, chirps, yips, and scratches at my door.

He would not be deterred. He would go where he wanted, and he did not stop until he was granted access to my room. I thought Baby's antics were hilarious. It pleased me if just a bit.

During this time when I am being 'punished' in my room, I find that I have started my blood days. It means I am not pregnant. I don't know whether to feel happy or sad. The maids mutter about one bad omen following the other. I feel that I am once again cursed.

Yanmei is delighted, and she giggles loudly when Catherine gives her my bloodied bedding. "Looks like the Queen has made quite a mess in her sleep." The maids debate on whom they should inform, Rhys or the Dragon King.

In the end, I don't know what they did, but if I am to guess, it would say it must have been Yanmei who broke the news to everyone in the Kingdom, taking great pleasure in my misfortune.

I know what is next, another ritual.

A horrible ritual...

I will have to feel not only his eyes once again but also theirs. I can beg the Dragon King, but it will do me no good. I am without child, and the King requires an heir.

The Dragon King enjoys tormenting others. He will not spare me. He didn't with Dakari and I start to dislike the King. Though maybe I fear him far more than I hate.

He has harmed a man who was nothing but kind and gentle to me. I have no one in this Kingdom, and Dakari was someone whom I actually considered a friend. But now I am not allowed to see him. I hope he is okay, and no further trouble has befallen on him since the incident.

The man, the Dragon, my husband, is *evil*.

All the rumors I've heard about him are most definitely true, but I cannot escape him. I am bound to him as he is to me. I wonder what he truly thinks about me. Probably all bad things.

Maybe even he thinks of me as evil. He always has something snide to say about what I am or about my people. No dinner passes by without him mentioning the word 'Mage.' He uses the word as a racial slur, to belittle me. *I hate it.*

A week has now fully gone by, and I cannot help but feel an over-whelming amount of sadness. Being alone in a single room with no one to talk to does that... The tower was the same.

The loneliness has cloaked me in obscurity once more. Again, I am a prisoner. I am a queen, yet I am locked away, unable to talk to my friend.

I will give anything to see him right now. Though I'm not sure if Dakari thinks the same of me. Maybe he was forced to be nice to me. Maybe everything was a lie.

My chest feels tight, and tears begin to prick my eyes. I do not want to cry. It is not fitting for a queen as Dakari would say. I am interrupted when a door swings open.

One of my maids, Catherine, enters. I turn my head away from her and wipe my eyes with a finger. "Yes?" I ask, trying my best not to reveal my grief. I swallow, but the lump in my throat is hard.

"I am told to give you this, my lady," Catherine says, approaching me.

"What is it?" I ask her.

"Dragon's Cane," she murmurs placing the gift in my hand. It has a ribbon around the stem as I feel the silk material brush against my hand. "It's a flower. A single one."

"A flower..." I mutter, confused. "Who sent me this?"

"I'm not sure," Catherine replies. "No one's sure. Seeing it's not a dozen of them, just a single one, it means this person is asking for forgiveness, whoever they are. They are sorry about something."

Forgiveness...

Maybe Dakari has sent it.

The Dragon King is not the one to send a flower. He will never ask for my forgiveness when he doesn't even care for me. He is the one who locked me away in this room after nearly choking my friend. He is mean and cruel.

I sniff the flower, and it smells extremely sweet.

"It is also edible in a way," she explains, knowing I have very little knowledge about the plant life in this land. "Dragon's Cane is where our sugar comes from. Though the stem is hollow, it's already been drained of its sugar, the flower itself is still sweet. You can eat the petals if you wish."

"I see," I mutter. "Who do you think could have sent me this?"

"Someone who has wronged you... I don't know. Perhaps someone who knows nothing of flowers. Maybe someone who just wanted you to have something sweet," she replies.

Wronged me... Dakari did not. He is knowledgeable about flowers. But then again, he can be saying he is sorry for everything. This is a mystery. One I may never figure out. I would like to know who sent me the flower and their reason for sending it.

"Well, thank you," I say, twirling the flower in between my fingers ever so slightly.

"You're welcome, my lady," Catherine says. As she turns to leave, she informs, "Oh, the King has given me orders to bring you down to dine with him tonight. He says that he has given you plenty of time to think about your actions and that your punishment is over after tonight."

I listen to her words and find them strange. *The King has asked me to dine with him? My punishment is over? This is unexpected.*

"I will be back with Ava in a bit." Catherine closes the door behind her, and I hear her footsteps disappearing down the hall.

I feel the ribbon around the flower, and I pull it to where it comes undone. I rest it at my side while I sit in a daze.

Perhaps I should wear it in my hair or on my wrist, signaling I am grateful to whoever sent it. For now, I tie it on my wrist next to my wedding bracelet. A flower is innocent, but the meaning behind it can also signify other things.

My mother once told me flowers are a symbol of a man's love. However, a prisoner I knew had said gifting of flowers meant a man wanted to give the woman a good dicking with his icy prick.

I recall the many weird and odd conversations I've had with this specific prisoner. He was not mad when he was first brought to the tower, though the years in prison made his mind disappear and warp into something different. His name was 'Chew' coz he liked to chew everything – boots, belts, clothing, rocks, bones, anything he could get his hands on. He just loved chewing.

I'm surprised I didn't turn out like Chew. Perhaps because he had experienced freedom previously, I had not. I wonder how he is... did he get hanged, or is he still bantering about ice whores and other things? I suppose I won't ever know.

I don't see myself going back to Yulor or anywhere near it, though it will be nice to live in the cold again, have my own home, be with my liwolf, and live peacefully with friends I make.

I will not have to worry about pleasing the King or being scared anymore. I do not wish to have anyone else get hurt like Dakari. But it is a fleeting dream. I am here, and I must live in reality. A harsh reality of kings and queens, Dragons, Mages, hatred, and potential death at every corner.

I lie back in bed with the flower next to me to prevent it from getting crushed, glad that I am at the end of my blood days. The cramps and emotions that come with it seem to be worse than ever before. My body is punishing me for not being with child. It is a curse upon the Mages. The Dragon women don't bleed but receive almost pleasurable heats and sweats, unlike the Mages who suffer the sins of our ancestors.

The woman who killed Kari and was the first to eat his flesh was cursed with pain and blood each month. It was the Dragon's punishment to her for violating his dead body. All her female descendants would feel Kari's wrath each month until she no longer is of child-bearing years.

If we don't suffer during our blood days... we will be cursed with infertility. There is no escaping the torment. So, because of this, the Mages always complain that a tiny Dragon is clawing at their bellies, purposely twisting their insides, punishing them for what their ancestors did.

Lately, I have spent most of my days like this, pacing, lying on the bed, pacing some more, bathing, short conversations with the maids, and eating. Lessons have been put on hold until further notice.

Eating and bathing are the only exciting things I have done in the last week. It is nice to eat two warm meals a day instead of just one small one. I am thankful to have enough food every day to sustain my body.

The maids have said that I am beginning to look healthy, and my appetite is increasing. It is good that I can feel the changes in my body and am no longer skin and bones. I feel more like a woman every day.

As I lay waiting, the door opens. Thinking it must be my maids, I sit up. My eyes narrow when I sense the presence that has entered my room. It isn't them, but someone else entirely.

Completely unexpected. Heavy and pronounced footsteps approach my bed, grabbing something off it. I assume it is the flower. "I hear you've received a sweet gift. Do you like it?"

I can't answer for a few seconds. I was not expecting him to be here, of all people. The maids have only bathed me. I feel messy and unkempt. I run my fingers through my hair that hasn't been brushed since this morning and hit a small snarl – *how embarrassing*.

"Yes... I suppose I do," I mumble.

I don't understand why he is here.

The King takes a few moments to respond. "So, you like these sorts of things?"

"Yes. I can't exactly admire its beauty like most. But I can tell whoever sent the gift, it came from their heart. It has a calming scent, too... I enjoy it," I reply in a rush.

"Hm. It seems all women like flowers. Give me your hand, Mage," he orders.

"No. You have hurt Dakari with those hands."

When I deny him, he grabs my hand and forces the flower into my palm. He does not give me a choice.

"It wasn't a question. Do you think he gave you this flower?" he scoffs, letting go of my hand.

His warmth not fading right away, I can still feel it. "I don't understand why you like something that will die and shrivel up so soon."

"Who else would? And if you must know, it is the meaning and thoughts that go behind the flower that is special," I say. "I guess this is why I, and other women, like them. I am told this flower means forgiveness when just given only one."

"Is that what it means, and you think Dakari is apologizing? For what? Being pathetic? He withered underneath my touch so easily," he snaps.

He is making me angry. How dare he! He is a repulsive creature! A vile slime of a Dragon!

I stand and raise my hand to slap him, thinking not of the consequences. But before I can strike him, he grabs my wrist and pulls me forward. Crashing his lips into mine, our bodies temporary melding.

My first kiss...

The anger I feel for him is gone. It is strange. The tension is fading away as a new sensation takes over. Even though I lost my virginity before – with this kiss, he has taken the last shred of my innocence.

Fingers grasp my nape, his other hand tightening on my wrist. His lips are hot and demanding, pressing into mine, expecting the same in return, but I do not respond. I don't know how to. But my head is spinning with the effects of his presence. I move closer to his body. Something about him is magnetic.

Being so close, the King smells unusually sweet today. His clothes have a distinct scent that my sharp nose picks up on. I know this fragrance. He smells like the flower!

I take another deep breath to confirm and reel back in shock. My mouth gasps open, and he takes it as an invitation. His wet muscle slithers inside. Immediately, I feel like I am betraying Dakari and bite down hard on his tongue, a copper taste filling my mouth.

The King groans and pulls away. "Vile Mage."

I think the same, my lord.

But was it he who sent me the flower...? Truly, he?

He is the last person I expected to receive the flower from. Maybe I have been wrong about him all along.

"The flower...it was you," I say boldly. "This kiss smelled sweet and so were your clothes."

Silence before a low chuckle, he ignores my accusation and says, "I will see you at dinner."

He walks away, opening but not closing the door behind him. I hear his footsteps fade away in the hallway. I hold the flower stem more tightly, my fingers wrapping around it, unsure and confused about the King's actions.

It seems like he has two faces. One is mean, hotheaded, and cruel, and the other questionable. I have only just seen glimpses of this second face.

I feel the petals of the flower one by one. I don't want it to wither and die, so I use my magic to keep it alive. This is the first in a long time that I have tapped into my magic.

Ice crawls up the flower slowly, creating crackling noises and when there is nothing left to freeze, it stops. I raise the flower to my face, my lower lip touching the ice it is preserved in. *It feels nice.*

The flower is forever frozen, and even in the hottest of heats, it will remain so. It is connected to my soul, where my magic rests. It will melt only if I die because I have the strongest of ice magic... magic so powerful I can't control it.

Now I will have the King's first act of kindness toward me forever, if you call it that, though it does not mean I forgive him. Never. He will have to do a lot more than this to earn my true forgiveness, but I believe this is as far as his 'kindness' goes.

In my lifetime, I may never see the King's second face again. He is probably saving it for his true queen, a queen of his heart I will never be.

ELEVEN

THE LINE OF FIRE

I THOUGHT our dinner will be different after what happened, but it seems that is not the case. Well, I guess in a way you can call it distinct in a small way.

Instead of being just the two of us, I feel and hear the noises of others, some sounding gruff, some snarky, while others are intelligent sounding.

The only thing missing tonight seems to be the King. I can sense that his seat is empty. Perhaps I have arrived before him, or he is still preparing for dinner. I thought he would be here by now.

I find it strange since he seems eager to have me for dinner unless he wants me to take his place during such a large and unexpected social event. *I could never...*

They will never listen to whatever is I have to say. Besides, all these people at the table are men, the King's men.

My mouth goes dry, and I grip the arm of my chair tightly. Catherine left me; and I have none of my maids at my side. I feel uncomfortable without them.

In a brief moment listening to the King's men talk about a battle which was successful, and how they boast about it at the table, I wish for the King to be here at my side.

I cannot talk about battle, I have never experienced one or been involved with one. And the more I listen, the more I know they are targeting me. These men do not like me or want me as their queen.

A man who I recognize the voice of is humming softly, his finger tapping the table lightly. And in the darkness, I see his Dragon, it is dark-colored with a messed-up eye and spines projecting from all over its body except its long tail that is barren of them except the very tip.

Zachariah is his name.

He speaks up joining the conversation, "Yes that battle was before King Orval's time. His father, King Diarmind, and I fought this one together. It was a village on the border of Yulor and Oria. An Ice Mage by the name of Aldis, a woman no less, thought taking over a village of Thekas, was something of a victory."

He chuckles continuing his story, "The Mages soon took that land as their own, enslaving Theka women, men, and children, and tried moving forward. Nonetheless, Aldis and her men did not get very far and ended up facing King Diarmind himself. We wiped the shits off the map, reclaimed the village, and Aldis became a toy to the King, much to Queen Wera's displeasure at the time."

"Ice Mages have always been whores to us Fire Dragons if brought to Oria. If King Diarmind knew his firstborn son would take one as his wife, he'd shit himself." another man says gruffly, this Dragon being lighter but baring many scars much like the one-eyed Dragon, Zachariah. His voice too is familiar- Fonzell.

He's probably rolling over in his grave somewhere. If Diarmind wanted a Dragon born of ice magic, he would have done so with his whore Aldis, but no, when she became pregnant with his bastard, he gutted her with his claws in front of the entire Kingdom." Zachariah replies before taking large gulps of his drink before slamming it down.

His Dragon bares its teeth towards my direction, "Her guts spilled onto the floor with the tiny fetus that was once safely in its mother's belly. Such a pure sight to witness. Queen Wera was especially happy, I cannot forget the Queen's smile that day."

"All Rhys's doing, always encouraging both Kings to lay with one of the ice women. Sometimes I question his loyalty to the Kingdom and his plans. That hairless scalp should have stayed within the safety of the walls of Watergrale.... Him, the Doctor, and you, Cell." says Ukiah, he too taking a jab - his Dragon staying within the darkness only flashes of brightness here and there.

"I agree, Rhys is a traitor along with the others, plotting to destroy Oria from within," hisses Fonzell.

I hear General Cell laugh, his voice is distinct, and despite hearing all the rudeness the other men are saying about Mages, he did not once stick up for me, "Oh Fonzell, you only have it out for Rhys because he stole Selene's heart before you and all your ugliness could."

Another bout of laughter comes from Cell that is definitely mocking as if he can't contain it, "And Ukiah, you are pissed the King didn't take your sister as his queen, then you Zachariah, well not much to be said about you, stuck in your ways. And to be honest, here is so much more entertaining than Watergrale as you know, it is a peaceful country, unlike this one, which will rather start a war than make love. Oria is known for war-making, is it not?"

"I was not in love with Selene, you damn water shit. I will rather gut one of you peace making Water Dragons than an ice whore any day," growls Fonzell.

Ukiah hisses, "Watch your tongue, you filthy ingrate, the moment the King does not protect you, I will be-"

"Ukiah? Filthy ingrate? Look at you who has risen from straight shit, looking so posh..." Zachariah says waiting for Ukiah, to perhaps attack but nothing happens, and he continues, "But as much as we like to gut Cell someday and I will want to cut his tongue that seen too many fire cunts, the Fake Queen is our top priority. Maybe we should make a statement to our King that we do not like her..."

These men are ruthless. If left in the room alone any longer with them, I fear I will be the next Mage to have her guts spilled out onto the floor. My hand begins to shake, and I can do nothing to control it. Their words frighten me and I have no doubt they would carry out their threats to harm me.

The only truly good man I have met so far in this Kingdom is Dakari. How I wish he was here at the table with us... But it is only warriors, generals, and dukes of the Firelands or otherwise known as the Kingdom of Oria.

The doors to the dining hall open and two sets of feet can be heard, and I know who it is automatically. The King and his Advisor Rhys. I have not felt magic like theirs, so powerful it is like it has a life of its own.

Though the King by far outmatches Rhys, but this man can definitely win many battles. He is not weak like the advisor of my father, although I do not remember him well.

The room grows silent as he walks in, and the King walks towards the empty seat next to mine. Rhys follows behind him but keeps his distance and is much slower with his steps.

"Zachariah, you're oddly talkative this evening. I see that you have already chosen to cozy up to our Queen," comments Rhys.

Zachariah is silent choosing not to respond, and I can see that the face of his Dragon doesn't look any kinder than it had seconds ago with me.

"He wouldn't be the first to do so," says the King slipping into the seat beside me, his comment snide. "Well, did I miss anything interesting while I was gone?"

"No, Your Majesty," says Cell, being the first to speak up, his voice calm and collected. "You just missed Zachariah and Fonzell's lovely comments about the Queen you picked out and how lovely she looked in her dress."

I hear the King next to me lean forward, the chair creaking slightly, "I see. Do the men in my Kingdom want to die over a few touches or comments to the Mage? I will gladly kill anyone who dishonors thy King, in any way, shape or form..."

Silence overtakes the table once more, no one responding to him, then a servant comes in setting something down on the table.

"Am I a joke to you all?!" the King snaps and all I hear is something get stabbed into the table, a knife perhaps.

A startled gasp leaves the servant and my eyebrows knit, worried that he has hurt the servant for no apparent reason, but I hear no other sounds after that. It leads me to believe he just startled them with his anger or sudden movement.

More servants come in setting things on the table, and they scurry away once the dishes are set down. Their steps are quick and skittish and I can sense that they fear the King.

I know why now.

More silence follows until I hear someone say from the far end of the table, "Well, let's eat."

"Yes, let's," says Rhys taking a seat somewhere beside us. "And then we shall discuss more important matters."

I hear everyone pick up their silverware, the King is one of the last as I am. I do not feel comfortable with so many people in the room, and from what I am smelling, today's meal seems to be some kind of stew.

Stew reminds me of the soup I have eaten in the tower, and I get reminded of many unpleasant meals. Foul, moldy food that I would have to eat without cutlery. I do not miss those days.

I first eat the bread at the side of the bowl, and I hear the King make a disgusted sound next to me. *Is something wrong with the meal?*

"Couldn't you servants have prepared something better than this garbage?" he questions them not seeming to like what he is eating either, he drops the spoon into the bowl after what I presume is one bite. "I gag on the mere sight of it."

"Do you want something different, your Majesty?" a male servant asks quietly, the only one left behind as the other servants have long since left and gone back into the kitchen.

"Yes. Anything but this shit." he hisses, pushing away his food, and I hear the servant collect the plates quickly, taking it away, and he too disappears behind a door.

"That wound on your tongue I spy does the stew burn it? Did a skalagin get your tongue?" asks Cell.

"Damn pervert and that's a shitty joke! I am sick of you, watching my mouth like you want to fuck it. Not a-"screams the King.

"Besides accusing perverts which is justified and the not so great food, sire, I think we should discuss-" Rhys begins to say but he too is cut off.

"About the borders. I already know." The King finishes. "As there is no immediate threat from the Mages, it does not mean we can trust them completely. So, men will still be dispatched to patrol the borders by Yulor, just not as many as before. We focus now not on the North but to the East, South, and West."

"Do you still plan to send an expedition towards the east beyond the Silvertop Mountains?" A voice I recognize as Gregory asks.

"Yes," answers the King immediately without hesitation.

"Your father did not dare go beyond the Silvertop Mountains in the East. For very good reasons, sire," Rhys adds quickly.

"I am not my father," says the King sternly. "I am not scared of other Dragons that may be different. Whether serpent-like or not. Our country is powerful, and if they start a war, then so be it, we will bring them a fight. They will be idiots to do so. I will make their women common whores, their men slaves, and the royal members suffer far greater than any of its people."

He sounds cruel... *but then what king isn't?* A king is the one to make cruel decisions, *or is he just a sadist?*

"As I said, Oria is known for war-making, not lovemaking," says Cell towards the two Dragons, Fonzell and Zachariah, from their earlier conversation.

A servant enters with a new dish, and they set it down in front of the King. A dish that smells much better than ours, it smells like steak. My mouth waters a little at the thought. I have never eaten steak, but I know the smell of it.

"Is this better, my King?" the servant questions.

I hear him pick up his silverware for the second time, and he cuts into the meat. I hear him say before he even tries it, "Its fine. Now go away. I can't eat with you staring at me with high expectations. I have none for these cooks."

Once more, I hear the servant leave through the door, and before they can go on to discuss other politics, I hear Lucius speak up, the one who I vividly remember got punched after our ritual, "Queen, you're so quiet... Did the death threats from earlier scare you?"

I reply, seeing as I got brought into the conversation now, "Not particularly..."

A lie... But am I supposed to say... Yes? That I was trembling in my seat, which I actually was. Their words bothered me greatly. I wonder if the King would stand up for me and reprimand them for their comments, but I had just bitten him during our kiss.

I hear the King put down his silverware, and he chews a fatty piece of steak. I find it hard to swallow the bread in my mouth, the tension rises.

Once the King swallows, he speaks up, "Threats? It goes from flirting to fucking threats? What kind of conversation was held here during my absence? Is someone dumb enough to plot treason in front of a whole fucking table of my men, one obvious traitor, maybe two... Three?"

"Yes. Actually." Cell says quickly, saving his hide from lying earlier to the King as Lucius had purposely brought up these threats, or perhaps he did so by accident. "Fonzell and Zachariah seem to be intent on gutting the Queen and me. They don't like foreigners, Water Dragons, or Ice Mages."

The King grows silent once again, and he picks up his cup and starts drinking. I am confused as to why he hadn't mentioned Ukiah, he was also speaking of treason.

"I expected no less from them," Rhys comments snidely putting his spoon down into the bowl of stew as if knowing something unpleasant is about to happen.

Once he finishes whatever it is in his cup, he slams it down on the table, and before he can speak, Zachariah growls out, "You will displease your father with what you have done! Making peace with the Mages, bringing an ice whore into our Kingdom and taking her as your wife, fucking her, and having whatever abomination she spits out as our next in line. You will disgust him, you disgust me, and you disgust your people with what you have done, they just don't have the balls to say anything! I do!"

The King stands from his seat, and I can tell he is getting ready to attack Zachariah. The others too raise quickly from their seats, preparing to get away from an inevitable battle.

But before he can attack Zachariah, I somehow get in the way and grab his arm, which is by far one of the most foolish things I have done.

Why do it? Zachariah was horrible not kind like Dakari. I suppose I did not want to see anyone else hurt.

But I end up in the line of fire, literally.

His skin is feverishly hot already, hot from boiling with rage, and I can see within my mind upon touching him, how angry his Dragon is. Unlike before in this vision, the Dragon bites at me, trying to swallow my arm whole. The vision startles me.

His skin is equivalent to touching fire, and my hand burns as it keeps on holding his arm, preventing him from attacking or lunging at Zachariah.

The Dragon inside my head snarls at me; the swallowing of my arm is not enough to spook me. The burning of my hand sparks my powers against my will, my ice tries to naturally cool off my burning hand. It tries to heal what hurts and protect me against the Dragon King's magic.

Upon feeling the littlest of ice touch his skin, the dark Dragon inside my head goes berserk, and before I know it, claws that feel like knives rake across my chest, making me scream.

A close-range attack is the worst for me. The most frightening by far. Imagine being in a dark world and feeling only pain, not knowing where the attack is coming from and when the next one will hit.

I long since let go of him, falling back from the force, and I feel blood escape my chest wounds. It splatters on the floor as my dress is torn, a flap of cloth hanging loosely on me.

The room is silent, but I feel the ease of the Dragon King's anger after he has lashed out against me, but it won't stop the trembling of my body. My breathing is shaky, the impact nearly steals my breath.

It is hard to comprehend what has just happened, and everything is blank and quiet as I continue to feel and smell the sharp scent of blood. My blood.

Then I feel the Dragon King's magic grow closer, reaching out to grab me, and all I can think of is his hand hurting me.

"Stay back!" I scream, trying to make myself bigger than I am. My hand that is burnt also cannot cease the trembling from the trauma it has suffered. Burns are the worst for my kind.

I hear another set of footsteps, the magic seems to be Cell's.

"Ok... Everything's fine. I apologize, my King, but you are the last person she'd probably want touching her." Cell explains as his hand wraps around my arm, which does not hurt me or bother me.

So, these are the hands of a Water Dragon, soothing... And not at all like the fiery hands of the Fire Dragons.

When I stare towards the faint magic of the King, all I can see is something that wants to consume and hurt and conquer. Just like when his magic wanted to consume Dakari and hurt him, it now wanted to hurt me. The Dragon that is dwelling inside the King is no better.

I hear the King back away from us, and he hisses at everyone, his attention focusing on them. "Get out!!"

Everyone listens to him, Zachariah being one of the last ones to leave.

I hear Cell next to me say as he tucks his arm under my legs. "I'm going to take you to my brother, Viggo. He can help you."

He lifts me off the ground and into his arms, and the King does not say a word to us, or specifically at me.

Maybe he is feeling shame... Regret ... Anger. It is hard to tell. *Is he pleased at how he has reacted?*

As General Cell carries me in his arms, it is then I see why women like him so much. He is a caring man, unlike the Dragon King.

What did Yanmei see in someone like the King? What kind of face is he making right now?

I hear expressions can tell a lot about what someone is feeling, especially during a moment such as this one.

For all I know he can be making the worst of faces.

What face are you making right now... my King?

TWELVE

THORNS OF THE THRONE

DOCTOR VIGGO's hands are surprisingly rough, though he takes good care of me. My breath hitches as he examines my wounds and the blood oozing steadily.

I take a good look at the Doctor. His level of magic matches that of his brother, and he appears strong enough to fight and win the battle. I wonder why he is a doctor and not a warrior like Cell. Perhaps he has chosen to work in this field to help others, his true purpose in life.

I can tell the Doctor has a good way about him. He asks his brother to leave the room, amidst Cell's protestations that he has seen many breasts in his life and mine are no different from the others and that he has already seen mine on the first night.

The first night ceremony... It has slipped my mind that Cell had been there. Learning this, Viggo not only sounds disgusted with his brother but he also decides to remove him manually from the room, all the while hissing that first night will be the last time he will ever see my breasts and that I was a queen, not some common whore.

At least, the Doctor respects me.

All I hear is the slam of a door, and I can no longer sense Cell in the room, his presence further away but lingering nearby. My attention is pulled away from that to the Doctor when he pulls the dress away from my chest, my breasts visible only to him as he goes about cleaning and dressing the wounds. I wonder how the King will react to him touching me in this manner.

A viscous cold substance washes over my chest, making me squirm in pain. It hurts as he mops the depth of the slashes with a clean cloth. The coldness of the solution is the only thing that is good about it, bringing comfort to my overheated skin.

Then comes the stitching, the needle going back and forth, joining my separated flesh, is a nightmare. I can feel every single prick, each drag on my skin as the thread passes through the wound, the Doctor pulling the edges together.

It is pure torture; I am frayed and restless. He tries to distract me from the pain with his small talks. "Queen Vrai, I believe we haven't met before. I'm Doctor Viggo if you haven't heard my name already."

My fingers curl into the table as I struggle to answer him. "I've... I've heard about you." I breathe, trying my best not to focus solely on the pain, but it doesn't stop the occasional tear from spilling down my cheeks.

"Well, I'm glad to make your informal acquaintance," he says, grabbing something and snipping the leftover thread. "That's one done, two more to go."

His hands steadily work on the second wound, this one being long and tender as it runs across both my breasts.

"Tell me, Vrai, what is your fondest memory?" The Doctor's voice seems to be coming from the end of a tunnel, and I have to force my brain to concentrate. I find it an odd question during a time like this. But I am also thankful for the distraction. He has a good personality, something every healer should have.

"My fondest memory..." I repeat. I try to think of what this loving memory may be, and all I can hear in my heart is the voice of my mother.

I remember the coldness of the snow and how it fell from the skies, landing on my skin, nothing like the cruel heat I now face. My mother called them snowflakes. She was by my side during one of the gentler snowfalls of the season.

My homeland... The Icelands - The Kingdom of Yulor.

I have many good memories from the days before the tower. Mostly, the ones with my mother and the ones where I faintly remember my father's good side, his visits few and far between, but he never treated me cruelly then... Not ever, not until that incident.

"Well?" questions Doctor Viggo, his hands constantly moving to seal the wounds.

"My fondest memory is being with my mother, out in the snow... playing," I reply honestly, recalling the memory of how we enjoyed that day, the thoughts calming me down from this incident. "What is yours, Doctor Viggo?"

"Hmm, that is quite a good question. I would have to say it is when I became a doctor. I studied for many years under my mentor – famous and well known in Watergrale. I was selfish back then and only interested in healing my sight," Viggo replies, finishing up the second wound with the sound of the thread being snipped, which makes me wince.

"You have no vision?" I question him, confused.

Then how can he be a doctor?

He chuckles softly. "I suffer from what we call fuzzy eye. It is one of the many reasons why I cannot be a warrior like Cell. My vision as a Dragon is much worse. I must wear reading sea glasses to focus on objects, words, really anything."

He begins on the last wound, his voice putting me into a trance. Talking to him is working... I am not focused on my pain much.

"Have you learned of any magic to heal vision?" I ask him, feeling a sharp pain in my chest as he brings the frayed skin together.

"No. Else I would not be wearing glasses," he replies. "I have studied many things about the eye, and I have found modified sea glass to be the only cure for fuzzy eye. In your case, Vrai, no set of glasses can make you see."

He sighs, "Total blindness is something I cannot help you with. I have heard rumors of magic being able to repair the eyes, and I have searched high and low for such a thing for many years, but I have come to the conclusion those are just rumors."

"I see..." is all I can mutter, my heart crushed with disappointment. My mother was wrong, perhaps. I hear another snip followed by a clattering noise as he puts down his instruments.

"There, all done," he says, fixing my tattered dress and covering my chest back up. "I will ask

Cell to call for your maids. I'm sure you want to rest. I can give you something to help with the pain, but I recommend not moving too much or wearing any corsets or tight-fitting clothes. You will need to rest for the next couple of days to ensure your wounds won't open."

I nod and sit up slowly with his support. He holds my hand and keeps the other at my waist to help me get off the table.

General Cell knocks on the door, and a few seconds later, opens it without an invitation. He starts walking toward us. "I see you are finally done. Took you long enough, I was bored waiting. It's a shame our beautiful Queen will be left with scars. The King has such a temper. He's marked such beautiful flesh... A shame indeed."

Scars... Will these wounds always linger on my skin even after they're healed? An everlasting reminder to never get in the way of the King's anger. *I don't want that... I want to forget; I never want to think of those moments again.*

Viggo jumps in. "Enough, Cell. Send for her maids. She needs to rest, not listen to your babble."

"Yes, yes. I will take my babbling elsewhere. I'm just saying it's a shame what happened. I know

I know... You don't need to start with your bitching. Relax, I will call for the maids right away. I only do the maid service because she is a woman." Cell is already beginning to move away from us. "I wish you get well soon, Queen. Hopefully, you're all healed up for the festivities next month. I look forward to them."

Festivities...? I suppose I will find out soon enough.

"Cell, out. Last warning." Viggo suddenly sounds angry.

He shuts the door, heeding his brother's warning, and Viggo helps me to one of the chairs in the office.

"I will get you some pills. They will help you sleep, not just get rid of the pain," Viggo informs me, walking away. I hear him digging through the cabinets, pills rattling, bottles moving.

He uncaps one, then puts it back. Taking my hand, he places two small pills in my palm, then gives me a small glass of water. I take both together, swallowing them with water. I really hope this makes me sleep after everything that has happened.

He puts the glass away and hesitates, facing me. "Forgive the King... I'm sure in these moments, he is fretting about what he has done, somewhere in silence. If there is one thing you should never do, it is to get between two fighting Dragons; you're destined to get hurt. Especially with your power, the King was most definitely spooked."

Forgive him?

I am unsure what to feel about this. *He hurt me, and I am the one who has to forgive him?*

Nonsense.

With everything he does, he shows what my people have feared about Dragons to be true. He is like an out of control beast that needs to be caged or locked away.

What he's done to Dakari... what he has done to me. He is becoming a monster, his Dragon not helping. I am going to be plagued by nightmares, night after night.

My maids come to collect me, not saying a single word. They help me to my room, change me into a loose dress, and prepare my bed for the night.

After such a long day, I am glad to be under the covers, thankful to have the coldness of the silk sheets against my skin. With the help of the medication, I fall asleep in no time, and the nonsensical dreams about Baby fill my head.

Come dawn, I am awoken by someone entering my room. Bold,

heavy footsteps make me sit up, nearly startled. The wind blows through the open window against me.

I grab the sheets, my heart thumping in my chest, and I can feel the presence. They linger in the corner, and I finally recognize the fiery magic.

"What do you want?" I question him. It is hard to sense the presence of his Dragon.

The King is quiet, almost... *remorseful*.

"You shouldn't have gotten in my way with Zachariah. He has pissed me off one too many times. He expects me to be my father, which I am clearly not. The only reason why you're hurt is that you laid your hands on me when you were using your magic. A foolish move, Mage... I didn't expect you to be so dumb."

"Is that all you've come to say?" I hiss at him, narrowing my eyes at the magic I am seeing, feeling hurt, though I expected no less from him. "I know now never to touch you, or you will lash out against me. Don't worry, my King, it will be the last time I will make such a foolish move... Forgive me."

Of late, my mouth has become bolder along with my actions. I'm surprised I still have a tongue after our kiss.

More silence follows, and I am unsure if it is a good or a bad thing. He moves next to my bed from the corner of the room, and I become worried about what he may do. I shrink into my pillows, away from his touch.

However, he reaches out and grabs my face, his fingers cupping my cheeks. "To be clear, Mage, I didn't hurt you because I am afraid of your magic... It is a warning to never get in the way of any of my battles."

It is my turn to be silent. My wounds are aching more just with his hand being near.

'Forgive the King....' is what Viggo said, but I'm unsure if he knows how evil this man truly is.

Forgiveness is out of question, it seems.

"I hear you've bled.... When your wounds heal, we must attempt another time. The people demand an heir, so we must give them one." His voice does not sound joyful.

His fingers slip from my face before he grabs a strand of my hair. "You're a queen now, Mage. No longer an innocent princess... Expect to be hurt, betrayed, and to be hated. You can never run from any of those things. The wounds you have on your chest are only a glimpse of what being royal does to you. Things do not get easier from here."

Suddenly, I feel Baby climb up on the bed to come close to me and begin growling low at the King, something that has never happened before. Baby is usually well mannered. He must have snuck in through the open window, scaling the ledges. He does not seem to like the King anymore.

"It seems I'm being told to leave." The King lets go of my hair. "Keep the mutt close. I have never seen a liwolf forge such a strong bond with its keeper. The only thing Cell has ever done right is gift you this creature." The King steps back and leaves the room.

Baby starts grooming me, his rough tongue licking my arm as he lies down next to me. He smells of fresh air and Dragon's Cane. He must have been exploring the same spot where the King plucked my flower.

He is unbelievable, that man! Picking flowers, then tearing my chest open.

I lie down with Baby, thinking about what the King has said and that being a royal will only get worse. Perhaps he has spoken from experience, but I will never know of the King's past with his people.

Rumors only spread so far to my country. I have no one to ask – no one willing to share. I shut my eyes again, the medicines making me drowsy once I relax with the creature at my side.

Dragon's Cane, the King, and our kiss weigh heavily on my mind. It feels like a distant memory from long ago when it has only just happened.

How things can change so quickly here.

THIRTEEN

THE DAY OF BLOSSOMS

Four weeks have passed since the incident and my subsequent healing, marking today as The Day of Blossoms.

A day where spring is rejoiced in the entire land, a time when flowers bloom and flourish. The air is vibrant with colors, and there is a sparkle in these Fire Dragons.

All join and gather to celebrate this festival. Typically, hosted by the king and queen, the day will abound with singing and dancing.

This day also worships women and girls of all ages. Dressed gaily in colorful clothes, flower crowns adorn their head to show their love and devotion to earth. Men carry no weapons; it is strictly prohibited.

No blood shall be spilled on the land during this day, else the Kingdom is at risk of being cursed by the Gods. The King spares no one who doesn't follow this rule. It is more a day of love than anything.

Apparently, this is the day that only the Earth Dragons celebrated once, but soon the Fire Dragons, more than two hundred years ago, decided to join in.

They too wanted to honor their love for the flowers, trees, and land as they were well bonded with Earth. A certain queen in the past made this a full day celebration amongst her people, her name forever remembered today.

The King and I are forced to interlink our arms as we walk together, sending a fake message of love and devotion between us just to make his people happy.

This is the first festival I have ever attended, and it is difficult to remain calm when my senses are constantly being bombarded with loud noises and magical vibes.

Almost everywhere I turn, I can see the magic in all living beings, its presence strong, its colors merging and intertwining, then separating to join with the others to transform into different shades like the dancers swaying to a different rhythm. There is pure joy in being in the center of such a powerful force.

But all my mind is focusing on is that small area of contact between our arms, leading me to remember what had happened more than a month ago. Two weeks post that incident, Viggo had removed my stitches, which hurt more than having them in, and soon after, a cleansing ceremony was held between the King and me when Rhys deemed me to be completely healed.

The King and I had sex once more, but this time we were alone. Things felt even more awkward and suffocating than the first time when we had his people in the room with us. I couldn't respond, and the King too had a tough time performing. There was no love or affection or lust.

We are not even good mates, let alone soul mates.

The act had been forced on us once more, but during this time, I felt no pain as I did my first night. Toward the end, I felt the beginning of something more inside me, but the spark faded when the King pulled out upon releasing, his duty done.

He rushed to get out of my room, hurriedly donning his pants and running out the door. He had not even finished buckling them when he bumped into a maid in the hallway.

He cursed loudly and asked her to get the fuck out of his way – I remember it vividly. Ava felt almost sorry for me after her run-in with the King.

Holding his arm now is all a lie. We are lying to each other and his people. It does not feel right to be by his side like this.

I am tempted to pull away from the King, but when I move my arm away just a smidgen, I hear him grumbling in a soft voice at my right, "Bear with it until the end of the day. Today is important to my people."

I frown in sullen acquiescence as we descend the stairs together. At the bottom, Catherine places a flower crown upon my head.

"You look beautiful, my lady," she says, and I know she is also lying for the sake of her people, or should I say, our people.

My frown deepens at the propagation of this untruth. I do not wish for anyone to pretend to like me. I am their queen. I should be respected, but this whole thing has been a farce right from the beginning.

"Thank you," I say to her, my tone flat, resembling my step-mother's.

Will I turn into someone like her?

I doubt she loves my father... just like I don't love the Dragon King. I know my father will never get over my mother's death, which means he does not love my stepmother.

Perhaps love between a king and his queen is impossible and eventually, the King will find someone to love, just like my father found my mother – a lowly Mage not born into royalty.

Maybe the Dragon King is already in love with a woman... What is her name? Yes. Red, the whore who was mentioned long ago, perhaps.

We move together and join the crowd of people, some making way for us while others stayed close to the King. I guess they are his close men.

We stop, and I hear beautiful singing from a woman. The kinds I have never heard before, a melodious voice. I feel a new presence within the castle, one that I have not come across before.

Suddenly, a different kind of Dragon appears in my mind.

This creature does not look like any other I have seen before, though I know it to be a Dragon. It is stocky, its limbs shorter, and its body is low to the ground.

Its scales are like a coat of armor, and it has a dreadful club for a tail. The more I stare at the strange Dragon, the more I liken its build to a dumpy person. The most remarkable thing is that the Dragon does not bear any wings.

The woman continues to sing, her voice growing louder as more gather around her. The crowd gives her a boost of confidence, though she needs none. Her voice is lyrical, and she must know the Gods have gifted her with song.

I wonder how I sound when I sing?

She sings about the land of the Fire Dragons, how sometimes the land is so barren yet can be filled with new life in the spring season, the summer heat is yet to kill anything.

The song is catchy, and I'm sure she is more beautiful than her voice. She is a woman whom everyone stares at longingly, her voice drawing them in.

I enjoy singing, but I am in no mood to sing, though it does help to soothe my nerves. Singing is all I knew in the tower. Pitching together the perfect tunes and finding out which sounded the best was how I spent my time.

The woman's singing stops, and everyone claps around us, including the King. He has clearly decided that it is something worth applauding. At the song's end, her Dragon disappears into the smoky blackness, having a sleepy and lazy look to it.

I see her magic move from the center of attention, and I hear the crowd pay her compliments for her singing, both women and men.

The King growls beside me. "Can you act normal? Perhaps try smiling more, people are already beginning to stare at you."

Smile, smile, smile... I am no longer a doll.

Is smiling really that important? I'm sure he is scowling.

"I will smile if it makes you happy," I say, forcing one upon my face.

The King sighs and once more, we begin moving through the crowd. However, we stop right before the strange Dragon.

I hear her introduce herself, no more than a foot away from us, her speech fast and nervous. "Your majesty," she greets the King and bows down. "I beg your pardon I haven't had time to properly introduce myself yet. My name is Chi. I've come all the way from the land of Earath to your beautiful Kingdom. I am honored and humbled you have allowed me to take part in your cultural festivities despite our countries' differences. Well, I hope to educate more young people from today about the importance of the land we stand on." Turning to me, she continues, "And it's also a pleasure to meet you, Queen Vrai."

I am at once charmed by her. Chi sounds like a woman who is full of kindness. I have learned to listen to the nuances of a person's voice to understand who they are on the inside. Her voice comes across as soft and gentle. I believe she has good intentions and is true to herself.

"I'm glad you wanted to be a part of the culture of the Kingdom of Oria. I hope to someday establish a treaty between your country and mine. King NuJu certainly cannot hold a grudge forever over something that happened so long ago, before he or I were even born. Perhaps when you travel back to your country, you can relay how civilized and good my people and our intentions are," the King expresses, standing next to me, and I force myself to keep smiling.

"Ah, I will try, King Orval." Her words seem high strung before she laughs apprehensively.

"You know King NuJu... It's so very difficult to get an audience with him."

"Ah... Yes, I know from experience." The King's tone in public is completely different to how he is with his soldiers, me, and those around him. "Your singing is wonderful. I would love to have you sing for us each holiday but, of course, you must go back home eventually."

"Thank you, King Orval. I agree I do have to go back home some-time, unfortunately, but I think I will stay just a bit longer on this visit. Well, it is nice to finally meet you. And you as well, Queen Vrai."

I hear her footsteps travel away from us, and the King tsks softly, under his breath. "I wish her King would just die. He's nothing but a spoiled brat, too young for the throne. He doesn't even give me the time of the day to restore our countries' alliances."

I am curious, so I question him as the King moves closer to me. "If I may ask, what was done to originally destroy your alliance with his Kingdom in the first place?"

The King huffs out his answer. "Forty years ago, my father, King Diarmind, promised he would help them go to war with Watergrale, and when the time came for the battle to happen, Diarmind betrayed him and joined forces with Watergrale. He hoped to conquer their lands. This forced the Earth Dragons to retreat since Oria has and always will be the country with the most Dragons and weaponry, so they had no choice. We are a strong ally but a stronger enemy. So Earath continues to shut us out, even this young prick, NuJu. I wish we'd conquered their lands, but it was a failure as their defenses were quite admirable."

"How old is NuJu?" I ask next.

"Fourteen years old," replies the King bitterly. "Fifteen in a few months. He gained the throne after the passing of his father, King Quimton. Ever since he has claimed the throne for himself, he has done nothing but sit on his ass and act like the child he is. He refuses to speak to the other kings or me. The only thing he has done right is trade, and I'm sure his advisor handles such matters. I should cut our trade deals until he accepts to meet me in person. Why should we continue to deal with a country that hates us and won't speak to us and will probably try and start a war with us once this Child King grows some balls?"

I find the King to be quite talkative about this suddenly, ranting almost. He is dealing with a child that happens to be a king, and he doesn't know what to do, that is for certain.

In my opinion, if I gained the throne so young, I would be scared, too. I wouldn't want to meet kings who could possibly kill me, especially the King of Fire Dragons. If the Earth Dragons have heard the same rumors as the Mages, they would be terrified.

"Perhaps this King is frightened to meet the other kings, especially being so young and naive and unprepared for the throne. I don't think he means any harm, and I am sure he won't be thinking of starting a war at fourteen. Maybe he feels threatened by all of you and will prefer to deal with a woman. Someone non-threatening and calm," I suggest.

The King stops and stares at me, nonplussed. We have reached a place near the fountain where the children are playing some game. Their giggles and tiny flames of magic are all that I can hear and feel. It feels inviting to go and play with them. But I am a queen. I have to behave like one.

"Are you suggesting that I send you to another country to try and deal with a King I cannot even get an audience with? I cannot, and will not, trust you, Mage. That is out of the question. You could betray me when you stand in the land of Earath, getting your country and theirs to go to war against me," he snaps quietly in my ear.

The King sounds paranoid... thinking I am still in league with Yulor and can get the Earth

Dragons to go to war against him. I can only shake my head at his line of thinking. I wasn't suggesting I'd go; I never gave it a single thought. It was just an idea.

I start to further explain myself, "I wasn't—" But we get interrupted.

A child runs up to us, a little boy from the sounds of his voice.

"Are you the King and Queen?" he asks innocently but sounds excited.

"Yes?" replies the King. His voice is monotonous as if unsure about the boy's question.

"Really?" he chirps, "I didn't think you would attend the festival. Mother says it is rare for the King to attend. Guys, come look. It's the King and Queen!"

All the children run and flock around us, staring in admiration. Their eyes say that they want the things we have, but they have no idea they lead happier lives than us. They have love, respect, and freedom. The very things I do not have.

"You're so pretty," a girl at my right says. "Is it true you're an Ice Mage?"

Another child asks the King, "Why did you marry a Mage? Father says they're our enemies."

"Maybe because she is pretty," the girl counters, giggling.

I can feel the King become irritated, and a small growl leaves his throat at their innocent questions.

Before the King can get angrier, I make up answers to spin an even falser lie, "It is true that I am an Ice Mage. The King married me because he wants a future with no war between all the countries. So we can all live peacefully together. A life with no war is a happy one, isn't it? War only causes unnecessary sorrow."

"I suppose it is," mutters a child.

"War is great! Zachariah is so cool. I want to be a warrior like him!"

"Everyone is amazing! Beheading Mages, lighting them on fire, and stomping on them like gnats. I want to be like them," hollers a young boy, reminding me of the vile man by my side.

The King snorts at the boy's remarks. He feels no shame at his actions when I, his wife, a Mage, is standing next to him and listening to how the Dragons torture Mages and kill them, that too from the mouth of a child.

My dear Dragon husband clears his throat. "This is much too inappropriate for a boy your age. Where is your father? Call him here so I can behead him since you enjoy the act so much."

"I'm sorry, please," whimpers the boy in fear, his mood souring.

"He is joking. There will be no beheadings or executions. Next time, be careful with your words. It is easy to hurt someone," I say softly placing my hand on his head and ruffling his hair. "The King wishes only for you to understand this."

The boy's mood seems to lighten up. "Your hand is like ice. That is so cool."

"Are you really cold all the time?" a girl chirps in, reaching out to touch my hand.

Her small, warm fingers grasp my hand. The flames hidden within the tiny Fire Dragon do not bother me at all. Her fingers are like a hot cup of tea, just right to drink.

"Yes, we Mages are born cold, and we continue to be cold for the rest of our lives," I reply.

"Wow, you really are cold," she says, feeling up my hand. "And can you not see?"

"I can't see, but I can hear and feel you," I reply.

"It must be hard," she says, letting go of my hand. "Unable to see and so cold all the time. At least you have the King to keep you warm."

I smile slightly. "It isn't bad. I promise. I enjoy singing and dancing and even some forms of reading. The cold does not bother me, just as the warmth does not bother you. And the King... He does his best to warm me if I get too cold."

Here, on this land, I can never feel cold, and I definitely don't want him warming me.

The girl goes to ask me another question, but I hear a woman call out, "Come on, children! Do not bother the King and Queen any more than what you already have. You're rude! Come! I heard you, Jack. Wait until your father hears about this."

The children begin to run toward the woman, the boy pulling away from my grasp, but the little girl lingers. "I wish I could be as beautiful as you someday." She reaches up and whispers in my ear, "Tell the King to smile some more. He looks so grumpy."

I hear her take something off. She reaches for my hand, wrapping my fingers around a small flower crown, "So you don't forget me. My name is Carrie."

She runs off to whoever that woman is to her, and I sigh. I hold the flower crown tightly in my hand.

"Damn these noble children... They are all spoiled and ask too many questions; their mouths are uncouth. It is the parents' fault. At least you're good with children, even when you have to lie," the King grumbles once the children are out of earshot.

"Sometimes, it is better to lie to a child than tell the truth," I respond. "Tell them how things really are, they either won't get it or become frightened. If a strange man or woman says something odd to you as a child or tells you something you don't want to hear, you probably won't go near them again. Try not to threaten children. They look up to you, you know."

"I see. I will try." The King resumes walking through the busy and loud streets. "Perhaps you're right, Mage, and that Child King just needs to be treated as one. You suggest I send out a woman?"

I am surprised he takes my advice. "Perhaps... or someone with intelligence but not a lot of power. A woman with a lot of power might make him think twice. You might make him feel insecure, so he would not do what you intend."

He is quiet as he absorbs my words.

"Maybe you aren't all that dumb after all," he hums. "Maybe that tutor... Dakari, is it? He was doing you some good."

"Well, I don't think it is because I am particularly smart or have taken lessons. I believe it's common sense as he is just a child," I explain.

He snorts. "Are you calling me dumb? You get bolder with each passing day."

"No. I think you've overthought your situation, worrying about war and betrayal. If you'd thought calmly perhaps, it would have eventually come to you," I placate him. "I don't believe you're dumb."

"You're getting too honest, but I suppose honestly is good," he agrees, and we descend another flight of stone stairs, going down further into the town.

I hold on to the small flower crown, grazing my finger over the hard work of the little girl. "What do I do with this?"

"You're supposed to wear it," he sneers as if I don't know what to actually do with it.

"I'm already wearing one," I say, then recall men don't wear them.

I take the flower crown that the little girl has given me and reach over, placing it on top of his head. His hair is stiff and dry from the beeswax but smells good as I stretch my body to reach his head.

He seems shocked as he slows his steps and snaps, "These aren't for men to wear."

I can tell he takes it off as I feel his body move and before I know it, he places the smaller crown also on top of my head.

"Why not?" I question. "Can't men enjoy flowers? It's just for today..."

"No, it reeks of feminine appeal and weakness. No king in history will wear one, it will be mockery," he replies, making me move with him. "I'll become a laughing stock in the whole Kingdom, something which I'm sure will please you."

"No, it won't..." I whisper.

"Why won't it?"

"Because I know what it feels like to be laughed at and looked down upon," I respond honestly, tightening my arm around his due to nerves.

I hear someone approaching from my left, and I look toward the sound, seeing a faint glow of twisted magic. This person is furious. Their magic is off and flaring wildly much like the King's most of the time.

"You're not our queen! Go back to your country!" screams a man from a distance. He picks something up and chucks it in our direction, targeting me.

The King grabs me by the waist, pulling me to his side rather quickly, and I hear a loud thunk, the rock hitting something or someone but not me.

It then bounces to the ground at our feet. It sounds relatively large, not some small pebble, perhaps being the size of my palm.

There's silence, and the King lets go of my waist. I hear the man begin to run, two people chase after him.

It seems we have been followed by the King's guards. I didn't even feel or notice them.

I hear something drip on to the pavement and smell the familiar scent of blood, lingering in the air.

"You're hurt," I say, surprised, not knowing where the rock hit him but having a good idea it is his head.

I reach out to him, but he grabs my wrist and warns, "What did I say about touching, Mage? Be a good woman and keep your hands to yourself."

The King chuckles darkly. "So much for a peaceful day without bloodshed... It seems we are all cursed now because of one stupid peasant."

"You should see Doctor Viggo," I suggest as he does not want me to touch him.

I shouldn't care as he did not care about the wounds I once suffered, but some part of me cares. After all, he is dripping blood. The sound of his blood hitting the ground bothers me.

"No. It's just a gash, nothing that won't heal on its own," he says. "Once the man is found, he is dead. I think we are all due for a good stoning."

I make a face, and the King starts going back to where we came from. I follow close to his heel. I do not know the layout of these streets.

"Must we stone him to death?" I question. "Yes, he hurt you, but I don't think he deserves death. Perhaps some other form of punishment but not that... It's too cruel."

"Everything is cruel to you, Mage. If they're willing to strike you, they will be willing to strike me someday, then why not our children?" he asks, sounding angry.

I grow silent, not knowing how to respond to that. He is right, but how will this help to protect us from any future pelting? It won't.

I don't think I can reason with the King, especially in the mood he is in now, so I follow quietly behind. Tonight had been going rather well. It is such a shame we have to end it like this, so many food and activities we have yet to partake.

But, as usual, nothing goes as planned. The night ends in blood being spilled and the lands potentially cursed. Let's just hope the Gods are lenient this holiday.

FOURTEEN

LOVELESS

THE WEEKS PASS FASTER than I like. Ceremonies between the King and I have been pushed up to a weekly routine rather than monthly. The desperation for an heir becoming more urgent.

Rhys has started to believe I am perhaps infertile while the King says nothing in hopes of it not being true. The man who pelted the King rather than me died the following week when he was spotted in the city.

Rumors said he was buying food in the market for his family, which spilled out on the ground when he was apprehended, sending fruits rolling everywhere. The paper bag holding the man's items were trampled by the guards as they dragged him to his doom.

Apparently, the reason he tried to hit me with the rock was that he'd lost his wife to one of my people, the man in question being Dr. Goodfella. His name only sends shivers down my spine for some reason.

Dr. Goodfella was an Ice Mage, whom my own people didn't dare trifle with, let alone my father. He was a cruel man, exiled from the Kingdom of Yulor because of his obsession with Mage and

Dragon experimentation. Many did not know this and thought Good-fella was still in league with us.

I have heard horror stories where he combined a Dragon and Mage, the abomination forever kept as a pet of his. The pieces of their bodies were sewn together crudely with ugly and large stitches. And it is said the head of the Mage has been sewn to the Dragon's chest.

I have also heard that he switched their minds, the Mage stuck in the Dragon's body as she did not know how to shift forms like the Dragon, while the Dragon was stuck in the Mage's body—well, her head—and therefore, no magic could be used to end their pain.

Cruel and endless torture for both of them, but Dr. Goodfella is such a powerful man, not many live after crossing paths with him.

So, the man had lost his wife due to the madman Dr. Goodfella and was looking to exact his revenge.

The King made me attend the man's execution. His death was to set an example to the rest of the country – anyone who harmed the royal family will be executed publicly.

Before his death, he spewed his venom at me. "You will never be my queen! I promise you, even in my death, a whore will always be a whore! No one will truly ever see you as a queen! You're only a lowly Mage!"

His words struck me like a lightning bolt, hitting my chest with a current of pure anguish, his last words so focused on me. He was then pelted.

I still remember his screams of agony with each rock and how his body finally gave up, hitting the ground, and even then, the pelting did not stop. I had thrown up on the floor by the side of our thrones, unable to take the sounds of a man being tortured to death.

The King said nothing, just stood rather than sit. He watched in silence until the people stopped. Only then did he leave. My vomit did not faze him, and not even a snide comment surfaced from his lips.

When I was alone, I kept feeling thankful I wasn't brought up as a

Princess but rather an illegitimate living with my single mother, and soon after, spending most of my life in the tower. I think I would have been a different person, had I been brought up by my own royal family in Yulor.

Then there is the sex between the King and me. It is as strained as ever, never passionate or leading to anything pleasurable. I start suspecting more and more that his love is secreted for another when we have sex, perhaps the only thing making him find his release is this woman.

The ladies of the court always have questions about the sex, and I begin to falsify, describing it pleasurable, but Beatrix caught me in my lie. She called me out on it, saying she has heard from my maid, Yanmei, that it is as dull as ever and that the King lasts no more than ten minutes in bed before exiting in a hurry.

It hurts worse when they say it aloud. The only comfort I find is in my tutor, Dakari. My lessons have resumed with the King's consent, stating that it is good for me to learn.

I am happy to be back in his company.

In our time together, I have learned how to read using the bumps and can even sign my own name, and I learned all that rather quickly. I then moved on to learn more about the land, the plants, and the past kings and queens. I learned that Ori named the Kingdom after his firstborn daughter.

He even taught me lessons on the colors that are associated with certain things like snow is white, grass is green, and blue is the sky. Not that I can ever see those colors and appreciate them.

It is then I finally get a name for the color of the King's eyes – red – as Dakari explains to me.

He says his eyes are often compared to rubies, and it is true. I have begun to remember the colors and their comparison but can never find a visual outside of my visions of the Dragons lurking in the darkness.

Dakari is a kind man, and my yearning for a kind and gentle man grows. I slowly begin to fall in love with him with each lesson and I grow closer to him. He is a friend. Someone whom I can trust. Someone who genuinely cares about me.

But my fantasies come to an abrupt halt during one of our times together when I confess my love to him one day. The memory is all but painful.

"Vrai, I cannot return your feelings," he says to me. *"You're the Queen, and I have a lover. I will love no other."* His words are soft, but they still hurt me.

Tears have begun to form in my eyes as I ask, "Who is your lover? Have I met her before?"

"No. And if you do not mind, I will not discuss it," he turns to face me, *"I can no longer continue our lessons. These will end today. You're too dangerous to be around. I almost died once because of you."*

I feel a surge in my magic but control it by holding my trembling arm and leave the small room before finding Baby in the hallway. I hug him tightly, a creature who cannot help but soothe the sadness I am feeling. The only being who can, and will, do so willingly. I am thankful at this moment that I accepted him as a gift and that the King allowed me to keep him.

I soon realize in the following days that my love for Dakari has been foolish, no more than a crush, just a result of the hatred around me, for me. A man being kind and gentle is probably all lies; they are all the same. They never truly care. Maybe I just needed a gentle anchor in this land to deal with the Dragons.

And even if he had accepted my love, it would have ended rather quickly. The King is a jealous man, possessive, so no doubt Dakari's throat would have been in King's hands once more.

My complete commitment is to the King. I know this now. No other man can own my heart and being like he does. Perhaps once the ten-year treaty is over, he will let me have my freedom, but I doubt it. Even if I am let go, I will be a target, an ex-queen wandering the streets blinded by a curse.

I'm certain I will be dead in no more than a year, perhaps sooner.

Listening to the rumors of the castle, I hear the King often spends time with this woman, Red, at the whore house. Also, I've discovered he ventures there more frequently, perhaps he too has fallen in love with a woman who does not see him as he sees her. Eventually, he will figure this out and be lonely once more.

There will be no love for us, of this I am sure.

The King's frustrations grow with the land of Earath. His request to see King NuJu has been denied in a simple letter. He did not take my complete advice and sent a man to their Kingdom along with Ambassador Chi, the woman who sang for us back during the Day of Blossoms Festival.

The King throws the letter down in disgust, and it catches fire on the table. I'm sure it is due to the King's magic, which flares even worse with anger, but I do not glance his way, focused on my plate and drink.

"It seems kindness does not work well with negotiations," he hisses to the men at the table, with me next to him, doing my best to keep quiet at these types of dinners, worrying about another fight like the previous one.

"I told you we are wasting our time. They will never forgive you or us for what your father did to them. The only thing we can do is start a war and force them to submit to Oria, and we will have all our negotiations solved," Zachariah says, throwing the cutlery on his plate, signaling he was done.

"It seems all we do is start war," growls the King. "You people convinced me that starting a war with the Ice Mages would solve our problems, but in the end, all that happened is a treaty and me gaining a wife."

Bastard, acting as if I am a thorn on his side.

"She is important for our future," says Rhys. "An Ice Dragon can make the Mages submit fully to us, making them fall under our rule. A power once lost to us fully restored and the lands we forfeited, we will have them back."

Rhys thinks I am important, but I hate him too.

"I've heard that story enough fucking times," snarls the King. "I could have killed every last Mage with the army I had prepared at their borders. Time and time again, I am not sure why I listen to you. Things could have been different, and if I wanted, I could have taken any Mage and given you your stupid Ice Dragon, the heir all of you so desperately want."

"Well, things have taken a dark turn, haven't they, Queen Vrai?" says Cell. "I'm sure listening to the ways of exterminating and ruling your people unsettles you along with the King going off on a rant about fucking any Mage he wants to."

"It does not bother me," I reply coolly, drinking the wine in my cup, which I find to be a comfort lately after Dakari's rejection. "Things turn out the way they do, and there is no changing it. You have ten years to decide what you want to do with my people or me, and no matter what the decision the King comes to, I cannot change it. I'm just a face and voice at this table."

Cell chuckles, taking small sips from his cup, "Well said, my Queen."

The King begins tapping his fingers on the table; he seems to be thinking about something.

"Hm, did you say something, Cell? Mage?" The King is deliberately being obtuse, despite listening to our conversation. He knows that we know it. Yet he toys with us. "Hmm, nothing important? So, as I was saying, before being so rudely interrupted..."

"War is no good," I declare, cutting in for once and putting down my drink.

"What?" questions the King, his voice more aggravated with my interruption. The more time I spend here, the easier it is to speak my mind. The wine also helps to loosen my lips.

"If you start a war with Earath, it will be tragic. Trade will temporarily stop in your Kingdom, and what I've heard from your talks, the coin has increased greatly due to trade with Watergrale. All that will go away. You will be too focused on your war and will end up investing all the increased coin in the battles ahead, thereby decreasing the trade further in your country. Other places like Watergrale will prosper in their businesses during this time. Even if you win and conquer their lands, all the Earth Dragons will become your enemies. The Fire Dragon King will be the most hated in the land, and you will have a massive target on your head. I say we don't go to war unless we have to."

The King is quiet after my impassioned speech. He leans back in his seat, and after a while, he says, "You all heard the Queen. No war unless we have to. Focus on trade and expedition. I want all the Dragons learning the layout of the lands and air currents and places we cannot fly. Understood? For any countries beyond the mountains, we can attempt to make allies and trade with them before anyone else."

I hear Rhys click his tongue at my side, a little agitated with the King's decision to go beyond the mountains, never coming to an agreement with him.

"You can't be really be considering what she has to say? She is a woman... She knows nothing of the prospects of war," says Gregory, astonished.

"My decision is final. Now all of you are dismissed, or you can stay and finish your dinner. I don't care." The King stands from his seat at which almost everyone follows suit, not saying a word. Rhys is the first one to walk behind the King, right at his heel.

I finish what is left in my cup, the rest of the wine slides smoothly down my throat, and I feel Zachariah linger at the table alongside Fonzell.

"You're getting a little too comfortable in that seat, Queen," mocks Fonzell, almost disgusted, and I hear him still chewing, finishing the remaining food on his plate.

"I would have said the same, but after our first dinner together, the Queen has earned a little of my respect. Not many have the courage to get in the way of the King's fury," chuckles Zachariah, which makes my heart skip a beat.

He stands, still grinning. "And I like staring at her tits. I guess it is a nice thing to have a woman at our table even if she is an ice whore;

it helps to pass time more quickly. Come, Fonzell, we have things to do."

Zachariah leaves, followed by Fonzell, who grumbles softly before finally leaving me alone. I do not catch what he has said as he intentionally whispers the words. Or maybe he has spoken in a different language and that is why they were intelligible to me.

I wasn't expecting those words of support to ever leave Zachariah's mouth though... I suppose I have earned his respect. But it feels as if I am being tricked.

Yanmei enters the dining room. "Queen Vrai. I have come to bring you to your quarters."

She is probably bowing right now, pretending to respect and honor me, but everyone knows her hatred for me runs deep. Of all my maids, she is the most dangerous despite the fact I feel no strong magical presence within her or even her Dragon.

Her name also sounds foreign. I have never heard a name quite like it. *Where is she from exactly? Certainly not the Water Kingdom or even Earath.*

I stand up. "This is unexpected. No Ava or Catherine tonight?"

"No, they are busy preparing your bath. The King is coming to visit you again if you have forgotten already," she says, her hatred starting to seep through her words at the mention of the King.

Yanmei loves the King, but it is still no excuse to treat me as she does.

"I haven't forgotten." I walk forwards, coming to a stop before her. "Then lead the way."

I begin to see a faint outline of a Dragon or perhaps something more... *It looks odd. I can't quite tell what it is.*

I hear her begin to walk, and I follow. I know the layout of the castle well now, the halls, stairs, and even where my room is. I no longer need the assistance of the maids, but they say it is important to have a maid at my side unless I am with the King, my tutor, or the ladies of the court.

"The King does not love you. He only visits you so often

because you can't get pregnant. Perhaps Dragons cannot impregnate Mages, and if that's the case, you won't be our Queen for long," She takes great pleasure in telling me this truth. "Our King needs an heir."

She does not know of Aldis then. *Do any of my maids?*

"If that is the case, Yanmei, will you treat your next queen with kindness or the same as you've done me?" I question.

She snorts softly and says, "Of course I will treat her with more kindness as she will be a Fire Dragon. She won't be a Mage, or perhaps you're just a bad egg. If that's the case, I may have to deal with another Ice Mage."

"And what are you? You aren't a Fire Dragon."

"I'm nothing, Queen. If you haven't heard already, I am a Theka."

"What is a Theka?" I am curious about the word but have never asked anyone until now.

"One without their Dragon. We are unable to transform; our Dragon is trapped within us," she replies, climbing a set of stairs. "Even a Theka queen will be better than you. I'm sure the people of Oria would agree."

So this is what it means. Yanmei, Ava, and Catherine are unable to transform, and it must have been how they ended up as maids. It seems the Dragons treat them like peasants even if they are born in royalty as I remember the conversation with the ladies of the court. One of their sons was born a Theka... I wonder how he will be treated.

"I'm not so sure that is the case, Yanmei," says Ava once we reach the top of the stairs, "We Thekas are considered worse than Mages. And when it comes to sex, no Dragon wants to fornicate with someone who will not add to their bloodline. The only ones for us are Theka men."

Yanmei growls at Ava. "I will love no Theka."

"Why not when we ourselves are one?" Ava persists. "Loving a Dragon is taboo, including the King. He took you in as a maid because of pity, not love. We all know whom the King loves, and it is not our Queen or you. So, you need not take everything out on her anymore."

My heart sinks in my chest, and my fingernails dig into my skin. So, he does love another. It has to be Red. Red is the woman whom he has visited the most... The whore!

The next few words that leave Ava's mouth confirm my suspicions. "Red will always win the King's heart, despite what her job entails. Now, we must not speak of this any more than what we already have so out in the open. We might have already lost our jobs if not our heads."

Ava turns around and heads back to my room. "Come, we have to move quickly. We are already behind schedule."

I hear Yanmei huff and grumble, following Ava. "Hear that, Mage? We both will never be loved by our King. It seems a whore is better than both of us put together. The King is a strange man..."

I follow my maids back to my room, where they have a bath prepared for me. I can't stop thinking about this woman, Red, whom I have never met before.

Perhaps she loves the King, and he loves her. A secret love affair that really hasn't been a secret after all if my maids know of it. I would like to know the woman who's captured the cruel Dragon King's heart.

Red... I would like to meet you someday, even if it might cost me my head.

FIFTEEN

THE QUEEN'S BEDCHAMBERS

I AWAIT the King in just my robe, my hair wet and freshly scented with aromatic oils as both Ava and Catherine are aware of his hair fetish.

Most nights, it is what instigates sex between us. The King loves to run his fingers through my hair, taking a good whiff of the strands before pushing me down on the bed. But one thought holds me captive.

Red.

I can't stop obsessing about her for some reason. I may be jealous of the fact that the King has found love when I cannot seem to. Dakari made it clear that he wasn't the one for me. From what I hear around the palace, the King spends most of his nights with her.

She probably gives him the pleasure I can't seem to. Her hair must be longer than mine, and with a name like Red, it probably matches the King's ruby eyes. I'm sure she will make a better queen than me.

I hear the door to my room open and shut, and footsteps march right in, heavy and confident. It is the King. I sit with my head bowed, refusing to look toward his magic.

Lately, it feels as if I am staring at his being even when his magic does not have a face. He walks toward my bed; I can feel his gaze on my face. His fingers reach for my hair and start playing with it. He normally does not say anything.

I too am quiet, breathing in the essence of him, letting him do what needs to be done. But unlike other nights, today, I feel the need to speak to him. I want to, before things go further.

"Have you ever loved anyone, my King?" I question him at which his fingers abruptly stop playing with my wet strands.

"Why do you ask, Mage?" His fingers leave my hair completely.

"Simply curious."

He is quiet as if refusing to respond to my question. He draws away from me slightly; I know this in the way his magic moves.

"I have," I begin, the words coming naturally to my lips. "I have loved a man before, but he refused to accept it, turning me down because he loved another... Now, I am alone."

"Why are you telling me this?" he snaps, aggression marking his words. "What is the sense of it? I'm just here because I need an heir, and now you're making it difficult to perform. I don't want to hear about whom you have loved."

"I simply want a normal conversation with you, my King," I say. "Have you loved another...?" I pause, taking a deep breath, before plunging on. "Is that why it is so hard... hmm... soft... I mean, difficult for you to perform?"

He growls and draws closer to me before grabbing my jaw, holding me still, making it impossible for me to speak as his fingers dig into my cheeks "You're quite mouthy tonight. Do you want to be a mute queen on top of blind?"

I grab his wrist and mumble to his idle threat through squeezed cheeks, "No, my Lord."

He lets go of my face and pushes me back on the bed. "Good. Let's just get this over with, Mage, and no more talking this time."

He covers my body with his, placing his weight on his elbows, fingers hovering on either side of my face. I am confused by the change in routine. Usually, he climbs up on me with his trousers open, crushing my body, and shoves his member into me without a single kiss or caress.

He asks suddenly, "Are you fussing with these questions because I never cared to please you those previous times? Is that what you want? To feel like the other women who have enjoyed my cock inside them?"

I twist my body away from him. "I don't care about pleasure." His hand runs up my leg, dragging the robe away from my body, before slipping in between my thighs and inside my underwear. I feel something odd as he touches me there, a hint of pleasure.

"I can make you eat your words," he whispers.

My brows furrow in confusion, eyes close as if in want of something more. My breath gets stuck in my chest when his fingers graze my folds before parting them. I can feel the moisture collecting where he touches me. Two of his fingers enter my slit, warm and full, while his thumb touches the apex of it, sending a shock down my body.

He begins moving them, first the circular actions then pulls out of me, with only their tips in the folds. His digits enter me once again, the movement gaining speed and force as he begins to pump them in and out, making me wetter and wetter. I stop breathing. A wave of pleasure crashes into me.

"You know, I can make you beg and writhe under me, desperate for my touch like a common whore. They can't get enough of me and soon you will be the same."

Yet he likes a whore more than me. My thought disappears when he begins to move faster within me.

I gasp, and moan for the first time, when he rubs something inside of me which makes my insides squeeze. The pleasure builds deep within my belly, slowly becoming intense, making me tremble. I have never felt anything like this in all the other times.

My fingers grab the blankets, twisting them, confused by what I am going through. This is so different. And so good... His fingers are... talented... perhaps better than his manhood. Another moan drifts past my lips, and just like that, he stops, lowering his mouth to my ears. "Beg, Mage, or you get no more."

The fog lifts off my brain, and it takes me a moment to collect my breath. I don't want to beg and humiliate myself. That is most definitely the King's intention. He will become more arrogant than ever. I shake my head, refusing his command.

He laughs softly, moving his finger back and forth inside me, my hips follow his action. He taps the apex of my folds; I scream with pleasure in my mind. "Time is ticking, Mage. Beg and you'll get it all."

"No." I exhale.

"No?"

"I won't beg," I finally manage to say it out. "Not for you... Not for anyone."

His fingers leave me, empty and full of longing. I can hear him wiping them on the sheet; I can smell my essence on them.

"That is unfortunate. Let's get down to business, shall we?"

My eyes water as the ache inside my body demands fulfillment. This is his doing. I want the feeling of emptiness to go away. All I have to say is a simple word 'please,' and the craving will stop... *but will it actually?*

Is he playing me, teasing me initially, then going on to say that real women don't get to feel pleasure...? I don't know, and now I will never know. I won't ever say 'please,' will I?

He pulls at the tie of my robe, opening it, laying me bare to his eyes. His fingers move up my abdomen before sliding below my body and unclasping my bra, the straps loosening. He drags the robe down my arms along with the bra, throwing it away carelessly.

His hand gropes my breast, squeezing it not so gently before he kisses the other one, his lips moving feverishly against the skin. He sinks his teeth to the underside of my breast, which is painful, makes me yelp yet gives me pleasure when his tongue slides across the abused flesh, soothing it, making in burn in a different way. I feel marked by the King.

Is this payback time? For the bite I gave him the last time.

"Your scars are ugly," he says, running his fingers across the ones he gave me, his fingers stopping at my nipple, where one of the scars ends. I want to say something sarcastic, probably thank him for giving the 'ugly' scars, when his finger encircles my nipple making me shiver. I can feel his arousal against my thigh, pressing and rubbing against my body. I have never felt it so hard before.

The King continues rubbing my nipple until it hardens, then pinches it firmly with his thumb and forefinger, his nail scratching the tip. My chest arcs in pleasure, and he says smugly, "Your body craves touch, Mage... It's a shame you won't let yourself beg."

His hand moves lower, caressing my sides and belly, and his lips follow suit, licking my skin. A kiss is placed on my hip bone along with a nibble, then on my lower thigh.

My underwear is dragged down until it is off my ankles. His fingers go back and forth over my lower region, his breath heating my skin as his mouth hovers over my opening.

Will he kiss me there?

"You even weep for me here. Your wetness leaks," he says, further teasing me. I can picture his red eyes within the darkness of my vision blazing at me with passion and something more, which makes my cheeks flush with color.

"You're cruel," I mutter out, and he finally moves up and places himself between my legs.

"How so, Mage?" he asks me, "I think you are enjoying it. Isn't this what you want? Maybe it will change your mood, which has been so sour lately."

He grabs my face, tilts it, then presses his lips firmly onto mine, which shocks me. They are warm and smooth against my cold ones with just the right pressure. They feel nice, and I get lost within the feeling. His lips move against mine, gentle kisses, then soft bites, and I am eager to follow his lips and repeat his movements. Like sex, this is better.

Between his kisses, he asks me once more, his breath fanning out against my lips, "Have you changed your mind, Mage?" His hips rock into mine, his arousal undeniable as his still-clothed member rubs against my aching womanhood. He runs his tongue against my lips, sucking my bottom one. I gasp. "Act like the ice whore you are."

He is definitely provoking me. Does he want to be bitten again?

I remain silent as he unbuckles his pants and pushes them down, letting his erect member press against my opening, the heat from it intense. I have never felt it so hot and pulsing before.

I long to open my legs and press myself shamelessly at his hard rod, yearning for it to fill me, right up to my core. I shudder, and he pushes the tip in before pulling it back out. The tease!

He is persistent. "Beg, Mage, or all you get is just the tip."

Noooo... I want it all. And I want it now!

"Please," I finally whisper, unable to hold my tongue. Digging my nails into his back, I squirm to get closer to him, the ache unbearable.

"Please what?" he asks smugly, getting what he wants like the spoiled King he is.

"Please... I want you." I shudder with intense longing. I want to bite my tongue for such needy words, but I am helpless. It is the truth. I want him inside me, above me, crushing my body, making this pain go away. I am sure he will embarrass me in future, reminding me of this moment or maybe not. This is his own private victory, too. He has never been this hard for me.

He pushes his full length into me, and I arch my back slightly, my stomach pressing into his hard and muscular frame. He is so hot inside of me... But, surprisingly, he doesn't burn me. His entire body is warmer than usual, a heat that is new to me.

"See, Mage, that is all you had to say." He grins as he lets his hot organ remain inside of me, unmoving, shivering slightly from the cold that has crept up on him from me. He pulls out before thrusting it with force back inside. "It wasn't so hard, was it?"

No, it wasn't. I am glad I said the word. I wouldn't have found this ecstasy, otherwise. *This heat... this longing...*

He wounds my legs around his back and holds my hips down,

pinning them to the bed as he pulls out before thrusting back into me, his movements and rhythm picking up speed. His breath hitches and trembles with his movements. He is also as affected by this as I am.

I whimper, longing for the full movement of my hips so I can push against him, closing any space between us, but he doesn't allow me this pleasure. He pounds into me like the Dragon he is. I am his prey. I begin to breathe heavily. Each thrust causes me to tighten around his length, unlike all the other times.

The headboard begins to bang against the wall as he picks up speed; our breaths enmesh and grow heavier. Suddenly, he crushes his lips to mine, groaning against them as he plunges back into my body. His claws sink into me, their tips burning. My fingers scratch at his jacket.

Even in this moment of passion, my thought goes to Red, and I begin to wonder if he truly loves her. He is being unfaithful to her with me, a cruel King.

Then all thoughts disappear when he pushes back inside of me roughly, his movements quickening. Pleasure overcomes my body as heat squeezes my insides. I have never found heat enjoyable until today. He pulls his lips away from mine before trailing them down my neck, his thrusts become erratic filled with desperation.

A wave of pleasure hits me. It feels nice, and I finally understand what the ladies of the courts brag about.

I am wound tighter than a spring, and my moans turn into screams as the King's hot member continues to plunge in and out of me. His curved length hits all the right places.

There is a swirling in my stomach; I do not quite understand it, but it is demanding. I feel like I am burning slowly from the inside out. I can't think straight.

"Ah. Hhhhmm ah ah ah." Unintelligible noises slip past my lips, louder when my magic combats the King's, and a mixture of cold and hot gathers in the pit of my belly.

I begin to lose control of my magic, and ice creeps up the King's jacket. He growls and slams my wrists above my head. My hips are now free to move.

The King wants to sound aggressive, but his voice turns huskier. "Control yourself." A groan follows his warning, and I wonder if he feels my magic as I felt his.

I thrust my hips into his, desperate to get as close to him as possible. He pushes deeper within me as my fingernails dig into his jacket. I am sure I am leaving gouges.

"Such a dirty little thing you are, so full of surprises, Mage." He pulls out and slams back into me again and again, pounding me with all his strength. "Better fit to be a whore than a queen." He exhales, a grunt leaving the back of his throat.

I can't take this any longer.

"AH," I scream right before grinding my teeth together as the pressure, heat, and cold in my belly all come undone. My body shakes to its very core and makes me release juices on to the King's member. A liquid that feels very cold.

Everything becomes hazy then. The King gasps, his magic also sparks, heat like a real fire nearly burns my wrists as he holds them above my head.

I wiggle my hips, still feeling the intense pleasure, and the King pushes me against him, groaning with his last thrust. He releases inside of me like so many times before, but this time, it feels different. His fluid reaches deep in my core, in my womb. A drawn-out moan lingers by my ear as he pushes his hips into my own as if he is desperate to become one with me, too.

With his release, I expect him to pull out as quickly as possible like he normally does, but he pants slowly and collapses on me gently. After a few minutes, he lets go of my wrists and places both of his hands on either side of me again on the bed.

"We missed out on so much... my Queen." He breathes heavily, pulling his torso away from mine but still within me, his member slowly becoming softer, no longer scorching as it was just minutes ago.

Queen... Not Mage or whore or some other nasty term?

I wheeze softly, my lungs still desperate for air.

He lingers on me, and his fingers run through my hair one last time before pulling out of me. His warmth leaves me, but his essence remains.

I close my legs, my heart thunders in my chest, yet to calm down from the experience I just had. I hear the King fix his clothes, the sound of ice hits the floor as he stands up. Once regaining his composure, he walks toward the door, opens it, and leaves silently. My maids, who usually have something to say, are so quiet outside my bedroom door.

I turn on my side, thinking of the experience the King and I just shared. It is definitely a new feeling and a memory I won't forget. I believe that is what people talk about when they discuss sex.

One of my maids hesitantly walks in. "Do you need anything, my lady?"

It is Catherine.

"No," I reply, my voice still hoarse from sex. "I want to be left alone until morning."

I assume she accepts my answer as she closes the door to my bedchamber again, giving me the privacy I sought. Perhaps the night ceremonies between the King and I wouldn't be so deplorable henceforth, I think I could come to enjoy them.

It is the only thing I can possibly enjoy with the King.

SIXTEEN

CONJURING

I THINK OF TWO MEN, Dakari and the King.

The more I think about my confession to Dakari, the harder it is to sleep. Somehow at the same time my mind keeps drifting to the night of pleasure I shared with the King. That too weighs heavily on my being. But both men share something in common; their love isn't for me but for another.

I lie awake, the night insects chirping and singing loudly outside the window I keep open in hopes of making it cooler. The liwolf, too, is overheating. He sleeps on the floor hoping it will be cooler, but he is born for this climate and the heat does not have the same affects on him as it does me.

It's only been a few days since that night. The events happened exactly where I am lying, and I can't stop thinking about the pleasure. Every time I sit with the King for dinner and breakfast and social gatherings in the palace, my mind drifts to what we've done.

But Dakari... He wants nothing to do with me. I try approaching him in the halls, but he only evades me, taking another route.

I remember his last words to me that I am going to get him killed. If I continue to approach him, it will not be far from the truth. The

King also knows now I love another. My foolish mouth will get Dakari and me into trouble.

I can't stop replaying in my head what and how it happened.

He was teaching me about the plants of Oria, an innocent subject. I wished I'd kept it that way. He was so close to me, looking over my shoulder, letting me touch the leaves of a plant. A heat emitted from his body which sent my heart racing and chills down my spine.

Then I let the words slip past my lips, "I think I may have fallen in love with you..." Words which will haunt me till the end of my days, I'm sure.

Foolish... I really am. I can never repair what I've done. As Dakari has said, I am a dangerous woman. Dangerous only because of the King.

The King.... his heart belongs to another woman, Red. I scrunch the sheets that have been washed since, but I swear I can smell his scent upon them. Sex, commitment, and love are all lies.

The vows I gave the King on our wedding night are false. I betrayed him with my love for Dakari, and he betrayed me with Red. Yet we still lie with one another and will continue to do so until I carry an heir.

I sit up in bed, unable to sleep, and my feet carry me to the door of my bed chambers. My hand lingers over the handle of the door, and I wonder if this really is a good idea.

I have never left unattended, much less at night, but I take a chance and open my door quietly.

I hear the liwolf roll over, a soft thump on the floor telling me that, and I slip out of the room before he can follow me. He will make too much noise, but I suppose if he really wants to be with me, he will find me by escaping through the open window as he normally does. Nothing stops him, ever.

As soon as the doors click shut quietly, I hear him on the other side, scratching at it before throwing his body against it. He is displeased that he is left alone.

Hopefully, he will settle down soon. I never left Baby alone at night. He has always been either with me or one of my maids or exploring the outdoors in his own time.

I walk through the halls quietly, knowing this part of the castle by memory now. I can also see magic, so if any person comes around, they will not escape my senses.

Though I don't expect much from my little exploration, it feels nice to be by myself, roaming the halls, without other people or maids following not too far behind.

It isn't very often they leave me alone since becoming queen. They rarely let me enjoy my time in the courtyard, which is highly secured, and many march back and forth, guarding me.

My feet eventually carry me to a part of the castle I have never visited before. The hallway is empty and soundless. I get a feeling I shouldn't continue forward, but a part of me wishes to explore further, a sense of false freedom.

So, I carry on, clicking my tongue softly, waiting for the sound to come back, and upon doing so, I avoid bumping into a small table to my right.

My hand runs along the wall to my left, and I feel that unlike the rest of the castle, these parts are unkempt. Especially when I feel how damp they are. There must be a leak of some kind.

I draw my hand back and nearly trip on a bunched-up rug at my feet, but I manage to catch myself by gripping what feels like a curtain – a soft and heavy velvet material clutched in my hands.

A sigh softly escapes my lips, and I let go of the material. I straighten my back and continue forward. The halls are getting narrow, and before I know it, my feet hit a stone step, leading some-where upwards.

I take careful steps up the winding staircase, entrapped by walls on either side of me. It reminds me of my old tower, and I begin to wonder if this is where it is leading me. I know it is not true, but I cannot stop my thoughts.

Do they keep someone trapped up here? What is the purpose of this part of the castle?

It is rundown. Do they still use it? Or is it a thing of the past?

When I reach the top of the stairs, I find a door and push it open. The howling of the wind is strong in here which means perhaps a window is open, or the walls are beginning to crumble and break down.

I need to be careful of my steps, though my curiosity gets the better of me and wants to know more of this place. It feels familiar... Yet it is so different.

My hands find a small bed, then a desk. And not too far away, a chest. I kneel on the ground opening it up and letting the lid hit the wall. I reach inside to find stuffed animals, wooden toys, and other things.

A child has been here.

I pick up a stuffed animal and bring it close to my heart.

My fingers learn its texture, and I feel it is threadbare and worn out. One button eye is hanging on by a thread, and its fur is no longer soft but stiff with dust and disuse. It also smells stale and musty.

I shut the chest and place the stuffed animal on top of it, then I stand. I retrace my steps, my fingers ghosting over the walls once more. Then I feel an engraving.

I step back, letting my fingers slide against the first few letters.

K...I...SMET.

It is a girl's name, Kismet. There is also more underneath, a heart or another similar symbol followed by another arrangement of letters.

O... RVAL.

Orval... the King?

I draw my hand away in surprise, and thoughts run rampant through my head.

Who is Kismet? Whose room is this?

Is Kismet a lover, sister, or friend? There is a heart, so it has to be a crush... Or a childhood love, right?

Suddenly I hear the flapping of wings, a Dragon is nearby or just coming back from wherever it's been.

Dragons coming and going out of the castle in their shifted form is normal, especially at night. I often hear just the flapping of their powerful wings, launching themselves into the sky or descending to the ground.

But instead of landing where it is supposed to, in front of the castle, it comes toward the tower. The beating of its wings draws closer. I know instantly danger approaches.

I need to leave.

The situation is no good if this Dragon, whoever he is, has seen me from a distance. I don't know how good the sight of a Dragon is... I have never heard anyone mentioning it.

Where is the door? I must leave quickly.

My hand locates it and whips it open. It smashes against the wall and before I can race down the stairs, the claws of the Dragon latch to the sides of the building, shaking and disrupting everything around me.

Fear strikes me. I can feel the heat of the Dragon through the cracks of the wall. Its breath is like hot steam, pressing against my skin, caused by a fire brewing in its chest.

I hear a low and menacing growl, followed by a screech. It is so close; I can identify it by its aura. It's the King.

My ears! I clasp my hands over them. The shrieks are powerful and loud, and I drop to the ground, trying to get away from the awful noise.

He is doing this on purpose!

The sounds stop, and when they do, I rise to my feet and flee quickly. He does not want me here. I hear more shrieking sounds as he scales the building, trying his best to follow me wherever I go.

I nearly trip a couple of times going down the stairs as my feet are rushed. The King knows his castle much better than I, and he will find me no matter where I hide. Escape is impossible. I wish I had never made the decision to explore this part of the castle.

When I reach the bottom steps, I don't hear much noise from him anymore. I want nothing more than to go back to the safety of my room and be with Baby.

I should have just stayed in my room!

It is then something big crashes through the hallway in front of me. I do not need to imagine what it is. I know.

I scream and begin to shout as I step back. He is only a few feet away from me, blocking my path. "I'm sorry!" I scream. "I'm so sorry. Please."

He doesn't listen to my pleadings. He moves forward, his claws scraping the walls as he tries to fit his body in the hallway. His growls are vibrating the air as his steps rumble the ground. The sound of his claws dragging on the floor produces an awful screech. I know he wants to pierce me with them.

"I'm sorry," I say again. "I won't go near the tower again... Ever!"

He stalks forward, the air growing extremely hot. I can feel his escalating ire. I'm going to be burned alive as in my nightmares.

My magic stirs, my body temperature lowers, and the air becomes cool around me. I am unable to control my powers. It is coursing through me, attempting to protect me.

Ice crawls up my arm, becoming a shield of defense. If the King truly wants to burn me alive, I'm not quite sure how long I'll last. It's crushing too! My ice will crack under the weight.

I'm nearly positive this is how most Mages die while battling the Dragons. Being stepped on or crushed doesn't sound very pleasant. I don't want that for me.

I've heard stories of their clashes from the guards in the tower. I do not know if I can do it, but other Mages have done it. If I have to and I push myself, I can spike my magic, causing spear-like blades to pierce through the flesh of a Dragon.

The ice causes the Dragon to recoil slightly, and he bellows in anger. I close my eyes, concentrating on my magic. I will die if I don't this – I know I once promised myself I would never use my powers again, but the King has not made that option possible.

I'm so sorry, mother. I betrayed you not once but twice; the flower was childish of me, but this time it is needed. But my survival is at stake

In front of me is all the King's magic, flowing and flaring wildly. Never at his angriest times have I seen it before like this.

In the past, my magic could never form shapes like the other Mage children I once associated myself with. They were far more advanced than I; the teachings of the school proved to be easy for them.

Some children were able to create cave spiders, quincats, and some forms of snowlingbears, which are the most difficult because of their size, but some could master the art.

I did not last a week at the school. The professor gave up on me, saying without sight, I could never learn the right way to use magic.

Devastated, I tried repeatedly at that time, but nothing ever came of it. Then there was my mother's death, and I promised thereafter I would never use my magic again.

The Dragon advances and I panic. I don't know what to try and form. I feel like a small child, sitting at my desk, sniveling, because I can't make a surprise for my mother.

I need to concentrate; I am not that child anymore. And I will do it! I am strong, so I tell myself.

The magic of the Dragon gets fiercer, an unbearable heat trying to combat with my ice magic.

A Dragon...

How can I be so dumb? I am able to see something. How can I forget?

I once heard of an Ice Mage who could conjure a Dragon made out of ice a long time ago. He used them to fight the actual Dragons, his artificial ones winning many battles, but he is one of the rarer ones.

"Don't come near me!" I warn again, but the King does not listen. I furrow my brows in concentration when he does not stop, attempting to visualize a Dragon for my magic to duplicate.

Ice crawls across my skin, and it takes everything in me to push my magic out from within my body, attempting to materialize and copy the Dragon I envisioned.

I hear the crack of ice as something forms before me, but I do not know if it takes shape. I want it to, so I push more of my power into it until it moves. And every time it does, it replicates the heavy footsteps of a Dragon, the same noises of a living one.

I did it! I think excitedly, the thing, whatever it may look like, Dragon or not, is moving on its own.

I try to focus on keeping what I have created going. A little more of my magic fuels my creation, and it charges forth toward the Dragon King, almost like a puppet loosely strung.

The Dragon who is my husband shrieks once more as my Dragon made of ice pushes him back, forcing him to dig his claws into the stone floors, creating more of those wretched noises.

My goal is to force him away, out of the hall and back outside. Fear makes my throat constrict, and my thoughts turn awry. I want to fling him out into the open sky and have him tumble to his death, impaled by the sharp rocks below.

My creation can protect me and more. I am desperate. I can be rid of him; I need him gone. His entire Kingdom will laugh at his demise, killed by an ice conjuring, liken his image.

The Dragon King breathes fire on the creature I control, making me cry out. I am able to feel whatever my creation feels. It is as if I am burning all over.

The King stops the fire abruptly, and I hear his voice echo in my head, using his magic, "Mage! Stop your stupidity; it is you who is getting hurt, not I."

I hear a growl follow his sentence, becoming more enraged. He always belittles me with his words, and he is speaking falsely. He is having difficulties combating my creation.

"No!" I scream at him, my hand shaking from the vast magic I attempt to control, "You're the one who didn't stop! I warned you to stay away! Why do you act this way? Benevolent then cruel? You confuse me, my lord!"

"You shouldn't have been in that tower! No one is allowed near it," he screams in my head, maddened by rage. He pushes my Dragon back toward me, his magic becoming more chaotic than mine. "Your maids are supposed to keep watch of the halls at night. They failed, and they deserve to die!"

"I can't fathom this. Are you planning to keep me trapped in my room night after night and make the maids my imprisoners for the rest of my days?" I hiss, feeling disgusted. Tears fill my eyes as memories of always being kept hidden in a house, locked in the tower, or barred in my room surface. "Why does everyone want to lock me in somewhere... be it a tower or a room? Why can't I have freedom? Even the smallest amount, I will be happy with. Why can't I have that?"

My creation once again pushes back at the King, this time biting him as I feel warmth invade my teeth and tongue, and another bellow emanates from the King, not in rage but in pain.

"Royalty has no true freedom, and you are a queen! I did not lie, Mage!" the King screams back in my head, his voice louder than ever. "Even I do not have the freedom I wish for. I am shackled and chained just like you! Do you think you're the only person in the world to be locked in a tower, hated and loathed?"

Before me, the vision of an evil Dragon begins to disappear. What stands instead is a man, although I cannot make out his facial features. Before I can concentrate, the visual is disrupted, and the King shatters some of the ice off my creation, destroying a small piece of it.

He is now winning. But only because my mind has become distracted by the first humanoid figure I have ever seen in my entire life. I wish I had the time to gaze upon it, study it, but the simple pleasure is lost.

Why did such a visual come to me?

I am getting further distracted, and more ice shatters off my creation, falling to the stone floor and breaking into smaller pieces. The further I back away, the more the King wins against me. I feel the pain my creation feels, it and I are one and the same. I gave it life using my magic, and so I will feel its pain.

I grit my teeth as the King rips a limb off my creation, the ice upon my arm cracks off me and inflicts me with small injuries. I know I have been wounded when I feel the warmth of my blood running down my arm.

"Mage, you have proven your point!" the King bellows. "Now give up!"

I contemplate it, the pain searing where the limb is torn off the Ice Dragon, and I hold my arm. I didn't want to feel any more pain like this unless necessary.

"Only if you grant me more freedom than what you have," I declare loudly. "I want to be able to roam the halls and castle freely and have access to the outside world with my maids."

"Done.... Just stay away from the tower," snarls the Dragon King, and I release my magic with a sigh, the ice crumbles to the ground and loses the form it once had.

The ice separates from my skin, my adrenaline beginning to decrease, and small aches and pains make their presence felt. The King must feel the same. I recall I bit his shoulder, or my Dragon did.

The King shifts back to his human form. I hear the same sounds as when he first shifted in front of me, and before either of us can discuss what we did to each other or even the castle, I hear footsteps draw near.

The King growls softly as if he knows the person just by the click of the shoes.

Rhys speaks once he comes to a stop, "Are you two done with your lover's quarrel? AND, sire, do you not realize how much it will cost us to fix these damages?!"

"Just get me a pair of decent clothes. I am in no mood to deal with you," hisses the King.

"You never are," says Rhys snottily. "You are always in a mood of some sort."

The King scoffs, and Rhys says to me, "And, Queen, it is past your bedtime. Hurry along now, that thing you insist on keeping in your bedroom calls for you quite loudly."

Rhys walks toward me, offering his hand which I take. He knows I will have trouble with all the rubble littering the ground.

Touching Rhys's hand feels nothing like Cell's and the calming effect it has. I get no feeling from his hand as he guides me through the hallway only to let go of mine when we bypass the debris.

"Everything is fine from here on. Now go. My matters lie with the King, and if you need, have one of your maids take you to see Viggo, but I think you will be just fine." Rhys makes it obvious that he wants to talk to the King alone or argue about what he has done to the castle.

I nod and hear no words come from the King as I move down the hall, away from him and Rhys.

As I walk, it is hard to imagine what I have just done. But for the first time in my life, my ice is finally able to take the form of something. I've fought a battle no other Ice Mage has and lived to tell the tale. The cuts on my arm are nothing compared to the secret happiness I feel while traveling back to my room.

SEVENTEEN

TO LOVE A MAN

Talk amongst the nobles, generals, and even civilians spread fast that the King and I fought. And everyone knew our fight was not a simple dispute of words.

The rumors are terrible, and no one but the King and I know the true story. This is a perfect opportunity for those opposing the King to speak in false tongues to cause mischief and further problems amongst the people and the court.

Some say I am a wicked Ice Queen who has plotted against the King, forcing him to a corner and leaving him no choice but to shift to his Dragon to defend himself from my great magic.

Others say I've lost control of my temper and as a result, my magic almost killed the King. If the King had not been as quick as he was while shifting, he would have been dead along with half the Kingdom. This one did shake me a little; it is frightening how one person's imagination is so close to the truth.

However, the stories always end in the same way. They speak of how the King overpowers me, then either spares me since I am with child or falls in love with me, a woman wanting him dead, so this makes him insane.

There are so many variations of the story, I lost count. They do not interest me past the first few I heard. Meanwhile, the King is not happy about how they twisted the real truth.

The rumors paint him in a false light, making him appear weak and powerless. The King rants every time he hears of a new one and becomes paranoid. He complains loudly at dinner about how others are trying to spoil his name. I have learned to tune him out.

I think of it as nothing but a story spread by bored Dragons and not a conspiracy as he believes. Overall, it means more work for the Dragon King.

I must say it feels nice to appear strong in the eyes of the Dragons. I was frightened of them when I first arrived but not so much now. They seem to respect me more, even if it is just a little.

More time has passed – another long and horrible week in Oria. I don't think I've ever had a great or relaxing week here. There's always something happening.

I would normally be preparing for the King and my night ceremony, but he has made it clear that he will not be coming tonight, saying he is tired and wants to rest. I believe it is an excuse to avoid me, but I am more surprised by his lack of rudeness.

Well, I don't care at the moment as I have been granted all I ever truly wanted... Freedom. I should rephrase that, I have been granted more freedom than I ever imagined for myself, even if it is nothing compared to others.

I am thrilled when he barked orders at Selene that I am to be given space to roam. I will not need an escort unless I ask for one, which makes me so happy.

Once Selene has dispersed the King's orders to the maids under her, not one of them disobeyed his command. If it were me ordering them or asking them, they would have challenged me.

The only part of the castle I cannot wander is the tower where the King and I fought. The hall is under repair, and it leads to the place where I promised not to venture.

I can't even go there if I wanted to, the tower obviously is a personal and private place for the King, and he has made it clear I am not to be seen anywhere near that hallway.

Instead, I walk different hallways that are unfamiliar to me; these are kept neat, smelling fresh and new. The atmosphere feels different, too. It feels like a calm place to be. I get no strange feelings from this hallway, unlike the last one I entered.

My hand runs along the wall as I walk absentmindedly and eventually, it leads to an opening, which means another room.

I start to enter the room but stop when I see the King's magic behind the door along with another person. It seems he is with a guest, one that I know well. I push my back against the wall, listening out of curiosity.

I should continue moving. But I don't, especially after realizing I can hold my own in a fight with the King if need be.

I hear the cabinets opening and glasses clinking together before being placed down on a surface.

"Dakari, I am curious about one thing, and I will be rather blunt. Why reject the Queen? A woman of high power, whom you can easily take advantage of and manipulate. She is daft after all, and eventually, you could've tried to come after me in some way," the King questions him directly, and my heart stops. "Is it simply because she is a Mage?"

I begin to feel a bit unsettled now, not knowing what the King's plans are with Dakari. *Does he plan to hurt him?*

I hear liquid being poured into a glass, and after a few minutes, Dakari shakily responds, "I didn't think you would know, my K-King. I not only refused out of respect for you but because I love another. I am no one in power to try to do something to harm you."

"I agree... There is nothing attractive about you. You're quite plain... powerless, and least I forget, pathetic. Your only good feature is your smarts," the King says, sitting down on a chair from the sound of it. He sighs. "Maybe she likes your voice but even that, I find annoying. Perhaps it appeals only to females."

"Have I done something more to offend you, my King? I don't understand why I am here," mutters Dakari, sounding fearful.

The King ignores his question. "And why wouldn't I know about you and the Queen, Dakari? She told me what conspired between both of you and that she confessed her love for you and thereafter, you rejected her."

Sweat beads on my forehead. I was worried about that. The King must have figured it out.

"I just didn't think she would tell you," Dakari responds quickly, "but I don't and will never love the Queen. I promise you I have stopped our lessons in light of the situation."

My heart sinks on hearing it a second time, then the King says, "Oh... didn't think she would tell, huh? But, of course, she would. However, the important question is, if she were to throw herself at you like a whore, her body nude as the day she was born, would that not drive you to temptation?"

"No," Dakari replies quietly. His single-worded answer only makes the King pester him more.

Why is this so important to the King?

"I find the Queen has a very nice pair of breasts and as a man, I find it difficult to resist her. So, let me ask you again. If she were to beg you, would you not fuck her?"

"No!" replies Dakari sternly. "Even if such things were to occur, I would never touch the Queen."

"Well, this woman you're in love with must be very beautiful, if the Queen does not faze you. Tell me, what is her name? I am quite curious. Perhaps I know of her." The glass filled with ice clinks noisily as the King lifts it.

Dakari is caught off guard, and the more I listen, my curiosity grows. Dakari did not tell me about the woman he is in love with, I too am curious. But I imagine now he will have no other choice but to tell him. The King is much more dangerous at the moment; there is an edge to him that wasn't there before.

He is quiet. And the King comments, "Well, Dakari. Do not keep your King waiting, or I may just start to assume that the time I have seen you in the courtyard holding her nude leg is something much more and that you and the Queen have been having an affair behind my back."

"I will tell you," says Dakari very quickly, his voice sounding solemn. "She is... a he. His name is Demos. He is in charge of training new recruits for your army."

My eyes widen upon hearing this. Dakari is a man lover? I've heard rumors of there being such people who love the same gender openly in the country of Oria. It does not faze the Dragons much as it does my people. I still don't know the rules or laws for the same-gender lovers in Oria.

Back in Yulor, if you are a lover of the same gender, you are branded with fire and cast aside, forced to live in the wilderness or exiled. I knew of this. One of the few times I traveled to the capital with my mother, a man begged and screamed for them to stop, and my mother pulled me close, reminding me to never love another girl, or it would be me screaming instead of the man.

I hear the King shift in his seat as he probably moves toward Dakari. I hear him laugh and say, "I see, so that is why a pair of tits and a love confession from the Queen does not, or will not, faze you. You're a lover of men. I just knew something was off about you, but I couldn't place what it was. You know... This is the first time someone has admitted such a thing to me."

I hear the King stand as he walks around the room, "Demos... I've only met him a couple of times through General Cell, but I did not peg him as a man lover."

"Demos does not know of my love for him, my King," mutters Dakari.

That is a lie... Unless what he said about having a lover is a lie. I'm not sure. *Maybe he is trying to protect the other man?*

"I see. This only gets more interesting. Why don't you prove to me you aren't lying and confess your feelings to him by tomorrow night?" the King asks cruelly. "During dinner, I will invite you and him to come to sit with me, the Queen, and some of my men."

"You can't be serious, my King. I will be ridiculed by everybody if not executed by the others!" says Dakari, panicked.

"There is no need to be frightened of being who you are," says the King smugly. "There was once a King in our past who was a man lover, which is why it is mostly accepted by us Fire Dragons. Thank King Radames for outlawing hanging because of what gender someone likes or prefers. Radames's story is truly fascinating, don't you think?"

"Yes..." Dakari says, unsure where the King was going now with his discussion.

"You know, he made such a law because his own wife found him tangled in the sheets with another man, one of the men on his council. His poor lover... King Radames made the law to protect himself, but now a couple of hundreds of years later, he is protecting you and many others like you."

Dakari is silent, listening to the King's rants and ramblings. It is best not to interrupt him until he has finished.

"This leads me to the question – if you do not know of the notorious same gender-loving King Radames, you aren't a Fire Dragon, are you? What are you...? Or rather, who are you? I do not like your magic, whatever you are. Don't try to argue that you know of King Radames. It will only irk me more; your eyes haze over with the mention of his name. But that is the least of your worries. I looked into you and found your fake documents and names of parents who do not exist in the country of Oria."

I hear Dakari stand up, startled, ready to flee, and seconds later, I hear a huge crashing sound. It makes me jump, my back stiffening, and I whip open the door, irrespective of any consequences I may be subjected to.

Once more, I see the King's magic nearly devouring Dakari's as he has him pinned against a surface. Like always, it doesn't take him long to notice me.

"Mage, are you eavesdropping on us?" growls the King.

"That doesn't matter. Let him go," I say confidently, my love for Dakari still present despite his inability to love me. I will protect him if need be.

"Why should you care about him?" questions the King. "Did you not overhear he is a man lover?"

"I heard, but I do not care. Dakari is a friend, and I do not want to see him harmed. He is the first man in this Kingdom to show me an ounce of kindness!" I say, trying to remain confident like I was during our last fight.

The King is quiet, before asking, "Tell me what you are and why you are here. You will be spared, but not by me, by your Queen if you do as I ask. If you are not truthful with me, I will have you hanged but not because you are a man lover. Be grateful to her. If it were my decision, your fate would be much different... "

Dakari breathes heavily. "I am an Air Dragon; I mean you no harm. It's a Kingdom up in the skies. A couple of years ago, they threw me to the land and stole my wings as a punishment for being what I am. From there, I wandered through the land of Earath until I found Oria."

He speaks faster despite being winded, "I knew everything about your country, well, from books mostly. So, I lied about being a scholar and slept with a man of power by the name of Kingston. He forged a couple of documents so I could live here and teach others like the Queen in return having sex with him whenever he wishes it."

"Air Dragons..." mutters the King, almost fascinated, finally letting go of Dakari and moving away, forgetting his anger. "How come I don't know of your kind then?"

"We are normally discreet, and the King and Queen of the Skies do not want their presence known by others like you. If they knew I told you, I will be killed by them," he says, his breathing labored before he has a coughing fit. "I was never expected to live!"

So that is why Dakari's magic has always been different to me, light and airy, like the air we breathe.

"Kingston... I wonder how many others he has forged documents for personal favors," says the King, suddenly switching from fascinated to angry. "He will surely be punished for his crimes. You can go now. But I still want to know more about these Air Dragons. Do not flee, eyes are watching and ears are listening and you will be dead the moment your feet attempt to leave our soils or skies."

Immediately, Dakari gets up and hurriedly walks past me but mutters, "Thank you," before running out of the King's office. At his 'thank you,' I can't help but feel a small pleasure in it; that makes me feel good.

I am left alone with the King afterward, and I back away slowly. The King snaps before I can slip out of his office, "Mage, this is exactly why I did not grant you freedom before. It has only been a week, and you've managed to find and barge into my office during a meeting that is supposed to be private. Do not make me revoke these privileges I so kindly granted you."

I narrow my eyes at what I see, his magic, and say, "It won't happen again but only if you keep your hands off my friends."

He scoffs. "Royalty does not have friends. Stop living in a fantasy."

Didn't the King have friends? I am sure he is fairly close to Cell and a couple of others.

"And you lied about needing to rest," I say, thinking of how he skipped out on the ceremony because of it. Just because he wanted to possibly kill Dakari.

"I did not lie about needing rest, Mage. I just had personal matters like your love interest to solve first. For all I knew, he could have been some terrorist or assassin sent to kill me or harm my country or even spy on me." He waits for a couple of seconds. "He can still be a spy. I need to keep a watch on him, now that I know what he is."

The King knows very well he isn't a terrorist or assassin. Dakari is far too weak, a spy maybe at best. I have a feeling it is more of a personal thing for him, just like the tower. I still wonder who Kismet is, but I am too afraid to even speak the name after the reaction last time.

"Then rest now," I say. I just know he is glaring at me; I can just feel it because my words come off as an order. "I will not stop you. But I am curious about one thing, my King, as you love to know who everyone else has a passion for. Whom do you love?"

"Again, you bring this up. Why are you so curious about it?" he asks me. "What happens if I tell you I don't love anyone?"

"I don't believe you."

He sneers, "Of course." He pauses briefly before he continues, "Then listen well, Mage, the girl I used to love, if you can call it that, is dead. Other than her, I don't think I am capable of loving others. So, go away. I want to fucking rest now."

I am a little surprised the King has told me anything about himself, especially since the girl whom he loved is dead. It has to be the same girl whose name is carved in the tower, Kismet, but what about the rumors with Red?

Is the King lying to me?

"Leave instead of standing there stupidly," he hisses, interrupting my thoughts.

I back away but before I can leave, I mutter, "I'm sorry she is dead then. Perhaps you would have been a much happier, if not a pleasant man with her by your side."

I then slip out of the room, knowing he can take what I've said as something negative, or maybe not. I do believe the King's past lover is dead. Some part of me thinks it's the truth from the way he acts.

I am not about to pry any further, but it doesn't mean I am no longer interested in the whore, Red, and the girl, Kismet. These two women know the King better than I ever can as his queen.

The King is neither lover, friend, nor foe, then why am I always so curious about him?

EIGHTEEN

THE GOOD & THE BAD

"Is Kingston really a man lover?" Catherine questions Ava, who walks behind me, each set of footsteps soft against the stone. The two women hold their own conversation and not once involve me, the one who knows the actual truth... But they don't know that.

"So I hear from everyone in the court," Ava replies. "It seems it has replaced the stories about our King and Queen... For now."

"It's a shame really. I always thought he is kind of hot," Catherine murmurs. "Maybe he likes the ladies, too? Just because he has slept with a man or two doesn't mean he can't like women as well."

"Forget it. Even if Kingston does like women, he will never come near you the way you are," Ava taunts, being cruel with her friend as usual. "Not until you lose a few inches around your waist."

"I did!" Catherine fusses. "I cut back on everything, such as cakes and buttered biscuits. You can measure my waist if you want to."

Ava scoffs, "Perhaps you did, on closer inspection, but every time you lose weight, you gain it right back, not after a couple of weeks. It won't be long until you're back as you were last month with an extended waistline."

"Shut up! Just because you have the luxury of being skinny all your life gives you no reason to pick on me the way you do! You're a cruel woman." Catherine snaps.

"Oh, maybe because I don't stuff my face come dinner time is why I am still thin today. I told you to never date the baker all those years ago. You used to be quite thin before him, and you still would be today."

"Well, he was an Orc. And you know how Orcs are, they love to eat, and he was the only thing dateable who wasn't a Theka man," Catherine answers.

A baker and an Orc? Now that sounds like an odd yet interesting combination. I know Orcs exist, but I have always been led to believe they stayed in their own land away from Dragons and Mages alike. It isn't every day that they willingly become something in another community unless they are a Halfling.

"I know very well how disgusting Orcs can be, especially with their appetites... Anyway, speaking of men, I found myself quite a looker, and on top of it, he is a Dragon," Ava says smugly, showing off.

"A Dragon?!" questions a surprised Catherine. "Who is it?"

"Demos," she gushes, "I literally can't pull him off me at times. When we get time alone, he is like a liwolf during their first rut... Sometimes I have to punish him." She giggles.

Demos... The man Dakari is in love with? Was this man and Ava really together? I think curiously as I try to avoid bumping into a pedestrian on the street. I feel and see their magic; the maids are not doing their job of guiding me through the streets as they are suppose to.

I wonder if Dakari knows or the King... There are so many questions I have yet to find the answers to. I should just enjoy today, being out of the stuffy castle and in public.

It is getting hotter each day as it gets closer to summer and its unbearable heat, which kills everything as the Earth Dragon sang about. I believe it. The night is the only time of the day I find comfort in my skin. The air is cool if I leave the balcony doors open.

The King... He was the one who granted me this freedom, but

when I wished to leave the castle grounds, he went back on his promise, stating he would grant me permission if two maids accompanied me. I am supposed to have total freedom, but in the end, I didn't. He lied to me.

He even fussed afterward, making condescending remarks such as, *"You're blind. Why go out?"* and *"Royalty shouldn't go out roaming the streets. It's just asking for unwanted trouble."*

There were other things that I tuned out after a while. I left the room before he could rant more. I am sure I made him angrier when I dismissed myself before he could do so.

The maids continue walking behind me, and I pull my hood up on seeing other magical presences on the street, though I doubt I am able to hide much... Especially with the two loud and bickering maids following me.

As we walk down the street, I begin to hear whispers following me, some anxious, others amazed. Most are frightened due to the King killing in my honor, and they are worried about what will happen to them.

"Isn't that the Queen and her maids?"

"Look at her eyes. They're quite unsettling; it's as if she is dead."

"Why is she here?"

"She's already got a man executed. Trouble always follows her kind."

I'm used to it by now, so I continue forward, ignoring everything around me. I find the street booths and run my hand over the vendor's tables, feeling hairpins and other jewelry.

Suddenly a woman's voice next to me says, "I think, my Queen, you will look quite lovely with this hairpiece. I have an eye for them."

Her fingers bump into mine, halting them. Her voice is soft yet alluring, and I glance at the woman's radiant magic. It is very soothing to me.

"I think so too," Ava responds from behind. "We may even purchase it for her."

"No need. I plan to already. It will please me so much to purchase a gift for my Queen," she insists. She picks up the hairpin under my fingertips and turns to the vendor. "How much for the hairpiece, madam?"

"Twenty-four coins," replies a worn voice, most likely belonging to an elderly woman.

"Done," the woman responds. I hear the jingle of coins followed by clicking when they fall into the open palm of the old woman. It is how I pictured it in my mind by watching the interaction of their magic.

Before I know it, a silk pouch is placed in my hands by the mysterious woman. The bag is light but certainly contains the hairpiece.

"This is a gift for you, my Queen," she purrs, touching my hair and running her fingers through it. "The King loves hair, and this would look lovely in yours. It would have been a shame to let someone else purchase it at such a reasonable price."

It seems that everybody knows about the King's hair fetish, even common townsfolk. She is also very touchy for a stranger.

"Thank you," I murmur as I hold on to the bag, quite shocked that someone approached me so boldly while everyone else remained so afraid to speak to me. "May I ask your name?"

"Red," she sings out, and my eyes widen as she pulls her hand away. "I'm sure you've heard of me by now. My name is quite well known in these parts of the city and the castle."

"Red..." I repeat, still in shock. "You are—"

"The King's whore," Ava says harshly, cutting me off before I can finish my sentence. She grabs me by my forearm, pulling me away.

"Did you come to smother your ugliness in our Queen's face?" Catherine squeaks out, wedging herself between Red and me.

It seems they are protecting me.

"How bold of a whoring wench," Ava snarls.

Red laughs and the whole town seems to have gone silent seeing the confrontation. She replies, "No. I have come with no such intent. I just wanted to meet our Queen and see if Yanmei is available."

"Yanmei?" Ava is bewildered.

"Yes..." Red lets out a disheartened sigh.

"What do you want with our Yanmei?" Catherine hisses.

"I have some matter I wish to speak to her about, but it seems she isn't here. I was hoping she was running behind as usual," Red says, her words seem gloomier as she speaks.

Why is she sad?

"Yanmei is back at the castle," I venture. "What do you wish to speak to her about? I can perhaps pass on a message to her."

She is quiet for a couple of seconds. "I don't want to burden you with this. Yanmei is a... friend. I just want to see her, but I should be on my way now. It seems your maids want me gone. It is nice to finally meet you, my Queen."

She starts to leave, but I throw Ava's hand away and push past Catherine.

I grab her wrist and inquire, "May I speak to you alone? I have questions regarding the King."

"my lady, I would not do that," advises Ava sternly.

"It can be dangerous. More so, the whore's words will only trouble your ears. There is a possibility you will not hear anything you like from her dirty mouth," warns Catherine.

Since when do they care about me? It must be fake, a show they are putting on because of the people surrounding us. It is starting to annoy me.

Red finally responds, "If you wish... We can speak privately. I know of a place."

"Good." I push the hairpin into Ava's hand. "Both of you stay here. I want our talk to be private without listening ears."

"My lady," Ava starts, but I cut her off.

"Quiet! Stop acting like you care about me in front of these people. I know you are not bothered if I live or die. " I snap. "So, all I ask is the two of you stay put and break your orders. Tell the King I threatened you both, if you need to, upon our return to the castle."

Neither Ava nor Catherine speak, and I walk away with Red, leaving the crowd behind as she leads the way. It doesn't take us long to find a private spot, a couple of turns and slips between buildings, and we stop.

"Here is a good place," Red says when we reach what I presume to be an alleyway. "No one will listen to us here... What do you wish to know?"

Her voice is hesitant, and I question, "First of all, who are you to the King? Does he love you? Tell me the truth."

I am beginning to sound like the King himself and the way he spoke with Dakari just a few weeks ago. The thought is *a little unsettling*.

She laughs before she responds, "The King and I are not lovers, I assure you, and least of all, I am not a rival. He is yours. What I am, is a friend to him."

"A friend?" I question with uncertainty, something I certainly didn't expect to hear.

"We were childhood friends, way before I became what I am today – a whore. We never slept with one another until a few years back. To ease your mind further, I turned him down when he proposed I become the queen of Oria. I do not love him just as he does not love me. What he is seeking is companionship and familiarity, something he does quite often."

"You turned down the title of queen just because you do not love him?" I ask astonished.

Wouldn't a woman like her do anything to become a queen? She wouldn't have to be a whore; she would be respected and powerful.

"Yes. Well, mostly because I cannot bear to tell him I do not enjoy sex with him." Her response is shocking, to say the least. She exhales sharply before I can ask why. "I do not like men. I only have sex with them for money," she continues.

"You're a woman lover..." I murmur.

It seems the King and I have something in common. We are both attracted to same-gender lovers. *What a weird play of fate...*

She laughs. "Yes, I am. Do not tell the King. I don't want him to know quite yet. I will tell him when I am ready; it is something only I must do."

"Is this why you wanted to see Yanmei?" I ask quietly, beginning to make the connection between the two.

She is quiet for a moment before nodding. "Yes... I only met her a couple of times, but it seems I am developing rather pesky feelings for a far more troublesome woman."

"Yanmei is in love with the King. You do know this... Right?"

"I know. I comforted her more than once after the King's rejections."

"The King rejected her?"

"Yes, many times. It is not only my bed he frequents but many others, including Yanmei's. He is young and handsome, and there are many who seek his affections, but he will never sleep with anyone more than once beside me, unfortunately."

"Has the King ever been in love?" I interrogate.

"Ahh, yes... Do you know of the name, Kismet?"

"Yes," I answer automatically, my heart pounding the more I hear.

"She was our first love. We were all friends. Before I became a whore, her parents bought me specifically to be Kismet's friend as I was an orphan. She was a duke's daughter. At the time, King Diarmind and Kismet's father were on good terms. So, King Diarmind wanted them to marry when they came of age. Kismet was to be our original queen," Red explains.

"So, what happened?" I am intrigued by the information she is telling me, but I have a feeling the story will not end well.

"Well, King Diarmind found out soon after that his son was a Theka." Red's response shocks me. Yanmei had said Thekas are without a Dragon, but the King has one.

"A Theka... Isn't that someone without...?" I start and stop. I have seen the King's Dragon plenty of times, fought with it firsthand, a terrifying experience.

"Yes, that is right. King Diarmind believed strongly that his son was without a Dragon, so did Queen Wera. Orval, when he was younger, had trouble calling forth his Dragon. No matter what he did, he could not shift into one. All began to suspect he was a Theka. They did not treat him well because of this. It was as if his parents abandoned him overnight. And so, it was only Kismet and I who treated him no different; everyone else betrayed him," she recounts.

She pauses briefly to take a breath before continuing, "Kismet soon fell in love with Orval and often or not, snuck into the tower he had been confined in. His parents perhaps tried to forget about his very existence because of the speculation he was a Theka. I can only remember watching her from below, climbing desperately to be with him. Kismet truly was a brave girl."

The King was confined to a tower by his parents. Once again, the King and I share more things in common than I thought. It explains the tower, the names carved into the stone, and why that place is personal for the King. It is a piece of his heart if I so dare to say.

"What happened to her?"

"One day, like any other day, she climbed the tower in order to reach Orval. It was raining, so the wall was wet and slippery. I advised her not to climb that day, so did Orval, who screamed from the top of the tower during the rainstorm. He kept yelling continuously for her to stop. I remember the panic visible in his eyes as he watched our stubborn Kismet climb. All I could do was watch as usual... And just like that, her foot slipped... It was like time had slowed for both Orval and me... But there was nothing we could do. Somewhere in our heads, we hoped Kismet would grow her wings and fly... But she did not... In a turn of events, it turned out Kismet was the Theka. Her parents hid this information. Orval just happened to be a late bloomer." She finishes the horrible story with a deep, shuddering sigh.

"I still want to call her stupid... To scream at her for what she did or why I let her do it... But we were just a bunch of stupid kids who made poor decisions back then." I hear the sorrow still evident in her voice. "But I know Orval blames himself. As a child, he was always too scared to climb down from the tower as he thought he did not have wings to save him from a fall when he actually did. Times like Kismet's death, I wish I were like you, to be spared of the horrors of her death. I might have then slept better at night. I suppose life has spared you from seeing the ugliness."

"It also took away the beauty," I remind her gently. "I did not know the King had suffered from such an experience. I guess I know very little about him. I am also sorry I brought back bad memories... I know about the pain and suffering caused by the death of a loved one so early in life."

I know first-hand what it is like... *Though my story is much different.*

"Unfortunately, Orval has suffered much more than that. This was only the beginning for him, but I think I have shared enough about him, my Queen. I hope one day he will open up to you and tell you these things himself. It's bad enough I've already shared so much without his consent. He will be very displeased if he knew I spoke to you about Kismet and his parents. He hates more than anything when people talk about his past because he lives in the present, and that is all he is willing to talk about."

I doubt he will ever open up to me and tell me these things himself.

"I understand. Thank you for sharing so much with me." I am so grateful to her.

"You're welcome. As a favor, please tell Yanmei I wish to see her," she says, sniffing. The way her voice cracks and how she coughs a little, I assume she is crying.

"I will." I start to move away from her and return to my maids when Red stops me one last time.

"Queen, you may think of Orval as a cruel and heartless Mage hater, but he actually isn't. Trust me, he is very kind."

I am unsure how to feel on hearing that. I am left speechless. Red takes off down the alley, leaving me alone, and I start to walk back, clicking my tongue as a way to not bump into anything.

Some people always know a different side of someone, whether it be good or bad. Red knows the good side of the King as I know only the bad, ever since coming to Oria.

Perhaps someday she will be proved right, and I will get to know this side of the Dragon King, but only time can tell... And my time is running out.

When will I become pregnant with an heir?

NINETEEN

DESIRE TO LIVE

MY HAIR IS WOVEN up on my head intricately, and the hairpiece that Red gifted me is placed neatly in the bun. Yanmei is doing the final touches before I am to meet the King for dinner.

She is quiet while working, without a single taunt to me. I ventured, "The woman, Red, wishes to see you."

Yanmei flinches, dropping the hair pick, snarling, "What nonsense do you spew?"

There she goes. I spoke too soon. I pause briefly to think of my next words to her.

"I met her today when I was out in the city with Catherine and Ava. She asked for you and desired to meet with you."

"I do not know Red, other than she being the King's whore. So, I don't know why she wishes to see me. Probably confused me with someone else," she retorts and refuses to look at me. Her tone is defensive, and she behaves oddly hearing that woman's name, making me sigh.

Why do people lie...?

Is she ashamed of Red or herself or perhaps of the act that occurred between them? Maybe she likes Red but refuses to accept that she is a woman lover, or maybe it is all one-sided, and she doesn't like Red in that way. Perhaps the times they comforted and held each other was a simple pleasure on Yanmei's side and nothing more. It is all so confusing.

Nonetheless, it is none of my concern. I have repaid the favor for the information Red has given me about the King. She didn't say I had to force Yanmei to see her.

I lean down to collect what she has dropped. As I stand, the flowy dress clings to my arms and legs. This fashion is different from what I usually wear.

I press the hair pick against Yanmei's chest until she takes it from me, and I move away from her, not wishing to continue talking about Red. I slip into a pair of flats left out for me by the door.

"Do I look decent?" I question her, not wanting to leave before I have her approval.

I want to know how I compare to all the other women the King has seen and dined with. The maids do say that, no matter what, they will remain truthful with me, though Yanmei did lie about Red...

"Yes, for a Mage..." Yanmei remarks before barking out, "I didn't expect you to be sniffing around for compliments. And you look much better now that you don't look like a corpse."

"Well, thank you," I say, smiling a little and opening the door, "I can walk myself... And you should perhaps consider speaking to Red. There is no point in denying that you know her; it just makes you look foolish, Yanmei."

I slip out of the room, closing the door silently, and I hear Baby following me. The click of his claws against the stone lets me know where he is.

Confidence... This is a new emotion. Perhaps after holding my own with the King, it gives me something I never had.

Baby is close on my heels, pushing past me when I open the doors, being the first to enter the dining room. I am surprised when I don't see the King's magic.

"Is the King going to be late again tonight?" I ask one of the servants nearby.

"No, ma'am. He says he wishes to eat alone, and he will be in his private quarters. Perhaps he does not feel well," the servant replies, acting as if I will snap any moment and show him my nasty temper like the King. He forgets I am not like the King. And I swear I'll never be like him.

"I see. Will anyone else be joining me for dinner?" I question him further. I do not sense anybody in the room other than this boy.

"Just you. Do you want me to call someone, my Queen?" the servant asks. "Your maid or a lady friend of yours?"

The thought is very tempting to dine with someone with so much food at my fingertips and complete privacy. I would have invited Dakari, but after everything, it will be awkward. He will probably think I am trying to poison him or something. It will also be inviting the King's wrath. I feel Baby brushing against me, and I know I will not be alone.

"I am good, thank you. And what about you? What is your name?" I walk forward and sit in the chair I am normally assigned to.

"Nathan," he replies, pushing my chair in place. "And if you are asking me to dine with you, I am terribly sorry, but it would be rude for someone of my status."

"I see, but it will be rude not to talk to your Queen, too. And if you don't mind me asking, how old you are? You sound very young." I am strangely curious about him.

"Not all that young, my lady, about seventeen winters now," he replies. "Do you wish for something in particular to eat? I'll fetch it at once."

It was cute to hear him say he isn't young when he isn't even a man yet, though the palace does seem to have many maids and servants who seem awfully young.

Selene says she will be employing a fourth maid for me soon, one who is more talented in doing my hair unlike the other three. They all took offense at this. I wonder if she, too, will be as young as the boy, if not younger.

"No. I will just have whatever the King has had for dinner. What is good for him is fine with me," I say as the boy fills my glass with wine. I like him already.

"Of course." He puts the canister down and walks away toward the kitchens.

I pick up the glass and begin drinking, thinking about the boy's words.

Is the King unwell? He has been acting... odd. Skipping out on ceremonies and now dinners?

Maybe I should check on him.

My fingernails tap lightly against the glass that I set down, thinking more about the situation. He can just be saying he feels unwell to get out of the ceremonies and dinners with me, making excuses. Yet it doesn't seem like a thing he would do. He normally just says it to my face that I am a miserable ice cunt, and he doesn't want to be around me. He doesn't hide from me deliberately.

The servant doesn't take long to come back, the food already being prepared, and sets it down on the table. "Let me know if you need anything more, my Queen, maybe just a friendly ear."

"I will. Thank you." I pick up my silverware.

He doesn't say anything more, just stands silently to the side of the room, and I can feel Baby against my legs under the table, silently begging for food from my plate. Though he does prefer raw meat most times, he is a strange creature, seeming to enjoy our food as well.

I begin to eat the food that was served. It feels nice to have peace during dinner without the King's snide comments, whatever they may be, but at the same time, it feels perplexing not to have him around me.

"Nathan," I call out to the boy as I place down the silverware on my plate.

"Yes, my lady? Is something wrong?"

"No, not at all. I want to know where the King's chambers are located."

He is quiet for a couple of seconds as if reluctant to tell me before he agrees, "I can show you, my lady, if you promise not to tell it is I who showed you."

I smile softly, rising from my seat, "I won't say a word. I want to know if he truly is unwell or not."

"You don't have to explain it to me, my lady. Do you need me to guide you?" He starts to come closer as I push my chair away from the table.

"It's difficult to explain, but I can see your magic," I say, approaching him. "So, I can walk on my own."

"I see. Very well, follow me, my lady." Nathan turns around, heading for the door.

It is unusual but his magic feels off or strange. Like for a second it is there and the next it completely vanishes. I don't recognize his presence either, so I assume they had perhaps just hired him, or I have never noticed this servant Nathan before.

I expect Baby to dog my footsteps, but he is much too focused on taking advantage of the opportunity presented to him, all the food I have left unattended. I hear him leap onto the table, his body tipping my chair over. Then comes the crashing of plates and silverware as he walks across the table to get to the spread bounty. A feast for him to devour, more like inhale. His powerful jaw snaps and crunches what he can swallow whole. This one is a glutton, my liwolf.

If the King were here, he would not be pleased... at all. But he isn't, so I suppose I will let Baby get away with it just this once, at least the food won't spoil.

I walk behind Nathan, leaving the dining room door open just a crack for Baby to follow me when he is done gorging.

We walk through familiar halls together, taking lefts and rights, then through unfamiliar hallways. Nathan's shoes sound heavier than before, as he takes a sharp right, his footsteps echoing in the narrow hall.

He is a few beats ahead, and we are presented with ascending stairs. I have never gone up them before, this being a part of the castle I have yet to explore, though I have seen most of it. Perhaps this is apt, the King's chambers at the very end.

I grab the railing and climb up, wondering if the King likes being so high up because of his Dragon. Or probably because he can lord over us.

We walk down a long and quiet hallway, and I begin to feel queasy. *Where are all the servants?* I press my hand against my stomach, hoping to calm it down. I stop walking when I sense the bile rush to the back of my throat. I feel I am going to vomit.

Is this what my maids have been telling me about? Am I finally carrying the King's heir after all this time? I squeak in joy.

"Is something wrong, my Queen?" Nathan enquires, stopping.

"I'm fine. Please, let's continue forward," I mutter as I force myself to walk toward him, the nausea stronger than I could have ever imagined.

I keep my hand on my stomach, waiting for the feeling to go away. Maybe it is a bad idea to continue going ahead if I am feeling so unwell... Especially if the sickness gets worse and I end up vomiting all over the King. I bet he will not like that, heir or no heir.

The maids did warn me about sudden triggers and what to look out for. Certain smells, amongst other things, I should have been more careful.

Nathan stands still at the end of the corridor, waiting for me to catch up. Suddenly I begin to feel light-headed as well, my mouth goes dry, and the hallway spins. I trip on my dress, but Nathan catches me in his arms.

"It seems you aren't alright, my lady," he says. "You look pale..." He brushes his fingers against my cheek, then my hair, and I feel the Dragon claws. This servant is no Theka, my heart flutters. *How did I fail to see his Dragon?*

I am also not pregnant...

The realization hits me as I see him truly for what he is. An enemy, who has perhaps poisoned me at dinner. Maybe he has even given it to the King, and that is why he isn't here. I am unsure of what is happening.

I strive to push away from him, but my arms feel too weak and heavy. I try to use my magic as a last resort, but that too is weak. Some ice forms, but it is unable to keep its shape, and it cracks and crumbles to the floor, defeated.

"What did you do?" I yell at him, feeling the uncomfortable cramps in my stomach worsen. A pained whimper leaves my lips.

"Ah, ah. Quiet, my sweet Queen," he sings, adjusting me in his arms. "It's nothing you should worry about. It's just a poison, not a very strong one, but I'm sure you already suspect that. So, before the others find the dead servant, your real Nathan, in the kitchen, I need to hurry. If you are curious, he really was a kind boy but when has that saved anyone?"

He starts to drag me as I am unable to walk properly, my legs feel heavy like my arms. I start to scream, the only thing I can do, but that is cut off when I feel a strike against my cheek, making the dizziness worse. A strong metallic taste soon fills my mouth.

"Stop it. You act as if I'm going to kill you," he scoffs before lifting and placing me on a flat surface, a table perhaps, as I hear things get knocked down. It also smells of old books and paper.

Are we in a library?

"I just want your heart, Queen... Oh wait, will that kill a Mage? I'm not really sure. It's best to ask one. SO SWEET Queen, can you replace it with ice as you would a lost limb?" He rips the front of my dress, leaving me bare. "Don't answer, I don't care. If you are dying to know what I am about to do to you, I am after the heart of the strongest Mage. So, after hearing about your battle with the King, I believe that qualifies you. Money is money, sweetheart."

The boy... or perhaps the man... laughs, he's even lied about his age. I feel a cold metal press in between my breasts. "You should be grateful to me for sending you off to the afterskies since no one here will miss you. You're no different than Aldis though the question is can one enter the after skies with no wings? I suppose your kind goes wherever your kind goes."

He stops and sighs almost sadly. "Look at what the King has already done to you, scarring such pretty skin. I guess I really am sparing you from a life of suffering."

"Stop! I want to live!" I manage to scream. "Please!"

I do not wish to die, not after all this! I feel the metal tip of the knife press into me, blood oozing from the cut.

A strong need to survive sends magic pumping through my veins. I feel a sudden burst of it down my body as ice travels from my fingers and is thrust into the room, living and expanding, hitting the boy solidly, encasing him in ice, making him curse one last time. My power flares up as ice crawls up the walls, the floors, and even the table I am on, coating the cut inflicted on me, leaving me unharmed, otherwise.

Before I know it, the temperature has dropped well below the freezing point, and the whole room has now become an ice chamber, sealing in its occupants completely. I breathe heavily and feel something shatter to the right of me, bursting and exploding, fighting my power, trying to get to me.

My magic attacks the only living creature besides me, the Fire Dragon, before I can stop it. Bile pours out, my body rejecting the poison given to me, and I puke. I slip off the table, the room still spinning around me, the smooth ice floor not helping.

I land on my rear, my foot coming in contact with what feels like a head, and suddenly I remember the King once telling me that royalty does not have friends, and I should not trust anyone.

Tears run down my face, turning into ice on my cheeks.

I kick the head, and it saddens me I am not standing to send it flying. I listen to it roll and skid across the icy floors, then a shatter followed by a loud crunch.

It makes me think someone has stepped on it, and I see his magic.

It flares in a roar with chaotic swirls and bursts of color. It seems enraged. It is the King.

I am too weak to fight with him or say anything and I slump against the table's leg. I see no more magic, everything is a blur, then darkness takes me under. And the world stops.

TWENTY

A CURSED BLOODLINE

KING ORVAL'S POV

I PEEL BACK MY SHIRT, at least I attempt to, the top half sticking to my right shoulder. The more force I use, the more it resists. I slip my fingers carefully between my skin and shirt to separate it. A single tug is near impossible.

The friction of my shirt causes excruciating pain, and a pungent smell of rot clings to me. I need patience and a few calm moments while dealing with this wound.

Once the shirt comes off, I take a deep breath, preparing myself for the sight which will greet me in the mirror. I stare at my reflection, shocked at how ugly my flesh has turned.

The fang from the Mage's ice Dragon is still wedged deeply into my muscle, and the area around it has blackened. Angry looking red streaks radiate from the site with pus and foul colored fluids draining from it. No wonder my shirt was stuck to it. Another damn thing I will be forced to burn.

Today marks three weeks since my fight with her, and my wound still continues to worsen and fester. Every time I try to remove the fang, it sinks further into the body, like the roots of a weed spreading into my healthy flesh.

I can barely manage to function most times, the spasms nearly making me lightheaded and unsteady on my feet. I fear if I try to extract it again, I will lose consciousness which will be dangerous. Perhaps the only one who can remove this wretched thing is the Mage.

I underestimated her entirely... Her magic is strong enough to do something like this. I have never battled a Mage who has the power to do this.

The Dragon she conjured is a new experience, although not unheard of. I have read an old account in a history book, detailing how an Ice Mage used them in war. He won every battle he fought until he encountered one of our past kings and was slain most horribly.

However, the written passage described the dead Mage's conjuring similar to a Dragon, but the drawing in the report looked nothing like it yet had the qualities of a Dragon. But hers, that was completely different.

She replicated her Dragon to the finest detail, and at the time of the fight, I had been too enraged to acknowledge the beauty of her creation. A blind Mage getting every tiny detail of the Dragon right. *Imagine that!*

I have to admire her; she has the gall to fight with me when I'm sure her own father doesn't have the guts. I know not many Dragons who will take me on, let alone the Mages.

It is hard to imagine her as the same feeble, sickly bag of bones that she was many months ago when she lined up with her sisters. Today her strength and inner powers shine, and she seems to see much more than others.

This is my error, a foolish mistake on my part, because I know the more abused one is, the wilder and far more unpredictable they become. I took everything from the Mage and forced the title of queen on her from the moment our wedding bracelets were placed upon our wrists. But she managed splendidly. I expected my relation-ship with the Mage to be strained and exhausting and more work than I have time for. But she made it easy. Though I am still not convinced about her smart mouth.

It is true having a wife is something I never wanted...

Now Oria finally has its long-awaited queen, despite her being an Ice Mage. As a king, I know this duty must be fulfilled as the Kingdom is in need of a legitimate heir. Many disagree with the idea of having a child with a Mage, even I am not entirely sure how I feel about it. As Dragons, we have been warned since childhood about how wicked and sneaky Mages are, as from the beginning of the world, they have always been evil.

Stories are told how the first Ice Dragon, Kari, loved humans and did all he could to protect them from the wicked colds of the young world. He even went as far as giving a piece of himself to a human woman he pledged his heart to so he could keep her alive and well.

Kari's brother, Ori, disagreed with him, warning him of the dangers of mingling with humans and how it would only bring about death. When Ori learned his brother had gifted a human female with magic, he abandoned him, leaving him with the prophetic words.

'You have doomed our people with a plague.'

A mass exodus of all Dragon kind from Yulor followed, Ori and the others he led deemed the Icelands as dangerous.

The woman Kari loved, unable to keep the magic a secret, told her family what he had gifted her with. She did not think of the consequences of her words.

She revealed that by eating a single scale from his body, she was able to obtain his magic. The cold was no longer deadly, and she could now command ice, even showing them how it danced upon her fingertips by just using her thoughts.

The story spread until all humans knew the truth, and when the brutal winter continued well beyond spring, the woman's twin sister, Raine, ventured to the tallest mountain in Yulor, where Kari slept. And as Kari relaxed, thinking her to be his lover, Rosa, Raine crept close, using this to her advantage.

The two sisters had similar scents and appearances, sharing identical blood, and masked by smell and looks, Raine drove a sword into Kari's chest, where his heart once lay beating.

His last image of the world was of the woman whom he thought to be Rosa, the one he had loved and trusted, and he died thinking it was she who slew him.

The final moments of Kari's life were tragic, with him frantically trying to get to the sky, a sword impaled in his chest, and pain more than physical affliction tormenting him. His brother's words rang in his ears as he took his last breath, the betrayal having defeated his will to fight.

His wings faltered, his body failed him, and he tumbled down the same mountain he ruled to his death. If the stab wound did not kill him, the height, for sure, did.

Raine climbed down the mountain a hero after spreading lies about Kari, telling the humans it was he who had caused the brutal winters and that the Dragons had wished for the demise of human life so they could steal their lands.

The only one who hadn't believed in her lies was Rosa, Kari's lover. She was mad with grief and attempted to murder her sister whom she once loved, but it was too late as the people already had rallied with Raine.

When Rosa failed in her attempt, she was locked inside a tower, becoming its very first prisoner. There she sat, lonely and cold, reminiscing of the times she spent with her Dragon lover. Tears of ice fell to the ground as days became weeks then years.

It is even said her spirit till today haunts the infamous tower of Yulor, sometimes even the royal family. It is led to believe Rosa died of a broken heart.

The story usually ends there, but when I was all but a boy, I found an old book in my father's office, and unlike the stories I was read to by the maids, it documented a different tale.

The beginning was the same, but the ending was different. After Rosa had been locked in the tower, she had discovered she was not alone; she was with child, the last Ice Dragon dwelling inside her... Kari's child.

She promised herself that even in the cruel conditions of the tower, she would keep her child alive – her dreams telling her she was carrying a son. It didn't take long for Raine to discover her sister's pregnancy. She was not happy and being cruel and twisted, she plotted further misery for her sister and her soon-to-be-born child.

Raine promised Rosa that the child, too, would rot in the tower, and the last of the Ice Dragon blood would end there after it had lived a very long and miserable life as a prisoner. Raine kept her word, and even when the birth killed her sister, she did not shed any tears as she focused on her nephew.

Rosa's son was born blind, his father's power too much to harness, so it had left a defect. The more Raine studied the boy, the further she discovered he was quite harmless, unable to transform into a Dragon like his father could, and what was more, he was without vision.

Time passed and Raine lost interest, having much more important affairs to tend to such as ruling a Kingdom, she being the first queen of Yulor. The boy Rosa gave up her life for grew up in the tower, and at the age of sixteen, he craved love and affection.

He reached out to one of his maids, giving her gentle touches in secret and asking for her love in return. The maid was unable to turn away the nameless boy who had been punished because of his very existence, and it wasn't long before she was with child.

She then married a friend in order to protect herself and the child growing inside her. Before long, the nameless boy heard of the marriage, and unable to take the loneliness and supposed betrayal, he committed suicide. He froze himself to the very core, not once knowing about the child he had fathered.

Tragedy ever since had followed Kari's bloodline, cursing any who shared his blood with death and misfortune. Every man and woman born in the family never lived a long and prosperous life. The story continued down the generations, telling tales of how his descendants always suffered in one way or another.

The stories fascinated me as I sat reading in the farthest corner of my father's office until I reached a new page. It began with a woman who birthed a child who did not inherit the blindness the others did. Her name was Zola. She was supposedly special, unlike the others, and it was thought the curse of the Dragon had bypassed her.

I thought it was good the story ended on such a positive note, almost bringing a lifetime of misery to an end to the cursed family. But no story truly had a happy ending... I soon found that out myself after going to Yulor to end an ongoing war the past kings of Oria and Yulor could not.

Perhaps I would have been able to exterminate most of the Ice Mages, leaving only a few to rebuild civilization under my rule if I'd decided on such a path. Then there would have been no more wars between us, stopping all the stories of the original Dragons, Kari and Ori... No more bitter blood. I would have made sure of it.

Standing in front of the King of Yulor, he gave me an opportunity I never thought I would have. A deal and marriage that perhaps would unite our kingdoms for the next ten years. Rhys agreed with my choice to marry one of the Ice Mages, maybe he thought the same.

I had stared at the four daughters of the King of Yulor and realized one of them was blind. I couldn't help but think of that story I had read as a child, how the true descendants of Kari continued right under the noses of the royals themselves.

The book was all fiction or so I believed. After all, the Mage I chose was feeble and pathetic, like a mirromouse. She could not possibly be a descendent of Kari; she was nothing special. The writer had simply wanted to keep the story going.

But I started to doubt myself while spending more time with the Ice Mage, Vrai. She began to fascinate me. Now, as I stare in the mirror at the ice that refuses to come out, I truly believe the woman has the blood of Kari flowing through her veins. It was not a storyteller who wrote it but a true historian recording the past.

I dab my fingers in the salve made from the soldier's herb and smear it on the wound. It gives some relief and even cools down some of the heat from the infection. I cover the wound back up after applying more, feeling weary from it.

I suppose I can change my shirt later; I just want to rest... Rest makes it throb less.

There is a knock on the door, and my eyes narrow. I fix my jacket and bellow, "Who is it?"

"Nathan, sir. I have come to remind you, your dinner is almost ready," he announces behind the door.

Nathan? Oh right, the young boy we just employed as a servant, another Theka. His voice sounds different, and there is something off about him. I inhale deeply. He smells different, too, but puberty often changes scents and voices. I think about opening the door but feel extremely tired. I don't want the servants to see me like this, looking like shit and weak, not to mention the Mage, later on.

"I am tired and have some paperwork to finish. Just keep my food outside the door. I won't be coming down for dinner tonight. Have the Queen eat with someone, maybe Fonzell or Zachariah or both," I yell. Even standing too long is exhausting.

"Yes, your Majesty," Nathan says before slipping away.

I kick my boots off before lying back. My body is tired, but my Dragon is restless, making sleep difficult. I don't know if it is from the wound or the fact I have left the Mage by herself. I click my tongue before shutting my eyes and mutter, "The fucking Mage can protect herself. Who better than I to know that!"

I don't know how much time passes in between, but I wake up when I hear the servant place a tray of food down. His footsteps disappear then reappear at my door. *Is he pacing?* Then the sounds get heavy and muted. His walking away slowly is ominous as if he is spying.

My Dragon continues to feel uneasy, but when I sit up, my entire shoulder is hotter than usual. An intense throbbing sets off from the core, right where the fang is wedged. I groan before grabbing my shoulder, claws sinking in, hoping to relieve some of the agony with a different pain.

How long can I avoid Doctor Viggo?

I do not trust him.

The wound will heal on its own. It has to just as everything else does. *Weakness is death.*

Moments toll by before the pain begins to ease, and my claws retract from my shoulder. I open the door and stare at the food kept on the plate along with a single cup of wine. The pricks should know better by now. They know I like bottles and unopened ones... He must have not been trained properly.

The pain stabs me as I reach down to pick the tray up. Slamming the door, I place it on my desk. The food, I have no interest in, but the wine will take the edge off. A strange odor drifts from the glass. I sniff it and notice the smell seems wrong. I take a small sip before spitting it back into the cup. *Disgusting! Something is in it.*

A poison? A sleeping draft?

I run my fingers around the rim of the cup, finding a residue sticking to the edge. I bring it to my nose and take a deep breath, trying to decipher the smell. Amongst the many drugs I have come across, this has to be something I know. A bell rings in my mind.

The poison is kingwort, not deadly enough to kill a Dragon but would make one ill unless he were King Harriff, who continuously consumed it over the span of many months. The imbecile deserved death for being a gluttonous pig.

My thoughts suddenly return to Vrai.

What about a Mage? Can kingwort be deadly to them? They have a delicate constitution compared to Dragons.

I begin to wonder if she is dumb enough to not check her wine glass. *But will she know this poison even if she encounters it?* She shouldn't even be drinking, not when she is trying to get pregnant, but I have noticed how she is starting to acquire a taste for it. I usually check her food and drink without her knowing; it is easy to do when she is blind.

I place my cup down and rush to the door, then through the hallways and stairs until eventually, I reach the servant who has brought me dinner. The same measured steps.

The servant with dark hair turns around. "You needed something, my King?" He was being facetiously polite. My face darkens with anger, and a scowl makes its way to my lips as I grab his throat, slamming him against the wall. "Do you think you can get away with poisoning me, and I wouldn't know?"

I squeeze his throat when he fails to answer. His eyes grow wide as I lift his body by the throat. His toes barely graze the ground. His life is in my hands. He manages to draw a breath before shaking his head. I wish I could squeeze his scrawny neck and snap it. But I need answers, and I have to know what he has done with Vrai. I hold my patience. "Why did you try to poison me? Do you work for somebody? Who ordered you to do this?"

A hoarse rasp is his voice when he replies, "I... I didn't poison you, my King. I was just tasked with bringing the food to your room and making sure you eat it."

"Bullshit, you fucking Theka... You should know your place and not get involved in someone else's vendetta," I growl, and before I can break the man's neck, I hear a scream come from the dining room. A female... Does it have something to do with the Queen?

I let go of him— *will deal with him later*—and find my way to the dining room where I see one of her maids, Yanmei, holding the Queen's pet as it foams out of its mouth on the floor, its body quivering with each spasm.

"I don't know what to do... It's like it's having a seizure," she says, panic in her voice and visible distress in her eyes. She obviously cares for it despite calling it a terrible creature while feeding it.

My eyes go to the cracked plates and unfinished food on the floor. The food... The Queen's food has been poisoned, too. If her pet is here... So is she. *But where is she?*

"Take the liwolf to Cell or Viggo. Fuck, do something, it's been fucking poisoned. It won't live long if you do nothing," I lash out. "And do you know where the Queen is?!"

"I don't know," Yanmei replies, holding on to the creature, beginning to shed tears. "I got worried after she didn't return to her room. I came down here and found Baby convulsing."

I growl, not having any idea where the Queen is. She could already be fucking dead or taken or who knows what, but standing here would achieve nothing.

I storm out the doors, inhaling the air, hoping to pick up some kind of scent. But Dragon noses aren't as sharp as a liwolf. Baby would have been able to show me where she was if it weren't a fucking tigg.

That's it! Cell's liwolf, Liz, she should be able to find her.

I whistle, hoping the creature will respond to me as I quickly walk down the halls, looking for any sign of the Queen. It is then I see Cell around the corner with Liz, a black Liwolf with white spots on its scales, right behind him, its dark blue eyes narrowing at me.

Cell crosses his arms in front of his chest and glares at me, the Liwolf too tilting its head. "King, I am interested to know why feel the need to call out to my Lizzy. You know she only responds to me. It's futile."

"I need her," I growl, not in the mood to deal with Cell's snark. "The Queen and her pet have been poisoned. Baby is in the dining room with Yanmei. I do not know where the Queen is. Either help me or get out of my way!"

"Oh hell!" curses Cell. "Do you have anything of the Queen's on your body?"

Yeah right! The ice fang, perhaps. *Will it have her scent?* Besides, I don't want Cell seeing my wound. I am still not convinced of his motives. So I am better off being paranoid. Best not to give him more information than what is needed.

I give a single shake of my head and start walking.

"Wait, we can still try. Lizzy, go with the King." The liwolf walks to my side obediently on his order, a well-trained yet stubborn creature that it is.

Cell walks past me, saying, "I will try to help Baby. It'll be a shame if such a beautiful creature dies like that. King, go to the Queen's room. I'm sure you will find something of hers, or the maids will help."

I start to walk quickly to the Queen's room, Cell going in the opposite direction. I grab one of her blankets from the bed, letting the liwolf smell it. It isn't long that the creature gets a waft of her scent, and it puts its nose to the ground, working judiciously through the hallways and making its way upstairs.

The library... Why will she be up there?

I tread carefully, not wanting to make any sudden moves. As I reach the hallway, I feel a burst of magic, and the temperature drops almost immediately, the air cooling to the freezing point just like that.

This is definitely the Queen's magic. It startles the liwolf which starts growling, showing all its teeth. Something bad has happened here. *Is the Queen dead?*

I head in the direction of the magic. Anger and... panic fill my chest. *Is panic what this is? Why do I feel panic?*

Entering the library, I see that everything has been frozen. The books have all been entombed in ice. Taking a breath of the freezing air it burns my lungs. *Is the Queen alive?*

A head is kicked my way. Following from where it came, my eyes land on the Queen and her state of dishabille. Her skin is unusually pale, with vomit on her clothes. Her breasts have been laid bare, a stab wound between them.

On the floor, in front of her, I see a man's frozen hand holding a dagger, though perhaps it is a woman. It is hard to tell who or what it is as their body has shattered into a million little frozen pieces.

Did they plan to cut her heart out? Is that a message for me?

My magic starts to flare as anger takes over me. Everything turns hot, the room blazes. Where I stand, the ice beneath my feet begins to melt, turning it into a puddle. I stamp on the frozen head, crushing it under my foot.

Whatever happened, someone will pay.

I watch as the Mage loses consciousness and I hurry to her, scooping her up in my arms. I try my best to remain calm, remembering that the last time my magic smoldered like this, I ended up burning her.

I walk with her in my arms, my fingers curling into her thighs, leaving indentations. I don't care. *The Queen is mine....*

She is my treasure.

TWENTY-ONE

FATHER

KING ORVAL'S POV

THE ANTIDOTE IS WELL RECEIVED by the Mage. Dr. Viggo's skill and knowledge about science and medicine were impressive, so also was his ability to ratify cures. She has already gained her color back, looking healthy and rested. But she is still unconscious. Or sleeping. I need to ask Viggo.

Perhaps I can trust the man for my own malady... maybe not. I reach for my wound that has started throbbing since I carried the Queen out of the library, hoping to soothe it. It pulses with its own heartbeat, pain shooting down my body with each beat. I stop and force my hand back to my side, ignoring the agony.

I am a king, the Dragon King, the strongest of my kind. Weakness is not tolerated.

But I have allowed this to happen in my palace by being weak, and next time, she might not recover easily or even survive. My enemies are not idiots; they will not stop with this failed attempt. It is just a trial run to check us out, though I will never make the same mistake of trusting the new servants or anybody here.

Attacking us is treason against my Kingdom, and I will have their heads on a pike. My thoughts disturb me as I run my eyes down her still form, watching her take shallow breaths. The panic in my heart has decreased but not gone away. Only when she opens her eyes will I be at peace. I am changing where the Mage is concerned.

While I attended meeting after meeting, ordering everyone to get me the traitors, her maids have bathed and dressed her in a sheer white nightgown, the material hiding nothing from my eyes. Of late, they seem to be dressing her according to my tastes. Someone is surely keeping an eye on us. I get the feeling of being watched even right now. I turn around and rear back with a start.

It is Rhys at my back, and nowadays he is everywhere I go, always complaining. He never stops whether I am listening or not. My claws curl slightly into the bedpost as if seeking patience. The nagging of the bald prick is starting to worsen my headache.

"Are you listening, my King?"

"N... Yes," I reply, hoping he will tire himself out, listening to his own voice and leave me alone. But, apparently, he doesn't get the hint.

"So, when will you get back to fulfilling your duties? You can't expect the Kingdom to run by staring at her all day, sire," he mocks loftily.

How did he become my aid?

"Duties?" I hiss softly, my voice becoming a growl before turning to face him fully. The wood splinters with the pressure of my claws as they squeeze the bedpost, imagining it to be Rhys's neck. "Are there any other words you know besides duties and my title?"

His lips tightly purse before he kneels, bowing down to me. "Forgive my insolence. I think I overstepped my bounds."

"You think...? No. You did. There is a time and place for everything. And as for my duties, I will return tonight. And Rhys, anything else which is unimportant, you can complete in my stead. Now scram, your ugliness fouls my mood."

"My apologies. As you wish." His brown eyes narrow at me, then turn toward the Mage, taking in her sleeping form. "I pray for the Queen's swift recovery. Good day, sire."

That word again... sire... sounds like a noose around my neck.

"GO!" I warn him one last time, disliking the disdain in his eyes and tone. He slips out of the room without a word, shutting the door with a soft click.

Once I am alone, I take a deep breath and try to relax my tense shoulders, relieving some of my aches. I feel extremely hot, the infection raising my body temperature and causing havoc with my magic. The anger too does not help. It boils my insides as I remember the scenes from the night before.

I sit by the side of the bed, opposite to the Mage, my eyes gazing outside the window. A soft breeze sways the curtains. It is snowing in the middle of summer, no doubt a freak result of the Mage's powerful magic, although this isn't too terrible.

The children of Oria seem to enjoy it. They have never seen the soft flakes falling from the sky, and their excited screams while playing in the snow, though dampened, carries all the way here. Unlike their fathers who have ventured to Yulor for battles fought, they are not thrilled. I know they are blaming the Mage for it. Ah well, at least, the kids are happy.

My weary eyes wander back to the Mage, seeing her flinch in her sleep, and I wonder if, instead of dreaming, she is having a nightmare. After everything that has happened, I won't doubt it. This was too brutal an attack.

And how does she dream? All sound and no sight? I imagine so. And it isn't as if she'll have a conversation with me and answer my personal questions. She doesn't seem to like me much.

I sigh and lie next to her, careful not to disturb my shoulder too much. I wipe my forehead for the thousandth time; sweat seems to drip off me, covering my entire body and soaking my clothes.

This isn't right. I never sweat, especially not when the temperatures have dropped so... But the Mage is nice and cool. I can feel the sweet chill on the bed covers. I press my body against hers, instantly feeling better. She feels nice... It's all I can think of as I put my arm around her midsection and close my eyes.

I have never slept next to a woman like this, but the Mage's body... Well, mostly the temperature is inviting, but her body is, too.

Curvy hips, long legs, and especially those round, plump breasts. They are like succulent fruits, begging for a taste. But what I enjoy most is her hair. Completely white with highlights of silver, soft to touch like the silken strands, they billow around her head like a cloud while she sleeps. And when she walks, those tresses move in time with her hips down her back, drawing my eyes to her body. She is sexy... fuckable. I wish she were awake. Sex always relieves my stress, but it is best for her to recover first.

Viggo has said that the recovery would take up to a day or less as she is healthy. So far, he has been correct in his predictions. She looks better by the hour. I press my forehead against her, glad to have our bare skin touch. I caress her midsection, hoping she wakes up soon. I notice the temperature is different from the rest of her body... Her stomach is ice cold.

I press my hand more firmly against her stomach. I recall how some of the men in my council often spoke about their wives' bellies growing warmer every month and becoming hotter closer to their due date when they were carrying a child. And temperature difference is one of the first telltale signs of pregnancy...

So... Is it the opposite for an Ice Mage? Is she finally carrying our child in her?

I sit up suddenly, the restlessness building in me. I am unable to settle down. I stare at her, brushing her hair behind her ear as I think about how I never wanted to have children, and now she may have made me a father.

A father... Me... I remember how ruthless mine was with me.

Is it expected of a king to hit his son into obedience on every occasion whether it is to stop him from going outside or to discipline him at dinner to correct etiquette or while teaching him to fly and when he doesn't, he is to die if he was to hit the ground?

I recall the memory of my father pushing me from the top of the tower for the very first time. He watched me fall, wondering if I was going to spread my wings. But I was not ready. I expected death when I was plummeting to the ground, but Zachariah was there, catching and saving me. That was the first and the last time he had glared with both his eyes at my father.

Now it will all be different. I can barely keep an eye on her, and now I have to double up as she most likely carries my child in her womb. *My child... My wife...*

This woman is different. She is not jaded and bitter like the others in my court. She may have the air of a queen about her, but she will always be that gentle princess I have watched so many times from my room and office.

The soft singing, the feeding of the quincats in the courtyard, the visit to all the different flowers in the garden. She is not meant to be a queen. I am sure she does not want such a life for herself either, but family and blood tie us down. We are chained by our pedigree and now by fate.

And if she is indeed with child, she will need help from her maids. I doubt she will be cruel to her child... but it will also be of my blood. If she hates me, she could become cruel. Women are odd creatures, able to turn on something with cold ferocity, even if that something comes from within them. I have seen it with my own mother.

I suddenly remember the poisoning and begin to wonder how it will affect the Mage's pregnancy. *Will she have a miscarriage? Will the child become deformed? Ill in the head? Or will it be normal?*

I hear a knock on the door, and I stand, the sudden movement causing me to grab my shoulder with the pain stealing my breath from me. I force my hand down and dig my claws into my palm to distract me just in time as Viggo enters without permission.

His eyes are unreadable, the light from the window makes the lens of his glasses shine, hiding them from me. He creeps me out the way he is so perfect. His actions are always careful and his words, measured. He gives off the air of always being cautious.

We do have interesting talks, and his ideas for improving Oria are always welcoming and heartfelt. I am implementing some with his help, his input great in such matters. But I cannot shake the unease I feel. Maybe it is just me. So far, I don't have any reason to mistrust him. Just my instincts...

He wastes no time in informing me, "Cell managed to save the life of the Queen's pet."

That is another thing about him, he is all business all the time. I can find nothing of note besides his profession which seems to be his hobby as well, no whorehouses, no gambling, no love affairs, nothing. I look past him to see Cell walk in, holding the creature in his arms. It dwarfs him.

"He will be just fine. He is a strong one," he states, patting its chest after laying it at the foot of the Mage's bed.

Right behind Cell, his liwolf comes stalking in, the click of its claws quietly echoing in the room. It slips between Cell and his brother, staring at the Mage's pet.

For a moment, I am unsure of the mother liwolf. *Will it try to kill its own pup?* I don't have my sword on me, and I am unsure how I will fare with one so large in my state. I tense, seeing the nasty look in its eyes.

I have seen it kill its pups before, but it pads forward and instead of attacking, it licks its son's snout before climbing up on the bed. The mother liwolf lies down next to it as if knowing it is not well.

"Oh! This is quite rare, Lizzy," Cell comments, smirking. "You always hate your pups so perhaps you like this one's color."

I look at Viggo noticing that he too is distracted momentarily as he stares at the creature before turning to the Queen. He clears his throat. "Are there any problems?"

"No..." I reply. "But I believe she is with child. Will the poison affect her pregnancy?"

"There is a possibility of complications, especially so early on, if she is pregnant. The fetus is so delicate during these months," Viggo says and presses his hand against her stomach.

"I see..." I state.

"It seems..." Viggo pauses, making me tense before he continues,

"It seems you are right. I can feel the child's magic although it is hard to tell how it will develop. I will be able to tell you more in a few months. The fetus is still very small, around three or four weeks if I were to guess."

I knew it. Of all the times for her to be pregnant. He is never wrong about such things. He is able to feel the magic far more sensitively than the others.

I hear Cell talk from across the room, playing with the items on the Mage's dresser. "Congratulations on an heir, my King. I'm sure the people will be happy about hearing such news, especially Rhys."

"And what are the chances of a deformity or it being ill in the head?" I question Viggo, ignoring Cell's comment. "Should we terminate it? If the chances are high, others... It will suffer and so will the Queen."

"It is hard to tell if it will be deformed. It is too early for me to know; to be safe, you can terminate it. But it is your and the Queen's decision."

"The King is right in that fact. If the Queen births some deformed abomination, no one will accept it. Everyone will consider it an omen. After all, royalty has never given birth to a monster," Cells cuts in, walking toward us and sitting at the edge of the bed with a grin. "But I am speculating. Who knows how the others will react? But at least, now we know she is not infertile."

"Only time will tell... Though the chances of her having a miscarriage are high. If I may interject, it may be best if she doesn't know. It will be a burden on her mental health. I can acquire the medication and you can slip it in her dinner and she will just think she has gotten her monthly blood," Viggo suggests.

"That is very cruel," hums Cell, "very cruel indeed."

My eyes glance at the Mage, wondering what the best for her is, trying to assess my options. *Will it be better for her to know or not to know?* She and the child will suffer if it is deformed and if she were to miscarry, as Viggo has said, it can be just as bad potentially.

"You whole lot are cruel!" A woman's voice rings into the room with the force of thunder, surprising me and the others. I see Ava, the tall, skinny maid, slip into the room quietly. "You speak so confidently about killing her child because it might be a deformity... or having something being wrong with it. Let the Queen decide the fate of her child. One of you might be a doctor, one a general, and one a king, but none of you are compassionate. I won't let anything happen without her knowledge. She has the right to know. It is her body, and it will be her decision."

Cell laughs harshly as he mocks, "Wow! Who would have known Demos's bitch would tell the King off about what to do with *his* child? And here I felt you hated your Queen. To think a Theka feels so strongly about her Ice Queen... Never thought I would see the day."

"Enough, Cell!" I warn him, narrowing my eyes at him. "I assume she is right... I will let the Mage decide. It is her decision."

His eyes look at me, but he doesn't say anything. Then I see him give me a cold look for the very first time. As a general, I have given him much freedom to do what he wants. This is the first time I have stopped him, not allowing him to speak how he wishes. I grow tired of my men doing as they please, including letting anything roll off their tongues.

"My apologies, my King, if Cell has offended you... He too had a heart once, and he loved Ava with all that heart. But now she is with Demos, and he can no longer have her," Viggo explains, touching his brother's shoulder.

Cell smacks Viggo's hand away as he stands up. "Like I ever loved her. She's too ugly for my taste, and on top of it, she is a Theka."

He walks coldly past her, glaring at her, and calls out to his liwolf. "Come on, Lizzy. We are leaving." The mother liwolf lifts its head and stares at Cell, not wanting to leave the pup's side. "Lizzy. Now!"

It shows its teeth in warning at his command, and Cell's glare worsens. "Fine, you get nothing to eat tonight, especially for baring your teeth at me. Suffer."

Cell fists his hands before disappearing out into the hallway, his boots smacking the ground loudly with rage.

"I'm glad you understand, King," Ava says with her head held high, unfazed by Cell. "She is my lady, and I will not let any form of harm come near her... even if that form is you."

How daring! And how loving!

I see the eyes of a Dragon instead of normal Theka ones. Her loyalty now lies with Vrai completely. Her loyalty to me is long gone. I will assume Catherine to be the same. Maybe the Mage has affected them somehow over time. To think the orphan brats I picked up dare to bare their teeth at me much like Cell's liwolf.

Very well, I accept it. I like it, in fact. The Queen needs all the support she can get. The next few months will be tough on her with the baby on the way and a traitor amongst us.

"Good," I praise. "Keep it that way. The Mage needs her maids to rely on."

Viggo clears his throat once more. "Very well, I will be leaving now, but I suppose congratulations are in order. I will be in my office if you need me."

I see his eyes study me and begin to worry he suspects that I feel unwell. His magic works quite differently as a healer as he has practiced the art for many many years. He walks away, hands shoved into his long and flowy coat, leaving Ava who stares at me for a couple of seconds before she too exits the room.

Once everyone is gone, I sigh, easing my claws from my palm and pushing my fingers into my hair. I can feel my hand is wet with my blood, and I wipe it on my pants. I will bathe later and dress in a new set of clothes.

But really what was I thinking in asking Viggo to kill my child? Maybe I am already starting to act like my father. Maybe cruelty runs in the family.

My eyes gaze at the Mage who has slept on even with all the commotion. I find it hard to believe she is able to; I wake up at the slightest noise. I suddenly feel drained from all this thinking, and once more, I lie down next to her. I press my head against her shoulder.

Being a king and a father will not be an easy task. It will mean more work and less sleep and being alert all the time. I sigh.

"You are tiresome... You and this child yet to be born," I mutter to her. I close my eyes, hoping to get more rest while Rhys or my men or the maids aren't here.

Just for a little while, I want peace, and I am not sure if I will get it when the Mage wakes up. I'm sure all peace will be lost soon.

TWENTY-TWO

WINTER GHOSTS
MANY MANY WINTERS AGO

THE EAST WINDS whip through the barren landscapes; a keening sound follows its path, terrorizing me as I try to trudge forward.

The snow makes it harder to see any type of magic, obscuring my way, and the hard flakes pelt my shoulders and back, its weight keeping me bowed down.

It piles and blankets the ground, causing me to fall behind the taller woman ahead of me. I have no choice but to follow in her footsteps, taking care not to slip. The snow now is too deep, reaching as high as my knees.

The bitter cold of Yulor is everywhere, wrapping itself around me like a ghost, chilling my soul. These ghostlings come from the tall mountains and seas, stealing lives and reminding us Mages how deadly the winters can be.

I can't imagine what our ancestors went through before they had eaten the Ice Dragon, Kari, and developed a tolerance to the cold.

"Mother," I call out as I lag further behind. She is so far away from me now. "Please slow down," I beseech her when my nose is frozen and feels ready to fall off much like the icicles hanging from the edge of the roof of our house.

"Vrai, you must keep up." I hear her voice echoing in the distance. "Hurry. We do not have much time."

"But where are we going? Why hurry? My nose is cold, Mother," I whine, trying my best to follow. Her magic is my only guide and that too I can barely manage to spy.

"I will explain when we reach where we are going," she states loudly, striving to be heard over the howling winds. "But you must follow me. Quickly now."

I try my best to plod on with her encouraging words, but I only fall, my knees sinking into what feels like never-ending snow.

"I can't," I wail further. "It's too cold. I want to go home."

I hear my mother draw near, easing my mind that she won't leave me behind. She trudges through the snow, one foot in front of the other ,and scoops me up, holding me high in her arms. "It's okay. Don't be scared. We will be home soon, Vrai."

She moves ahead, still holding on to me as I shiver. "If you hear anything strange, just remember you HAVE to move, you can't collapse, or else bad things will happen."

My eyes well, and a tear runs down my cheek where it freezes halfway. My voice breaks as I hold back my fear. "What's going on? I'm scared. Why are we running?"

"Shh, don't be scared. Everything will be alright. Soon we will arrive at the Kingdom of the East, where we won't have to deal with the bitter cold or the extreme heat. Everything is perfect there. It's truly a kingdom of calm and beauty. They will accept you as you are; you won't be known as a bastard there," she whispers, in hopes that it will make me feel better.

I do feel reassured in her arms, listening to her words of a better life for us. I hold on to her fluffy jacket, not understanding the word 'bastard,' but I hear the word a lot, always being directed at me.

"Why am I a bastard?" I ask her as the freezing gales continue to blow against us.

"I was not married to your father when I had you. You are a special gift who came to me even when I thought I was unable to bear children. Dinacko, our God, wanted me to have you. He put you inside of me, so you're special, Vrai, and no matter what the others say, you are no bastard," my mother explains, caressing my face.

Dinacko is our God, our creator, a man who is worshipped amongst the Mages. Just hearing his name soothes me.

Suddenly, a woman's garbled voice breaks through the winds, bringing with it an air of wicked sourness. The words are not kind, and she sounds more malicious than the ghosts.

"Zola! Do you really think you can escape the Kingdom in such conditions? Only a true member of the royal family can withstand this degree of cold. Proof that your bastard isn't one of us. Look at her trembling like a newborn babe in your arms."

"Stay away, Lydia. I just want to leave. I promise to never step back on these lands again. I will not cast my eyes on King Amir again! I promise!" my mother says with panic in her voice.

"That does not guarantee you won't return to Yulor when your child is grown," Lydia mocks, she being the Queen of Yulor and my stepmother, too.

"Please!" my mother screams, holding me tighter against her chest, making me whimper at the desperation in her voice. "Lydia, I beg of you. We used to be like sisters."

"That was before you fucked my husband," Lydia growls in anger. "You betrayed my trust, Zola. I will never forgive you."

I feel wetness, not my own, on my skin that turns to ice immediately. It makes me shiver.

"Then kill me but spare Vrai." My mother loosens her arms around me. "Promise me you will spare her. She is innocent."

"Mother..." I protest, startled by what she has said, and I manage to cling to her desperately.

Kill her? Why would Lydia kill her? I don't understand.

I hear Lydia chuckle. "I will spare your daughter, but I can't promise she will lead a good life."

My mother goes on to plead for my life, but it isn't long before something splatters against my face, and she gasps.

"Vrai... run..." mother manages to say as she chokes and gags. I hear her use her magic, dropping me to the ground instantly and I can no longer cling to her.

I get up and begin to run as fast as I can, scared out of my wits, yet keeping a listen for my mother's steps, but the snow is thick and hard to traverse. I hear in the distance a battle, my mother and the Queen, multiple forms of ice magic being used, the sounds that would have been beautiful if they didn't carry with it danger and death.

Suddenly, I am running aimlessly not knowing where to go but just away from the area. I bump into someone's legs and sense the presence of spine-chilling magic.

I feel a hand on my shoulder and a gruff male voice in my ear. "Little Vrai. I presume?"

I swallow, not replying to him, filled with a different kind of trepidation.

"I'm Dr. Goodfella. We will be spending the next few weeks together, you and I. And I hope with all my heart we can be friends... Lydia says we can."

Fingers curl into my shoulder, hurting me, and I know he is a bad man, and terrible things are about to happen to me. I struggle and fight, frightened of the man who drags me through the snow, choking me with my winter coat. Panic clouds my senses, and I scream loudly.

"No! NO! LET GO! Mother! HELP!"

My last chance of escape is lost when my vision blurs, and I am dizzy with the lack of air in my lungs. He ignores me, whistling a song out of tune and bringing me to some unknown place. Much time and distance pass, enough for me to lose sight of mother's magic and for the air to be empty of the sounds of battle.

I can't seem to scream either, my throat burns, and I wheeze. The cold has gotten to me, numbing my fingers and toes where I can no longer feel them. I think I am going to die, too, until the man stops, and I hear him open a door. I feel a warmth wash over me but also smell the rot, which is pungent and nauseating.

Fear makes me tremble to my bones, and I barely manage to find my courage to ask the man in panic. "What is going to happen to my mother?"

"Dead, I suppose," is all he replies as he stops whistling.

"What do you mean?" More tears replace the ones that has already fallen.

"You killed her, Vrai," he tells me, pushing me to a chair and forcing me to sit. "Your magic is out of control, and when your mother tried fleeing from Yulor, you cried and became unstable, resulting in you freezing your mother to death."

"What? No. I didn't," I protest.

"You went L O O N E Y," he laughs, "looney!" His cackle reverberates in the room with an untamed wildness, piercing my ears and drilling into my brain. "Looney Vrai made her mother a popsicle."

"No! No! Lydia hurt mother! Not me!" I yell as I pummel him with my tiny fists, kicking his shin as hard as I can.

"No, child, I saw it all. You killed your mother." His tone suddenly changes, and he pins me to the wall after ripping me from the chair, his hands stripping me until I am in my underclothes.

"Don't! Pervert! No! Mother! SAVE ME."

Panic courses through me, and I become hysterical with fear. I scratch his face and stab his eyes with my fingers, all the while my body squirming under the force of his hold, wanting to escape a situation worse than my darkest nightmares.

A strike vibrates in the room, and my head jerks sideways. A singing burn on my cheek soon follows.

"Shut the fuck up!" he screams and spits on me.

He lifts me and straps me to the seat once more, then places sticky things all over me.

"I—" Before I can protest again, electricity runs through my body, making me clench my fists. A pain I don't understand and one that I am not prepared for.

After the current stops, tears run down my cheeks. "No... Please, no..." I murmur.

This results in a higher shock which makes my muscles spasm. The pain grows stronger, more stunning with each jolt, and it makes me wet myself. It continues like this, with me refusing to accept mother's death or a possibility where I have killed her, and at each of my refusal comes the electricity.

I don't know how long I spend in that chair, electrocuted every few seconds. My brain feels fuzzy, and I cannot articulate the words properly. Everything is so scrambled in my head. Time and place are lost to me as well, I know not where I am.

I recall the Doctor leaning over me, brushing my hair out of my face. "That's right. Accept your fate. You are a monster, a curse on the lands like the Great Dragon Kari!"

"Wha—" I never finish the word as another electrical current tears through my body, making me convulse.

Many more days I am tortured until I am begging, but only enunciating half the words, the rest have disappeared from my memory. I open my mouth to moan, and drool drips uncontrolled down my chin. There is the Doctor's magic in my face, whispering the words in my ear, again and again, every time I open my eyes.

"You have no control of your magic; a rampaging beast that you are, freezing anybody and anything... And what's more, you fear to use your magic now," he says softly, his voice slowly putting me in a trance.

I also overhear a woman's voice that is familiar.

"I assume everything is going well?" she asks.

"Yes, everything is fine. I am taking care of it as you ordered. Just understand, Queen Lydia, that I expect full payment soon. I find experiments such as this one tedious and boorish. Now off you go, you are disrupting me."

I don't hear the woman's voice again, but it doesn't matter. My mind is in pieces; she is a fragment of my imagination. I exist nowhere and everywhere. I am in a void, and my reality is the voice in my ear, speaking to me in deep, hushed tones. And I focus on it, hoping the truth wraps itself around me. I slowly start to repeat his words, beginning to believe them, and there is also no more pain this way.

"I am a curse."

I murmur the words, my head rolling from side to side, a painful throb emitting from the back of it. "My magic kills...I killed my mother. I won't use magic ever again."

"Good, my child," he praises, and I feel his lips on my forehead, giving me a kiss that is slimy and disgusting.

A part of me, buried deep in the recesses of my brain, shouts the words that leave my lips, unspoken.

Die, I want you dead. I want to hurt you like you did me.

I won't ever forget this.

I'll be back.

When he pulls away, the pressure increases in my head, my legs arc painfully, and my eyes burst fully open. I try to scream but can't, my throat is closing tight, preventing me from breathing or speaking.

"I know, I know. It hurts but just for a moment. You will soon forget this. All bad memories will be gone. Well... except when you wake up, your mother will still be dead. Also, you'll learn it is you who has killed her. Though I hope we can meet again one day when you are a lovely young lady." He laughs, and the pressure becomes too much for me.

Before my eyes close for the final time, he says something which chills me to the bone. "We will always be good friends, little Vrai."

Darkness envelops me slowly, in ever-narrowing circles until the pinpoint of light, too, disappears. Everything goes blank, and I wake up in the tower in my cell, screaming repeatedly.

"Mother?"

"Mother?"

"Mother..."

I sob one last time as I press my head against the wall of my prison, craving nothing more than the warmth and love of my mother's arms.

TWENTY-THREE

MOTHER

I LURCH FORWARD, screaming, my fingernails scraping against nothing but air, a single word from my night terrors expelled from my lungs.

"MOTHER!"

My chest tightens further, and a feeling of suffocation swells in me, the pressure unbearable, unsettling me further. The twin sensations of doom and dread fill my body where escape feels impossible, the impression of ice-covered walls still lingers against the flesh of my fingers.

Cold and ice fade and I feel hot, almost feverish. Pins and needles prickle my skin, especially my side and back. It is reassuring, the sweat covering my body tells me I am elsewhere and if this place is better or worse, I have yet to determine. I am no more a small child, a prisoner in the tower where my only company is a crazy man and cruel guards.

I touch my chest and face, trying to calm myself, and hear a voice from my left which spooks me. "Congrats... I already know... Now, be quiet. I have some time before I must return."

The Dragon King...

Only his voice can draw me away from my horrible night terrors and haunting memories. I frown, forcing myself to focus, trying to decipher the meaning behind his words. He seems to be talking about something altogether different. I am shocked to learn that his magic is so close... *Is he lying next to me?*

"What?" I ask, a tremble lingering in my voice. I haven't yet collected myself completely. I am still confused about what is happening.

"You're a mother..." he declares.

"WHAT?!"

The color drains from my face as dizziness closes in from the sides. I sigh tremulously, trying to take more air into my constricted lungs. I am forced back on the bed by him, his arm tightens around my shoulders, keeping me pinned down. "I assumed you overheard Doctor Viggo and I speaking before you woke up... Perhaps not, if you are taken aback by it."

Why is he lying so close to me...? And I am a mother...? I'm pregnant...?

Surprise and shock shake my core and my night terrors, repressed memories, and recent events begin to weigh heavily on me. The last thing I can recall is vomiting the poison fed to me by the servant who wanted my heart.

The servant... He must have been the trigger, the reason why I can now remember who my mother's true killer is.

Relief washes over me as my memories resurface, the moment as clear as the day it happened. The guilt I have lived with for so long is relieved. I begin to feel a rage come to life, a hatred I never knew I had until now. Even the King has never brought about such tempestuous emotions in me.

My stepmother, so she was the one who killed my mother, the reason I was imprisoned and the real cause of my father loathing me. She will pay for everything she has done to me and my family.

"Why are you here... King?" I whisper hesitantly, everything is still confusing.

"To sleep," he answers, sounding annoyed and winded.

"The real reason besides sleep," I demand, my brows furrow and my voice rises with every word. *The gall of this man!* "Or is it because I carry your heir that you now care for me? Is that the reason?"

"Did I ever speak of wanting a child, Mage?" he questions. "Did I ever ask you if you were with child? I think you are mistaken and confusing my words with the rest of the Kingdom. I told you the people demanded an heir, so I must give them one. I never once declared I wanted a child."

"What...?" I utter in shock, his words ripping my beliefs. All this is bewildering. My eyes widen as I start to process what he is saying.

He drags his hand down my chest to my stomach, skimming his claws over the material of my nightgown, making it ripple. "What you carry in your womb can very well be a monster, evil... Granted, if it survives its mother's poisoning. Never has an offspring of a Dragon and Mage ever been born. Being the last of my family, I need an heir, so this is what I am doing. Do not for a moment think I will walk outside the realm of what I as a king must do."

I push his hand off me, in disgust and repulsion, and shift away from him. I hiss, sitting up once more, "You're telling me, after all this time, performing the ceremonies and saying you needed an heir, you never once wanted a child to begin with?"

Exasperation and frustration, turmoil and anger, all chaotic emotions rush and broil inside of me. I want to pull my hair out. Actually, I want to pull *his* hair out. I want to punch and hit him for doing this to me.

I fling myself out of my bed, wanting nothing more than to get away from him.

"Maybe it will die," I say before lashing out, "I hope it does. I'd rather it dies than be born in such a miserable world and have you as its father, the one who does not want him."

All I feel is rage and sorrow within me. I can't seem to escape the fact that no matter what and where I go, misery follows me like a true companion, twisting my insides and leaving me defeated.

I hear the King get up from the bed and approach me cautiously. When he goes to touch me, I smack his hand away, my lips twisted in a scowl. "Don't. Don't touch me..."

"You asked for the reason for my being here, and the truth is I am hot... Even I, or Fire Dragons in general, get hot just as I assume Mages can get cold. Forget I said anything and come to bed. I can't believe my words affect you so." The King stretches an arm toward me, wincing.

I don't believe him. I can feel deceit dripping from his tongue. He is lying. He is too calm, too...

He abruptly grabs me, turning me around and pressing my back against his chest. Something I do not expect. It is terrifying, his hands encircle my forearms, pinning my arms against my chest. More than terrifying, it is enraging.

I begin to squirm, and the uncomfortable movement turns into a fight of arms. "Unhand me!"

"Listen for once, my Queen," he snarls low in my ear, his warm breath sending chills through me. His breathing slows down; he is calming himself. The rise and fall of his chest against my back feels hypnotic and soothing. I nod, waiting for him to explain.

"Maybe I am wrong, so why don't you prove me so? If the child lives, it lives. If it dies, it dies. And if it survives, maybe it will be the monster as I think it to be or perhaps something beautiful as you imagine it to be."

Monster... Beautiful...?

Continuing to grip my arms, he slides his hand down and rests it against my stomach, his claws gently sinking into the flesh through the flimsy cloth. "But I must warn you, my bloodline has produced nothing but vile monsters... I'm sure, so has yours. Nothing good is birthed from royalty. To live and thrive, you must become cruel and despicable."

I think back to how kind my mother was and even my father before he was manipulated by the bitch that is his queen.

"No, you're wrong..." I say. "My mother was a kind and gentle woman. She was no monster."

"And your father?" His claws start to ease from me once I stop my struggles. "I believe he locked you in a tower and treated you worse than the scum of your country. How can a father do that to his own flesh and blood, his little girl unless the stories are wrong? Well, are they, Mage?"

"It's because he believes I killed my mother," I reply, trembling. "He was manipulated by Queen Lydia into thinking I killed her... I know I didn't... Or maybe I'm crazy... Maybe I am imagining false things. I do not know. But you are telling me all this now, now when it is too late. I'm already with child, a child you do not want... or ever wanted." I begin to crumble within the King's arms, but he holds me up.

"Whatever his reasons were, it does not earn him forgiveness," the King hisses. "So put such thoughts away and come to bed, the poison still clouds your head. If you refuse to heed me, then listen to the Doctor at least. You need rest now. I do not care if you don't want your monstrous child because of my whim of never wishing to have children, but you will lie down now."

He manages to pull me back to bed, and his arms loosen further around me, giving me the freedom to sit down. I feel tears landing on my hands.

The King doesn't say anything but wipes them away before pressing his lips against mine. I turn my head quickly, not wanting such touches.

I expect a sarcastic reply, but he chooses to remain quiet, to my surprise again. I am guessing he is taking things for how they are, an improvement for him, even if it is only a bit. A tense silence befalls us.

"That woman, Red, you see so often... She doesn't love you... She never will. She's a same-gender lover." I keep my head turned away from him.

"Mage... Don't talk anymore," he warns. "Kindness for bitterness... It does not suit you."

"When have you ever shown me true kindness?" I snap in return.

"Rest," he says, not answering my question. His voice sounds strained, reminding me of how odd his magic is being, almost nonexistent. Maybe he is sick like the fake servant said.

"I don't want to..." I murmur, thinking about the nightmare I had about the night of my mother's death. "I will only have bad dreams."

"Don't sleep. Just lie down in bed." He sits next to me.

Again, there is silence and even though I crave to touch the King, to be comforted by him, I refuse to, not after what he has just said. I move away from him, lying down with my back toward him, still feeling as if I am being poisoned. Everything is spinning in my head.

Without saying anything, he lies next to me but doesn't touch me, knowing I will just refuse him. "I warned you, it does not get easier in this palace... Now you know, Mage, what I speak of."

I can only clench my teeth, holding my tongue in place, trying not to fight with him again. I do my best to ignore him. It doesn't matter if it is fighting or wanting to be comforted by him, I just want an outlet for these emotions.

I am confused, and perhaps I can blame it on the child.

I suddenly remember Baby, how the last thing I heard from him was crashing on the table in order to get to the food... My food which was poisoned.

"Baby!" I yell with urgency and prop up on my elbows. "He ate my food. Have you seen him? He was probably poisoned just like me."

The King sighs. "Your pet lives, Queen. I don't know what Cell did, but he managed to save him. Or perhaps he did nothing, and your pet just managed to survive all on his own. But he is here. At the end of the bed and breathing."

I sit up again and crawl to reach for Baby, relieved that he is alive, but I hear a growl, and it doesn't seem like Baby's growl. It is different.

The King grabs my wrist before I can investigate. "Cell's liwolf is here with us...I would not go near him. She seems to be very protective of him at the moment."

"His mother?" I query.

"Yes," he replies.

The King lets go of me as I sit back, craving to touch Baby but unable to do so due to his mother who will probably bite me. The growl is only a warning.

Cell says liwolves give one warning, a single growl. I can feel the intense stare of the animal now. She watches me, and I wonder if I would too become a mother like the liwolf, fiercely protective of my child.

Even if the King doesn't want him or her, I will love my child no matter what. Despite my words earlier about wishing it dead, it was only my emotions speaking during that time.

I do not wish it dead; I wish for it to live. *Live for me...*

Maybe I won't be so lonely then.

My eyes glance toward the King's magic as I begin to think about the memories of that night so many winters ago.

I will get my revenge against Lydia. I will do anything, even if I have to use the King in order to get to her.

The only question is how?

TWENTY-FOUR

BLOODTHIRSTY KING & SORROWFUL QUEEN

Snow in Oria...

I would have never believed such a thing was possible if I had not seen it with my own eyes. I reach up toward the sky, greeting the small and gentle snowflakes that land on my skin like a lover's kiss. My hands open to catch the wonder of them in this hot and fiery land.

It is a fleeting grace that I embrace because they soon melt on my palms as soon as they come to rest. They are too delicate, the cold of my skin not low enough to freeze them. I bury my feet and curl my toes into the softness of the snow. I know they will also melt; the terrible heat of this land will soon destroy my paradise.

Or maybe the King will. He lingers somewhere behind me in my quarters, not following me out into the balcony. I am sure he will like nothing more than to destroy any happiness I can procure for myself.

I let my hand drift to my side, then brush off this agonizing thought to just enjoy the moment for now. My fingers dance through the snow much like how I danced with the Dragon King on our wedding night, my fluidity though not as elegant as his. He is what he claims to be, a royal in every sense.

I have calmed down after the initial fight post waking up from poisoning, but I am still not happy with him. I turn around to stare at the King and his transcendent magic that never fails to declare its presence.

In some ways, I understand where the King is coming from. Nobody in history knows what our child will be. His thoughts about me bearing a monster and the fear he holds for the life growing inside me is justified.

He believes the child will be like him or the one before him. I have the same fear buried deep in me. But I don't think he realizes the strength of my determination. I refuse to let this child become anything wicked or cruel. A mother's love is stronger. That's where he is foolish and unwise even with all the knowledge he holds.

I recall how my mother was toward me. And remembering her brings out other nasty memories of Lydia and her cruel lies and torture. For so many years, I have held the belief that I deserve to be locked up in the tower, far away from everyone and hidden from the world.

The woman, Queen of Yulor, had the nerve to pretend she didn't know who I was that day when I was offered to the Dragon King as a part of the treaty with my Kingdom. She acted as if she barely knew of my existence, ignoring and pretending. But she will know me now. She will regret the sins of her ways when I come to exact my revenge, for both my mother and me.

And for this, I need the Dragon King and the power that he tightly keeps leashed in him. I have to make him more malleable toward my suggestions. If I tell him my desire now, he will never consider my words. He will immediately reject my proposal and perhaps mock me. I will not be permitted to leave Oria to tell my father the truth. I will need his support in the forthcoming days. I want to enjoy the downfall of Lydia and plan it accordingly.

To do that, the King and I cannot continue our standoffish ways, and it is I who has to take the first step. I am sure he is still angry over what I have said about Red. An apology it will be from my lips, though a lie and not heartfelt.

"I apologize for what I said earlier... about Red." I turn my back around, facing the Kingdom of Oria stretching in front of us. I brush the snow off my gown before stating, "It was not my place to tell you about Red."

A few moments later, I hear him stand from where he had been seated and join me on the balcony. "I had my suspicions about Red. Like men, she does like to ogle tits and asses for far too long. There is no need to apologize."

"Then why do you continue to lay with her?" I press on, wanting to get the truth from the King as I know I will not do the same with Dakari now that I am aware that he is a same-gender lover.

"Denial... I suppose, or maybe I just don't care. Red is a good fuck. She knows the art of pleasuring a man even if her interests are women." In return, his words turn on me quick as he questions, "But now when I think about it, Mage... Who told you of her being a same-gender lover? And what other secrets do you keep from me?"

I become quiet and don't respond to him, not knowing what else to say. The wind pushes my hair off my shoulders. I dare not pin it on anyone... And what he has said about Red irks me.

"If you don't answer, I will assume you are looking into my relationships." He draws closer to me and boxes me to the corner of the balcony. I know the ledge is close, and there is no railing to protect me. He is trying to scare me. I refuse to fall for his mode of intimidation and remain still.

"Are you jealous, Queen?" I feel his words like a hot breath in my ear as his chest presses against my back, the familiar heat comforting me, knowing he can scorch me anytime.

He bursts into laughter, mocking me as I continue to hold on to my silence. "I never thought a day would come when you would be jealous, Mage. I did not think Mages had hearts that could feel anything but the cold – especially for a Dragon. But is it true? Did your heart really beat for that man or was it lust? If it is, you are quick to change your affections to another."

"It isn't lust, and you're gravely mistaken if you think I feel jealousy in matters concerning you. If that is the case, you must be jealous of Dakari, speaking to him privately about his and my affairs," I hiss.

"So, you spoke to Red herself?" He lets his talon-like nails graze up my arms, stopping when he reaches my shoulders. "How interesting... And my talk with Dakari was for the benefit of my country, and it turns out my suspicions of him were correct. He wasn't who he said he was. I also found another traitor, another false face in my midst, so I will have to thank you for that, Mage."

I allow his threatening touches. They do not frighten me. Instead, they cause me to shiver, a gentle streak of fire. Parts of me are feeling good.

"My talk with Red too was for the benefit of my country as your country is mine as well. You forget, King," I dare to say.

He drags down the straps of my nightgown, and his lips press against my nape, causing me to tremble. "Are you saying what is mine is yours? Like a true married pair... To think the sickly Mage I brought here is speaking to me like this.... A Mage thinking that she owns Oria just because I married her and also fuck her from time to time. How laughable."

"I am the Queen. You decided that yourself the night you married me, so by all rights, Oria is also mine." All my senses seem to center on the warmth of his lips against my cold back. The contrast in temperature is robbing me of my thoughts, making it hard for me to focus. I wanted to appear confident and not waver just at the feeling of his lips against my skin.

"Tell me then, Queen... In your own words, how do you view Oria after having been once a princess of Yulor? Is it better than your country?" He pulls away.

"Are you being deliberately funny when you ask how I view Oria or are you mocking me? If you seek my thoughts, I will tell you. I find your country detestable. The heat is miserable, the people rude, and the King a beast. Yet, all things considered, I do enjoy some things here. But I do not know which country is more miserable - Yulor or Oria."

"What kind of things?" He lets his hand roam freely over my body. My father is right, the King loves women. He repeats the question, pressing his fingers deeper into my flesh, "What kind of things do you enjoy?"

He is hinting he wants me to say sex with him, or that is what I imagine. But I won't say it.

"I enjoy the animals, flowers, things that are able to grow without the bitter cold killing it first. Hmmm... I might have to take back my words as not all people are horrible... And perhaps the Beast King is tamable." I find myself flirting.

Flirting... And me?

This is new, but this may be the best way to recover our relationship. The King's downfall is women. I've heard that many times from my own flesh and blood and complete strangers.

He scoffs, "Do not get your hopes up too high about the people. And do not think so highly of yourself or so powerful. You've only had one attempted assassination. And for some reason, I detest you referring to me as some tamable beast. I would prefer you labeling me as just a beast. I have no idea what nonsense you are thinking right now. Dragons are untamable."

The air turns blue with his protestations; I hide a smile while listening to him prater on about the fiery of Dragons. The King does protest too much.

"And how many assassination attempts have you had on your person, my King?" I am curious, although I understand it may be a dangerous topic to bring up.

"Too many to count," he replies. "Again, it is the price you pay for being on top. As the most untamable beast."

He has to add that on.

I turn to face his magic. "And I think anything can be tamed with the right amount of generosity, kindness, and love. Look at Baby, for instance, his breed is usually nothing more than just animals."

"A liwolf is no Dragon. And I can tell you right now, no ice woman will tame me." The King has a satisfied purr in his voice as his fingers course down my body, making me tremble. "A wingless woman without vision and with blood as cold as snow."

His fingers hook on to the straps and lower my nightgown, revealing more of my cleavage. "But I do admit, her breasts are something to admire. And her body can possibly tame many men... Everything but true beasts."

Well, that confirms he is flirting... And I feel myself blush; my nipples turn hard. I want to touch him again. An urge suddenly overwhelms me as memories of our lovemaking crash into me.

What does his face feel like? Is it really handsome like the women speak of?

I reach up and touch his face for the very first time. My fingers graze across everything – his eyes, brows, nose, jaw, and finally his lips. They are soft for a man and smooth like a newborn baby.

"Is it true your eyes are like rubies?" I whisper.

My fingers return to his eyes, and I am surprised he hasn't stopped me. I find this very pleasing. I picture his Dragon's eyes when I think of it, their color.

Normally the King's reaction would be volatile, but he just closes his eyes. I find peculiarities, too. There are long stretches of his face that feel different, places where it sinks and dips in. The skin is unusual and not as it should be.

Is it from his tattoos?

I want to ask, but it would ruin the mood.

"I wouldn't say rubies, Mage. My mother used to say royals who inherit the blood-red eyes of the first Fire Dragon, Ori, foretell of the many we would slaughter as we age. The deeper the red, the more killing we will do." He further explains, "And she couldn't have been more right. I'm not sure if others have spoken about this to you, but eye color is important to Dragons. It tells us many things about a person."

"How will you explain mine then, King? Do they tell you anything?" I ask him, wondering what his thoughts were on my color-less eyes. My fingers return to his lips, caressing them, enjoying the feel of their shape and texture.

"Your eyes tell me a lot," he replies. "I see sorrow, misfortunate, tragedy, and a lifetime of darkness, but they're innocent, nonetheless."

Sorrowful... He can really tell that much by staring into my eyes? My breath hitches in my chest with the strength of my emotions.

My hands slip from his face, almost mesmerized by his words. "A bloodthirsty king and sorrowful queen. Oria will surely crumble."

"Let it." He pulls me inside.

Once we are past the balcony doors, he pushes his lips to mine, and I welcome it. I return his kiss with fervor.

Perhaps I should have let him kiss me earlier, but I was too angry and full of turmoil, not understanding the King at all. He pushes the rest of my nightgown off my body, his fingers dragging the straps all the way down, letting it crumple in a pile at my feet.

Passion. Eagerness. Need.

His mouth moves slowly over mine, tiny pecks and licks, gentle nibbles and rough bites, the King does a thorough job of exploring my lips. His tongue slips between them, inviting me to taste him. Our tongues dance to the old song of mating. Rough breathing breaks the silence as the air turns hot and heavy with our passion. Our desire to be one.

There is desperation in our need as time begins to slow down for the King and me. He reaches behind my back, and my bra loosens and falls. My breasts heave with a silent demand. Demand for his fingers, his mouth.

Ceremonies are no longer needed as I carry his heir already; the King knows this yet wants me. Pure lust envelops us. His mouth leads and mine follows. I suck on his lower lip wanting to get more of him. Our kisses continue to grow deeper when he suddenly pushes me, and my back collides with the wall. He grabs my hips and lifts me up so that our waists are at level. I can feel his hardness pressing into the soft core of me.

I grab hold of his shoulders in support, only for him to suck his breath loudly as he pulls away from our kiss. It sounds like he is in pain.

"What's wrong?" I ask, panting heavily.

"Don't touch me." He takes my left arm and slams it against the wall while his other hand holds my waist. "Just because I've been lenient with you and have decided to fuck you, it does not give you the right to touch me as you please. Your touch is disgusting and so is your magic. Why else would I recoil? Be coy and keep your hands off me."

What? What did I do? And disgusting? Wasn't he the one making those mewling sounds a few seconds ago? The King has gone mad.

"You are horrible..." I manage to whisper as my other hand curls into his shoulder. "If my magic is so foul, why bother doing this?"

"Because you had to go and ruin everything with Red. You wished her gone, so now you can replace her," he says cruelly, his fingers tightening around my left wrist.

I raise my other hand and strike him harshly across the face. There is more silence. The King is unfazed, continues to kiss me, this time with more aggression. The gentleness is lost on him.

I too act out, anger fueling my actions. I bite his lips, causing a guttural growl to arise from him. I savor the metallic taste on my tongue, my bloodlust appeased at his gasp, thrilled to have caused him some pain, wanting to elicit more.

I reach up and grab his hair, which isn't as gelled today. I pull the locks hard, making his lips move away from mine, a blood cry now leaving his throat. It has fueled his lust rather than the opposite. It seems me hurting him doesn't affect him as much as I thought it would. I still feel the warmth of his erection poking into my soft center.

His love for women is disgusting.

"Do you want things rough, Mage?" he asks as his hips rut against mine, making me whimper at the growing pressure against my already throbbing womanhood. "Because I can do rough."

I stop pulling his hair. The need for him is greater than my anger as he continues thrusting against me. "You're confusing... Why are you so confusing?"

He ignores my statement, and whispers in my ear, "Do you want it rough or not?" He lets go of my wrist, and I hear his clothes rustling. "I'm going to take it as a yes seeing how wet your little ice cunt is... How vulgar of you to like hurting me. Maybe you're not as innocent as I thought."

I am too embarrassed to answer such a question, and he doesn't give me much time to prepare before shredding the last piece of clothing from me. He tears my underwear off and pushes inside of me his full and hot length in one stroke.

My heartbeat thunders in my ears as blood pounds into my lower areas, sizzling with lust. I moan loudly as he catches me by surprise, and the King groans too, enjoying me to the fullest, his breath fanning out on my neck.

He pulls out before slamming back into me. I fist his hair, wanting something of his to touch and clench with each thrust of his hips.

"Guess you do like it rough then," he mocks, continuing to thrust in and out of me, his hand holding my hips tightly, fingers curling into my flesh.

He raises me higher up against the wall, lifting my thighs to wind around his hips, his mouth finding my breast, all at once. His tongue plays with my hardened nipple, sucking and biting it. I don't want his attention there; it is tender, making me whimper. He moves to my other breast, giving it his thorough attention.

His thrusts are hard, making me jolt each time he re-enters me. There is an urgency in him as he draws his hips back from mine, his cock leaving my folds almost completely, then rams hard into me, reaching my womb, filling me, making me wetter.

I arch. "Why won't you let me touch you?" My fingers curl into his scalp in frustration, wanting to dig them into his back, to feel and touch him.

He clicks his tongue in anger. "Is having me inside of you not enough?" One of his hands grabs my ass, groping it, while the other lingers at my hip. "I think this is more than enough contact. Stop being a greedy whore. Red never asks for anything, be like her."

His hand groping my rear slips down to where he is inside of me. His finger circles the stretched opening, which makes it more sensitive, and I stop breathing. His thrusts temporarily come to a halt, but his length remains hard.

"It's not enough," I murmur, a hatred growing for Red when she is innocent. I cannot help it.

My hand slips under his jacket and shirt, not caring about what he had said earlier. "I am not Red, and I am not a whore. I am your Queen and your wife. I want to feel you."

"No, you are not Red, she is your opposite. But wife and Queen, think as you wish, those are just titles. You will never have my heart if that is what you seek to possess; it is something you cannot have." He grunts and pants as he utters the words. I can feel his need to move, but he controls his yearnings.

I feel his muscles tense when I slide my hands to his back, going further up until I feel two large lumps. I caress and press on them, making the King go rigid.

"What is this...?" I question, angrily digging my nails into the hard lumps. I will make him see me; I will make him love me. That will be my revenge on this terrible Dragon King for his torment on my heart and mind.

"Wings... Even as a human, I have them. Every Dragon does, some just don't know how to use them. Now you've had your fun, put your hands back to where they belong." He begins moving inside me once more.

"No," I say, getting closer to him again. "If you're going to lay me as you are doing now, I have the right to touch you."

He growls, trying to be threatening, then shivers when I press my lips against his neck. I can smell and taste his sweat.

"Fucking Mage," he curses at me, and his thrusts become rougher. He has reached the point of no return. He now has both his hands on my hips, keeping me pinned against the wall.

I don't respond to him, moaning against his neck. My nails curl into his back. The King seems to respond more as I feel him begin to leak from his tip, even though he said earlier he despises my touch. I claw his back. He arches and groans, his thrusts becoming more erratic.

Is what he said another lie to leave his lips? What is the truth and what is false?

I question it but only briefly as he hits that particular spot inside of me which makes me cry out.

"Fuck." He continues to curse in my ear, a low moan leaving him after he releases a shaky breath.

It doesn't take him long to release inside of me, making me shudder, a warmth flooding my insides, coating everything it can. The King quickly pulls out, and I feel unsatisfied. I have not had my release.

He lowers me, his seed slipping out from within me onto my thighs and down my legs. My hands leave his body from under his clothes, and he suddenly turns me around. I was not expecting him to continue... I am not sure if he is going to... He never has before.

"I'm not done with you yet." He pants heavily, and I hear his jacket drop to the floor. More curses leave his mouth, and he sounds to be battling with the removal of his clothes.

I am ripped to him, then bent toward the wall once more. My arms cling to the wall for support. He re-enters me, his seed spilling out. His length is extremely hard.

He pulls in and out of me rapidly and I moan.

He questions me gruffly, "Now what will you hold on to, Mage? Huh?"

He's such a... But I am unable to complete my thought as the cold in my belly rises, overcoming the heat that has come with the King's release.

I lay my hands out flat and push back as the King's length continues to slam into me. Magic slips from my fingers, freezing the wall the more I feel pleasure, and he laughs. "You feel that good you let your magic seep from your body like that... See, you are a whore. My whore."

He grunts and continues to mock me. "If I let my magic out every time you make my cock feel good, the whole castle would be burning... And then I wouldn't have a place to rule from. Isn't that right, Mage?"

I make him feel so hot that he can burn his precious palace?

He lays his hand on top of mine, and the ice begins to melt, but the heat coming from him does not burn me as it should.

"Nnnngh, ah." I bite my lip, not wanting any weirder sounds to leave me.

Slap

Slap

Slap

I focus on the noises our bodies make, we meet and separate repeatedly. My lower region begins to clamp around him. He pants heavily, and his breaths fan out against my back.

My stomach tightens, preparing to release. Extreme cold is coiling inside me. I am feeling good and so is he, the mix between hot and cold delightful.

I finally snap as he too releases inside me for a second time. The warmth floods my belly, and with my release, comes the cold. I practically scream, and the King holds my hand tighter as I climax with him.

This time, it takes the King a few minutes to recuperate, and we hold each other in the afterglow of sex.

His fingers begin to loosen from mine, and he presses his face against my back. He admits, "I have never fucked one like you before..."

He slides out of me slowly. Again, I feel the King is ever so confusing, becoming angry or aggressive one moment and fine the next.

I am not fine.

I may feel bliss and my body may be relaxed, but my mind strays to Red and how he has touched her like this but gently like lovers. She had earned his love, yet I am treated like the whore. Red will receive retribution.

TWENTY-FIVE

AN UNBEARABLE HEAT

ALL I CAN SMELL IS the scent of roses. It perfumes the room with a sickeningly sweet smell that nauseates me. As if the heat is not terrible enough, I am coming to hate the smell of flowers.

I lean forward, and a sponge drags across my back slowly. Lukewarm water trickles from it, rushing down my flesh to join the bath again.

"We should have spotted it sooner." Catherine washes my back. "In the end, I think we fail as maids for the King to notice such things before us."

"I agree," replies Ava, who takes a cool washcloth and cleans my face. "I should have observed the changes beforehand. We're lucky Selene didn't fire us on the spot at such news. Her breasts have already started to swell. I thought it was just my imagination."

"I knew," Yanmei declares as she comes into the bathroom.

I recall the first time I met her and how she attempted to drown me. I am always wary of her and alert about her movements. She is not to be trusted, but now I know the moment she tries something, I will turn her hands to ice so that she can never lay them upon me again.

I am not the same woman who originally came to Oria.

It is hard to believe I was timid and frightened, especially to use the powers my people and I were gifted with – whether it was from my ancestors eating Dragon flesh or from something else. It is my legacy, and I am duty-bound to respect it.

Now I look forward to finding out what else I can do with it and where its boundaries lie. I want to learn the extent I can wield it and how long I can sustain it. I need to practice and hone it well so that it protects me and my child from all enemies, mine and King's. I am no longer scared to use my powers against anyone – whether it be an assassin, maid, or the King himself.

"I informed Selene that day, but she never got to inform the King as he retired to his room early. Then with the assassination attempt, I assume she thought it was best to wait on such news. But the King notices everything... and he soon found out," continues Yanmei.

"I see," Catherine sighs heavily, "I wonder why we weren't strung by our hair."

Things turn silent again, and Yanmei leaves the room, but I can still feel her eyes lingering on me, perhaps with jealousy.

"How is your nausea today, my lady?" questions Ava.

"Fine," I reply, neglecting to tell her the smell of flowers makes me feel ill. It is not entirely their fault for my foul mood. "The ice seems to make me feel less sick during the night."

"I assume the child will be of ice magic," says Catherine excitably. "The little Prince or Princess definitely won't be a Theka. Its magic is already plenty strong. I'm starting to feel it more and more with each passing day. And craving ice is strange. Especially eating it. What do you think, Ava?"

"It can still be of fire magic," argues Ava. "Though, for the Queen to carry a Dragon of fire magic, it can be risky, if not deadly. We best pray to the Sky Gods it is a Dragon of ice instead of fire."

"That is true... We never had such a thing occurring before, did we?" murmurs Catherine. "What can a Fire Dragon do to her if she is of ice...?"

"I'm not sure. From what I hear from Demos, Zachariah mentioned Aldis carried a Fire Dragon from King Diarmind. According to him, she was ill most days and had taken to bed from mid-pregnancy. Slowly she looked like a corpse with her face paler than death. The child caused her body to become hot and clammy, and her stomach burned and blistered. That is the only account we have of an Ice Mage and a Fire Dragon conceiving and what could potentially happen." Ava sighs as she finishes the tale, her voice petering out.

"That sounds horrible." Catherine wrings out the sponge, her voice barely a whisper.

The silence is overwhelming.

Fear stops me from voicing my worries; a frown mars my forehead as I begin to think. If this child is of fire like the King... I will suffer just like Aldis through a painful pregnancy. Not to mention Rhys and the others expect an Ice Dragon and a son, not a daughter. This child needs to be a son. I can have nothing else. He needs to be an heir to the King's throne. The pain is going to be all mine. I will suffer if it is a Fire Dragon, and I will suffer greatly if it's a girl.

What will happen to me and this baby?

Pangs of disquiet shoot through my chest, and I feel Ava place her hand on my shoulder. "My lady, it is time to get out of the bath now. Take my hand and be careful not to slip."

I reach out for her, taking care.

"You have a busy day today," says Catherine, who helps me further.

Standing up, I begin to feel more bouts of nausea as my dizziness increases, but I ignore it.

Worry is the emotion that holds my attention now.

I just hope what's inside of me isn't a Fire Dragon...

Breakfast is quiet, and all I can hear is the scraping of silverware against the plate. The smell of food is tempting, but I still feel the nausea welling in me. If I eat normal food, I'm afraid it will result in vomiting.

I chew the ice I requested, and I find the King back to his usual self. "Do all Mages not have taste buds? They eat such bland food, to begin with. And now you eat ice. Maybe that is how your ancestors survived when not dining on the Great Dragon, Kari." He decides to laugh at his own joke.

Things get silent when I choose not to respond to him. I am more focused on the turmoil the baby has caused my body. How things have changed. A few days ago, I had no idea I was pregnant or if I would become pregnant. And now I feel nothing but anxiety over this unborn child.

I lean back in my chair, trying to take deep breaths to ward off my nausea, and sweat collects on my forehead. I swallow the last of the ice. It must be the heat... It's amplifying my morning sickness – which in my case is mostly night sickness. This is the first time it has continued into the morning.

"King..." I murmur.

He puts down his silverware and looks up, his voice unpleasant. "What is it?"

"I can't take the heat, not like this. I need a cool place to stay today. Do you know of any such location?"

"Not in Oria," he replies, still eating his breakfast as I continue to hear the fork and knife sliding across the plate. "You will have to endure it. If you need to, have your maids run you an ice bath."

I want to roll my eyes at his answer. *What does he think I have been doing the whole time?*

I mutter, "I already had one this morning... Thank you. If you don't mind, I'm going to excuse myself now."

I stand up and exit the dining room and as soon as I leave, I hear the King toss his silverware on the table with a clang. He seems angry that I've left or perhaps at how abrupt I was with him. I'm not sure which as I don't hear him curse or trail after me. He just allows me to leave. And now, frankly speaking, I don't care. I am feeling too warm and growing hotter by the second.

IT IS A SHAME HOW QUICKLY THE HEAT RETURNS TO ORIA, conquering my magic and quickly melting any remaining snow in its path. I find myself yearning for it again. It will make things a lot easier for me. How I miss the cool atmosphere already.

I trace the teacup in my hand, liking the bumpy ridges on its side. Usually, I am unable to drink it until it is time for me to take my leave.

To make conversation and for the time to pass, I bring up Red. I explain to the women of the court that she isn't a whore of the King any longer and is actually a same-gender lover.

Things are silent as they hear this. They seem to be soaking in the information until I hear Beatrix scoff, "Ha, you think Red is a same-gender lover." She begins to laugh loudly. "What a joke. Any woman would rather say that than say she is constantly fucking your husband, that too in front of you. She is a whore; I am sure she has fucked women also. That is what she does and gets paid for. Don't get me wrong, Queenie, she's played you."

Beatrix's words get more vulgar each time we meet. I imagine this is how she speaks to others regularly outside of the castle, too. I do not mind her honesty, I enjoy it. Most days. Today, not so much.

I narrow my eyes and take a sip of my tea. "So you know Red personally?"

"I have seen her enough times bouncing on men's penises to know how lewd she looks, her enjoyment in being a whore. I mean why else would she turn down the King's offer to be a queen as you said?"

"Isn't your husband one of them?" questions Amelia, cutting her off. "Well, not your husband, the one who fathered your bastard."

As usual, Amelia and Beatrix don't get along, and they start bickering. They are always picking on each other's husbands, lovers, and even children. None of the ladies of the court truly enjoy each other's company. They are all very cutthroat with one another. But they are upfront about it.

"Yes, I blame her for stealing him away from me. Now it's like he doesn't even see me anymore or his son for that matter. I promised to make that Theka bitch pay. I still haven't got around to it yet," she complains.

"And how will you make her pay?" I question.

I see Willow's Dragon from the end of the table wrinkle its snout at me, showing she is displeased with my question. She is always quiet, not saying much at all. It seems she is forced to be here much like I was in the beginning.

Maybe Willow likes Red or dislikes the women being cruel or perhaps thinks I would take cruelty to the next step and have her killed. Alas, I am not sure of my intentions, but I remember the last time the King and I had sex, he kept telling me to be like her which infuriated me.

I did promise to make her pay in the heat of the moment...

But do I truly want to do such a thing? The King is right. Sweetness has changed to bitterness, and now anger.

"Men like redheads... Especially Dragons, I'm not so sure about Mages. Red has great hair," mentions Beatrix. "So, I always imagined my revenge would have something to do with her hair... Maybe put something in her drink to make it fall out. If you pay Viggo enough, he has the medication to do so. He made it for Rhys and other men who like baldness. The only reason I haven't done it already is because of the King. If he finds out I, or my household, have had anything to do with such a thing, he will kill us all. I can't risk the life of my son."

I hear Amelia speak. "But you're pregnant, my Queen. If you ever were going to do something so rash, I would suggest you do it now. You will be spared as you carry his child, and the King will no longer have any sexual attraction to Red. Hair is very important to him. It will be justice for all women, even if you are a Mage. I think it's vile for any man to stray from his wife's bed."

I continue to rub the side of my cup and don't respond directly to Amelia. "Mages like black hair or so I hear..."

"Oh." I hear another lady of the court speak up. "Interesting. So that means a lot of the Mages will like us Dragons. Most of us have dark hair, only a seldom few have light hair and usually, those who do, are foreigners."

"Yes..." I murmur, continuing to feel light-headed. "If I had sight, I assume I would like the King's hair."

"It's a shame you can't see our King, he really is a beauty," so says another one of the ladies.

"Indeed," someone else pipes up.

I recall the King's face when I touched it about a week ago and how everything was finely sculpted like one of the statues in the courtyard. And I cannot agree more, eyesight will make everything a lot more real to me.

What is it like to see?

I will not even have the luxury of seeing my own child, and that thought strikes agony in me, but I can't do anything about it. It is something that can never be fixed. *Never.*

No magic is strong enough to cure a curse or an illness this powerful.

I just have to live with it.

"DOES THAT FEEL BETTER, MY LADY?" ASKS CATHERINE, WHO takes a bag of ice to my body, placing it on my forehead like I am ill.

"It's still hot," I complain, feeling uncomfortable even during the night when things usually are much cooler. My skin is covered in a thin layer of sweat as I lie on the floor with the pillows, a place where Baby usually sleeps, but now I have usurped him.

"This is all we can do." Ava attempts to fan me. "It might be summer... But it is only the beginning."

"She will only continue to suffer. The heat will grow worse each passing day into the season. You wait and watch. She will be miserable," Yanmei warns as she attempts to get Baby to eat. "Her kind should have never been allowed in a place like Oria, much less carry a Dragon child, but this is what the others desire."

"How do you explain Kari? He was an Ice Dragon, and he was born here!" I snap, the heat getting to me more and more. And now I couldn't care about what should have or not have happened. I need a solution, or I need her to shut up and leave.

Yanmei is silent, not used to my outbursts, but only for a second. She continues, "That was long ago... Maybe things were different back then."

What does she know!

I'm sure Oria was just as hot for him, and that is why he took to the cold places like Yulor.

Ava replies, "This is not a time to be fighting, just try to relax, my lady. Anger will cause you to overheat. Sleep if you can. It's getting late."

"How can I when I am being boiled alive?" I complain as if they can do something more for me. I don't even know why I am like this.

Why am I?

"The heat isn't that bad, my lady, now that it is nighttime," says Catherine who also picks up a fan to cool me off.

I glare toward her magic, which is faint, and I want to say something, but my tongue stops as a coil of heat forms in my stomach.

No No NO!

I sit up, the weird feeling of heat settles and stays. The bag of ice falls off my head and onto my lap.

"What is the matter, my lady?" questions Ava as she stops fanning me.

"There is heat in my belly, and it is intense." I grab at the fabric of my dress, my voice expressing the worry I feel.

There is silence, and Catherine mutters, "Fire magic..."

"The others won't be happy. Her only job is to produce an heir of ice magic," says Yanmei. "I'm sure the King will be disappointed."

"As I said this morning, the baby's magic can change, nothing is confirmed yet. It will only be confirmed after the eight-week period," Ava explains. "It's only been four weeks now, so four more to go."

I inhale heavily, feeling as if the King's magic is trapped inside of me, and in a sense, it is. This is his child as much as it is mine. Therefore, his vile and disgusting magic is inside of me.

"Please revert back to ice magic," I say out loud, speaking to the child inside of me.

The heat does not die down then, and it doesn't for the rest of the night. As the days grow longer, its magic grows stronger. Where it was just a small flame at the beginning of summer, now it is a raging ball of fire.

TWENTY-SIX

FALSE YET TRUE

THERE IS a strange container and another. My fingers run over an oddly shaped glass slowly. It is wide at the bottom and narrow at the top. The next object I touch is long and narrow with a cork. I even trace a tightly coiled glass tube that connects the two vials together.

They were all very peculiar.

Some of these are filled with powders; others rattle when shaken, something solid, I suppose. Yet there are others that contain liquids. This place is a combination of magic and chemistry.

As I move to the inner bowels of the room, I discover a few containers which hold heat within them yet have no source of magic or fire. The best are the ones that are ice cold permanently. I am more than astounded when I come across them as they are the ones that cool my flushed skin, and my touch lingers on them for the longest. I have no idea how all these have come about.

My fingers reach the edge of the table, which marks the end of my exploration of Doctor Viggo's exotic workroom, packed with interesting objects. But what holds my curiosity is how he has trapped magic and made it work for him. The Water Dragons are certainly different.

I entered the room a little over an hour ago with the same wonderment as I could not smell anything including Doctor Viggo. *How can this man modify magic?* Though, when he comes closer to me for the examination, I can perceive it is barely there.

The smell is distinct and familiar, but I cannot place it despite how hard I try to recall. I turn my head, seeing his aura, the essence of his magic, approach me. It is as interesting as him.

It reminds me of tranquil water, where the ripples, though present, are barely seen. His personality seems to be stoic and level-headed, a man of reason, much like Dakari. Perhaps men of knowledge are alike in this manner; it takes a certain mold of a person to have that much of patience.

The last time I was here on this same table, I was getting my wounds stitched by him, lying bare and vulnerable. The memories are unpleasant and speak of a haunting pain, but now I am here for a better reason. I touch my stomach feeling my baby's magic - fire - through the fabric of my dress.

The clunk of a lid closing followed by the clasp of a lock precede him. His steps are soft and almost indecipherable from others. He stops in front of me and soon, I feel his hand on mine, comforting me. It is soothing and cool, just like the touch of an Ice Mage, the more that I think about it.

He presses into my palm a wooden egg with a flat bottom and narrow mouth. "Inside are the vitamins, the pills needed to keep you and your baby healthy. Take two every morning with breakfast. And here is the other thing you requested." He sets a bundled cloth in my other hand, the shape unwieldy, causing my brows to knit. "Wrapped in it is a jar with ointment. It is used by a lot of Water Dragons. We are easily burned from fire magic ourselves."

I hold the jar to my chest, my mind now at peace. I think about Red and what Beatrix and Amelia had spoken about at tea. The King's words even now make me flush with jealousy. I nearly open my mouth to ask Viggo for something to deter Red.

But I stop, envisioning the many unpleasant scenarios involving the King and me. Also, I cannot do that to her. She was nice to me, and she is the King's childhood friend. What Red told me sounded authentic – she is in love with Yanmei. I need to let this go. I have to for her, the King, and my sake. My child deserves better. I find myself veering away from cruelties and pouring my thoughts unto my unborn child.

"You promise to keep this a secret?" I question him. "About the baby possibly being of fire magic..."

"Yes, I am your physician. I will not inform Rhys or the others what occurs in my office." His kind voice assures me, and I hear him adjust his glasses. "Not even the King."

"Thank you," I say and when I start to leave the room, Viggo touches my shoulder, stopping me from walking any further.

"Vrai?"

"Yes?"

"Has the King... Has he mentioned anything about Earath? Specifically, about Chi?"

The person whose name he alludes to escapes my memory. I frown, trying to bring the Dragon into my mind. "I..."

"She is their ambassador. She sang at the festival. You met her briefly," he reminds me.

"Ah yes, now I know who you speak of," I reply, finally putting her name to her person. "She has such a beautiful voice."

"Yes, she does. Though do you know if the King has mentioned about her return here?" he asks.

"I'm not sure. Last I knew, King NuJu angered our King as he kept denying his request to meet. I assume things aren't well between the two countries. Why?"

"I see." He doesn't say much else. "That woman... You can say she and I have some unfinished business. If you can, keep me updated since my brother has a tendency to forget to mention things to me about what is happening in the castle."

I nod, wondering what he means by unfinished business, and his hand slips from my shoulder as I turn to leave.

He calls out to me once more, "And don't hesitate if you need anything, I'm always here. Or if you need someone to talk to. Our discussions and dealings will always be private even from the King and others."

I nod once more and slip out. I walk down the hallway and up the stairwell that is seemingly void of even servants today as I head back to my room.

I am glad my child is okay during his examination. Though Doctor Viggo did explain it is still too early to tell and sometimes impossible to know if the poison I ingested will have any adverse effects.

Upon returning to my quarters, I place the vitamins on a small table next to my bed and in its drawer, the ointment. It needs to be kept a secret for now; I do not want anyone else finding out. Not even my maids. Too many people knowing about it is dangerous. Secrets have a way of escaping in this palace.

Behind me, my bedroom door opens. I know my maids do not bother to knock anymore, but it is too early in the day for them. The only one besides them will be the King and sure enough, when I turn, I see his magic.

Strange...

Normally he isn't around during this time, always too busy with his duties.

"Do you need something, my King...?" I ask of him before correcting myself. "My lord?" It feels strange to call him by this title. I find myself slipping at times.

I hear Baby stand from his favorite pillow and walk over to him as if greeting him. After the poisoning, he seems to enjoy the King's presence as much as he likes me.

That is new...

"A few days ago, you asked me for a frigid place to stay," he says quietly, and I wait for him to continue, wanting to know where this is leading.

"There is a place, not frigid but cool," he adds, with a bite in his tone. There it is, his usual pleasantness. Politeness seems to be lost as a virtue in this Kingdom.

After a pause and gauging my response, he continues without the harshness in his tone. "It is located along the borders of Oria and Yulor, and it is where a lot of Thekas have gathered and built their villages since the last king. And as it is before, the same Duke with Dragon blood governs them. I have contacted this man in hopes he has somewhere decent for us to stay, but his behaviors are quite queer."

"It's cold... And both of us...?"

I cannot believe this is the King speaking. *What's wrong with him? He is being too nice.*

"Yes, I am not lying. It is known to snow there, but don't expect much as I said this man is eccentric and bizarre. He does not even have the courtesy to show his face at gatherings since..." He falls quiet before snapping at me. "What were you going to say, Mage? Why are looking at me like this? Do you think me ill in the head?"

"No! This is just so unexpected. It's just taken me by surprise, that's all." More like shock, I would say. But I am not going to say anything, else he withdraws the offer.

"I would be a fool to send you off alone when pregnant with one or a few of your maids. Now more so than ever when there has been an assassination attempt on your life already and that happened when they did not know you carry my heir. But again, do not get your hopes up, I doubt the Duke will welcome us. He should since I am his king, but I will not force my hand if he doesn't."

He told me not to expect much, but I am thrilled at the idea of what might be a reality.

"Who will take care of the Kingdom?" I ask. "Rhys...?"

He chuckles, his amusement so evident in his aura I couldn't help gazing at it, and he walks toward me. "No, I will appoint Zachariah in charge while we're gone. He's a bit rough, but he's to be trusted. He won't betray me, and I will give him specific rules not to start any wars. He's served my father and never once has he betrayed him. He is loyal to my family."

Trusting a man who wished to gut me the first time he met me doesn't leave a good taste in my mouth. It seems the King trusts him for some reason. So, a bond might exist between them that I haven't seen before as most times, they seem to be at each other's throats because of disagreements.

Zachariah, in the end, did say he respected me... So perhaps that is a side the King sees more than just the gutting one.

He stops a few inches away from me. "But first, I must do a few things, like take care of that pesky Child King and once again, postpone the expedition to the East... I'm sure Rhys will be thrilled with that one. I just got everything mapped out. What a waste. Then I also won't be here to monitor Kingston and Dakari as I have been doing." He 'tsks' and says to himself, "I will have to inform Zachariah of what is going on between the two... Everything will have to wait until you give birth."

"I told you to send a woman with Chi when it comes to Earath. You didn't listen..." I start.

"Women are far too delicate to be meddling in affairs involving entire lands. Earath only sent a woman because they belittle me, I'm sure of it." He fusses again, growing agitated as he usually does.

"Or they trust Chi and the other women to hold their own," I say. "Not all women are delicate just as not all men are strong. I know quite a few women since coming here who can definitely fight and are intelligent enough to speak to officials or a king himself."

The King is quiet, so I give him more advice. "Call for Ambassador Chi again. She is still our ally in this situation and perhaps select a trusted female to go with her, one who is charming but also loyal to you. Let her work her way inside the Kingdom as she is a Dragon woman and not perceived much of a threat like a man. My King, let her speak on your behalf. The whole thing can be resolved so simply."

"I will think about it," he says. "I will need to find such a woman... However, I can send for ambassador Chi again in the meanwhile." He tilts my head up, his fingers tucking under my chin, and lays a quick kiss on my lips before pulling back. The small action has me blushing.

"Tonight, come to my room after dinner. I believe you know where it is," he says as his fingers slip away and his claws trail against my skin.

My first invite to his room... I never thought he... And to kiss me like that...

I absent-mindedly hear him leave, the closing door telling me he is gone, but he has left me with so much to think about and focus on.

I can't help but recall the flower which I had frozen. Tucked away safely in my drawer along with the ointment now, my secrets are hidden from the world. I feel excited and joyous, more than just about the chance of going to the cold border.

Perhaps I might see more glimpses of this King.

And perhaps I am no longer the False Queen I thought I was.

TWENTY-SEVEN

RISE

In the late afternoon, the first rains of summer descend on Oria, pouring and pounding against the stone fortress relentlessly.

The winds whip through the tall towers, leaving behind wicked and despicable howls that sound like they originate from the belly of a yokjok, a creature of legend that haunts both this land and Yulor. These creatures are said to mimic the cries and screams of tormented souls, dead and living, and their sounds are often likened to the noises of the thunderstorms, so Yanmei says.

I am not certain if she speaks the truth or makes up tales. If it is the latter, I gather she is trying to frighten me along with Catherine. Ava is more practical than us and calls it nonsense, but either way, I cannot help but think of the tortured souls, especially when the thunder rumbles and shakes the stones of the castle. Every crack of lightning has me jumping up and the roar of thunder makes me want to clap my hands over my ears.

I am not used to the loud noises caused by thunderstorms yet, though Yulor does have rains but not like this. They mostly have blizzards and the blustery winds that accompany them, but now when I think about it, I begin to recall the last storm I had last experienced with my mother.

It sounded as if yokjoks were lurking in the squalls, screaming. I had nightmares about it for many years, alone in my tower.

The King... I wonder if he believes in such things and glance in his direction. He has been oddly quiet and again unpredictable. He chooses to stand a distance away from the dining table, next to the large glass doors which open onto the balcony. He is most likely watching the beautiful, but dangerous, outdoors. The stormy winds probably call to the primal nature of the Dragon.

Emotions are going to be wild today at the table.

A bolt of lightning strikes the ground, rattling the plates and silverware, meaning it has hit nearby, followed by the boom of the rolling clouds along with the heavy showers.

I feel the remnant vibrations under my feet, a sudden fear making the hair on my neck rise. It is eerie to think that nature has such powerful magic; kings and queens cannot rival against them, not even my husband in his Dragon form.

The King breaks the silence, being the first to speak, "Never leave the castle when it is raining, Mage. Storms like these in Oria are dangerous, even to Dragons. I'm assuming your kind, too, won't fare greatly in these conditions."

"Yes, such nasty weather, especially lightning. It has been known to strike even Dragons dead," Cell speaks up. "Except Zachariah, by some miracle. He should be dead by now with the number of times he has been struck. I am hoping one day he stops being lucky, but each time he surprises me by surviving. The bastard refuses to die."

"Nasty!" Zachariah bellows, his mouth full of food, "Storms like these are what keeps me alive! I am no pussy afraid of the damn rain or lightning."

"I think your brain has been damaged from it," mutters Gregory derisively.

"It gives me vitality, perhaps you should give it a try, boy. The way the whores speak of you, a little shock might do you some good."

Snickers escape some of the men, Fonzell being one of them. "Inso-"

"King, will you not eat?" questions Rhys, making Gregory stop his retort midway. He, like the rest, is interested in the King's reply, picking up on his strangeness like me.

"I am not hungry," he says, annoyance lancing his tone. "And does it matter if I eat or not?"

"No... I thought it would be nice to announce the—" Rhys begins.

"I know what I must do, though I am sure they have all heard about it by now," sighs the King.

"What have we heard?" questions Lucius.

The King stops when he reaches his seat and announces, "The Queen is pregnant... There, are you happy now, Rhys?"

Rhys is silent, probably angry yet hiding his ire, if I were to guess, as I see his magic flare at the King's comment but die shortly after. He is one man to keep a watch on. *Is the King right to trust him so much?*

The King sits down after his abrupt announcement and fills a glass of wine. The sweet smell of heart fig hits my nose, making me crave the liquid, but it is temporarily forbidden because of the pregnancy.

"Oh, this is definitely old news," remarks Cell. "Once she told Beatrix, it spread quite quickly. That woman loves being one of the first to share any news or gossip."

"I knew nothing of this," declares Fonzell. "You've probably only heard because you fuck everything with tits."

Cell scoffs, "Not everything. That would have to include the Orc women. I am not that low. And actually, I was one of the first few people to hear about it, and it wasn't from that woman. I heard the news from the King himself."

"So that means you've fucked Mages like the Queen?" Fonzell interrupts, sounding disgusted.

"Yes. Just one, though. And I am so glad you're interested in my sex life," mocks Cell. "Maybe because you don't have one."

I hear Zachariah laugh at his friend and Fonzell growls, his magic flares more wildly as he stands, flinging his plate at Cell, but it smashes against the wall, shattering into tiny pieces. So, I assume Cell has dodged it.

"Must we fight like savages every time we gather?" Rhys stands up from his seat, and I am surprised he is the one snapping instead of the King who remains relatively quiet during everyone's conversation at the table.

"Well, tell your fucking water rat to shut his trap," growls Fonzell.

"I don't control Cell or Viggo as they're not my children," Rhys says. "But if one more plate smashes against the wall, you will personally be buying another or have it subtracted from your earnings at the beginning of the month. Oria does not give you title, land, and coins to act like an animal."

Rhys sits down in his seat, and Fonzell is silent at this rebuke but obviously peeved as he has never been reprimanded before, not when so many other bad things happen when they gather together.

"Well, now that everyone is fucking quiet, I can finally speak." The King sighs heavily again. "I want to inform you all that I sent for ambassador Chi again in one last attempt to contact King NuJu from the lands of Earath."

"It is useless, my King," says Gregory. "The Child King has made it apparent he wants nothing to do with Oria. Why will this attempt be any different from the last?"

"This is not my plan but your Queen's," responds the King. "She suggests we send a woman back with Chi as this is what she believes King NuJu will feel most comfortable with."

"And where will we find such a trusted woman in Oria? She would be representing us. One mistake can be fatal for us and our people. She has to be trained before we can send her," wonders Lucius.

"Not to mention we are to trust the Queen on this?" mocks Fonzell, sarcasm dripping in his voice.

He does hate me so...

"And me," snaps the King. "I would not have put forth this idea if

I hadn't thought about it from all angles. Sending a man has been disastrous as seen last time. I knew it, yet I did it anyway."

"Do you have a woman in mind?" questions Zachariah.

"I have thought of one," the King replies. "But there is always a chance of betrayal, especially with this woman. But I have something she wants... that only I can give her."

My curiosity peaks at the mention of the woman by the King. *What is this thing the woman wants – money or something else from the King?*

"You're not speaking of her, are you?" mutters Rhys as if knowing who the King has thought of. He sighs distastefully. "I'd rather trust one of the Queen's maids than her."

"Shall we go with the choice of a Theka since that seems to be your preference?" the King asks Rhys.

Rhys remains quiet, thinking of his choices, and Cell speaks up, "I'd rather go with this mystery woman than a Theka."

"I agree," says Gregory.

"Me too. As long as she has her Dragon... Thekas are much too spiteful and more likely to betray." Erik is usually quiet during dinners, so it is strange to hear him speak up.

Erik is another mystery just like this woman they speak of. He does not have many opinions, comments, or suggestions. He is just there every time at the table – I know nothing of him.

"Who exactly is this woman?" I turn to the King.

"None of your concern, my Queen. Only Rhys and I need to know." I frown at the abrupt tone of his voice.

I hate it when I am not allowed to know anything but snippets.

"Well, I think it's decided," the King pushes on as if I have not spoken. "Though I don't expect everything to go well, it is our only choice. As far as I can tell, there are no other candidates to fill this position to travel to Earath and attempt to speak to King NuJu."

"Now, I think we are done with our discussions unless anyone else has something to say," the King concludes.

"What about the expedition?" questions Fonzell.

"Postponed," the King mutters.

"May I ask why?" Fonzell continues.

"Personal reasons, Fonzell... No, obviously, it is the Queen's fucking pregnancy. Assassination attempts will be higher now, though once my heir is born, I will be able to leave in peace, knowing I do not have to risk being overthrown. As long as I have loyal men to watch over the Queen and the child," the King snaps. "Is there anything else?"

Someone clears their throat after a moment of silence, and they speak up, "Actually yes. I have matters concerning Yulor and the Ice Mages."

"What of it?" The King's voice is stern and seems to be serious, concerning my people.

"Princess Alana, the Queen's daughter, has requested she has the right to visit Oria as part of the ten-year treaty you signed with their King during the winter. Technically, Mages can come to our land just as we can go on to theirs. It just hasn't been attempted before... by anyone," the man explains.

Alana... My half-sister, her mother is Lydia.

"Then we can't deny her?" questions the King.

"No," replies the man.

"If she or any other Mages arrive, I can deal with them. They're my people," I interrupt their conversation. Through my sister, I can learn about Lydia and get to her more easily.

"Good. My Queen, you will be dealing with Princess Alana when the time comes. I do not want her wandering about freely without being watched," commands the King. "Except you will also be accompanied by someone here at the table everywhere, never alone."

I silently agree with him, knowing the King will not change his mind about me being watched with her. He is stubborn and especially so with his men surrounding him. Pushing him will get me less than more.

"I think we're done now. If there is anything more, it can wait till tomorrow." The King stands.

"Orval. I do have something to discuss with you in private. What we discussed earlier..." Ukiah speaks up, and I see his Dragon for the first time.

Its eyes match the King's – ruby red. While his body is smaller than the average Dragon in size, it is quite an odd sight. *Maybe Ukiah is young? I can't tell from his voice.*

What has me curious is how this man, or boy, addresses the King by his first name. *I am not allowed to do so...*

"We will discuss it further. And for the rest of you – you can go," orders the King, and I hear the boyish Dragon, Ukiah, follow him out of the room.

Once both of them have departed from the group, I question some of the men at the table, hoping one will answer. "Is that a boy who left with the King? Do you let boys in the army?"

Zachariah laughs. "Ukiah is secretly one of the King's favorite men, Queen. And he is far from a boy. He's almost as old as I. And to answer your other question, yes, we do, but they have to prove themselves."

"He's short, is all," remarks Cell as he stands up from the table. "But not to be taken lightly, criminal blood runs in his lineage."

Criminal?

"He's like fire, wild and insane, true to his nature. Though whatever you do, do not mention his stature or call him boy by mistake. It is a sore spot for him as the rest of his family is tall..." Gregory cautions.

"Criminal blood!" scuffs Zachariah after taking a swig of his drink. "The man comes from a line of warriors, and he is unlike some of the sniveling shits who parade around here acting as one. Half the shits around me should be sucking on their mother's tits."

"If you want to believe fighting in the arena makes you a warrior, that's fine. It's a matter of opinion, nothing to get so heated over," says Cell.

"Arena?" I question.

Lucius speaks up before anyone else can. "It is a place of entertainment during the summer solstice. Anyone can participate, including criminals. They have a chance of freedom if they win, which hasn't happened in a long time. And as for the rest of the year, it is used solely to punish criminals... You have been there before when the King had that man stoned to death for pelting a tiny pebble at you."

His snide remark – it's meant to antagonize and belittle me, which sours my mood slightly. *A tiny pebble... indeed.*

Gregory gives his input. "To sum it up, Ukiah's ancestor, Carnelian, was a criminal who earned freedom in the arena. But that isn't the interesting part of the story. Carnelian was said to have kept coming back to participate year after year despite gaining his freedom. Some said he'd developed some sort of sick fetish, others said he was insane, but his descendants are like him, drawn to the arena year after year. Eventually, one of the kings made this an event to participate in and watch for fun."

"I don't understand the point, to potentially die over something so frivolous..." Cell says.

"He enjoys sparring with the King and also battling," Zachariah concludes.

"Still seems foolish..." Cell hums.

"He is also the first one to join the council without having any royal blood," Fonzell comments, "He has earned his place, unlike some."

"Will it happen this year? And does the King participate?" I ask.

"Of course," answers Zachariah. "You will have to attend with him. The King fights the winner of the arena."

"No doubt that will be Ukiah," says Cell, shaking his head. "If the King didn't enjoy women so much, I would assume they were lovers."

Zachariah laughs loudly. "I dare you to say that to the King's face. You won't be left with a pretty one to shove under the women's skirts."

"Yeah! I would like to see that," agrees Fonzell, his Dragon leering at Cell's.

"I'm not the one who picks fights with the King," Cell sasses.

"Well, no... You say things behind his back like a weaselly fat water rat. At least we speak to the King truthfully," growls Fonzell.

I can see Cell's Dragon, its head rising insidiously from the darkness which seems to ripple like water. The snout tears through it, lips peel back, and the mouth opens in a snarl. The teeth are thin and pointed; they are like the bristles of a brush but are in fact needles, sharp enough to shred the flesh in one bite. A low guttural growl comes from it as its neck pulsates and flares. Its huge evil eyes, filled with malice, dart everywhere taking in the scene.

This is the first time I have seen his Dragon, and I watch as it dips behind the darkness slowly which hides its entirety. The only evidence it is still there is the ripples that grow closer to Fonzell's Dragon.

Rhys intervenes, "Cell, think logically. If you start a fight here, you will die. We are not of their kind."

"No, you and he aren't," hisses Zachariah, standing. "If he starts a fight on land, he will die. He's a fucking water rat who doesn't realize he's surrounded by Fire Dragons!"

"And we are just itching to tear him apart," adds Fonzell.

All around me at the table, I see the Fire Dragons jeering the ones who are different from them, teeth bared, their bodies in defensive postures.

"We can fight on land. I can prove it to you." Cell is offended by their words. "Not just the water..."

I see the one-eyed Dragon of Zachariah, drawing its lips back further as if smiling, but not in a friendly way. "Oh really... Prove it," he challenges.

Just when all hell is about to break loose, I stand up from my chair. I do not want there to be fights and discrimination just because there are different types of magic, Dragons, species, and people.

It sickens me...

It reminds me of the times in childhood when I used to approach the other children during play, only to be left behind. A disabled child was one no one wanted to play with.

I had to be helped at times. I could not run without caution like they could. All my life I have been treated differently by my own people and now by these Dragons.

"Enough!" I yell and all the Dragons' eyes turn toward me. "Just because he is a Water Dragon and I am an Ice Mage, you hate and despise us! You're like little kids picking on a child who is different. I know because I used to be that child, a Mage without sight. If you're going to work together, be ruled under one kingdom, you will have to accept the people inside if they're good, however different they might be!"

Zachariah hisses, "Queen, I was just beginning to respect you... But I think these are matters you should stay out of."

Gregory stands up, walking toward me before his Dragon leers. "Zachariah is right. Stay out of this, Queen, and leave!"

He reaches out to grab me, probably to push me out of the room. When his hand just grazes my skin, I automatically spike my own magic, not wanting to be intimidated, as I am above these men as their queen.

I am no longer that princess who has been neglected, abused, and bullied. I am a woman, a strong one, much more than these men can ever be. I am a queen, though not one like Lydia, and nobody can deny my right anymore.

I am the true Queen of Oria and the Dragons better heed. My magic surges ahead with a wave of ice, sharp and hard. He screams, and I assume his hand has been pierced. His Dragon retreats, screeching.

I command the room when I see the other Dragons grow nastier by the minute, though some are cautious. "No. I will not leave. I am your Queen, and you are duty-bound to respect me!"

I bang my hands on the table and my magic rips through me with the force of my anger and everything in its path freezes over – the tabletop, plates, glasses, chairs.

"If you think we would let you hurt one of our own without repercussion, you're wrong, little Mage," mocks Lucius as he starts to approach me, but someone stops him, and I hear Zachariah speak next.

"Leave it be. She is serious. Her magic equals the King right now. If you want to die, then be my guest."

I see all the Dragons in the room staring at me, waiting, watching but not moving forward. Some recoil into the darkness when my ice grows across the table.

Once none of them makes any other move, I continue. "As Rhys has said, you are Noblemen, but you act like animals. Perhaps you Fire Dragons need to start learning from the other lands and behave correctly. You are no better than the Mages or the Water Dragons you despise."

Their magic is flaring dangerously but in response, I make mine do the same, and I see more Dragons slink back into the darkness.

"Now start with no fighting. It will do you some good."

I see some of the King's men submit to me, though many still have the bloodlust. I loosen my control over the ice magic and turn to leave when I feel the air shimmer, and one of the Dragons charges at me from behind. I notice his magic as I turn.

The one from before. Lucius. *They never learn, do they?*

I close my eyes for a second and think hard. I don't want to kill him, the King will not like it, but I want them to stop attacking me once and for all.

I have no other choice; words have no effect on them. I need to show them how to respect each other. The only language these Dragons understand is power. My need to survive produces a surge in me, and ice courses through my blood producing thin bands as they reach my fingertips.

I focus my magic on Lucius and within seconds, tendrils of ice, smooth and flexible like a rope, leave my fingers and wind around him.

I know shock must be flaring on his face as each strand tightens around him, making it difficult to move. His magic wars with mine, but as I keep feeding more ice into the strands, I can see mine taking over.

His Dragon tries to break free, but the ice stops its struggle midway. It writhes in pain, roaring and wanting to spew its fire, then all of a sudden, it quietens.

Silence echoes in the room once the screeches stop. The men halt in their tracks, their Dragons unsure. I look at their magic, ready to take them on. I want to show them what this queen can do, staring at their Dragons right in their eyes.

It takes a few seconds to have my command over them, and each of the mighty Dragons bows down, their eyes downcast, submitting to the magic in me.

Lightning strikes at the very moment. They have completely surrendered.

"No more fighting... I tire of it." I repeat, mimicking the King.

"Yes, my Queen." Zachariah is the first to say as I hear him sink to the floor. Once he does, the rest follow suit. Even Rhys. They're bowing to me as they should.

Complete fealty to me. All the councilmen except one have pledged to me, accepting me as their queen.

I don't believe it. I have their loyalty. My heart pounds as I see no signs of their Dragons or magic. There is nothing but silence.

I walk out the door, and no one else attempts to attack me. When I shut it, I lay my hand over my heart which is thundering. Thrill, amazement, and some traces of fear course through me.

That was... exciting.

I smile before continuing forward. My heart will not calm anytime soon. I know now I can become a true Queen of Oria. It all starts with power.

TWENTY-EIGHT

BLOOD IN CHAINS

KING ORVAL'S POV

The amber-colored alcohol falls into a see-through glass without a drop splashing out. Ukiah always has a steady hand, no matter how much he drinks. And the bastard has no respect, none as usual, going through my liquor cabinets and taking whatever he wants.

It is something I will not tolerate from others, but this behavior is normal for him and his family. They take what they want, whenever it pleases them, from the poor to the rich, they do not care.

At least the alcohol he selects is inexpensive, common liquor found in all the households of the noblemen and rich merchants. He considers his taste to be fine when he actually has the taste of a criminal, his roots bleeding through. It is amusing to watch, especially when he starts defining a quality woman.

The man is short in stature, my other generals loom over him, but I have to admit, he is strong, his build muscular and lithe. It will be ignorant of anyone who does not think this man to be dangerous, and tragedy will befall them.

Women fawn over his looks, power, and status.

His hair is long but styled in a certain fashion, shaved on both sides and pulled up in a ponytail, something I often see in the slums of the city. Though what fascinates me are his eyes – a dark and dull red like that of dried blood. Not many have such colored eyes.

Tattoos cover his body, black ink which is similar to mine. And a single marking decorated his face, a line starting from his chest and ending at his lower lip, revealing he is on my council.

In Oria, it is illegal to have any designs on the face unless directly under me or having royal blood. There is also a requirement that you battled in the arena at least once to prove yourself to the royal family and the people that you are worthy of such tattoos.

"So, what news do you bring me of the Duke, or is it something else?" I question from my desk.

"It's about the Duke. He is, of course, as strange a man as he has always been," Ukiah says, drinking. He is nosy, his eyes scan my office and private collection of books, which irks me slightly. "I spoke about you and your Queen staying there, but he didn't respond to me or acknowledge I had even spoken..."

"So, I can assume his answer is no." I continue to watch Ukiah.

He walks over to the bookshelf, running his finger over the many spines before selecting one and sliding it out. "Yes, I guess it would have been a no, but I persuaded him enough to say he has a small, old castle in which you and the Queen can reside temporarily."

I am quiet, not liking the impression Ukiah has made of me, but what did I expect when I sent him out to the Theka villages governed by a slightly eccentric and unstable Duke?

"Good, but next time listen and do not use threats," I warn him, but he doesn't give me much of a response and only a small glance in my direction.

"I am curious about something, Orval. You mentioned sending a woman to Earath this time?" he questions me.

"Yes, and thanks to you and your *persuasive* ways, my ties with Earath are strained now more so than ever." I look away from him, still angry over the fact he has failed me when I had sent him with Ambassador Chi.

He had terrorized some of King NuJu's councilmen, threatening to burn them alive if their King continued to refuse a meeting with me. Fortunately, the ambassador stopped him in time from committing an act of war.

And now he has the audacity to explain the benefits of war!

"War is the only way you will make them amenable to you, all through pure power and domination. Sending a woman based on the Queen's advice might just push Earath over the edge." He slides the book back on the shelf after looking at a few pages and losing interest fairly quickly.

He finishes what's in his glass and puts it back on my desk, instead of the coaster. I know he glanced at it previously, and this irritates me more. His way is always deliberate provocation, even if it with me, his king.

He stares down at me as he questions with narrowed eyes, "Why listen to that Queen of yours all of a sudden?" I look up at him in askance and he continues, his tone dipped in suspicion, "You haven't begun to love and trust her, have you? Love is not for a king. This is what gets kings killed. You cannot love, especially a woman of ice. Their hearts are cold, and she will betray you the moment she can. I have watched her from time to time. She grows confident, and she yearns for power. Now that she bears a Dragon child of your royal blood, you're giving her even more power over Oria. Do you truly want this?"

"I have never wanted children, but it is needed. You know this. If I find the Queen a threat, or if she becomes one, I will handle her. I am not weak, Ukiah. Or do you perceive me as such?"

He gazes at me, using the silence to belittle me, as if the question requires deep thinking. "In my tribe, an heir is chosen not because of blood but because of power. If you're strong, you are chosen to be the next in line."

"Why are you mentioning this now?" I am inquisitive about what goes on in his mind.

"Because I think Oria should change its old ways," he declares with a slight grin as he sits on the edge of a leather chair. "Your heir to the throne should not be that child your Queen bears, but someone young and full of power. Take the arena, for example, we use it every year. Why don't you choose who will succeed your throne by whoever wins this year or the next? Can you really trust a child that an Ice Mage bears and whom she can manipulate until she eventually kills you and gets your son to take everything you worked so hard for?"

I never thought about it before... And my shoulder wound begins to ache. Vrai can betray me in the future... My child can betray me. Children listen to their mothers more than their fathers. It is a bond that can never be broken, although I had broken mine. But my mother did not have any love for me, nor I for her.

But can Vrai ever do such a thing? The woman who was afraid of me on her arrival to Oria.

"Queens are evil, Orval, because they are women." He watches my reaction carefully. "If you do decide to keep to your old ways, don't let that child bond with its mother... It could be your downfall."

Things grow silent between us as I mull over his words and wonder why I never thought of this solution before. But it is too late now. Rhys and the others will never settle for someone random being my heir, and he, too, can betray me in the end. Everyone can, and some of the people closest to me can and they have. I doubt everyone's allegiance and loyalties.

"Anyway, who is that woman you will be sending to Earath?" His curiosity knows no bounds. "I have not seen any woman worthy of such a task in the castle."

"Do you really want to know...?" I push away from my desk and stand up. He is quiet as I move toward the door, wanting a distraction to take my mind off the things I had just thought of. "If you do, follow me."

I can hear Ukiah's footsteps behind me as I leave my office. Today he seems to be the most curious I have ever seen him, and his eyes are drilling into the back of my head.

We go down many flights of stairs until we reach the bottom of the castle where the dungeons lie. Cobwebs mark the corridors, and only the guards and the most unfortunate lie sequestered within these walls where even the sunlight does not penetrate.

I walk ahead, ignoring the traitors, criminals, and the grunge of Oria who are barely alive, their eyes slowly watching the movement outside their cells.

It is dark and damp, musty filled with dust. The air is pungent down here, the bowels of the castle. I crinkle my nose when I step in a puddle that is not water.

Ukiah seems unfazed as he peers at the men and women in their cages that have been designed specifically for them. I'm sure he has seen things worse than this. The arenas being the bloodiest place in Oria and that is where he thrives.

I stop at a guarded door, and the soldiers move aside, bowing to me. "My King," one says softly. Even they do not know who or what is behind the door they guard so carefully.

I open the door, ignoring them, and step inside to see two red eyes, leering at me, through the matted hair which covers most of her face. Time has not been kind to her. Her face is heavily lined and body scrawny and starved. I feel revolted just by looking at her, and I assume she feels the same for me. Heavy chains tie her to the ground she sits on.

She smells like piss and shit.

Once Ukiah steps beside me, he stares in awe and shock as he crouches down. He is smart enough to keep his distance, feeling instinctively the power that flows through her veins, despite her wretched condition.

"I didn't know that she lives..." His eyes are still wide as he takes in the entire scene.

"Yes, the true Queen of Oria lies here, rotting without her wings, and if she wants her freedom, she must help to restore my ties with Earath first... Won't you, Lilou?"

Her eyes watch me like the animal she is, but she doesn't say a word. She does not even acknowledge her first guest besides Rhys or me in such a long time. She just continues to stare, but I know she will bite. *Which prisoner wouldn't try at the chance of freedom?*

She is the only Fire Dragon skilled in combat and intelligent enough to go to Earath. She can handle herself, and I do not care if she were to come back alive or dead. I have no plans of letting her live once she completes the task.

She is another usable pawn in my game of chess. Even if she does betray me, I will have her killed easily. She cannot fly anymore and to Dragons, that is no better than losing your legs, a fate worse than death.

She is immobile, and the people who once followed her are no longer alive. If she does manage to survive, she will live in shame and isolation. A Dragon without wings is worse than a Theka.

There is no place in the castle for her but death or dungeons. I am the King now and Vrai is my Queen, and the child in her belly my heir.

Lilou, the first child of Queen Wera and King Diarmind, the successor to what I now rule by pure power and strength. Her husband was supposed to take my place, but he is long dead after attempting to flee to Yulor the day he saw the previous King and Queen at my feet.

Lilou's husband was such a coward.

He tried to escape without warning her, so he did not have a place on the throne. As to why she selected such a man to be her husband, it is still beyond my comprehension. He is the reason she is wasting away here. If he had been stronger, she would have been standing where I am.

Our parents were nothing but bodies underneath my throne, their blood flowing beneath me. They were just like many others who dared to defy me. Family means nothing to me anymore. Usually, they are the first ones to betray and hurt you, just like this one, but I have broken her.

The day Rhys bowed to me as king and recognized me as the new ruler of Oria, he gave up Lilou almost immediately. He even helped to remove her wings and throw her into the dungeons.

This has been her place for all these years, and now I am giving her a chance at freedom...

So how can she refuse?

TWENTY-NINE

TO BE HURT

A servant led me to the King's room, since I do not know the way, but also the King does not want me to walk the corridors alone. There was no one waiting for me, apparently, he isn't back from speaking with the Ukiah, a man whom I believed to be a boy.

Taking advantage of this opportunity, I begin to explore the room. It is the largest in the palace with many statues and books. Large shelves line the wall; the King seems to be well-read.

The floor is tiled, hence, smooth and cool under my feet. He even has his own attached bath. Unlike mine, which is separate from the room itself. His is obviously bigger, a lot bigger, to accommodate his Dragon.

His room fascinates me as it gives me an insight into him. My fingers caress the items from books to bed, from statues to tiny figurines; the King is enigmatic in his collections. I hear the door open, and I am almost giddy with excitement when I see and feel the King's magic.

I start to approach him, but I hear him stomping toward me, his aura wild and raging, which confuses me. Before I know it, he shakes me and barks into my face. "Idiotic Mage! Do you know what you have done?"

Why is he so angry with me?

I was so happy in his room. *Is it because I was touching his things? Is there something dangerous here?*

It must be my curse; everything I touch turns to dust. The more I want to touch the King's heart, the further it goes away from me. I don't say anything when it finally dawns on me. He wasn't angry at me for touching his belongings.

"I leave you with my men for no more than ten minutes and come to find one of them bound so tight that he cannot breathe and another ill because your ice will not leave his hand," he growls at me. "Do you think you have the right to punish my men?"

My hand goes to my chest to calm my heart which was pounding hard, and I spit hatefully, "Your men were out of control... They were ready to attack one of their own like animals, then they turned on me."

"They always threaten each other and fight, you imbecile," he hisses. "Another thing to ponder in your tiny brain is that you are not the one to deal with this man's family. They will be breathing down my neck the moment they find out he is bound like a criminal in my dining hall, and even worse, my Queen is the one who did this to him. He isn't a nobody! He is from a noble family of Dragons and the last male of his bloodline! They will ask for retribution."

"He came after me! Ask any of the men in the room!" I yell back. "And Gregory was just a warning... My ice only hurt his hand...Then came Lucius, readying to cause me bodily harm. I did all this to protect our child."

"After you provoked him! I don't think you understand just how deadly your power is, my Queen! It's no better than poison to us! You have never been trained how to use it, and we don't know its side effects." He grabs the front of my nightgown. "The ice will not leave from my men's bodies just like your damn ice won't leave my fucking shoulder!"

I narrow my eyes. "My ice is in your shoulder?"

My ice Dragon... it bit him during our fight.

"Yes, and I tried everything to get it out," he snaps. "That is the reason why I called you here tonight... But then I found out about your destructive behavior in the dining hall! I do not need another person who does not listen to me!" he growls, and I can see his Dragon irritated.

He lets go of my nightgown and shoves me, sighing heavily. "Just leave. You've caused me enough problems."

I stumble back and hear him take off his jacket and whipping it to the floor.

I plead, "At least let me take the ice out... Or try to."

The King is quiet as I hear another article of clothing hit the ground, followed by the sound of his boots being taken off. "I told you to leave," he roars at me once more.

"You did, but I am not going to listen to you," I say quietly.

I see his Dragon bare its teeth, almost lunging at me, and he snaps. "I said get out, Mage!"

I may be testing the limits of the King, but I continue to walk toward him. The closer I get, the more his Dragon goes into a defensive posture with eyes full of hate like when we first met. Pain grips me, knowing we are back to where we were a few months ago. I walk closer, and I see him rear back. I wonder what his men have said to him about me. Now I have lost his trust too.

Not knowing how to calm the enraged Dragon, I put my arm around his back and embrace him, which causes him to tense. Anger flows like molten lava, and his skin is like hot embers. I am uncomfortable and sweat drips off me, but I continue to hold him, even when he protests. His Dragon snarls at me, treating me like the enemy.

"Let go of me, Mage!" he bellows.

"You don't trust me anymore," I whisper.

"I have never trusted you!" he hisses before grabbing hold of me in an attempt to pull me off him. "I don't trust anyone."

"At least trust me once!" I feel his wounded shoulder, making his Dragon hiss at me like a quincat. The sound coming from his Dragon is much more threatening.

I can feel my magic while touching the open wound directly, and I delve my fingers into the site. This causes his Dragon to shriek and howl, and the King's breath hitches in pain.

"You fucking bitch!" he yells, fingers curling into my shoulder and his claws rip my flesh. I take his mauling silently as I know the King is only lashing out in pain, the pain that I've caused him.

The only thing he knows to do...

"I feel it," I say. "I just need to pull it out."

"Don't!" he yells, but I do not listen to him. I do not even have to attempt to grab it as my magic is naturally drawn to me. It begins easing out the moment I concentrate on his shoulder.

Just as the ice starts to come out of the King's body, he snaps and shoves me away. It is violent this time and causes me to stumble and fall back, hitting the ground harshly.

I let out a startled yelp, placing my palm on my lower belly to protect my child. His outward rejection hurts me more than the pain of connecting with the floor.

"I told you to stop!" he hisses, and I hear him step back, falling into what sounded like a chair or sofa.

I feel an ache at my hip and backside, but I push myself up, determined to finish what I have already started.

I see his Dragon's chest heaving, growing weary and tired. I'm sure he doesn't feel a single ounce of remorse for shoving me or care that his baby might be hurt. His Dragon is selfish and primal, just as he is.

Once I stand, his Dragon growls softly at me, and the King snaps at me. "Why can't you just leave me alone?"

"Because I am the one who caused it, and I am the only one who can remove it," I retort back. "Just let me do it!"

He is silent for several moments, then sighs heavily. "Fine! Just get it over with! You're not going to leave me alone until it is done anyway!" he bitches.

I walk to where he is and put my hand over his shoulder. I concentrate harder, and he winces as the ice begins to slide from his body. All my energy is focused on removing it.

"Fucking cunt!" he curses. I hear the squeak of leather as he grips the chair and squeezes it, probably wanting to do the same with my neck. I wish he would just scream and not try to be so brave.

More ice begins to slide out. Blood leaks from the wound, and the metallic smell fills the air. The King seethes in agony. Half the ice is out, and I wrap my fingers around it, gripping it hard, trying to remove it gently.

There is only a tiny bit left inside, but I will need to yank it out. It is twisted into his flesh, and the King will be in extreme agony. It is going to be brutal.

"It's almost out," I begin to pull harder, and I hear the most gruesome sounds coming from the wounds, but I try not to concentrate on them.

Instead of pushing me away, I feel his magic flaring before falling. It starts to go back and forth as if his magic is conflicted by his emotions.

I continue to focus on my magic, and more of the ice leaves his wound. Before long, it rips away from his body and shatters as soon as it is released.

The King screams, and this is the first time I have heard him do so. At the same time, I see his Dragon bellow in sync with him; it too has felt the pain from the extraction.

I feel blood ooze from the wound, running over my hand as I grab his shoulder. I shout excitedly. "It's out! I got it all out!"

The King does not reply, and I feel his body growing limp. His Dragon too disappears from my mind within seconds, and my heart stops. I start to feel panic.

"King?" I question, and I feel his body lying still, head rolled to one side.

"King!" I ask more loudly, the smell of the blood giving me bad memories like the last night I was with my mother.

"Orval!" I snap again, calling him by his name, but he does not reply.

All I can think as I hold on to him is, *What have I done...?*

THIRTY

DARKNESS

"To THINK he was hiding such a thing. What did he think would happen?!" Rhys snaps as he paces the room, his footsteps loud and heavy. He keeps asking me questions instead of helping Doctor Viggo, who is trying to understand the situation and what the King is inflicted with. Neither he nor I can understand what caused the King to become unresponsive.

Rhys came along when he got to know that the King was hurt. After that, many people sauntered outside the room like vavultures, wanting to know of the King's status, dead or alive or somewhere in between. Most seemed to delight in malicious gossip.

He cannot be dead or dying... Not from something as silly as my ice.

Kings died greatly in every tale I have heard, either in a battle or after many accomplishments, finally succumbing to old age – especially a Dragon king!

Surely, this is not the first time he has suffered wounds from an Ice Mage?

Why would mine be any different? Why is he sick from mine?

I am worried.

When the King collapsed, in my panicked state, I called on Viggo first but failed to see the other person in the shadows. Word then spread of the King's condition, and that led to something I have never seen – CHAOS! Another thing that I have done which the King won't like. A sigh escaped me when I saw too many people swarming about, throwing questions my way every time they saw me. Questions that I could not answer.

Fortunately, the shock had held my tongue, and I have said very little publicly. Only Rhys and Viggo know the truth about the ice fang and what had occurred.

"So, when you fought, you're saying your ice lodged into his shoulder much like it has done for Gregory and when you pulled it out, he lost consciousness?" Viggo interrogates me.

"Yes," I reply, standing against the wall, my legs shaking, and stomach in knots. I wring my fingers in worry. I wish I could escape and hide away from this situation. I am so confused and scared of everything. Answering question after question, usually the same ones repeatedly, that does not help anyone.

The King cannot die. I forbid it.

But I cannot see his magic.

"The infection is much worse than what a normal Dragon can withstand. I'm not sure how he was up and walking with something like this," Viggo murmurs, incredulously. "But it is dire, and he will need constant care from this point forward if he is to survive."

"How long will he be unconscious for?" questions Rhys.

"I am not sure." Viggo sounds irritated for the first time with someone who isn't his brother.

"What do you mean?" snaps Rhys, and I can sense his annoyance. "You are a doctor. You should know."

"I am not a miracle doctor. The King should have died long ago with this, but he hasn't... yet," growls Viggo.

"What do you mean yet?" I lash out, pushing away from the wall, my heart in my throat.

The King cannot die, that too by my hands. He is the father of my child. *What have I done?*

A keening sound fills the room, the pain in it reaching directly into my heart, breaking it further until I realize I am the one making that sound. So miserable was I.

Viggo looks sharply at me, the feel of his gaze strong. "Queen, get a hold of yourself. I am not saying that the King will die but I cannot say that he will live either. It is touch and go. The only thing I can do is to keep his wound clean and hope for the best. But if he were anyone else, he would have been, in fact, dead already."

"Great! Now to deal with the men outside..." grumbles Rhys.

"It will be in our best interests to say the King is fine and resting," Viggo states. "Anything else will cause an uproar."

I hear Viggo leave the King's side and approach me. "Queen, do you think you can handle such an announcement and speak confidently in front of the King's men? Other than the King, only you have the title and power and as you carry his heir now, you can rule in his stead until he recovers."

I swallow, uncertain, but also think back to how I was able to handle the men at the table and how everyone, except Ukiah, bowed to me.

Can I be the Queen of Oria? I was so confident before. *Can I do this? Can I lead the men? A country?*

"I think I will be able to handle it," I say.

I must for everyone's sake. I will be the ruler of Oria until the King wakes up. He has to.

"Good. Rhys, stay by her side as you do with the King," Viggo suggests. "That way, the men will understand the situation as clearly as possible."

"Yes, I plan to anyway. I do not need you telling me what to do. I will follow anyone in charge for it is my duty," Rhys grumbles grouchily. All three of them, including Cell, act like family. I can tell they love the King, *but will they feel the same about me?*

I sigh heavily and turn to Viggo's magic. "Will you stay with the King and make sure he is well?"

"Of course. Now both of you go. You have more important things to tend to. We're lucky Zachariah hasn't tried breaking down the door in order to find out what is going on. Right now, they fear the King's anger and will not dare, but that will soon end."

I nod and walk toward the door. I see the magic of many Dragons flaring wildly with their emotions. This will be hard to deal with, but Rhys follows me, much like he does the King. It seems he accepts me as a temporary ruler.

I just need to be strong... In mind and presence. I never expected things to lead to this when I removed the ice from his shoulder. I thought things would become better, not worse.

I open the door to the King's quarters, and Rhys shuts it behind us to keep the prying eyes out.

"The King has fallen ill temporarily but is currently fine and in recovery," I say, expecting many more questions to come my way.

"What do you mean ill?!" questions Gregory snidely, still angry over the wound in his hand. I don't blame him. "The King has never once fallen ill since childhood!"

Before I can answer the question truthfully, Rhys speaks on my behalf. "He is ill with the duorlox flu and just because he is a king, it doesn't mean he is invincible. He is not a God as many describe him to be. Others have died of sickness and plagues, but he will prevail. The Royal Physician Viggo is uncertain how he obtained such a disease, but he advises everyone to be clean and stay out of the King's room to avoid getting sick."

"The flu... If I recall, Duke Orlow not too long ago had such a thing," mentions Cell, who comes out of the crowd, his magic approaching us. "And he died, how unfortunate..."

"He died?!" I hear a surprised reaction from the people in the room. "Since when, Cell?! I did not hear news of such sickness in the Kingdom or Duke Orlow coming in contact with it. Last I knew he was healthy and living."

"Last night, unfortunately, and Viggo is the only one who knew along with the King. Viggo tried saving him, but there was nothing left to save... It is unfortunate indeed. Such a strong and powerful man brought down by an illness. I hope such a fate does not befall the King as well. He must have fallen sick after our visit with him."

What Cell says is all but eerie. *How can he create such vivid lies within seconds without knowing what is going on?* He is doing every-thing to protect his brethren, Rhys and his brother.

But is the Duke truly dead as he says, and how did he die if it wasn't in fact from this flu they speak of?

"I see. This is troublesome," says Erik. "If there are any more ill, take them to Viggo immediately. We cannot have this get out of control. The sick will go into solitary."

"If the King is ill, who will be in charge?" questions Zachariah gruffly. "And I should have known. The King was not acting his usual self lately. We should have eased his burden."

"I will rule," I say immediately, "temporarily... until the King is healthy and ready to take charge."

There is silence, and Fonzell is the first to question me. "You? We've just accepted you as a queen, but we cannot accept you as our ruler, Mage! First, you're a woman and second, a Mage. Third and most importantly, I do not trust you."

"Why not?" I ask, looking at his magic as it rises to fury. "In all these months, have I not proved that I am loyal to the King and the lands? Besides, I carry the royal heir."

He backs away, having no answer to that, but his Dragon bares its teeth, wanting to snap me off my feet. It is clear he is feeling threat-ened by my presence.

A hand on my shoulder startles me; it feels like a shock from the lightning bolt as this is the first time I have been shown support publicly by any of the King's men. It belongs to Zachariah. *How did he move so fast?*

"Enough. I accept the idea as long as it is temporary. She is right, Fonzell, we forget she is pregnant, and in her, she carries the future ruler of Oria," he speaks in my support. "My instinct says she will not betray us. I'm sure the King will be better soon and back to ruling the Kingdom."

"And what happens if he isn't?" Ukiah cuts through the group, his voice low and threatening. "Will we just accept her as our ruler so easily? Let her control Oria when her true origins are with Yulor, a Kingdom we have been at war with for almost as long as the beginning of time? I don't trust her."

His magic begins to move toward me, and even though I know his Dragon is small, much like him, his power is immense, and he is distrustful of me, more so than the others. He was the only one not to bow to me.

And I have never felt so small...

Ukiah continues. "She will do anything to merge Oria and Yulor when the ten-year treaty ends, and it will be her kind who rules over us. We will be servants, slaughtered and preyed upon just like the Great Dragon, Kari. Every country strives for power, and allowing her to rule us will give them the advantage they have been seeking for so long. Besides, is it just a coincidence that her sister is coming for a visit and the King falls ill?" His voice is filled with poison.

"You speak false," I protest, seeing more Dragons appear in support of him. They distrust me more under Ukiah's influence. "My country and I have no ties, and I have not called for my sister."

"Why is that?" he questions as he stops a few inches away from me. "And not only that, you gather within your close circle, Viggo, Rhys, and Cell... All Water Dragons. Did you make some kind of deal with their country? Watergrale, in my opinion, is to never be trusted... For all we know, you have killed the King and are using this illness to cover up a royal murder. Let us inspect him for ourselves to ensure he is well before we take such a rash decision of making you our ruler." I can smell his breath on my face.

They will find out. *What do I say now? How do I act?* I am not like Cell; I can't think of any more convincing lies.

Cell comments from behind me. "Go ahead, Ukiah. See for yourself and risk getting sick, and another council seat will become vacant."

"I was with the King, just an hour ago, before this mysterious illness overcame his health. He seemed fine to me. Not only that, but he also said he was meeting with the Queen before all this happened. Don't you find that just a tad suspicious? Alone with an Ice Mage who thinks she is superior to everyone because she carries an heir which a Fire Dragon should be carrying," Ukiah puts forth his point smoothly, and I can tell from the thick tension in the air that the men who were supporting me have sidled toward him.

"She did side with the Water Dragons earlier at the dining table," mentions Gregory. "Protecting them as if they are allies... Then she bound a councilman as well as infected me with her ice."

"See, things aren't adding up anymore," Ukiah protests loudly. "I think the Queen is getting a little sloppy and feeling good about herself. She's finally tried finishing the King off in order to take full control of Oria."

"It's possible. I agree," says Fonzell immediately. "The Queen shouldn't be trusted with this type of power. With her magic, she can kill any of us."

No! Don't side with Ukiah. Don't, please! I am your Queen!

Rhys clicks his tongue scornfully. "You all sound so ridiculous. Why will we want to side with the Ice Mages if they are so willing to slaughter all the Fire Dragons? Won't we be next in line then? You men do not use your brains. You are listening blindly to one person."

"For all we know, you think you're safe because you made a deal with the Mages. Ice and Water Magic are very similar, to begin with, so it is obvious you will get along with each other. And was it not you who always wanted the King to take a Mage as his wife?" asks Ukiah.

"Ukiah..." warns Zachariah, interrupting the argument between the two, obviously having something more to add. "If you don't want the Mage to be the ruler, whom do you suggest? Yourself? I do not think so, and I would not let you rule. Warrior you are, though deep down like your father and his father before, I see a criminal. I have not turned a blind eye to your ways."

Ukiah casts his evil eye then on Zachariah, his laughter mocking him and my only support. "You seem quite attached to the Mage, Zachariah. Why is that?"

"The King seems to trust her, and she doesn't seem to be like the rest of her people with whom I have battled multiple times before. I have no reason to trust Mages; they are the ones who took my eye... But our Queen is nothing like them," he says. "I do not believe she will betray us as you suggest."

"Well then, let all of us see the King," Ukiah demands.

I immediately know things are going to escalate quickly and badly.

"You may not!" snaps Rhys. "Ukiah, you are nothing but a barking grod. I have served King Diarmind and now King Orval and never once have I betrayed either and I certainly would not side with Yulor. They are the last country I will take my knee to. While you, on the other hand, sneak around like a rat!"

Ukiah laughs again, dark humor in his tone. "But am I not the King's favorite and most trusted? If you deny my right to see the King, it just proves that everything you've said has all been lies!"

All the Dragons are tense, especially Rhys, Cell, and Ukiah. They seem to be ready to battle each other. Rhys and Cell stand close to me. Looking at their Dragons and sensing them, Ukiah suddenly seems to lose steam.

"Forget it..." he says, sighing loudly, then looks down, muttering something. I can catch only a few words. *Matters... hands... quicker... efficient... can't trust.*

What is he saying?

Just when I think he is about to give up and leave the room, he lunges and charges at me. Suddenly, I am grabbed by the throat and thrown against the wall, his fire magic pressing and burning my neck. It makes me whimper in pain and shock. I can't breathe.

I claw at his fingers, trying to loosen them. The power that is vibrating in him tells me he is not to be trifled with. He will not let go until the end. My death. That is his aim. I am going to die here, against the wall. And so is my baby.

"Queen, tell me the truth, or I will burn your throat," threatens Ukiah evilly. There is so much darkness in his Dragon. Its hot breath fans my face, waiting and desiring to melt everything that I am. Its lips peel back, revealing the sharp teeth. When it opens its mouth wider, I can see the tunnel of its throat. There is something brewing in its gullet; a ball of fire that can dissolve flesh and blood. Mine. It seems to think of me as the enemy, and even the other Dragons in the room recoil seeing its vicious force. Some like Cell, Rhys, Zachariah bare their teeth, not liking the turn of events and rush to pull him off me.

I hear Zachariah yell, "Ukiah, even I have never gone so low! Attacking a pregnant woman and our Queen! What is wrong with you?! Let her go! Now!"

"I wouldn't be attacking her if she'd just told us the truth. Now don't get righteous with me, you are just as bad as I. Now, Queen, I give you ten seconds," Ukiah warns before he starts the countdown, "10... 9... 8..."

I attempt to use my ice magic to freeze his fingers and unclench them from my neck, but for some reason, I fail. Maybe his magic is more powerful than I would have imagined. I shift restlessly. Thought about my baby's safety is foremost in my mind. I attempt to kick him, but my force is pitiful. It does nothing to him. I have to get him off me for my baby's life.

Why can't I use my magic when I could before? Is he really that strong? I fought against the King, and I was able to use my magic! This is impossible! I need to tap into my powers. Please.

"7...6...5...4..." he continues his countdown, his hand tightening around my throat with each number.

Suddenly, a voice cuts in from the other side, and I feel Cell's magic threatening Ukiah. "Let her go, or you will be dealing with me, boy."

At the choice of his words, I feel Ukiah release my neck, and I can take the first gasp of air. He then throws his fire magic against Cell, the heat in the room doubling, becoming boiling hot, only to suddenly cool off with Cell's water magic from the other side. The energy of the magic incites the other Dragons, who begin to growl and bare their teeth, wanting their chance to join in the battle. With no leader guiding them, they are as blind as I am. The magic makes them restless, and there is a lot of shuffling of feet in the room.

The warmth around my neck dissipates, but I feel the aftermath of burns. I cough and try to take in as much air as possible. My ice magic does not seem to soothe me or heal my burns.

I back away from the warring Dragons, and Rhys is at my side, pulling me down the hall with him, with everyone distracted by the fight. "We must go now. Things are not looking good for you and me."

From somewhere behind, I hear a window cracking and the screech of inhuman beasts with the power unleashed by the transformation of the two Dragons. The deadliest of magic is being pitted against one another. Fire and Water are equally balanced. I can see that, and I am blind. They had eyes but blind to it all.

I hear a crashing sound and assume it is the door to the King's room. Suddenly, Gregory yells, "They're gone! Arrest Viggo and search the palace and grounds for the King! They must be somewhere close."

The King is gone? Where has Viggo taken him? Is he alright?

My heart sinks right into my stomach at the thought of losing my King. "Will they be safe? What will happen to Cell and Viggo?" Rhys continues to pull me down the different corridors, and the most awful noises made by the Fire Dragons fade away.

How can they fight against so many Fire Dragons?

"Cell will be fine; he has been through worse." Rhys holds onto my arm tightly as we move quickly through the known and unknown hallways. "And Viggo can handle himself. He will keep the King safe. He is not pitiful and weak as the warriors make him out to be. I would be worrying about yourself, my Queen. Things are not looking good for you. We must secure your safety first. Everything else can wait."

"I can't just leave!" I yell, tears of panic and fear filling my eyes. "I have no place to go! And Baby is here! I can't leave him behind. They will kill him if they think of me as a traitor!"

"Now is not the time to be worrying about silly pets!" Rhys lashes out and drags me down a flight of stairs. I have trouble keeping up with him.

"And my maids?!" I question, thinking perhaps they may kill Ava or Catherine and even Yanmei...

"They will be fine. Selene will protect them if need be. They're like her children."

When we make it down the flight of stairs to the first level of the castle, something above us crashes, and I feel the presence of more Dragons fighting. It is Zachariah and Fonzell.

The air then gathers energy, a static build-up of a different kind of magic before I hear yells followed by claps of thunder which shake the foundations of the castle, making it quiver.

The windows rattle with the pressure of the winds, and the glass cracks and bursts into the hall we have run down. Massive gales of wind and rain flood the castle with the storm which chases after us to the floor below.

Faster.

We must run faster!

One of the Dragons bellows, and Rhys pushes me behind him, debris falling everywhere around us. I cannot perceive most of the dangers surrounding me; the energy of the place is in an uproar. Completely a sensory overload.

Rhys tugs me to the right, doing his best to guide me through the chaos. We eventually make it to the outside. The rain pelts against my skin in sheets, drenching me in a heartbeat.

I suddenly remember the King advising me at dinner to never leave the castle during such conditions, but I am left no other choice.

It does frighten me to be outside, but the inside is a danger to my child and life. I just hope that Rhys continues to guide me to safety.

As we make it to the edge, he is not given enough time to transform as a Dragon crashes into the earth in front of us. It is Cell. His magic is flickering and the smell of blood is strong.

My heart stops as Rhys halts in his tracks. He is no longer focused on me, but on Cell, who seems to have been beaten nearly to his death.

From above, I hear a Dragon rage with bloodlust as it screeches its power over the others. A sound of victory and triumph for another battle won. Another horrible screech and I know it has spotted us.

It descends with great speed in our direction. We are briefly blanketed from the rain by its massive wings as it flies above it and hits the ground, shaking the earth with its impact. The small pebbles vibrate around my feet, announcing its proximity to me.

Its magic flares as it gracefully grips the stony earth, its wings extended out in a frightening display, and even if its form is smaller than others, it dwarfs me.

It is Ukiah...

I hear his voice in my head. "It seems Water Dragons are weak after all, Rhys, as I'm sure you are, too. I will rip your head from your body with great satisfaction. I hope you give me a better fight." His eyes look at me with sick joy, he and his Dragon both enjoying the fear that emerges in me. His words are tinged with sadistic pleasure as he imagines what he will do to me. "And, Mage, I will rip you apart from head to toe with my bare claws, my teeth tearing your flesh and bones until your innards are scattered on this earth. Your shrieks will be louder than thunder, and your blood will rain over this ground. All of Oria will know you have died. At my hands."

"How dare you!" snaps Rhys from above the roaring skies, and before I know it, he transforms and flies into Ukiah. I only have such sights of their Dragons and it comes to me vividly.

Bodies crash into each other, the claws striking the flesh with a vengeance. The smell of blood grows thicker in the air. They meld into one another in their vicious fight. Their aura seems to be conjoined and weaved together. I cannot tell where one begins and the other ends. It is a confusing clash of colors that move too fast for me to keep up.

The only hope I have is Cell being alive. His magic and his Dragon are not yet gone from my world of darkness.

Fire magic is used, I can smell the scorching flames followed by the hiss of water. I am pushed back as the steam envelops around me, burning and blistering my skin. I cover my face and belly, turning away from the force of the hot air.

They meet and clash, again and again, their magic burning bright, the elements trying to make the other surrender to their superior power. It is hard to breathe, the flames are burning the remaining air and diluting it of rich oxygen. The rain pours, and the water counters the flames.

It appears Rhys is winning, though that does not last long. Soon the water is not forceful enough to stop the raging fires that hurtle toward him from Ukiah's Dragon. The fire smites the water that attempts to counter it. What is left of the flames hurl toward me.

I step back in an attempt to escape what seems like sure death, but for the first time since arriving in this land, my foot comes into contact with nothing but air.

My heart drops, and my hand moves to my lower belly where my child is nestled safely in me. I am reminded of a distant memory of the King's warm fingers, wrapping around my wrist, saving me from a horrible fall, but not this time. As I fall, there is no one to grab my hand and protect me, especially not the King. It will not just be my death but also our child's.

The only thing I can recall in these very moments is the King's words months ago. "I wouldn't run if I were you... It's useless... You will either die from the cliffs or by the hands of my people."

And his words couldn't have been more right... A mixture of both it is.

It is all I can think of as I fall from the cliff, and I know it won't be long before I hit the bottom. My body broken, bones shattered. My child slipping out of me silently in obscurity as the blood drains out.

The King, if he survives, will come for us, but it will be too late. I will lie soon in the embrace of death, knowing my child and I will soon be a part of the earth.

I breathe once. Twice. And I breathe no more. I will die only knowing only this.

THIRTY-ONE

THE DOCTOR'S SONS

Thoughts plague me as the winds buffet my body, the rushing air causing an ominous silence in my ears as I am pulled down to a rocky bottom. The grounds rush in eagerness to lead me to my inevitable doom.

In my final moments, all I can think about is the Fire Dragon King and the storms and destruction surrounding him, and how pitiful my existence is where I can't do anything to protect him or our baby. My life is going to be snuffed out like a candle's flame along with our unborn child.

I close my eyes in the final moments, unable to do anything. I cannot scream or fly or even pray for a miracle. Just the night before, I had expected greatness, but in less than a day, I have been led to my doom. A tragedy that has always been my fate has led to this...

How unnerving it is to think these are my last thoughts and that I will be no more. I can barely recall the tender moments with the King, such as him gifting me a flower, us dancing the night of our wedding, or the last time we made love. My tears fall down my cheeks as my body gravitates to my end, wishing I could have had more time with him. Time to have gotten to know the King or become the Queen I should have been or the biggest regret of all, a chance to greet my child. But I will have none of that. I will never get to hold my child, soothe him or her, or sing a lullaby before bed.

"Let it be quick," I whisper, but the winds steal my words and the air from my lungs.

I hit the bottom.

Pain... Every cell of my body feels it. Absolute agony takes over and envelopes my being. It feels as if I am melding with the earth, and my body is crushed in this terrible last moment. I can't breathe. Everything is blurred, and I feel as if I am being submerged in water.

Water...

I move my limbs, and it is, in fact, water. The fluid around me just like during my baths.

The storm... It must have flooded the area. I can feel the pain in my muscles, but there is enough water to soften my fall and for it to be not as deadly as it would have been, had there been rocks and stones. I sink to the bottom, air escaping out of my lungs. There is a burning sensation in my chest as my body craves for air.

I begin swimming in an attempt to reach the surface. I manage to come up and take a big gulp of air, but the heavy flow of the water pulls me down, and the current carries me downstream with it, nature not giving me a break. I continue to struggle within the waters, surviving for my baby, the only thing keeping me going as I fight against all the odds, trying to cling or grab onto anything nearby.

I am scared out of my wits when the branches slip by, more than I've ever been before. I was so close to death only to be spared, and now, I find myself in a new and dangerous situation – one where, yet again, I do not know if I am going to survive.

Water fills my empty lungs, causing me to cough each time I come up for air, only to be pulled back down, a frustrating repetition. My clothes too are heavy, sodden with water and seem to drag me to the bottom. My limbs grow tired, trying to fight the rushing currents.

I just want to be on land, safe from the horrors which I cannot comprehend or protect myself from. Even on land, it's a worry that

Ukiah will hunt me down for treason and tear into me, keeping his promise to rip me apart above Viss.

I should have just spoken the truth, but even the truth would have led me to a situation like this, if not worse. *What will happen when they discover that I am the reason the King is unconscious?*

Fearing my fate, I thrash in the water wildly, recalling the time when Yanmei had not so long ago attempted to drown me and I was ready to give up, but now I fight for my life desperately. I have a reason to live, my child.

I must live... I can't die like this.

I hear a loud splash as I surface. Something dives or falls into the water from above, and I notice the magic belonging to a Dragon but not one of fire.

I do not focus on it for long, knowing it would have to be either Rhys, Viggo, or Cell. It swims closer to me, and as it nears me, I grab on to it, my nails digging deep into its flesh, causing it to twitch in response.

It moves fluidly through the water, going against the current with ease. It is only when we reach the land that I let go, slowly discovering my legs after being in the water for so long. I focus on its magic, not having the slightest clue with whom I was or even where I was.

It is Cell. He is alive.

Never have I been so happy to see him.

I fall to my knees in relief, taking in air and expelling the water in my lungs, glad to have been spared once more. The sounds of his transformation reach me. It is so different from when the King's scaled flesh turns into skin, Dragon to man.

"You saved me," I rasp, my voice still hoarse. The water rages behind me still, and the skies continue to weep from above.

He coughs painfully, followed by a groan, as he collapses in the dirt some distance away from me. "I am not the one to let a beautiful woman die even if I may have been pathetically beaten. Humiliated and brought down to the ground like a wee babe. The first thing I see when I open my eyes is you falling. Perhaps you won't spread rumors now that I have saved you."

"How badly are you hurt?" I question him as I get closer. He still has his humor despite the situation.

"It's nothing..." he responds grumpily. "Especially nothing a lady should worry about. It should be me asking how you are. "

"I am fine," I say as I touch him, trying to figure out where he has been gouged and bleeding from.

He grabs my wrist. "Your touch would be most welcome another time. I can even take you up on it, but we should move before Ukiah gets bored with Rhys and comes looking for you. I do not know much of what is going on, but I do know you and I are currently branded traitors."

"Can you even walk?" I question him.

"Yes, as I said, I will be fine." He slowly rises from the ground.

I follow his actions, taking time to become steady. I know I have not been honest about my injuries. But he doesn't need to know that now.

"Where will we go from here?" I ask him, unsure.

"I own property and land not far from here. No one knows about it but my brother and Rhys... We will go there and hope things resolve themselves. If it doesn't... Well, we will figure something out then." Cell walks with a slight limp.

He utters a groan and grimaces as he continues forward, but I say nothing. There is little to be said. I walk close to him, my only ally, as I think about what has happened to my magic when Ukiah attacked me. I could not use it even though I fared just fine in the dining hall.

Perhaps I went a little overboard and used all my powers... Or it has something to do with my pregnancy. I pray my child is unaffected by all this. It would need a miracle.

And the King... I hope he is all right, as well.

I worry about his health. *Is he okay?* I wish to be by his side. I am scared, hurt, and alone with enemies everywhere. I want the warmth of his body, security of his arms, and the sweet kisses I've rejected numerous times. He makes me feel safe.

I do not know of anyone's status anymore or if Ukiah is plotting to usurp the King while he is unconscious as he wants to kill me. If the King and I die, he can rule Oria. There will be battles and injuries, war and more death. The world will be covered with fire from land to sea, and ashes and smoke will block out the skies, making it forever dark.

All life would perish.

Things will turn ugly faster than I could ever imagine. I hope the King opens his eyes soon and get this under control. I imagine he will be in no condition to fight. He is weak because of me... He's unconscious because of my actions.

Strength is all that matters to these Dragons, and if they see a weakness, they will attack.

All our fates and lives are in jeopardy, and I wonder how things will go from here since I have barely escaped death. Cell and I continue walking, though his pace is slow due to his injuries. He needs help, so I approach him silently and lend him my support. "You're injured... Do not be like the King and fight me on helping you."

He tenses at first, not liking me being so close to him or having to show vulnerability, but he doesn't say anything and allows it as he puts some of his weight on me as we walk. "Do not ever speak of this if things go back to normal. The ladies of the court will think very little of me."

"I won't," I respond, knowing men and their pride. He is no better than the King in the end, trying to mask his injuries.

We continue walking some distance, my dress is drenched and feels heavy on my skin, weighing me down and slowing our pace.

I notice tremors in Cell's body, causing it to shake from the cold rain, unlike mine. "You wouldn't know it, Queen, but Viggo, and I are part Ice Mage... Much like yourself. Viggo has tremendous control over his other half. He has always been a cool bastard. If you are wondering, let me tell you, our mother fucked an Ice Mage. Don't take it the wrong way, our father was a prick. I have nothing against you or your people."

My eyes widen briefly, shocked by his revelation or more like his confession, and I mutter, "You're part Dragon and part Mage?"

"Yes," he answers. "I thought I'd tell you something I've never told anyone just in case I were to die. I wanted someone to know who I truly am."

"Do not speak like that," I murmur. However, the possibility is there; he is just overly truthful about the near future.

He laughs. "Yes, very well, Queen. I'll continue. You see, good old Viggo, always so clever, crafted something to suppress certain magics in our body to hide what he and I are. I have never developed ice magic, but I take them nonetheless, just in case this magic were to suddenly develop. It would be most terrible for it to happen when I am surrounded by Fire Dragons. I'm sure the experience will not be very pleasant."

So that is how Viggo hides it, but his words seem unreal. I think I am in shock hearing this confession. I nod, wanting him to continue. I would never have guessed that he and Viggo were part Ice Mages.

"White hair is not common in Watergrale as some may have told you. It is a rumor I started with the ladies of the court. Many didn't believe me – like your maid. She thinks I strip my hair of color – for looks and vanity." His voice has become sluggish. He is very tired. "She thinks the same about my stick-up-the-ass brother. But why would he? Sometimes the bastard skips baths. Yulor is the only country to have such a unique color."

"I see, and what of your father? You seem to dislike him."

"Yes, you may know of him as he is definitely famous in Yulor and even parts of Oria. So, I'm sure you've heard his name before, but as I said, I am not very fond of my father. Viggo was always closer to him than I; he even followed the same path in life." he says.

"What is his name?" I ask out of curiosity. The man, although a bad father, seems to have done some good, inspiring Viggo to help people.

"Doctor Goodfella. He is mostly known as an evil man, and I do not blame them. I myself think of him as such. In Watergrale, he is known more as a miracle doctor," he replies, and my heart stops beating as I recall that day in the snow when my mother died, the day my torture by this doctor started. I remember Viggo mentioning that he'd studied under a well-known doctor. He must have been speaking about his father.

To think his sons were so close to me... And they didn't even know of my past ties with their father and what he had done to me.

"Are you still close to him?" I ask, my fingers grasping Cell's clothing.

"No, like I said, he is a prick. I do not want anything to do with him. I do not see him as my father either," he replies. "When Viggo and I left Watergrale, we left our parents behind. Our mother was quite a hard woman to love as well."

I feel Cell tense up again, and he curses loudly, "Fuck."

"What?" I question, startled, but then I feel Ukiah's magic from above along with many others. "I can't seem to use my magic against him, Cell. I can't fight him."

"Yeah, that happens. Mother had the same problem when she was pregnant. Your magic will be erratic during your pregnancy."

"Oh. Now what?"

The earth trembles as they land in front of us.

"We're fucked. That's what... Rhys must have been beaten. If not by Ukiah, then by the others who follow him. Ukiah is much too weak to beat Rhys..." says Cell loudly so our common enemy can hear it.

It isn't long before I hear Ukiah's voice once again, and my heart fills with dread on hearing it. I'm sure Cell too is hating our situation. "I thought you were both dead, but it seems I am mistaken. It is a good thing I was scouting the area for you two after your bodies mysteriously disappeared. General Cell, oh yes, that's right, you're not a general anymore. You were stripped of your title and status and marked as a traitor."

Another Dragon speaks up, and I recognize the voice as Erik's. "We will not kill you, but we are placing you under arrest for possible treason and plotting to kill the King. Both of you."

"You will rot in the dungeons until the King awakens... if he ever does. Yours will be a much slower death," another Dragon says gleefully. I never heard or seen him before, but his magic is similar to Ukiah's.

A friend of Ukiah. I am sure many more will come.

I feel magic approach us from behind, and we are surrounded. All Cell and I can do is stand there helplessly. There is no chance of us fighting; the odds are stacked too high against us. Two of us versus ten of them.

We will lose. *Badly*.

"You are wrong. All of you," I say. "When the King awakens, you will all regret throwing me in the dungeon! He will not be pleased!" I really hope that the King does wake up soon and that he will defend me.

I feel a man roughly grab me, tearing me away from Cell and twisting my arms behind my back. He is deliberately causing me pain as he growls in my ear, "Shut up, ice cunt."

I hear Cell laugh as he too is arrested. "Ah, I would love to imagine how the King will react to not only throwing me but his pregnant wife into the dungeons..."

Cell is right; they will regret it. The King will kill them, rip their limbs from their bodies, then scavenge the innards from their bellies and use it for decorating the castle's halls once his health returns.

They will not be forgiven for their grievances. They will pay dearly for the hurt they cause me but also for the potential harm they are causing to our child – mine and the King's.

He grimaces, but they do not care about his wounds. He is manhandled as much as I am, pushed and pulled to wherever they were taking us. Then I hear Ukiah say. "If the King does not wake up in sixty days or dies within this time, I will exile or execute you myself after I become the King of Oria. And Ice Mage, know this. I think exile lacks excitement."

I hear faint laughter echo in my head, and that is the last thing I hear before the powerful beating of wings, and I am left cold at the thought.

Just when I got out of my prison, I am placed in another for another crime I did not commit. I am not sure how, but one thing rings through my head at these moments.

Cursed.

THIRTY-TWO

CONFINEMENT

THE DUNGEON AND TOWER.

They are alike yet so different. Instead of the bitter cold, it is the unbearable heat that makes it insufferable. Below the earth's surface, it is not cooler as one would like to believe; it holds the temperature of the oven, and the unwashed bodies in the cells disperse rancidness in the air.

I wholeheartedly swear I can feel the warmth seep from the stones lining my cell, making them weep. I, too, wish to do the same, but I will not shed my tears until I am free.

I press my hand solemnly to the wall, feeling it covered in slime. The grit and filth seem to move under my fingertips as I learn this small place. Water seems to be a scarcity here.

I discover many have been imprisoned in this very cell. Their names carved into the stone spoke of their own story, their lamentations and anger, all mixed with sweat and tears.

Sadness fills me up when I think about these souls and how some of them could be innocent like me but condemned by all. Alone and finding no comfort in the cell but for the others who have come before them and etched their names on these walls, announcing their existence. The only proof of their lives.

Unlike them and my time in the tower, I am not alone. Across from me is Cell and adjacent to me is Rhys. Cell has been resting since our capture yesterday, unable to do much, his body collapsed in exhaustion. Rhys, being who he is, has been pacing nonstop, screaming at the guards with threats of beheading them once when he is back in his position next to the King.

He promises to make them pay and weed out the ones siding with Ukiah and kill them. He does seem to know many ways of death, some heartening, but many are sour and scary. I do not doubt that if the King were to wake, there will be no hesitation in his judgment, and heads will roll. He will definitely act out the words as Rhys screamed. Their fates will be worse than the man who had thrown a stone at me.

If only I can escape, *but where can I go?* Leaving this treacherous land seems to be next to impossible. The guards are constantly watching us. I have already been hit once by a baton-like thing when I objected to living conditions.

Rhys says these cells are designed to hold the Fire Dragons, suppressing their magic, but the Water Dragons can use theirs, but it is subdued. He attempted to use his magic, and I did feel water flooding the floor of my cell, but he, too, was hit by the guards many times. I like his determination; he is still going strong with his threats and promises. I can use my magic here, but my powers are being temperamental in my pregnant state. We seem to be in a fix.

From one end of this long corridor, I hear nasty and vulgar screams directed at us as to how we all deserve to be here and the King to rot in his bed and die. We are even pronounced to be the worst King and Queen in the history of Oria. None of them like me for being an Ice Mage. All of them seem to support Ukiah, chanting his name, happy that someone from their clan will be ruling the Kingdom.

Not too long after being confined, Viggo joins us and is thrown into his own cell, adjacent to mine. He has said nothing since being tossed here, but from the little I've heard from the guards, I know he had tried to flee with the King using a secret passage. However, it was in vain as Ukiah, being the King's favorite, was privy to the knowledge and had sent his men with Gregory to get them back.

I hear noises from down the hall, familiar footfalls of two people followed by the clunk of the heavy treads of the guard. I rise from my bed and walk to the bars, turning my head to the direction of the sound.

It is Ava and Catherine, and I am completely surprised. *Were my maids rounded up too?*

I am warned as I hear my cell door opening. "If you try anything, I have the right to burn you and your maids alive, Mage."

The door protests on its hinges, opening wider to allow my maids to walk in, then slams shut behind them. I cannot contain my curiosity, feeling both joyous and fearful. "What are you doing here?"

"We convinced Ukiah to let us bathe and dress you as we normally do, given that you're still rightfully the Queen at the moment," Ava responds, and I hear Catherine place down a bucket beside me. "So, undress, we do not have much time."

I start to remove my dress, but I feel the watchful eyes of the guard in the dungeon. I hear Rhys tsk, and he sits down somewhere in his cell, feeling my pain and embarrassment.

Catherine is the first to warn the guard. "At least give her some privacy, you dirty mongrel! Do you not have any shame? She is your Queen!"

"Prisoners are not given privacy, and she isn't my Queen," he spits back.

"Catherine, it doesn't matter." I begin to undress, my mood hindered already from the heat. "When this is all over, I will have the King gouge out his eyes. The guard will then know how to live life without sight, just like his Queen. The last female body he will see will be mine, never his wife's. His days are numbered."

I drop my dress right down to my undergarments, and the guard scoffs, "If Ukiah wishes, he can finish off the King, but he is loyal. Nevertheless, the minute the King is dead, you will have every guard and soldier shoving themselves inside your every hole and filling you with their seed. Then you won't have such a privileged Princess cunt that has only ever suckled a royal cock."

I narrow my eyes at this guard, detesting his disgusting tongue. "Do you forgot I still carry the King's heir inside of me? Ukiah will never be a ruler as long as I am with child!'

He laughs louder as he nears my cell again. "And do you know how quickly I can abort that baby inside you? It only requires one punch to the gut."

"You sick bastard," I growl out. "If you come anywhere near me, I will freeze your cock and break your arms off, and I will be the one gouging your eyes out with my ice, not the King." Heat rushes through me as my anger grows. *How dare they speak to me in this manner?*

"Queen, enough!" bites Ava as I hear water drip down from the washcloth into the bucket. She runs the cloth over my body, and I feel the grime slowly disappearing. "Let him wank off looking at you, he will get what is coming to him soon as they all will."

"Shut it, Theka bitch!" The guard spits at us. "I can keep you in here if I fucking want."

"Okay, quit provoking the guard. Both of you," says Catherine nervously as she too begins sponging me with a wet cloth. Both my maids try to keep my body hidden from the guard's lusty eyes. She whispers to me softly, "I really don't want to be locked in here. No offense, my Queen."

"None taken," I say. "Where is Yanmei?"

"She was with Baby earlier this morning, but we know little of her whereabouts since then. She tried to gain entry to the King's quarters but was denied. You know how fiery she is. She did not take their refusal well, so the other servants say," Ava informs as she washes under my arms.

"What happened next to Yanmei has the other servants acting like mirromice," added Catherine.

"It was terrible. They beat her until she was unconscious, but after that, we do not know what happened to her. Baby has vanished, too. These are truly frightful times," Ava whispers.

"But how are you and the baby, my Queen?" asks Catherine.

"I..." I say before correcting myself. "We're fine."

"That's good," mutters Ava.

"Have you eaten?" asks Catherine.

"Yes, this morning," I reply. "For now, they're still feeding me."

There is a brief silence as they clean me up, and I pry more information from them. "How is everything else?"

"A disaster," states Ava even more quietly. "The people are divided now more than ever. Loyalties have been challenged, and many have turned sides. We have no idea of the King's status, especially with Yanmei being turned away so brutally."

"What else?" I ask.

Catherine answers quickly, "Some of the nobles have sided with Ukiah, and he continues to bring people from the slums to the castle." She washes my back. "But there are others who disagree with the decisions being made – Zachariah being one. They believe your child should rule especially if it is a male. But—"

Ava interjects, "Don't tell her such news, it will only cause her distress. She is pregnant, Catherine!"

"What? What news do you speak of? Tell me, it is an order." My heart pounds in my chest.

"If it is a girl you birth, she will marry Ukiah. It won't be the first time such a thing has happened in the history of Oria, though the huge age gap will be terrifying for the Princess. Most of the council and nobles seem settled on this idea. They do not care," Catherine says.

How foul and disgusting. He will never touch my child, my baby.

There is a pause, and Catherine continues, "If it is a boy, I worry that supporters of Ukiah will assassinate him so he can ascend as the only possible king to the throne."

"Either way, my baby won't be safe," I state. "Whether it's a girl or a boy, they will have to pry it from my dead and cold body first."

"Ukiah doesn't seem to be worried, though," Ava reveals. "He seems to be keen on just executing you and your child, going against some of the wishes of the others."

"He appears relaxed, not worried about his ascension to the throne, almost like he has a plan of his own." Catherine says.

"Do you have a guess to what it may be?" I ask.

Before Ava or Catherine can respond, Rhys shouts from his cell. "Yes, his sister still lives. Ukiah must know she breathes. King Orval is such a fool to reveal her existence to him. Ukiah must be planning to marry her. What an awful turn of events this is because if this reaches the rest of Oria, it will make Orval's claim to the throne illegitimate since she is the true ruler and so also any man she marries."

"You mean Queen Lilou is alive?" says Ava, almost shocked.

"Yes, indeed, right in these very dungeons we are in. She has been chained, rotting away for many years," replies Rhys. "This was never to be known; it was supposed to stay hidden. But it's best everyone here knows what we are dealing with. After the King challenged his parents and killed them when he was a boy, he had to go against the newly appointed rulers, Queen Lilou and King Leroy, his sister and her husband."

"No..." Ava whispers and stiffens, squeezing the washcloth.

"I never liked them, Leroy was a wimp and Lilou... The best description of her is that she was more like a king than her husband—"

Ava sputters, "Her love for him was so great she married one who was of a lower class. He was a commoner, born of a Theka. All of us in the lower class know of the story; it's an inspiration."

"Yes... And as your maid said, he was far removed from anything of noble lineage. But so also was she. She bore illegal tattoos on her body. Women never dared to have such markings, especially from the royal family. It was a disgrace, and furthermore, she never was open to any advice. She never listened to me, always on some grand scheme of making a new and grander Oria. Absolutely ridiculous. If she marries Ukiah like I believe will happen, it will be a terrifying union," Rhys says disgustedly

"So, if he marries her... The King will be executed or exiled anyway?" I ask horrified.

"Yes, and your heir will be proved to be illegitimate just like its father. We will be executed most horribly, especially Cell, Viggo, and I. She has no love for anyone from Watergrale."

"This can't happen," I reply, thinking of the story Zachariah told me about King Diarmind ripping the Ice Mage's still growing baby from her stomach.

"It will happen... and the only offspring that would matter will be what Lilou produces from Ukiah. That will be the heir to the throne. I told the King to just kill her, but in the end, he didn't have the heart to do so. He doesn't even know her all that well. It seems my words did not reach him that she is more treacherous, evil, and crazed than any ruler in Oria before. He has always been strange about killing women, instead choosing to lock them up. If she is set free, it will be she who will kill King Orval first, not Ukiah."

Everybody becomes silent as the maids continue to wash and dress me, and I can only be told more bad news.

"Cheer up, Queen," says Catherine as she ties the strings of a loose dress while Ava picks up my old one. She puts her hand on my shoulder to comfort me. "You have sixty days to figure out something. The King may just wake up and put everyone in their rightful place. Stay hopeful."

Ava begins braiding my hair and whispers in my ear. "You are good and kind, Queen. We will figure out something. Do not forget I still have Demos up my sleeve."

"Enough whispers, ladies," the guard opens up the cell door, "come out now."

"Oh, and Dakari did offer to come down and teach you still...

Even in these conditions. He is a sweetheart," says Catherine as she picks up the bucket of dirty water and rags.

"Ukiah turned him away, though," says Ava as they exit. "See you tomorrow, my Queen."

They both leave, and the guard locks the door before walking behind them. I sit on the bench in the only ray of sunshine coming from what I feel is a small window.

I have to think of something, else we all will die. My mind drifts to the King, and fear grips me. *Is he all right? Will he be safe. How will I live without him?*

Tears roll unchecked down my cheeks as my mind travels to our memories together. As the wetness falls on my hands, I realize I want nothing more than him sitting next to me, even if he is being rude. I miss him.

———

NIGHT FALLS QUICKLY, AND ALL I HAVE DONE SO FAR IS absolutely nothing. Nor could I think of anything. I lie on the hard bench, finding it difficult to sleep as my hand gently caresses my belly, which feels cold now. I begin to wonder if this is how my last days are going to be, and across from me groans Cell who is in pain.

He needs proper medical attention, else he will die, faster than all of us. Perhaps an infection just like the King or some other cause. I can't even begin to guess, I am no doctor, unlike his brother who has strangely remained silent.

Almost everyone is asleep. I can hear the soft breaths of their restful slumber, but one person down the hall is awake. I can hear someone humming a tune that is eerie yet sad sounding, and it continues for a long time.

I listen carefully, the tune sounds familiar. Somewhere I have heard it, either here or in the past. Finally, I recall mothers singing such a lullaby to their babies, mine did too. I sit up and approach the bars of the cell, having nothing to occupy my mind now.

The person stops immediately on hearing my footsteps before a voice says to me, "Isn't it funny how not one but two queens have ended up in the same dungeon?"

I do not respond at first as I sense magic similar to the King's, yet different, though I can't compare it to his. It slowly creeps up on me, winding around my aura. I feel like I am being suffocated by it; the heaviness is oppressive. The feelings evoked are of dread, hatred, and destruction to everything.

Rhys is not wrong in the slightest.

I knew who this is, Queen Lilou... The woman who could possibly be taking my place after my inevitable execution. She also knows who I am, and I am sure she has been listening to us.

"Not really," I say, finding the situation not humorous, but to someone who has spent many years down here as well as being deranged on top of it, it probably is. "But I am sure you are overjoyed at the news of your possible freedom... Queen Lilou."

"No need to be so proper, call me Lilou. And to answer your question, I am afraid I am not happy with such a prospect. Which woman is happy to be forced in such an arrangement?"

"Why is that?"

"Freedom, I want to be free. I will say marrying that man or possibly becoming queen again, both cause me to be ill... It brings back memories that should be forgotten. And, new Queen, who has married my sweet brother... What is your name? I do believe the guards and others have not spilled it from their tongues."

"Vrai," I reply.

"Hmm... pretty name for such a sweet and delicate woman," she comments half-heartedly. "But enough idle talk, you and I both tire of such conversations. What I am after and what I seek is power. And queens are normally that. Aren't you?" she asks.

"I would like to think I am," I remark, my eyes narrowing at her magic, her sarcastic voice, and her total lack of respect.

"Good," she says, "And you are an Ice Mage, right? Please correct me if I am wrong."

"Yes..." I reply, wondering where this is going.

"Oh, what friends we could have been, although it's a pity I hate your kind. If the fates were different but alas, they are not. Though truly I really am in awe that my brother married you at all, I rather be frozen to death than crawl in bed with one. " she says, which irks me. "But I'll set my feelings aside for more important matters that we must hurry and discuss."

"Vrai, you do not have sixty days as you have been led to believe, you have only until dawn. They will come for me at first light, cutting the chains and bindings, and I will be brought to Ukiah and wed."

"And why are you telling me this?" I wonder if she is trying to provoke me.

"I can't run away or flee by myself," she says, "I am unable to fly, but maybe, just maybe with your ice, your power of creation, you will gift me temporary wings. That is my price, and I promise to set you free."

My fingers tighten around the bars, thinking about her offer and how I can be set free, but there is a chance she will turn on me, "What of the guards?" I question her, not agreeing or refusing her offer.

"They will die because I will kill them," she says nonchalantly. "They think I am nothing, that I am too weak from lack of substance, but I burn with years of anger. They will know my wrath. Also, these guards are not my brother, and the only reason why I have not picked a fight until now is that I had no chance of escape before, but with you – I might."

"You could betray me," I say.

"I could," she says. "But I am your only choice. Either this or face your own execution less than a day's time with little to no option for you or your baby. Think, you will be dead if you wait, and there is a chance you'll live if you trust me."

I begin to reply, but I hear shuffling down the hall and a door is opened. We both grow silent at the entry of the guards, who holler, "Stop speaking, or I will cut off your tongues!"

At his words, we do not speak anymore, and I go back to my bench, thinking about what she has said.

Either this or an execution.

I guess I have no other choice.

I have to help her.

THIRTY-THREE

EXECUTION

THE FIRST LIGHT sprawls across the back of my hand, warming it gently, and I know dawn has come. Fear grips me making my heart pound, and my fingers tremble at the uncertainty of my fate. I was unable to sleep at all. After my talk with Lilou, I am more disturbed. Though I have not much of a choice, I still don't know if I should agree to her deal.

Footsteps of the guards soon shatter the silence of the hall, two of them, their gait steady and in sync. I listen to them move swiftly past me to the last cell at the end.

A door is opened, its hinges squeak in protest, having not been in use. Then there is a loud push, and the bars smash against the opposing wall. Heavy metal – probably shackles are dropped to the stone floor – I soon feel the vibrations of it.

A rush of magic creates a wave in the dungeons. It flares wildly, having been freed at long last, its power much like a whirlwind of fury. It is similar to the King's energy in some ways – angry, fearsome, strong. So very strong, it washes over me. I feel the warmth of it, yet it doesn't burn. But there is a darkness to it. Where the King's magic is bright and pure like fire, this has undertones of evil dancing in it. I fear what this magic will unleash over the world.

She is released – Lilou is set free. I see her Dragon in the blackness. Its ruby red eyes snap open, seeming to glow in this dark world. It moves with a subtle sensuousness as it uncurls its body, stretching its neck and limbs, awakened from the captivity it has been in. Its scales glint and shine with every movement; dust and grime disappear magically. There is anger hidden under its very skin, vibrating with energy.

It is regal in every sense. The King and Lilou's Dragons are almost physically identical. The only difference between them is the wings or the lack of them.

Where wings once were on the previous Queen, it is now a tattered base, a remnant of the past. Two deformed stumps mar her back, with just a hint of the beautiful wings that were present before.

My mind wanders to dark places, picturing the King doing such a thing to his own flesh and blood. I truly know nothing of him besides the stories and gossip that were fed to me, but I have seen glimpses of such a man, ruthless in his judgment.

He had, after all, stoned a citizen of his country coldly, without mercy. And he had shown no remorse to me – his wife – threatening and even hurting me. I too bear the scars of his anger on my chest. And now there is evidence that he has amputated his sister's wings, though I am sure he is more than his cruelty. If the little what Red had shared about his childhood is true, then there is so much more to uncover and learn.

I draw close to the bars of my cell, eager to know what awaits her, a dreadful silence pervading the dungeon. It is not only I who holds my breath, but the other prisoners, too, know something is about to happen. Ukiah's plans to marry the rightful queen and become the new King of Oria, as prophesied by Rhys, have been put into action. Little does he know his plans will soon go away.

However, this will only come to happen if Lilou does not double-cross me. If she does, there will be mayhem. The gamble I take will be lost, and she will be the new queen.

And the King, I, and our child - *what will become of us?* Surely death...

I bang my head against the bars, hope fading away with each second. I cannot let us die; I refute the possibility of death. It will not happen. No... For my baby, I have to fight. I have to risk everything, including putting my trust in the King's sibling whom he had imprisoned years ago.

I hear the sound of bare feet and the footsteps of guards, prodding her on and slowing when she refused to move fast. The smacking of her feet grows louder as they near my cell, but there is some unsteadiness in the gait, almost sluggish. I hear Rhys click his tongue noisily while putting his thoughts to words. "We are all done for. All of us."

The more I listen, the more I begin to understand that she is limping, and my hope of escaping diminishes. *What is she capable of?* She cannot kill the guards in her condition; she can barely walk. I hear a thud just outside my cell, and my body grows tense. *Did she collapse?*

One of the guards orders, "Get up!"

"Damn it! She must have passed out. Help me lift her." The other guard grumbles before he and his partner go to her.

As they bend toward her, there is a burst of magic, and the heat flares up, which makes me shield myself with my ice and back away from the raging fire in the hall.

My powers... Are they back?

I hear the screams of the guards as the flames swallow them whole, and the blaze does not stop until their screams cease. Their bodies are no doubt crisped to cinders. Hot ashes drift past the ice wall I created, stinging my skin where it lands. The fire born from her magic is such a haze that I can barely sense her when she approaches my cell. A splashing noise, the only indicator, when her foot sloshes in the water with my ice melting from the powerful heat.

She stops in front of my cell, her voice soft. "So, this is me... How pitiful I look. I am just a memory of my old self."

She must be looking at her reflection in the ice wall. There is a brief silence as the rest of my ice melts and puddles the area around my feet, then I feel dual stares on me. Both she and her Dragon's eyes bore holes into my skin, scrutinizing me, not with hatred but with something akin to interest as if I am a puzzle she is unable to solve.

Before I can break the silence, she speaks, "That is the last of my magic, and as I am at this moment, a guard still green behind the ears will easily best me. Time is of the essence, Mage. Now give me my wings, and I will set you free."

I hear the rustling of clothes, most likely she's undressing and discarding her rags and I hear Rhys shout urgently, "Vrai! Don't! She will betray us all!"

"Betrayal... The word is so bittersweet on thy tongue, Rhys. Back down. I am almost tempted to become a queen again just so I can watch your beheading," Lilou growls out, "though that is of no concern now. Hurry up, Mage, stop fucking around. Your face says you are in a stupor."

Her mouth is exactly like the King's, tone and everything. Oria would have become very frightening if they had ever ruled together. But I can see that they can never work as one. They are too alike and too damn thick-headed. I approach her, my hands pressing against her and finding it to be her back. I feel no ridges as with the King, just rough skin around the deformed stumps, the flesh is almost constricted.

She seethes and flinches the more I touch, especially when I apply some pressure. I warn her as I continue to feel the area on her back. "I've never reattached something like this. I'm not sure I can do it. In my state, my magic comes and goes."

"Wondrous information for the ears, but I do not care, Mage. Now be quick and do not dare to say you can't. I am aware Mages replace their own limbs. You are a Mage, so I know you can create wings," she snaps at me.

I sigh and try to recall the King's wings, their shape and the way the tendons of the back moved to spread them before launching into the skies or close them to land on the hard ground. I push my magic on to her back, hoping for a good outcome. Please! I need to escape for my baby.

She lets out soft whimpers unable to bear the feeling of my ice on her ruined flesh as it travels and attempts to take the shape of her missing wings. I let my mind wander just as my magic does, and I think how lost and defenseless I would have been without my limbs. And to Lilou and other Dragons, losing their wings must be the same.

My magic flows down her back and embeds itself into her body. She rips away from me when the pain became intolerable, her cries growing louder. And suddenly, she stops. Just like that, I see her Dragon spout artificial wings.

The colors I cannot describe, but it is a stark contrast to her scales, though my creation is not perfect. One wing is slightly larger than the other. She takes in huge gulps of air as she stretches out her new wings; I hear the crackling of ice when she moves.

"Many thanks, Mage... I will not forget what you have done for me," she says after regaining her composure. I hear the patter of her feet, walking away from me, making my heart drop. She is not limping anymore. It was all a fake act to fool her guards... and me. "But, unfortunately, I cannot help anyone associated with my brother. It is too dangerous for me." Her magic moves further down the hall, only stopping briefly, but her words are not directed at me. "Doctor Viggo, if only I can repay your kindness, but alas, even I am not that cruel."

"You said you will release me! You promised!" I yell, but she ignores me and continues down the hall, which enrages me, knowing my baby and I are still in danger.

"I warned you," says Rhys, "You did not listen, just like the King, and now you have released her from her prison. What chaos she will bring, I can only fear."

I grind my teeth and freeze the bars of my cell. I throw in a proper tantrum by thrashing wildly against the metal. "Come back!" I scream, frustrated, when they don't bend or break. My cell is meant to hold Dragons; they are not malleable as I want them to be.

As she progresses down the hall, the other prisoners grow wild, screeching their insanities and trying to break free of their prisons, knowing the guards are dead, too.

The only hope I have now begins to dwindle slowly as Lilou travels further away where I can no longer feel her magic. She must have already found a place where she can escape to the skies.

I slump down, my knees hitting the ground, my fingers never once letting go of the bars. It feels like hours pass in this manner, a dreadful weight on my chest as the inmates in each cell shriek and holler as loud as they can.

Eventually, the guards storm the dungeons, and alongside them marches Ukiah, who heads straight for me. He knows it is I who has allowed Lilou to flee. His aura is suffused with anger, and he strides to my cell, his boots hitting the stones sharply.

He reaches through the bars, grabbing and pulling my hair and smashing my face against the metal rods. "You whore," he hisses through gritted teeth.

"What's wrong?" I say even though my scalp and face hurt, and blood pours out of my nose. There is nothing left now for me but torture or death. "Did your fiancé leave? Annul the engagement? Are your plans ruined?"

"Fuck you, cunt," he hisses, kneeling to my level, and I smell the scent of burning hair. He is slowly singeing me. He has a temper worse than the King himself; his emotions are raw and unchecked. At least the King hid his for the most part. The man before me, the one who is hurting me, is no king of mine and will never be. Although the Dragon King is not the best, he is at least better than Ukiah.

"Tell me, what are your plans now?" I ask bravely, and he pulls my hair harder, enough to make me whimper.

"My plans... Well, I guess my best option is to see what monstrous halfling you produce and marry it if it's a female."

"And if it's a boy?" My eyes narrow, waiting for his answer.

"I'll kill it," he responds coldly, "and marry you, who is still the Queen of Oria."

I hear Rhys laugh at Ukiah. "So, if it's a male, your plan is to marry the Mage Queen who the people are already not too fond of. What nonsense, Ukiah! You rebel against your own ideals, if there were any to begin with, to achieve what you want. You will be hated, especially for killing King Orval's child."

"The people do not need to know I killed it. A prince dying at birth is not unheard of, and she will have to make do in such circumstances," he says as he lets go of my hair.

I hear him stand up and announce, "Everyone here but the Mage will be put to death, including General Cell, Advisor Rhys, and Doctor Viggo."

"Yes, sir," the guards say.

"But what of the previous King?" questions another guard.

Ukiah is quiet. "If he does not wake up today, we will give him an honorable death. No king should suffer in his bed trapped in limbo. And we do not have the time to cater to his needs, especially after the execution of the Doctor."

"Yes, sir."

I am livid and hurt. I want revenge, and I want it now. Anger reaches a boiling point in my blood, and I want nothing but Ukiah to feel such pain that he will never forget. My magic surges into my fingertips, power dances in me. I reach out far enough to grab him by the leg and spread my ice on it. It is his mistake for being so close to my cell within my reach.

"And to think the King trusted you the most," I scream.

He hisses and tries to back away from me, then takes his other foot and stomps on my hand. He crushes it under his heel, making me cry out. And of all the situations to be in, my magic seems to stop working abruptly, so I cannot defend myself.

"And maybe while we are at it, we can cut off both of the Mage's hands, the suppressors of her cell is not working or likely it was never meant to imprison her kind. No hands means she cannot create such disgusting and foul magic," he says.

He puts all of his weight on my hand and twists his foot. Evil laughter echoes in my cell; he is getting sadistic pleasure at my pain. The entire air hums with it.

There is a loud crunch that resonates throughout the dungeon, and I seethe. A wave of pain travels up my arm making me writhe. I slap his leg with my other hand in panic, but it is he who draws away.

"Oops, did I break it already?" he mocks from afar. "Mages are indeed delicate."

I can feel the throbbing pain as I quickly pull it back through the bars, cradling it to my chest. The fingers are swollen and don't seem to work right.

"Fuck off, fire cunt," I growl.

He laughs at me as he, too, walks away, much like Lilou. "See you tomorrow."

With that, he exits the dungeon, and I hold on to my throbbing hand, unsure of what awaits me.

Is it torture or death? But knowing Ukiah, it will be torture first, death later.

And will I have to hear the King and the others being put to death by his new ruling?

After all these months with them, I think I will miss them.

The King, the Doctor, the General, and the Advisor.

All will be gone. Tomorrow.

I AM PULLED FROM MY CELL EARLY THE NEXT MORNING, FORCED into cuffs that bind my magic in them, and shoved forward. I know what is in store today, my fingernails bloodying my palm as the others are brought with me.

Viggo is quiet, Rhys is yelling hateful things, and Cell is much too weak to put up any fight. I cannot bear to listen to them, thinking these to be their final steps, the last time they would breathe or I would hear their voices.

We are taken to the King's throne, and each of us is pushed down to our knees, and at this, my heart feels heavy. My mouth is dry and cannot formulate any words, a feeling of sorrow and pain overcomes me.

"I've decided to make your executions private. So be grateful I did not bring you to be watched by pitying eyes as you piss and shit yourselves when your head leaves your body," Ukiah announces.

"I wish you the same..." Rhys says bitterly. "For an uninspiring and Criminal King like you, the end will come soon. People will riot, and it won't be long when you'll suffer the same fate."

Ukiah only laughs at Rhys's comments. "Since you seem so eager, let our first death of the day be you."

"Yes, let it," agrees Rhys. I hear one of the guards, who has accompanied us, raise his weapon, and every muscle in my body tenses, preparing for a bloodbath.

But before the sword can come down on his head, the doors to the throne room are pushed open violently.

A voice yells.

"That is enough, Ukiah!"

That voice...

That magic...

My heart lightens, and I feel tears run down my face. This has been the first time I have been so overjoyed at the feel of his magic.

The King!

He is alive.

THIRTY-FOUR

TOGETHER

COMPLETE SILENCE...

Shock.

I can feel everyone in the room freaking out at the turn of events, left speechless by his entry. The King radiates power, the colors he exudes are eye-blinding. I can see his health and vitality suffusing through my being, filling me with strength. Only the four of us are grateful. I may not have lost my head today, but I know my hands would have been severed. My joy knows no bounds at the fact that the King... no... *Orval is alive.*

Viggo lets out a burst of laughter, which startles everyone. This is the first time I have heard him laugh. And since his capture, he has not uttered a single word. So, it is a wondrous surprise.

The Doctor has changed but I hope he transforms back to the same person he was. His laughter rings throughout the room, none of our enemies join in. The guards seem to be terrified. The hand holding the sword shakes in naked fear.

I look at the King. His boots strike the ground with a steady beat, each vibrating with pure energy, and his coat flaps around him. His Dragon's eyes scrutinize every single person in the court and surely finds them lacking. All the people who betrayed him have shattered his trust, and the Dragon King is not ready to forgive.

"What have we here? Looks like everyone has gone insane, can I join in? And, Ukiah, I must ask, did you have fun playing king?"

He walks past me, casually plucking the sword from the guard's listless hands and moves toward the throne on which is perched Ukiah, his mind trying to find a route of escape when there is none.

Let the games begin... I suppose.

I hear Ukiah rush to his feet and kneel before the power that is the King. The Dragon King's hostility is subtle, his presence radiates in the entire room. Everyone is holding their breath, waiting to see what will happen next. Nobody knows, not even Ukiah himself, what the King will do to the man he once considered a friend and ally.

"My King, I thought these four..." Ukiah stumbles over his words, and I feel his evil eyes sweep over us before he speaks again. "I believed they plotted against you with their kingdoms."

Oh, the fool! Couldn't he have thought of a better answer than that? He can't possibly believe Ukiah?

"Stand," the King says, his voice commanding as he ascends the stairs to the throne, each step reverberating with a solemn force.

"My King, thank—"

"So respectful," the King mocks, and he takes one last step, finally standing in front of Ukiah.

"Forgive my in—"

"I said stand!" The King's voice booms in the room, and I hear Ukiah slowly rise to stare up at his ruler.

He must realize his mistake, that his power to sway the King which he took for granted is gone.

"I have seen, and I have heard. And now I know what I must do. Let me see your eyes, Ukiah."

There are more words whispered from the King, spoken so softly that no one can hear.

"Orval..." Ukiah breathes out the name almost too quietly for me to hear.

"There, you have finally uttered my name. Look at those eyes, so much like mine. We could have been brothers, if not for your intentions. What a gruesome day it would have been in the history of Oria had you ruled. You are not me, but you thought yourself to be in the same class as me. Your biggest mistake. And mine was trusting a criminal."

"I would never—"

"Enough! No more lies, Ukiah. Now stand up straight and bear the pain or bring more shame to your future descendants by shrieking in fear."

The King's magic flares in a burst of colors until it remains a steady yellowish-orange. I hear Ukiah scream, piercing and full of agony. The sound enters my brain and curdles my blood.

He tries to stifle it, but I have undergone the effects of the King's anger. I know he can never withstand it, even with all the magic he has. The rage I sense from the King wants him to writhe in agony, every wave attacking each part of Ukiah's body.

I hear the blood splatter on the floor while Ukiah screams, long and hard, and I feel not a single ounce of pity for the man. Because of him, the entire nation is in turmoil. He has caused riots and division in the hearts of the people.

The King's punishment for Ukiah is not quick. He is slow with his torment, and Ukiah's screams continue, echoing in the room. The guards cringe and try to step away to escape the room. But one look from the Dragon and they are struck motionless. The King is doing this on purpose, for the people to see and spread the word that treason will never be tolerated.

Minutes roll and the screams are replaced by labored breathing as the King speaks, "You will not hide these scars. You will display them for all to see, and today and onward, you and your blood, including everyone in your clan are not welcome in my council or my castle, the arena, or anywhere near my lineage."

"I understand," says Ukiah, his voice trembling in pain.

"Now go," orders the King sternly. "And take your men with you.

Anyone who stays behind will be hanged in Viss for Oria to look upon so that nobody ever dares to go against their King. Death will befall them along with humiliation for their entire family."

I hear Ukiah leave, his pace fast, and the King orders the guards next. "Release them!"

"Yes, my Lord." The guards approach us to remove our chains obediently. Ukiah was their leader but only for a short while – three days exactly – and they have immediately switched sides and chosen the King in order to survive.

"You let him off too easily," complains Rhys, brushing his clothes, seeming to regain his composure rather quickly. There is a spring in his step. "He should have been executed or tortured for his crimes."

"No... He will return to the slums. That kind of life is worse than any punishment or death I can give him." The King's voice is cold and harsh, almost bitter.

The guard releases my chains, cutting them off, and it feels good to regain my freedom once again. I automatically rub my swollen hand, waiting for my time with the King.

"You've only let him off so easily because he is your favorite, or at least he was... Do not lie, my King," Viggo says, and I see his magic move close to his brother to support him. "And as much as I would like to discuss everything that has transpired in your absence, I cannot. I need to get my brother to my office as soon as possible."

"Yes, go. We can talk later. Take care of Cell, I need him back with me as soon as he is well enough to resume his duties. I have Rhys and the Queen to fill me in on the details. But Viggo, do not overstep your bounds and question my judgment. You and I are not friends, and I do not consider you my equal."

Viggo looks at the King for a few seconds without responding, then helps his brother as they walk away. He does not bother to look at me or enquire about my baby.

"We have many things to talk about, sire," complains Rhys. "Many punishments and banishments. I would like to get some disloyal men into the court today. The biggest impact would have come from you executing Ukiah in front of everyone, but that opportunity is gone."

"Rhys, speak his name once more, and it will be I beheading you. He is banished, and his name is never to be spoken of hereafter. What I want now is a list of men who have been disloyal, and I will deal with them accordingly." The King descends the steps of his throne, walking toward me, before grasping my upper arm and helping me stand.

"I see... We also need to make arrangements, repairs, much cleaning, and such," Rhys says before sighing heavily, "We just finished repairs from the damages of your fight with the Queen, and now this. What a disaster."

"Leave me. I want to be alone with the Queen for a short while."

Rhys is quiet for a couple of seconds before starting again. "Do not delay much more, sire. We need law and order. The people must see you alive and well."

"I said leave. Everyone, clear out," the King bellows.

"As you wish, sire, but I will be back soon to call on you." Rhys's boldness never ceases to amaze me. He can talk around the King's orders. Nothing fazes him. I see him walking out with the guards. He closes the doors behind them, leaving the King and me finally alone.

"Fucking Rhys. He is just about to get his fucking head cut clean from his body, and he dares to give me lip, acting all nonchalant. If I had stepped in a moment later, he wouldn't be talking, or perhaps his head would still be blatting about shit, telling me I was late and how dare I. I am sure I will have such dreams if I ever get a chance to sleep again. He is going to ride me like a cheap whore nonstop for the next few days."

There is silence after he airs his complaints about Rhys and everything else, and I can't help but laugh, sounding as insane as Viggo, listening to his voice after so many days. I throw my arms around the King much to his surprise and even my own.

I hug him tight, glad to hold him within my embrace, and to be here listening to him speak just like normal days. It feels so good to hear him again that tears slide down my face. I am so happy he isn't dead and for my baby to possibly have a normal future ahead of him or her.

"Well... This, I did not expect. If I am to almost die the next time, should I expect this?" the King questions, jokingly.

"Maybe..." I giggle but soon become quiet. "I thought I had killed you. After I pulled the ice from your shoulder, you collapsed and were unresponsive. So, I went to Viggo's office telling him what happened, someone somewhere overheard, spread the rumors, and everyone ended up at your door, thinking you were dying. Eventually, the blame was placed on me and the Water Dragons, and Ukiah took clear advantage of the opportunity. Initially, he appeared to be genuinely worried about you, but now I am not sure if it was all a big plan. Everyone believed Ukiah," I rush through my words.

"Sounds terrible, literally a shit show," he says in response, not returning my embrace or touching me. Maybe he is unsure about what to do.

"I am sorry, you did say not to utter his name..." I begin.

"It is fine, don't worry. Just be glad one of the others decided not to do away with me while everyone else was bickering."

"However, it needed to be done," I say, grabbing the back of his coat tightly. "You were suffering with the ice fang inside you."

"I'm not the first king to suffer an infection..." he mutters. "You look rubbish, Mage."

"No worse than you, my King. Take a look." I keep my head pressed against his warm chest, upset that he is making light of the situation.

"You're probably right..."

"You stink. Of sweat," I comment while smelling his shirt.

"Enough mockery, I do not need to be belittled by you," he growls, pulling me forcefully away from him. He looks at me from top to bottom.

"You're covered in bruises," he says, his hand running down the side of my face until he reaches my hand, which makes me wince. "Your hand is broken, too."

"All his doing," I say.

"I should have killed him," the King laments, and I see his Dragon open its eyes menacingly.

"It's too late now, but I think you should know that Rhys and Cell tried helping me. Especially Cell... Even with his wounds, he kept me from drowning."

"I will keep that in mind... Of all my people, I was not expecting the Water Dragons to end up helping you when I wasn't around."

"Zachariah tried," I comment, remembering he, too, had stood behind me in support and tried to protect me.

"Of course, he did. I have never doubted his loyalty to me. And you should not also. He may be foul of mouth and appearance, but he would never harm anyone unless they asked for it. He won't even listen to me if I order him to slay an innocent."

Does a good person express his desire of wanting to gut me in the first five seconds of our meeting? I'm not so sure of the King's judgment with people. He had trusted Ukiah and look what happened. I find it hard to believe what he said about Zachariah.

But that doesn't matter anymore.

"What do we do now?" I ask, unsure of our next action since I have a title once more.

"We do as Rhys suggests. There is a reason why he is my advisor. But I want you with me, by my side as queen. It is your rightful place," the King says. "It seems they still do not think of you as that, given your state of appearance."

I feel my cheeks heat slightly. "I imagine you're right... They have never held respect for Mages."

"They will with time... Come now," he says, taking my unhurt hand in his. "We will walk together as king and queen, even though we do not seem very royal at the moment."

He pulls me forward, and we walk together, the King being my guide. A warm feeling envelops me; his magic is soothing since the time I embraced him. I never thought I would be saying this about any type of fire magic, but this is the first time it has comforted me, and his and my magic have not clashed. Instead, they are coexisting next to each other without causing either of us pain or discomfort.

I grip his hand tightly as we go through the doors of the throne room, and I reminisce about the time when we first walked through them together after our wedding, how I thought his magic to be foul. But it wasn't like that anymore. I feel like I am standing next to an entirely different person, and I like this person.

Perhaps there is something more to us than just the titles 'king' and 'queen.'

I would like to believe that.

THIRTY-FIVE

A NEW JOURNEY

THE KING IS TIRED.

After weeks of meetings, executions, exiles, and punishments, it is apparent now. But an easy remedy such as a good night's sleep will not cure him. He carries an invisible weight on his shoulders, which grows heavier as the traitors grow in number.

Name after name rang from Rhys's mouth, and his voice and the glee in it while announcing the traitors and their predetermined fate still echoes in my ears. He is happy to get his revenge and extract justice, but the King, I believe, does not feel the same.

In fact, he has not been the same since the Hearth tree incident. Actually, many weren't after the incident, not just the King.

The day Ukiah's reign of terror ended; it did not cease with the loss of a friend. Unspeakable acts had taken place that I or those locked in the dungeon were ignorant about. I could never have imagined Ukiah to conduct such an act. It was most devastating for the King, a crippling blow to his heart. He works with his mind unfettered, but his heart is lost, defeated.

While Ukiah was in power, he feared the possibility that the King had sired bastards because, like everyone, he knew of the King's lust for women. So, to ascertain his claim to the throne, he hunted down all the women who may have at one time been intimate with the King. He hung them up on each sturdy branch of the Hearth tree, deciding that to be their final resting place.

In the middle, and together, hung Red and Yanmei. Both, in the end, seemed to have found their love for each other as even their corpses held hands.

Yanmei's death is devastating to my other maids, Catherine and Ava. They were like her sisters. I am unable to shed tears for her, though I feel bad at the way she died. I may be called a cold and heartless Mage, but I can feel pain. No being deserves to die like this.

We were not friends, we never got along from the beginning, but what has happened to her is plain wrong. Yanmei's life ended too fast before I got a chance to know more about her. Her life will forever be a mystery to me. Maybe we could have been friends if things were different or in another lifetime.

The King, on the other hand, was stunned, not saying much at the scene. He was devastated and broken. He was the closest to Red since his childhood. Not only did he lose his best friend, but there were also many others whom he knew, many Dragon women and some Thekas.

Even a child was hung from the tree as Ukiah suspected him to be the King's bastard. But I am unsure. Only the King knows, and I am not ready for such a conversation with him. Not having my sight was a blessing in this case as I was spared the sight of the hanging bodies. The only time I was happy being blind.

Gloom and despair were swift after the reveal, and it clung to the very air of the castle – an emptiness in every hall and room. The place no longer felt comfortable no matter where I went, many of us sad, angry, or just confused. And while things were getting repaired, celebrations and holidays of the Summer Solstice were temporarily canceled. It was a time for mourning, and the King was not in any shape for festivities. The whole ordeal had taken a toll on him.

By that time, whispers and rumors began to gather pace about the

King, news traveling quickly. They spoke about his sister, the true ruler of Oria, and how she was imprisoned by her own flesh and blood, her brother, for many years. Some of the people's views changed along with their loyalties, though they never spoke aloud. Nobody knew if she was still alive.

Things are different at the castle too. Ava has changed. When the subject is brought up, I feel her loyalty has shifted toward Lilou rather than for the King or me. There is a distance between us.

Lilou is another mystery. No one has any idea where she is or whether she is still alive. But I worry that she will pose a greater threat to my baby than anybody else. Hopefully, she keeps true to her promise and has no desire to rule Oria. But I wonder if, like the unknown child that hung on the tree, mine will too in the future.

The child within me feels stronger with each passing day, and with that comes the change and feel of my belly, which is no longer flat but slightly rounded, proof of growing life. I am a little past eight weeks, my exact due date unknown.

Ava had said after this point, I would be able to tell if the child would be blessed with fire or ice magic. But much to my disappointment, the coldness in my belly has stopped completely and is replaced by an ever-growing fire. After days of suffering from the heat, sweats, and blisters, I know I am damned.

My suffering is silent. I want to keep the misfortune away from the King's ears as he already has much to deal with. Knowing me to be a failure in giving him the first Ice Dragon will not ease his burdens. It will cause problems with Rhys, who only wants an Ice Dragon as the heir.

It may even cause the King to grow distant from me, and I greatly fear the separation from him now that he appears closer to me than before. He even lies in my bed some nights to comfort me with kisses which taste of the wine I cannot have, falling asleep on me, his head resting in different spots on my body every night.

I think sadness is what brings him to me. He doesn't speak of it, but it is what I perceive. I selfishly don't mind; I like the King this way, staying close to me.

A new maid is brought to me by Selene, a young one, someone I already know of. It is that little girl who gave me her flower crown the night of the festival of the Day of the Blossoms. She asked me to remember her name, and I did not forget. "Carrie..." drifted from my lips when I met her the second time, and she was elated. I had somehow remembered her name even when so many months had passed.

There is a story behind how she ended up as my maid. Apparently, she was eager to serve me despite having her Dragon, and that caught Selene's attention. She agreed to give Carrie a try. That was the best decision.

With the gloom around Yanmei's death, Carrie is a breath of fresh air who blows cheer into the room, lightening everyone's mood. I am glad to have her around, her good nature rubs on to me, and she is very good at assisting me.

When it feels like things are going good, Ambassador Chi arrives at the broken shambles of a castle. The King and I had forgotten we had sent for her. Luckily, Viggo meets her first and becomes a stand-in ambassador of the Kingdom, so to speak, and is able to smooth out all matters regarding Earath, temporarily postponing the meeting with her King.

Baby seems to be the only one unaffected by the recent events. He leans his large body against my legs and does not let me move from my spot in the shade outside the castle. I pet him soothingly, knowing soon I will be leaving this place. Drasa is our destination.

The King has suddenly decided he wants to travel with me to the borders, saying it will be healthier for my pregnancy. He mentioned some such things earlier, but now it's an excuse... A lie. He is trying to rid himself of the ghosts he is forced to see in the castle and Viss every day.

"I wish you could come with me," I murmur to the liwolf, my

hands running over his scales. "But Carrie will take good care of you here. She seems to like you just as much as Yanmei did."

My eyes narrow slightly, recalling how close my maid had been with Baby and how I would never hear her feeding him during his dinner time. She really was gone... just like that.

So quick, I think.

Death is scary.

I should know... I've had many close calls with it.

I lean down, wrapping my arms around the now huge liwolf, who is stiff and doesn't like to be held, but I know I will be gone for a couple of months with the King. It will be the last time I will get to hold Baby for a while, the longest we've been apart since he was just a pup nibbling on my finger. He was my special wedding gift from Cell who has healed quickly from his wounds with his brother's help.

I wonder how Baby will fare without me. Just fine, I bet... He enjoys playing with Carrie, who is still a child. She is the only one keeping him up and moving.

"I will miss you..." I murmur as he pulls away from my hug and shakes his body, his claws clicking against the stone as he moves from the grass to the road. I just know I will be lonesome without him.

"You talk to that beast like he is your friend," the King says from behind me.

"He is... Maybe my only friend," I reply. "Baby will not betray me."

The King scoffs and starts walking forward. "Come on, Mage. The last of your luggage is in the carriage."

"Will I be riding alone?" I ask him as I follow his magic, wondering if my ride to the borders will be lonely.

"Yes," the King replies. "But I will be nearby."

"In the skies?"

"Yes... Where else?"

"I don't know. Maybe with me in the carriage. It will be a long ride."

"With you?" the King asks as he stops by the carriage with the two slender cryeaters, scratching the dirt, impatient to move, as their breed often is, wanting to cart and run.

Cryeaters are like horses, only more serpentine and odd-looking from how I was described during my learnings with Dakari. It is how Thekas got around the city faster as they cannot fly.

"I've never traveled in such a small carriage normally meant for Thekas," he complains as he opens the door, most likely checking the space. "Dragons don't travel like this for a reason... We like our space."

My hand finds the door, realizing the King is stubborn. "Never mind... I will be fine by myself."

I climb inside, hitting my head on the low entrance, and I wince as I slide into my seat. I should probably feel more of my surroundings.

I hear the King click his tongue impatiently as he reaches out to me, touching my forehead briefly before stepping inside. Then he complains. "You are helpless without your maids... Now you will have a nice bruise there for the Duke to see... You're always getting hurt somehow, and I have no doubt the Duke will accuse me of beating my wife. He does not know how to hold his tongue still."

The next thing I hear is him sitting across from me, then the closing of the carriage door, followed by a tap on the ceiling. It signals for the man to drive.

The carriage begins moving, and I ask the King, "What are you doing?"

"Riding with my helpless Queen..." he replies sarcastically. "Remind me to gift you a cane for your birthday if it hasn't already passed."

"I don't remember the day of my birth." I rub my forehead, which still throbs.

"You don't?"

"No."

"How pitiful. I will mark the day of your birth when I will buy you a cane. You need it. I'm not sure why it hasn't already been done."

I don't think birthdays worked like that, but I don't say anything. I like him when he tries to show his caring side. Instead, I think back to how he has left Zachariah in charge while he is gone, giving him the authority over everybody, including Rhys.

"Are you sure leaving Zachariah in charge will be okay?" I ask him, my hands curling under the seat as the carriage hits a large bump and rocks us.

"Yes. And what else can happen that is worse than what has already happened? Killing off a few good men?" he asks me in return. "I am not the only king who has gone to a different castle to wait for his firstborn heir."

"We can come back to worse." I shudder.

The King laughs in return. "Worse? Many of my trusted men have betrayed me, thought about killing me, then decided to go ahead and slaughter the women I had fucked. They thought it to be a brilliant idea to decorate my favorite tree with their bodies. Lastly, I had to look at a child I knew, a good kid. His death occurred only because I happened upon his mother's cunt. I don't even remember her! What's worse than that, Mage? What and who else can die? Oh, and don't forget. The real ruler of Oria roams the lands, looking to do fuck knows what!"

I sigh after he is done ranting. I know he has been holding it in. All this time, it has just been building up inside of him.

There is silence at first before I mutter, "I know we've had our differences. I am blind and troubling to you; our people are enemies; our magic is completely different so also our species; you, more or less, wanted to use me for a strong heir that you didn't even want but your country wants; and at one point, we have even loved others... Despite all that..."

I reach over, grabbing his hands and pausing briefly before continuing, "I will continue to be by your side. I won't ever leave it. Although I may be temporary, and the only thing sparing my life is a contract and the child in my belly, I will never betray you, even if you throw me away... Even then."

After all that has occurred, despite thoughts of betrayal once running rampant through my head, I now realize I can never be another disappointment in his life, even if it means giving up on my plans for revenge on my stepmother.

"Temporary?" he asks before pulling me by my wrist toward him. My eyes widen in shock. My hand lands on his chest and my face inches from his, his breath soft on my cheek.

He puts his arms around me. "I think you are mistaken, Mage." His embrace feels odd, and he rests his head on my shoulder. "If I get rid of you, I am no better than a fool."

My face softens, my heart thumping in my chest, and I sink into his embrace. I close my eyes, relaxed.

I love him, even if I bear scars of his love over my heart. Nothing can change that. A Mage's love lasts forever, and that terrifies me. Unknown and dangerous such a love can prove to be, our worlds will burn in it.

Only time will tell...

WEBTOON COMING SOON

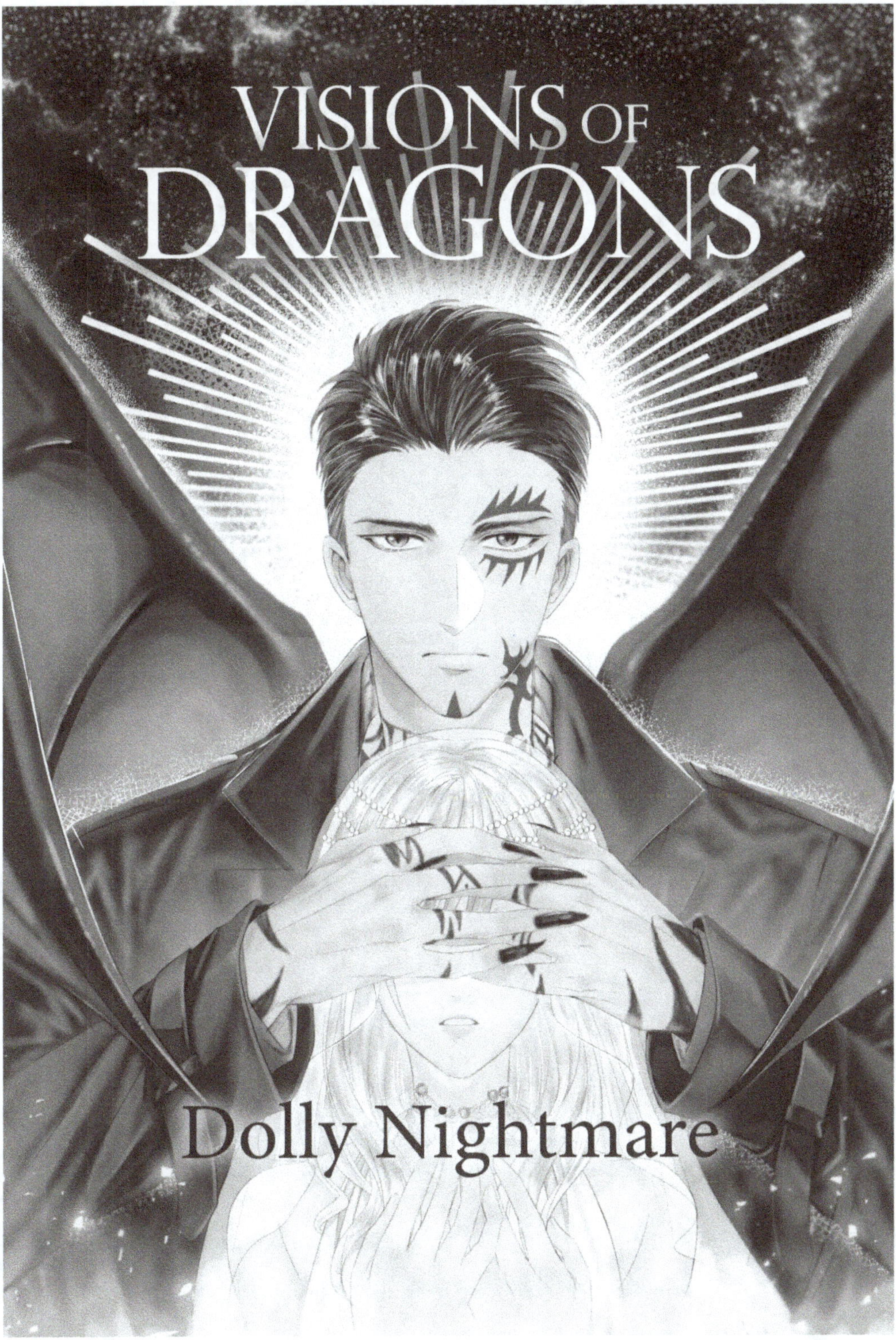
VISIONS OF
DRAGONS
Dolly Nightmare